Molly Bawn

by
Duchess

Molly Bawn
by Duchess

ISBN: 978-93-67147-23-8

Published by

DOUBLE 9 BOOKS

2/13-B, Ansari Road
Daryaganj, New Delhi – 110002
info@double9books.com
www.double9books.com
Tel. 011-40042856

ABOUT THE AUTHOR

Margaret Wolfe Hungerford, often referred to as "The Duchess," was an Irish novelist born in 1855, celebrated for her engaging narratives that frequently explored themes of love, social class, and personal identity. Her writing is distinguished by vivid characterizations and emotional depth, drawing readers into the lives of her characters.

One of her most notable works, "Molly Bawn," tells the story of a spirited young woman navigating romantic entanglements and societal expectations. This novel highlights the struggles women faced in society and reflects Hungerford's keen insights into human relationships.

Throughout her prolific career, Hungerford authored several other novels, many of which garnered critical acclaim and solidified her reputation as a significant literary figure of her era. She passed away in 1897, but her works continue to resonate, appreciated for their rich storytelling and exploration of the complexities of life and love. Hungerford's legacy endures as her stories still captivate readers today.

CONTENTS

CHAPTER I

"On hospitable thoughts intent."

"Positively he is coming!" says Mr. Massereene, with an air of the most profound astonishment.

"*Who?*" asks Molly, curiously, pausing with her toast in mid-air (they are at breakfast), and with her lovely eyes twice their usual goodly size. Her lips, too, are apart; but whether in anticipation of the news or of the toast, it would be difficult to decide. "Is any one coming here?"

"Even here. This letter"—regarding, with a stricken conscience, the elegant scrawl in his hand—"is from Tedcastle George Luttrell (he is evidently proud of his name), declaring himself not only ready but fatally willing to accept my invitation to spend a month with me."

"A month!" says Molly, amazed. "And you never said a word about it, John."

"A month!" says Letitia, dismayed. "What on earth, John, is any one to do with any one for a month down here?"

"I wish I knew," replies Mr. Massereene, getting more and more stricken as he notices his wife's dejection, and gazing at Molly as though for inspiration. "What evil genius possessed me that I didn't say a fortnight? But, to tell you the honest truth, Letty, it never occurred to me that he might come."

"Then why did you ask him?" says Letitia, as sharply as is possible for her. "When writing, you might have anticipated so much: people generally do."

"Do they?" says Mr. Massereene, with an irrepressible glance at Molly. "Then you must only put me down as an exception to the general rule. I thought it only civil to ask him, but I certainly never believed he would be rash enough to go in for voluntary exile. I should have remembered how unthinking he always was."

"But who is he?" asks Molly, impatiently, full of keen and pleasurable excitement. "I die of vulgar curiosity. What is he like? Is he young, handsome? Oh, John, *do* say he is young and good-looking."

"He was at school with me."

"Oh!" groans Molly.

"Does that groan proceed from a conviction that I am in the last stage of decay?" demands Mr. Massereene. "Anything so rude as you, Molly, has not as yet been rivaled. However, I am at a disadvantage: so I forgive, and will proceed. Though at school with me, he is at least nine years my junior, and can't be more than twenty-seven."

"Ah!" says Molly. To an Irish girl alone is given the power to express these two exclamations with proper effect.

"He is a hussar, of a good family, sufficiently good looks, and, I think, no fortune," says Mr. Massereene, as though reading from a doubtful guide-book.

"How delightful!" says Molly.

"How terrific!" sighs Letitia. "Fancy a hussar finding amusement in lambs, and cows, and fat pigs, and green fields!"

"'Green fields and pastures new,'" quotes Mr. Massereene. "He will have them in abundance. He ought to be happy, as they say there is a charm in variety."

"Perhaps he will find some amusement in me," suggests Molly, modestly. "Can it be possible that he is really coming? Oh, the glory of having a young man to talk to, and that young man a soldier! Letitia," to her sister-in-law, "I warn you it will be no use for you to look shocked, because I have finally made up my mind to flirt every day, and all day long, with Tedcastle George Luttrell."

"Shocked!" says Letitia, gravely. "I would be a great deal more shocked if you had said you wouldn't; for what I should do with him, if you refused to take him in hand, is a thing on which I shudder to speculate. John is forever doing questionable things, and repenting when it is too late. Unless he means to build a new wing—" with a mild attempt at sarcasm,—"I don't know where Mr. Luttrell is to sleep."

"I fear I would not have time," says Massereene, meekly; "the walls would scarcely be dry, as he is coming—the day after to-morrow."

"Not until then?" says Letitia, ominously calm. "Why did you not make it to-day? That would have utterly precluded the possibility of my getting things into any sort of order."

"Letitia, if you continue to address me in your present heartless style for one minute longer, I shall burst into tears," says Mr. Massereene. And then they all laugh.

"He shall have my room," says Molly, presently, seeing that perplexity still adorns Letitia's brows, "and I can have Lovat's."

"Oh, Molly, I will not have you turned out of your room for any one," says Letitia; but she says it faintly, and is conscious of a feeling of relief at her heart as she speaks.

"But indeed he shall. It is such a pretty room that he cannot fail to be impressed. Any one coming from a hot city, and proving insensible to the charms of the roses that are now creeping into my window, would be unfit to live. Even a hussar must have a soft spot somewhere. I foresee those roses will be the means of reducing him to a lamb-like meekness."

"You are too good, Molly. It seems a shame," says Letitia, patting her sister-in-law's hand, and still hesitating, through a sense of duty; "does it not, John?"

"It is so difficult to know what a woman really means by the word, 'shame,'" replies John, absently, being deep in the morning's paper. "You said it was a shame yesterday when the cat drank all the cream; and Molly said it was a shame when Wyndham ran away with Crofton's wife."

"Don't take any notice of him, Letty," says Molly, with a scornful shrug of her pretty shoulders, turning her back on her brother, and resuming the all-important subject of the expected visitor.

"Another railway accident, and twenty men killed," says Mr. Massereene, in a few minutes, looking up from his *Times,* and adopting the lugubrious tone one always assumes on such occasions, whether one cares or not.

"Wasn't it fortunate we put up those curtains clean last week?" murmurs Letitia, in a slow, self-congratulatory voice.

"More than fortunate," says Molly.

"*Twenty* men killed, Letty!" repeats Mr. Massereene, solemnly.

"I don't believe there is a spare bath in the house," exclaims Letitia, again sinking into the lowest depth of despair.

"You forget the old one in the nursery. It will do for the children very well, and he can have the new one," says Molly.

"Twenty men *killed*, Molly!" reiterates Mr. Massereene, a faint gleam of surprised disgust creeping into his eyes.

"So it will, dear. Molly, you are an immense comfort. What did you say, John? Twenty men killed? *Dreadful!* I wonder, Molly, if I might suggest to him that I would not like him to smoke in bed? I hear a great many young men have that habit; indeed, a brother of mine, years ago, at home, nearly set the house on fire one night with a cigar."

"Let me do all the lecturing," says Molly, gayly; "there is nothing I should like better."

"Talk of ministering angels, indeed!" mutters Mr. Massereene, rising, and making for the door, paper and all. "I don't believe they would care if England was swamped, so long as they had clean curtains for Luttrell's bed."

CHAPTER II

"A lovely lady, garmented in light
From her own beauty."
—Shelley.

The day that is to bring them Luttrell has dawned, deepened, burst into perfect beauty, and now holds out its arms to the restful evening. A glorious sunny evening as yet, full of its lingering youth, with scarce a hint of the noon's decay. The little yellow sunbeams, richer perhaps in tint than they were two hours agone, still play their games of hide-and-seek and bo-peep among the roses that climb and spread themselves in all their creamy, rosy, snowy loveliness over the long, low house where live the Massereenes, and breathe forth scented kisses to the wooing wind.

A straggling house is Brooklyn, larger, at the first glance, than it in reality is, and distinctly comfortable, yet with its comfort, a thing very far apart from luxury, and with none of the sleepiness of an over-rich prosperity about it. In spite of the late June sun, there is a general air of life, a tremulous merriment, everywhere: the voices of the children, a certain laugh that rings like far-off music, the cooing of the pigeons beneath the eaves, the cluck-cluck of the silly fowls in the farm-yard,—all mingle to defy the creeping sense of laziness that the day generates.

"It is late," says Mr. Massereene to himself, examining his watch for the fifteenth time as he saunters in a purposeless fashion up and down before the hall door. There is a suppressed sense of expectancy both in his manner and in the surroundings. The gravel has been newly raked, and gleams white and untrodden. The borders of the lawn that join on to it have been freshly clipped. A post in the railings, that for three weeks previously has been tottering to its fall, has been securely propped, and now stands firm and uncompromising as its fellows.

"It is almost seven," says Letitia, showing her fresh, handsome face at the drawing-room window. "Do you think he will be here for dinner, John?"

"I am incapable of thought," says John. "I find that when a man who is in the habit of dining at six is left without his dinner until seven he grows morose. It is a humiliating discovery. Surely the stomach should be subservient to the mind; but it isn't. Letitia, like a good girl, do say you have ordered up the soup."

"But, my dear John, had we not better wait a little longer?"

"My dear Letitia, most certainly not, unless you wish to raise a storm impossible to quell. At present I feel myself in a mood that a very little more waiting will render ferocious. Besides,"—seeing his wife slightly uneasy,— "as he did not turn up about six, he cannot by any possibility be here until half-past eight."

"And I took such trouble with that dinner!" says Letitia, with a sigh.

"I am more glad to hear it than I can tell you," says her husband, briskly. "Take my word for it, Letty, your trouble won't go for nothing."

"*Gourmand!*" says Letitia, with the smile she reserves alone for him.

Eight,—half-past eight—nine.

"I don't believe he is coming at all," says Molly, pettishly, coming out from the curtains of the window, and advancing straight into the middle of the room.

Under the chandelier, that has been so effectively touched up for this recreant knight, she stands bathed in the soft light of the many candles that beam down with mild kindliness upon her. It seems as though they love to rest upon her,—to add yet one more charm, if it may be, to the sweet, graceful figure, the half-angry, wholly charming attitude, the tender, lovable, fresh young face.

Her eyes, large, dark, and blue,—true Irish eyes, that bespeak her father's race,—shine with a steady clearness. They do not sparkle, they are hardly brilliant; they look forth at one with an expression so soft, so earnest, yet withal so merry, as would make one stake their all on the sure fact that the heart within her must be golden.

Her nut-brown hair, drawn back from her low brow into a loose coil behind, is enriched here and there with little sunny tresses, while across her forehead a few wavy locks—veritable love-locks, in Molly's case—wander idly, not as of a set purpose, but rather as though they have there drifted of their own gay will.

Upon her cheeks no roses lie,—unless they be the very creamiest roses that ever eye beheld. She is absolutely without color until such occasions rise as when grief or gladness touch her and dye her lovely skin with their red glow.

But it is her mouth—at once her betrayer and her chief charm—that one loves. In among its many curves lies all her wickedness,—the beautiful mouth, so full of mockery, laughter, fun, a certain decision, and tenderness unspeakable.

She smiles, and all her face is as one perfect sunbeam. Surely never has she looked so lovely. The smile dies, her lips close, a pensive sweetness creeps around them, and one terms one's self a fatuous fool to have deemed her at her best a moment since; and so on through all the many changes that only serve to show how countless is her store of hidden charms.

She is slender, but not lean, round, yet certainly not full, and of a middle height. For herself, she is impulsive; a little too quick at times, fond of life and laughter, as all youth should be, while perhaps (that I should live to say it!) down deep within her, somewhere, there hides, but half suppressed and ever ready to assert itself, a wayward, turbulent vein that must be termed coquetry.

Now, at this instant the little petulant frown, born of "hope deferred," that puckers up her forehead has fallen into her eyes, notwithstanding the jealous guard of the long curling lashes, and, looking out defiantly from thence, gives her all the appearance of a beloved but angry child fretting at the delay of some coveted toy.

"I don't believe he is coming *at all*," she says, again, with increased emphasis, having received no answer to her first assertion, Letitia being absorbed in a devout prayer that her words may come true, while John is disgracefully drowsy. "Oh, fancy the time I have wasted over my appearance, and all for nothing! I won't be able to get up the enthusiasm a second time: I feel that. How I hate young men,—young men in the army especially! They are so selfish and so good-for-nothing, with no thought for any one on earth but Number One. Give me a respectable, middle-aged squire, with no aspirations beyond South-downs and Early York."

"Poor Molly Bawn!" says John, rousing himself to meet the exigencies of the moment. "'I deeply sympathize.' And just when you are looking so nice, too: isn't she, Letty? I vow and protest, that young man deserves nothing less than extinction."

"I wish I had the extinguishing of him," says Molly, viciously. Then, laughing a little, and clasping her hands loosely behind her back, she walks to a mirror, the better to admire the long white trailing robe, the faultless face, the red rose dying on her breast. "And just when I had taken such pains with my hair!" she says, making a faint grimace at her own vanity. "John, as there is no one else to admire me, do say (whether you think it or not) I am the prettiest person you ever saw."

"I wouldn't even hesitate over such a simple lie as that," says John; "only—Letty is in the room: consider her feelings."

"A quarter to nine. I really think he can't be coming now," breaks in Letitia, hopefully.

"Coming or not coming, I shan't remain in for him an instant longer this delicious night," says Molly, walking toward the open window, under which runs a balcony, and gazing out into the still, calm moonlight. "He is probably not aware of my existence; so that even if he does come he will not take my absence in bad part; and if he does, so much the better. Even in such a poor revenge there is a sweetness."

"Molly," apprehensively, "the dew is falling."

"I hope so," answers Molly, with a smile, stepping out into the cool, refreshing dark.

Down the wooden steps, along the gravel path, into the land of dreaming flowers she goes. Pale moonbeams light her way as, with her gown uplifted, she wanders from bed to bed, and with a dainty greediness drinks in the honeyed breathings round her. Here now she stoops to lift with gentle touch a drooping head, lest in its slumber some defiling earth come near it; and here she stands to mark a spider's net, brilliant with dews from heaven. A crafty thing to have so fair a home!—And here she sighs.

"Well, if he doesn't come, what matters it? A stranger cannot claim regret. And yet what fun it would have been! what fun! (Poor lily, what evil chance came by you to break your stem and lay your white head there?) Perhaps—who knows?—he might be the stupidest mortal that ever dared to live, and then yet not so stupid as the walls, and trees, and shrubs, while he can own a tongue to answer back. Ah! wretched slug, would you devour my tender opening leaves? Ugh! I cannot touch the slimy thing. Where *has* my trowel gone? I wish my ears had never heard his name,—Luttrell; a pretty name, too; but we all know how little is in *that*. I feel absurdly disappointed; and why? Because it is decreed that a man I never have known I never shall know. I doubt my brain is softening. But why has my tent been pitched in such a lonely spot? And why did he say he'd come? And why did John tell me he was good to look at, and, oh! that best of all things—*young*?"

A sound,—a step,—the vague certainty of a presence near. And Molly, turning, finds herself but a few yards distant from the expected guest. The fates have been kind!

A tall young man, slight and clean-limbed, with a well-shaped head so closely shaven as to suggest a Newgate barber; a long fair moustache, a long nose, a rather large mouth, luminous azure eyes, and a complexion the sun has vainly tried to brown, reducing it merely to a deeper flesh-tint. On the whole, it is a very desirable face that Mr. Luttrell owns; and so Molly decides in her first swift glance of pleased surprise. Yes, the fates have been more than kind.

As for Luttrell himself, he is standing quite still, in the middle of the garden-path, staring at this living Flora. Inside not a word has been said about her, no mention of her name had fallen ever so lightly into the conversation. He had made his excuses, had received a hearty welcome; both he and Massereene had declared themselves convinced that not a day had gone over the head of either since last they parted. He had bidden Mrs. Massereene good-night, and had come out here to smoke a cigar in quietude, all without suspicion that the house might yet contain another lovelier inmate. Is this her favorite hour for rambling? Is she a spirit? Or a lunatic? Yes, that must be it.

Meanwhile through the moonlight—in it—comes Molly, very slowly, a perfect creature, in trailing, snowy robes. Luttrell, forgetting the inevitable cigar,—a great concession,—stands mutely regarding her as, with warm parted lips and a smile, half amused, half wondering, she gazes back at him.

"Even a plain woman may gain beauty from a moonbeam; what, then, must a lovely woman seem when clothed in its pure rays?"

"You are welcome,—very welcome," says Molly, at length, in her low, soft voice.

"Thank you," returns he, mechanically, still lost in conjecture.

"I am not a fairy, nor a spirit, nor yet a vision," murmurs Molly, now openly amused. "Have no fear. See," holding out to him a slim cool hand; "touch me, and be convinced, I am only Molly Massereene."

He takes the hand and holds it closely, still entranced. Already—even though three minutes have scarcely marked their acquaintance—he is dimly conscious that there might possibly be worse things in this world than a perpetual near-to "only Molly Massereene."

"So you did come," she goes on, withdrawing her fingers slowly but positively, and with a faint uplifting of her straight brows, "after all. I was so afraid you *wouldn't*, you were so long. John—we *all* thought you had thrown us over."

To have Beauty declare herself overjoyed at the mere fact of your presence is, under any circumstances, intoxicating. To have such an avowal made beneath the romantic light of a summer moon is maddening.

"You *cared*?" says Luttrell, in hopeful doubt.

"Cared!" with a low gay laugh. "I should think I did care. I quite *longed* for you to come. If you only knew as well as I do the terrible, never-ending dullness of this place, you would understand how one could long for the coming of *any one.*"

Try as he will, he cannot convince himself that the termination of this sentence is as satisfactory as its commencement.

"When the evening wore on," with a little depressed shake of her head, "and still you made no sign, and I began to feel sure it was all too good to be true, and that you were about to disappoint me and plead some hateful excuse by the morning post, I almost hated you, and was never in such a rage in my life. But," again holding out her hand to him, with a charming smile "I forgive you now."

"Then forgive me one thing more,—my ignorance," says Luttrell, retaining the fingers this time with much increased firmness. "And tell me who you are."

"Don't you know, really? You never heard of me from John or—— What a fall to my pride, and when in my secret heart I had almost flattered myself that——"

"What?" eagerly.

"Oh, nothing—only—— By the bye, now you have confessed yourself ignorant of my existence, what *did* bring you down to this uninteresting village?" All this with the most perfect *naïveté.*

"A desire," says Luttrell, smiling in spite of himself, "to see again your what shall I say?"—hesitating—"father?"

"Nonsense," says Molly, quickly, with a little frown. "How could you think John my father? When he looks so young, too. I hope you are not stupid: we shall never get on if you are. How could he be my father?"

"How could he be your brother?"

"Step-brother, then," says Molly, unwillingly. "I will acknowledge it for this once only. But never again, mind, as he is dearer to me than half a dozen real brothers. You like him very much, don't you?" examining him anxiously. "You must, to take the trouble to come all the way down here to see him."

"I do, indeed, more than I can say," replies the young man, with wise heartiness that is yet unfeigned. "He has stood to me too often in the old school-days to allow of my ever forgetting him. I would go farther than Morley to meet him, after a lengthened absence such as mine has been."

"India?" suggests Molly, blandly.

"Yes." Here they both pause, and Molly's eyes fall on her imprisoned hand. She is so evidently bent on being again ungenerous that Luttrell forces himself to break silence, with the mean object of distracting her thoughts.

"Is it at this hour you usually 'take your walks abroad?'" he asks, smoothly.

"Oh, no," laughing; "you must not think that. To-night there was an excuse for me. And if there is blame in the matter, you must take it. But for your slothfulness, your tardiness, your unpardonable laziness," spitefully, "my temper would not have driven me forth."

"But," reproachfully, "you do not ask the cause of my delay. How would you like to be first inveigled into taking a rickety vehicle in the last stage of dissipation and then deposited by that vehicle, without an instant's warning, upon your mother earth? For my part, I didn't like it at all."

"I'm so sorry," says Molly, sweetly. "Did all that really happen to you, and just while I was abusing you with all my might and main? I think I shall have to be very good to you to make up for it."

"I think so too," says Luttrell, gravely. "My ignominious breakdown was nothing in comparison with a harsh word thrown at me by you. I feel a deep sense of injury upon me."

"It all comes of our being in what the papers call 'poor circumstances,'" says Molly, lightly. "Now, when I marry and you come to see me, I shall send a carriage and a spirited pair of grays to meet you at the station. Think of that."

"I won't," says Luttrell; "because I don't believe I would care to see you at all when—you are married." Here, with a rashness unworthy of him, he presses, ever so gently, the slender fingers within his own. Instantly Miss Massereene, with a marked ignoring of the suggestion in his last speech, returns to her forgotten charge.

"I don't want to inconvenience you," she says, demurely, with downcast lids, "but when you have quite done with my hand I think I should like it again. You see it is awkward being without it, as it is the right one."

"I'm not proud," says Luttrell, modestly. "I will try to make myself content if you will give me the left one."

At this they both laugh merrily; and, believe me, when two people so laugh together, there is very little ice left to be broken.

"And are you really glad I have come?" says Luttrell, bending, the better to see into her pretty face. "It sounds so unlikely."

"When one is starving, even dry bread is acceptable," returns Molly, with a swift but cruel glance.

"I refuse to understand you. You surely do not mean— —"

"I mean this, that you are not to lay too much stress on the fact of my having said— —"

"Well, Luttrell, where are you, old fellow? I suppose you thought you were quite forgotten. Couldn't come a moment sooner,—what with Letitia's comments on your general appearance and my own comments on my tobacco's disappearance. However, here I am at last. Have you been lonely?"

"Not very," says Mr. Luttrell, *sotto voce*, his eyes fixed on Molly.

"It is John," whispers that young lady mysteriously. "Won't I catch it if he finds me out here so late without a shawl? I must *run*. Good-night,"—she moves away from him quickly, but before many steps have separated them turns again, and, with her fingers on her lips, breathes softly, kindly—"until to-morrow." After which she waves him a last faint adieu and disappears.

CHAPTER III

"In my lady's chamber."

When John Massereene was seven years old his mother died. When he was seventeen his father had the imprudence to run away with the favorite daughter of a rich man,—which crime was never forgiven. Had there been the slightest excuse for her conduct it might have been otherwise, but in the eyes of her world there was none. That an Amherst of Herst Royal should be guilty of such a plebeian trick as "falling passionately in love" was bad enough, but to have her bestow that love upon a man at least eighteen years her senior, an Irishman, a mere engineer, with no money to speak of, with nothing on earth to recommend him beyond a handsome face, a charming manner, and a heart too warm ever to grow old, was not to be tolerated for a moment. And Eleanor Amherst, from the hour of her elopement, was virtually shrouded and laid within her grave so far as her own family was concerned.

Not that they need have hurried over her requiem, as the poor soul was practically laid there in the fourth year of her happy married life, dying of the same fever that had carried off her husband two days before, and leaving her three-year-old daughter in the care of her step-son.

At twenty-one, therefore, John Massereene found himself alone in the world, with about three hundred pounds a year and a small, tearful, clinging, forlorn child. Having followed his father's profession, more from a desire to gratify that father than from direct inclination, he found, when too late, that he neither liked it nor did it like him. He had, as he believed, a talent for farming; so that when, on the death of a distant relation, he found himself, when all was told, the possessor of seven hundred pounds a year, he bought Brooklyn, a modest place in one of the English shires, married his first love, and carried her and Molly home to it.

Once or twice in the early part of her life he had made an appeal to old Mr. Amherst, Molly's grandfather, on her behalf,—more from a sense of duty owing to her than from any desire to rid himself of the child, who had, indeed, with her pretty, coaxing ways, made a very cozy nest for herself in the deepest recesses of his large heart. But all such appeals had been unavailing. So that Molly had grown from baby to child, from child to girl, without having so much as seen her nearest relations, although Herst Royal was situated in the very county next to hers.

Even now, in spite of her having attained her eighteenth year, this ostracism is a matter of the most perfect indifference to Molly. She has been bred in a very sound contempt for the hard old man who so cruelly neglected her mother,—the poor mother whose love she never missed, so faithfully has John fulfilled her dying wishes. There is no poverty about this love, in which she has grown and strengthened: it is rich, all-sufficing. Even Letitia's coming only added another ray to its brightness.

They are a harmonious family, the Massereenes; they blend; they seldom disagree. Letitia, with her handsome English face, her tall, *posée* figure, and ready smile, makes a delicious centre-piece; John a good background; Molly a bit of perfect sunlight; the children flecks of vivid coloring here and there. They are an easy, laughter-loving people, with a rare store of contentment. They are much affected by those in their immediate neighborhood. Their servants have a good time of it. They are never out of temper when dinner is a quarter of an hour late. They all very much admire Molly, and Molly very much agrees with them. They are fond of taking their tea in summer in the open air; they are not fond of over-early rising; they never bore you with a description of the first faint beams of dawn; they fail to see any beauty in the dew at five o'clock in the morning; they are very reasonable people.

Yet the morning after his arrival, Luttrell, jumping out of his bed at eight o'clock, finds, on looking out of his window that overhangs the garden, Flora already among her flowers. Drawing back hastily,—he is a modest young man,—he grows suddenly energetic and makes good speed with his toilet.

When he is half dressed—that is, when his hair is brushed; but as yet his shirt is guiltless of a waistcoat—he cannot refrain from looking forth again, to see if she may yet be there, and, looking, meets her eyes.

He is slightly abashed; she is not. Mr. Massereene in his shirt and trousers is a thing very frequently seen at his window during the summer mornings. Mr. Luttrell presents much the same appearance. It certainly does occur to Molly that of the two men the new-comer is decidedly the better looking of the two, whereat, without any treachery toward John, she greatly rejoices. It does not occur to her that a blush at this moment would be a blush in the right place. On the contrary, she nods gayly at him, and calls out:

"Hurry! You cannot think what a delicious morning it is." And then goes on with her snipping and paring with the heartiest unconcern. After which Luttrell's method of getting into the remainder of his clothes can only be described as a scramble.

"How did you sleep?" asks Molly, a few minutes later, when he has joined her, looking up from the rose-bush over which she is bending, that holds no flower so sweet as her own self. "Well, I hope?"

"Very well, thank you," with a smile, his eyes fixed immovably upon the fresh beauty of her face.

"You look suspicious," says she, with a little laugh. "Are you thinking my question odd? I know when people are put over-night in a haunted chamber they are always asked the next morning whether they 'slept well,' in the fond hope that they didn't. But *you* need not be nervous. Nothing so inspiriting——"

"Is that a joke?" demands he, interrupting her, gravely.

"Eh? Oh, no! how could you think me guilty of such a thing? I mean that nothing so hopeful as an undeniable ghost has ever yet appeared at Brooklyn."

"Are you sure? Perhaps, then, I am to be the happy discoverer, as this morning early, about dawn, there came an unearthly tapping at my window that woke me, much to my disgust. I got up, but when I had opened the shutters could see nothing. Was not that a visitation? I looked at my watch, and found it was past four o'clock. Then I crept into my bed again, crestfallen,—'sold' with regard to an adventure."

"That was my magpie," cries Molly, with a merry laugh: "he always comes pecking at that hour, naughty fellow. Oh, what a tame ending to your romance! Your beautiful ghost come to visit you from unknown regions, clad in white and rustling garments, has resolved itself into a lame bird, rather poverty-stricken in the matter of feathers."

"I take it rather hardly that your dependent should come to disturb *me*," says Luttrell, reproachfully. "What have I done to him, or how have I ingratiated myself, that he should forsake you for me? I did not think even a meagre bird could have shown such *outre* taste. What fancy has he for *my* window?"

"*Your* window?" says Molly, quickly; then as quickly recollecting, she stops short, blushing a warm and lovely crimson. "Oh, of course,—yes, it was odd," she says, and, breaking down under the weight of her unhappy blush, busies herself eagerly with her flowers.

"Have I taken your bedroom?" asks he, anxiously, watching with cruel persistency the soft roses that bloom again at his words. "Yes, I see I have.

That is too bad; and any room would have been good enough for a soldier. Are you sure you don't hate me for all the inconvenience I have caused you?"

"I can't be sure," says Molly, "*yet*. Give me time. But this I do know, that John will quarrel with us if we remain out here any longer, as breakfast must be quite ready by this. Come."

"When you spoke of my chamber as being haunted, a little time ago," says Luttrell, walking beside her on the gravel path, his hands clasped behind his back, "you came very near the truth. After what you have just told me, how shall I keep from dreaming about you?"

"Don't keep from it," says she, sweetly; "go on dreaming about me as much as ever you like. *I* don't mind."

"But I might," says Luttrell, "when it was too late."

"True," murmurs Molly, innocently: "so you might. John says all dreams arise from indigestion."

CHAPTER IV

"As through the land at eve we went."

—Tennyson.

Seven long blissful summer days have surrendered themselves to the greedy past. It is almost July. To-day is Wednesday,—to-morrow June will be no more.

"Molly," says Mr. Massereene, with the laudable intention of rousing Molly's ire, "this is the day for which we have accepted Lady Barton's invitation to go to the Castle, to meet Lord and Lady Rossmere."

"'This is the cat that killed the rat, that did something or other in the house that Jack built,'" interrupts Molly, naughtily.

"And on this occasion you have not been invited," goes on John, serenely, "which shows she does not think you respectable,—not quite fit for polite society; so you must stay at home, like the bold little girl, and meditate on your misdemeanors."

"Lady Barton is a very intelligent person, who fully understands my abhorrence of old fogies," says Miss Massereene, with dignity.

"Sour grapes," says John. "But, now that you have given such an unfair turn to Lady Barton's motives, I feel it my duty to explain the exact truth to Luttrell. When last, my dear Tedcastle, Molly was invited to meet the Rossmeres, she behaved so badly and flirted so outrageously with his withered lordship, that he became perfectly imbecile toward the close of the entertainment, and his poor old wife was reduced almost to the verge of tears. I blushed for her; I did indeed."

"Oh, John! how can you say such things before Mr. Luttrell? If he is foolish enough to believe you, think what a dreadful opinion he will have of me!" With a lovely smile at Luttrell across the bowl of flowers that ornaments the breakfast-table. "And with such a man, too! A terrible old person who has forgotten his native language and can only mumble, and who has not got one tooth in his mouth or one hair on his head, and no flesh at all to speak of."

"What a fetching description!" says Luttrell. "You excite my curiosity. He is not 'on view,' is he?"

"Not yet," says Molly, with an airy laugh. "Probably when he dies they will embalm him, and forward him to the British Museum, as a remarkable species of his kind; and then we shall all get the full value of one shilling. I myself would walk to London to see that."

"So would I," says Luttrell, "if you would promise to tell me the day you are going."

"Letitia, I feel myself *de trop*, whatever you may," exclaims John, rising. "And see how time flies; it is almost half-past ten. Really, we grow lazier every day. I shudder to think at what hour I shall get my breakfast by the time I am an old man."

(Poor John!)

"Why, you are as old as the hills this moment," says Molly, drawing down his kind face, that bears such a strong resemblance to her own, to bestow upon it a soft sweet kiss. "You are not to grow any older,—mind that; you are to keep on looking just as you look now forever, or I will not forgive you. Now go away and make yourself charming for your Lady Barton."

"Oh, I don't spend three hours before my looking-glass," says John, "whenever I go anywhere." He is smoothing her beautiful hair with loving fingers as he speaks. "But I think I will utter one word of warning, Ted, before I leave you to her tender mercies for the day. Don't give in to her. If you do, she will lead you an awful life. At first she bullied me until I hardly dared to call my soul my own; but when I found Letitia I plucked up spirit (you know a worm will turn), and ventured to defy her, and since that existence has been bearable."

"Letitia, come to my defense," says Molly, in a tragic tone, stretching out her arms to her sister-in-law, who has been busy pacifying her youngest hope. As he has at last, however, declared himself content with five lumps of sugar and eight sweet biscuits, she finds time to look up and smile brightly at Molly.

"Letitia, my dear, don't perjure yourself," says John. "You know I speak the truth. A last word, Luttrell." He is standing behind his sister as he speaks, and taking her arms he puts her in a chair, and placing her elbows on the table, so that her pretty face sinks into her hands, goes on: "The moment you see her take this attitude, run! don't pause to think, or speculate; run! Because it always means mischief; you may know then that she has quite made up her mind. I speak from experience. Good-bye, children. I hope you will enjoy each other's society. I shall be busy until I leave, so you probably won't see me again."

As Letitia follows him from the room, Molly turns her eyes on Luttrell.

"Are you afraid of me?" asks she, with a glance half questioning, half coquettish.

"I am," replies he, slowly.

"Now you are all my own property," says Molly, gayly, three hours later, after they have bidden good-bye to Mr. and Mrs. Massereene, and eaten their own luncheon *tête-à-tête*. "You cannot escape me. And what shall we do with ourselves this glorious afternoon? Walk? — talk? — or — —"

"Talk," says Luttrell, lazily.

"No, walk," says Molly, emphatically.

"If you have made up your mind to it, of course there is little use in my suggesting anything."

"Very little. Not that you ever do suggest anything," maliciously. "Now stay there, and resign yourself to your fate, while I go and put on my hat."

Along the grass, over the lawn, down to the water's edge, over the water, and into the green fields beyond, the young man follows his guide. Above, the blazing sun is shining with all its might upon the goodly earth; beneath, the grass is browning, withering beneath its rays; and in the man's heart has bloomed that tenderest, cruelest, sweetest of all delights, first love.

He has almost ceased to deny this fact to himself. Already he knows, by the miserable doubts that pursue him, how foolishly he lies to himself when he thinks otherwise. The sweet carelessness, the all-satisfying joy in the present that once was his, has now in his hour of need proved false, and, flying, leaves but a dull unrest in its place. He has fallen madly, gladly, idiotically in love with beautiful Molly Massereene.

Every curve of her pliant body is to him an untold poem; every touch of her hands is a new delight; every tone of her voice is as a song rising from out of the gloom of the lonely night.

"Here you are to stand and admire our potatoes," says Molly, standing still, and indicating with a little sweep of her hand the field in question. "Did you ever see so fine a crop? And did you notice how dry and floury they were at dinner yesterday?"

"I did," says Luttrell, lying very commendably.

"Good boy. We take very great pride out of our potatoes (an Irish dish, you will remember), more especially as every year we find ours are superior to Lord Barton's. There is a certain solace in that, considering how far short we fall in other matters when compared with him. Here is the oat-field. Am I to understand you feel admiration?"

"Of the most intense," gravely.

"Good again. We rather feared"—speaking in the affected, stilted style of a farming report she has adopted throughout—"last month was so deplorably wet, that the oats would be a failure; but we lived in hope, and you may mark the result here again: we are second to none. The wheat-field——" With another slight comprehensive gesture. "By the bye," pausing to examine his face, "am I fulfilling my duties as a hostess? Am I entertaining you?"

"Very much indeed. The more particularly that I was never so entertained before."

"I am fortunate. Well, that is the wheat. I don't know that I can expect you to go into ecstasies over it, as I confess to me it appears more or less weak about the head. *Could* one say that wheat was imbecile?"

"In these days," politely, "one may say anything one likes."

"Yes? You see that rain did some damage; but after all it might have been worse."

"You will excuse my asking the question," says Luttrell, gravely, "but did you ever write for the *Farmer's Gazette*?"

"Never, as yet. But," with an irrepressible smile, "your words suggest to me brilliant possibilities. Perhaps were I to sit down and tell every one in trisyllables what they already know only too well about the crops, and the weather, and the Colorado beetle, and so forth, I might perchance wake up some morning to find myself famous."

"I haven't the faintest doubt of it," says Tedcastle, with such flattering warmth that they both break into a merry laugh. Not that there is anything at all in the joke worthy of such a joyous outburst, but because they are both so young and both so happy.

"Do you think I have done enough duty for one day?" asks Molly. "Have I been prosy enough to allow of my leaving off now? Because I don't think I have got anything more to say about the coming harvest, and I wouldn't care to say it if I had."

"Do you expect me to say that I found you 'prosy'?"

"If you will be so very kind. And you are quite sure no one could accuse me of taking advantage of John's and Letty's absence to be frivolous in my conversation?"

"Utterly positive."

"And you will tell John what a sedate and gentle companion I was?"

"I will indeed, and more,—much more."

"On the contrary, not a word more: if you do you will spoil all. And now," says Molly, with a little soft, lingering smile, "as a reward for your promises, come with me to the top of yonder hill, and I will show you a lovely view."

"Is it not delicious here?" suggests Mr. Luttrell, who can scarcely be called energetic, and who finds it a difficult matter to grow enthusiastic over landscapes when oppressed by a broiling sun.

"What! tired already?" says Molly, with fine disregard of subterfuge.

"No, oh, no," weakly.

"But you *are*," reproachfully. "You are quite *done up*. Why, what would you do if you were ordered on a long day's march?"

"I dare say I should survive it," says Tedcastle, shortly, who is rather offended at her putting it in this light.

"Well, perhaps you might; but you certainly would have nothing to boast of. Now, look at me: I am as fresh as when we started." And in truth, as she stands before him, in her sky-blue gown, he sees she is as cool and bright and unruffled as when they left the house three-quarters of an hour ago. "Well," with a resigned sigh that speaks of disappointment, "stay here until I run up,—I love the place,—and I will join you afterward."

"Not I!" indignantly. "I'm good yet for so much exertion, and I don't believe I could exist without you for so long. 'Call, and I follow—I follow,' even *though* 'I die,'" he adds to himself, in a tone of melancholy.

Up the short but steep hill they toil in silence. Halfway Miss Massereene pauses, either to recover breath or to give encouragement.

"On the top there is always a breeze," she says, in the voice one adopts when determined to impress upon the listener what one's own heart knows to be doubtful.

"Is there?" says Luttrell, gloomily, and with much disbelief.

At length they gain the wished-for top. They stand together, Molly with her usually pale cheeks a little flushed by the exercise, but otherwise calm and collected; Luttrell decidedly the worse for wear. And, yes, there actually *is* a breeze,—a sighing, rustling, unmistakable breeze, that rushes through their hair and through their fingers, and is as a draught from Olympus.

"There, didn't I tell you?" cries Molly, with all the suspicious haste and joy that betrays how weak has been her former hope. "Now, *do* say you are glad I brought you up."

"What need? My only happiness is being with you," says the young man, softly.

"See how beautiful the land is,—as far as one can discern all green and gold," says she, unheeding his subdued tenderness. "Honestly, I do feel a deep interest in farming; and of all the grain that grows I dearly love the barley. First comes the nice plowed brown earth; then the ragged bare suspicion of green; then the strengthening and perfecting of that green until the whole earth is hidden away; then the soft, juicy look of the young blades nodding and waving at each other in the wind, that seems almost tender of them, and at last the fleecy, downy ears all whispering together."

"When you speak in that tone you make me wish myself a barleycorn," says Tedcastle, smiling. "Sit down here beside me, will you, and tell me why your brother calls you 'Molly Bawn'?"

"I hardly know," sinking down near him on the short, cool grass: "it was a name he gave me when I was a little one. John has ever been my father, my mother, my all," says the girl, a soft and lovely dew of earnest affection coming into her eyes. "Were I to love him all my life with twice the love I now bear him, I would scarcely be grateful enough."

"Happy John! Molly! What a pretty name it is."

"But not mine really. No. I was christened Eleanor, after my poor mother, whose history you know. 'Bawn' means fair. 'Fair Molly,'" says she, with a smile, turning to him her face, that resembles nothing so much as a newly-opened flower. "I had hair quite golden when a child. See," tilting her hat so that it falls backward from her head and lies on the greensward behind. "It is hardly dark yet."

"It is the most beautiful hair in the world," says he, touching with gentle, reverential fingers the silken coils that glint and shimmer in the sunlight. "And it is a name that suits you,—and you only."

"Did I never sing you the old Irish song I claim as my own?"

"You never sang for me at all."

"What! you have been here a whole week, and I have never sung for you?" With widely-opened eyes of pure surprise. "What could I have been thinking about? Do you know, I sing very nicely." This without the faintest atom of conceit. "Listen, then, and I will sing to you now."

With her hands clasped around her knees, her head bare, her tresses a little loosened by the wind, and her large eyes fixed upon the distant hills, she thus sweetly sings:

"Oh, Molly Bawn! why leave me pining,
All lonely waiting here for you,
While the stars above are brightly shining,
Because they've nothing else to do?
Oh, Molly Bawn! Molly Bawn!

"The flowers late were open keeping,
To try a rival blush with you,
But their mother, Nature, set them sleeping
With their rosy faces washed in dew.
Oh, Molly Bawn! Molly Bawn!

"The village watch-dog here is snarling;
He takes me for a thief, you see;
For he knows I'd steal you, Molly darling,
And then transported I should be!
Oh, Molly Bawn! Molly Bawn!"

"An odd old song, isn't it?" she says, presently, glancing at him curiously, when she has finished singing, and waited, and yet heard no smallest sound of praise. "You do not speak. Of what are you thinking?"

"Of the injustice of it," says he, in a low, thoughtful tone. "Had you not a bounteous store already when this last great charm was added on? Some poor wretches have nothing, some but a meagre share, while you have wrested from Fortune all her best gifts,—beauty——"

"No, no! stop!" cries Molly, gayly; "before you enumerate the good things that belong to me, remember that I still lack the chiefest: I have no money. I am without doubt the most poverty-stricken of your acquaintances. Can any confession be more humiliating? Good sir, my face is indeed my fortune. Or is it my voice?" pausing suddenly, as though a cold breath from the dim hereafter had blown across her cheek. "I hardly know."

"A rich fortune either way."

"And here I am recklessly imperiling one," hastily putting on her hat once more, "by exposing my precious skin to that savage sun. Come,—it is almost cool now,—let us have a good race down the hill." She slips her slender fingers within his,—a lovable trick of hers, innocent of coquetry,— and, Luttrell conquering with a sigh a wild desire to clasp and kiss the owner of those little clinging fingers on the spot, together they run down the slope into the longer grass below, and so, slowly and more decorously, journey homeward.

On their return they find the house still barren of inmates; no sign of the master or mistress anywhere. Even the servants are invisible. "It might almost be the enchanted palace," says Molly.

Two of the children, seeing her on the lawn, break from their nurse, who is sleeping the sleep of the just, with her broad back against an elm, and running to Molly, fling their arms around her. She rewards them with a kiss apiece, one of which Luttrell surreptitiously purloins from the prettiest.

"Oh, you have come back, Molly. And where have you been?"

"Over the hills and far away."

"*Very* far away? But you brought her back again," nodding a golden head gravely at Luttrell; "and nurse said you wouldn't. She said all soldiers were wicked, and that some day you would steal our Molly. But you won't," coaxingly: "will you, now?"

Luttrell and Molly laugh and redden a little.

"I doubt if I would be able," he says, without raising his eyes from the child's face.

"I don't think you are a soldier at all," declares the darker maiden, coming more boldly to the front, as though fortified by this assertion. "You have no sword; and there never was a soldier without a sword, was there?"

"I begin to feel distinctly ashamed of myself," says Luttrell. "I *have* a sword, Daisy, somewhere. But not here. The next time I come I will bring it with me for your special delectation."

"Did you ever cut off any one's head?" asks the timid, fair-haired Renee, in the background, moving a few steps nearer to him, with rising hope in her voice.

"Miss Massereene, if you allow this searching examination to go on, I shall sink into the ground," says Luttrell. "I feel as if the eyes of Europe were upon me. Why cannot I boast that I have sent a thousand blacks to glory? No, Renee, with shame I confess it, I am innocent of bloodshed."

"I am so glad!" says the darker Daisy, while the gentler looking child turns from him with open disappointment.

"Do you think you can manage to amuse yourself for a little while?" says Molly. "Because I must leave you; I promised Letty to see after some of her housekeeping for her: I won't be too long," with a view to saving him from despair.

"I will see what a cigar can do for me," replies he, mournfully. "But remember how heavily time drags—sometimes."

Kissing her hand to him gayly, she trips away over the grass, leaving him to the tender mercies of the children. They, with all the frightful energy of youth, devote themselves to his service, and, seizing on him, carry him off to their especial sanctum, where they detain him in durance vile until the welcome though stentorian lungs of the nurse make themselves heard.

"There, you may go now," says Daisy, giving him a last ungrateful push; and as in a body they abscond, he finds himself depressed, but free. Not only free, but alone. This brings him back to thoughts of Molly. How long she is! Women never do know what time means. He will walk round to the yard and amuse himself with the dogs until she has finished her tiresome business.

Now, the kitchen window looks out upon the path he means to tread;—not only the kitchen window, but Molly. And as Luttrell comes by, with his head bent and a general air of moodiness about him, she is so far flattered by his evident dullness that she cannot refrain from tapping at the glass to call his attention.

"Have you been enjoying yourself?" asks she, innocently. "You *look* as if you had."

He starts as her voice so unexpectedly meets his ear, and turns upon her a face from which all *ennui* has fled.

"Do I?" he says. "Then my looks lie. *Enjoying* myself, with a pack of small demons! For what do you take me? No, I have been wretched. What on earth are you doing down there? You have been *hours* about it already. Surely, whatever it is, it must be done now. If you don't come out shortly you will have murder on your soul, as I feel suicidal."

"I can't come yet."

"Then would you let me—might I——"

"Oh, come here if you like," says Molly. "*I* don't mind, if you don't."

Without waiting further invitation, Luttrell goes rapidly round, descends the kitchen steps, and presently finds himself in Molly's presence.

It is a pretty old-fashioned, low-ceilinged kitchen, full of quaint corners and impossible cupboards so high up in the wall as at first sight to be pronounced useless.

A magnificent fire burns redly, yet barely causes discomfort. (Why is it that a fire in the kitchen fails to afflict one as it would, if lit in summer, in the drawing-room or parlor?) Long, low benches, white as snow, run by the walls. The dresser—is there anything prettier than a well-kept dresser?—shines out conceitedly from its own place, full of its choicest bravery. In the middle of the gleaming tiles stands the table, and beside it stands Molly.

Such a lovely Molly!—a very goddess of a Molly!

Her white arms, bare to the elbow, are covered with flour; a little patch of it has found a resting-place on the right side of her hair, where undoubtedly one hand must have gone to punish some amorous lock that would wander near her lips. Her eyes are full of light; her very lips are smiling. Jane, the cook, at a respectful distance, is half ashamed at the situation of her young lady; the young lady is not at all ashamed.

"Do you like me?" cries she, holding her floury arms aloft. "Are you lost in admiration? Ah! you have yet to learn how universal are my gifts. I can *cook*!"

"Can you?" says Luttrell, with a grimace. "What are you making now? I am anxious to know."

"Positively," bending a little forward, the better to see him; "you look it. Why?"

"That I may avoid it by and by." Here, with a last faint glimmer of prudence, he retires to the other end of the table.

"Have you come here to insult me in my own domain?" cries Molly wrathfully. "Rash youth, you rush upon your fate; or, to speak more truthfully, your fate intends to rush on you. Now take the consequences."

With both her hands extended she advances on him, fell determination in her eye. Alas for his coat when those ten snowy fingers shall have marked it for their own!

"Mercy!" cries Luttrell, falling on his knees at her feet. "Anything but that. I apologize, I retract; I will do penance; I will even eat it, every bit; I will——"

"Will you go away?"

"No," heroically, rising to his full height, "I will *not*. I would rather be white from head to heel than leave this adorable kitchen."

There is a slight pause. Mercy and vengeance are in the balance, and Molly holds the scales. After a brief struggle mercy triumphs.

"I forgive you," says Molly, withdrawing; "but as punishment you really must help me, as I am rather late this evening. Here, stone these," pushing toward him a plateful of raisins."

"Law, miss, I'll do 'em," says Jane, who feels matters are going too far. To have a strange gentleman, one of the "high-up" gentry, a "reel millingtary swell," stoning raisins in her kitchen is more than she can reconcile herself to in silence; she therefore opens the floodgates of speech. "He'll soil hisself," she says, in a deep, reproachful whisper, fixing an imploring eye on Molly.

"I hope so," murmurs that delinquent, cheerfully. "He heartily deserves it. You may go and occupy yourself elsewhere, Jane; Mr. Luttrell and I will make this pudding. Now go on, Mr. Luttrell; don't be shirking your duty. It is either do or die."

"I think it is odds on the dying," says he.

Silence for at least three minutes,—in this case a long, long time.

"I can't find anything in them," ventures he, at last, in a slightly dejected tone; "and they're so horrid sticky."

"*Nothing in them?* Nonsense! you don't know how to go about it. Look. I'll show you. Open them with your first finger and thumb—so; and now do you see them?" triumphantly producing a round brown article on the tip of her finger.

"Where?" asks Luttrell, bending forward.

"There," says Molly, bending too. Their heads are very close together. The discreet Jane has retired into her pantry. "It is the real thing. Can't you see it?"

"Scarcely. It is very small, isn't it?"

"Well, it *is* small," Miss Massereene confesses, with reluctance; "it certainly is the smallest I ever saw. Still——"

By this time they are looking, not at the seed of the raisin, but into each other's eyes, and again there is an eloquent pause.

"May I examine it a little closer?" Luttrell asks, as though athirst for information, possessing himself quietly of the hand, raisin-stone, flour, and all, and bringing it suspiciously near to his lips. "Does it—would it—I mean does flour come off things easily?"

"I don't know," returns Molly, with an innocent gravity that puts him to shame. "Off some things it washes readily enough; but—mind you, I can't say for certain, as I have had no experience; but I don't think——"

"Yes?" seeing her hesitate.

"Well, I don't think," emphasizing each word with a most solemn nod, "it would come off your moustache in a hurry."

"I'll risk it, anyhow," says Luttrell, stooping suddenly to impress a fervent kiss upon the little powdered fingers he is holding.

"Oh! how wrong, how extremely wrong of you!" exclaims Miss Massereene, as successfully shocked as though the thought that he might be tempted to such a deed has never occurred to her. Yet, true to her nature, she makes no faintest pretense at withdrawing from him her hand until a full minute has elapsed. Then, unable longer to restrain herself, she bursts into a merry laugh,—a laugh all sweetest, clearest music.

"If you could only see how funny you look!" cries she. "You are fair with a vengeance now. Ah! do go and see for yourself." Giving him a gentle push toward an ancient glass that hangs disconsolately near the clock, and thereby leaving another betraying mark upon the shoulder of his coat.

Luttrell, having duly admired himself and given it as his opinion that though flour on the arms may be effective, flour on the face is not, has barely time to wipe his moustache free of it when Mrs. Massereene enters.

"You here," exclaims she, staring at Tedcastle, "of all places in the world! I own I am amazed. Oh, if your brother officers could only see you now, and your coat all over flour! I need hardly inquire if this is Molly's doing. Poor boy!" with a laugh. "It is a shame. Molly, you are never happy unless you are tormenting some one."

"But I always make it up to them afterward: don't I, now, Letty?" murmurs Molly, sweetly, speaking to Letitia, but directing a side-glance at Luttrell from under her long, dark lashes: this side-glance is almost a promise.

"Well, so you have come at last, Letty. And how did you enjoy your 'nice, long, happy day in the country,' as the children say?"

"Very much, indeed,—far more than I expected. The Mitchells were there, which added a little to our liveliness."

"And my poor old mummy, was he there? And is he still holding together?"

"Lord Rossmere? He is indeed, and was asking most tenderly for you. I never saw him look so well."

"Oh! it grows absurd," says Molly, in disgust. "How much longer does he intend keeping up the farce? He *must* fall to pieces soon."

"He hasn't a notion of it," says Letitia, warming to her description; "he has taken a new lease of his life. He looked only too well,—positively ten years younger. I think myself he was 'done up.' I could see his coat was padded; and he has adorned his head with a very sleek brown wig."

"Jane," says Molly, weakly, "be so good as to stand close behind me. I feel as if I were going to faint directly."

"Law, miss!" says Jane, giving way to her usual expletive. She is a clean and worthy soul where pots and pans are concerned, but apart from them can scarcely be termed eloquent.

"You are busy, Jane," says Mr. Luttrell, obligingly, "and I am not. (I see you are winding up that long-suffering pudding.) Let me take a little trouble off your hands. *I* will stand close behind Miss Massereene."

"He had quite a color too," goes on Letitia, mysteriously, "a very extraordinary color. Not that of an old man, nor yet of a young one, and I am utterly certain it was paint. It was a vivid, uncompromising red; so red that I think the poor old thing's valet must have overdone his work, for fun. Wasn't it cruel?"

"Are you ready, Jane?" murmurs Molly, with increasing weakness.

"Quite ready, miss," returns Luttrell, with hopeful promptness.

"I asked John on the way home what he thought," goes on Letitia, with an evident interest in her tale, "and he quite agrees with me that it was rouge, or, at all events, something artificial."

"One more word, Letitia,"—faintly,—"a last one. Has he had that sole remaining tooth in the front of his mouth made steady?"

"No," cries Mrs. Massereene, triumphantly, "he has not. Do you too remember that awful tooth? It is literally the only thing left undone, and I can't imagine why. It still waggles uncomfortably when he talks, and his upper lip has the same old trick of catching on it and refusing to come down again until compelled. Sir John was there, and took me in to luncheon; and as I sat just opposite Lord Rossmere I could see distinctly. I particularly noticed that."

"You have saved me," cries Molly, briskly. "Had your answer been other than it was, I would not have hesitated for a moment: I would have gone off into a death-like swoon. Thank you, Jane,"—with a backward nod at Luttrell, whom she has refused to recognize: "I need not detain you any longer."

"Mrs. Massereene, I shall never forgive you," says Luttrell.

"And is this the way you entertain your guests, Molly?" asks Letitia. "Have you spent your day in the kitchen?"

"The society of the 'upper ten' is not good for you, Letitia," says Molly, severely. "There is a faint flavor of would-be sarcasm about you, and it doesn't suit you in the least: your lips have not got the correct curve. No, my dear: although unnoticed by the nobility of our land, we, too, have had our 'nice, long, happy day in the country.' Haven't we, Mr. Luttrell?"

"Do you think he would dare say 'No' with *your* eyes upon him?" says Letitia, laughing. "By and by I shall hear the truth. Come with me"—to Tedcastle—"and have a glass of sherry before your dinner: I am sure you must want it, after all you have gone through."

CHAPTER V

"Gather the roses while ye may;
Old time is still a-flying;
And the same flower that smiles to-day
To-morrow will be dying."

—Herrick.

It is four o'clock, and a hush, a great stillness, born of oppressive heat, is over all the land. Again the sun is smiting with hot wrath the unoffending earth; the flowers nod drowsily or lie half dead of languor, their gay leaves touching the ground.

"The sky was blue as the summer sea,
The depths were cloudless overhead;
The air was calm as it could be;
There was no sight or sound of dread,"

quotes Luttrell, dreamily, as he strays idly along the garden path, through scented shrubs and all the many-hued children of light and dew. His reverie is lengthened yet not diffuse. One little word explains it all. It seems to him that word is everywhere: the birds sing it, the wind whistles it as it rushes faintly past, the innumerable voices of the summer cry ceaselessly for "Molly."

"Mr. Luttrell, Mr. Luttrell," cries some one, "look up." And he does look up.

Above him, on the balcony, stands Molly, "a thing of beauty," fairer than any flower that grows beneath. Her eyes like twin stars are gleaming, deepening; her happy lips are parted; her hair drawn loosely back, shines like threads of living gold. Every feature is awake and full of life; every movement of her sweet body, clad in its white gown, proclaims a very joyousness of living.

With hands held high above her head, filled with parti-colored roses, she stands laughing down upon him; while he stares back at her, with a heart filled too full of love for happiness. With a slight momentary closing of her lids she opens both her hands and flings the scented shower into his uplifted face.

"Take your punishment," she whispers, saucily, bending over him, "and learn your lesson. Don't look at me another time."

"It was by your own desire I did so," exclaims he, bewildered, shaking the crimson and yellow and white leaves from off his head and shoulders. "How am I to understand you?"

"How do I know, when I don't even understand myself? But when I called out to you 'Look up,' of course I meant 'look down.' Don't you remember the old game with the handkerchief?—when I say 'Let go,' 'hold fast;' and when I say 'Hold fast,' 'let go?' You must recollect it."

"I have a dim idea of something idiotic, like what you say."

"It is not idiotic, but it suits only some people; it suits me. There is a certain perverseness about it, a determination to do just what one is told not to do, that affects me most agreeably. Did I"—glancing at the rosy shower at his feet—"did I hurt you *much*?" With a smile.

There is a little plank projecting from the wood-work of the pillars that supports the balcony: resting his foot on this, and holding on by the railings above, Luttrell draws himself up until his face is almost on a level with hers,—almost, but not quite: she can still overshadow him.

"If that was all the injury I had received at your hands, how easy it would be to forgive!" says he, in a low tone.

"Poor hands," says Molly, gazing at her shapely fingers, "how have they sinned? Am I to understand, then, that I am not forgiven?"

"Yes."

"You are unkind to me."

"Oh, Molly!"

"*Dreadfully* unkind to me. Can you deny it? Now, tell me what this crime is that I have committed and you cannot pardon."

"I will not," says the young man, turning a little pale, while the smile dies out of his eyes and from round his lips. "I dread to put my injuries into words. Should they anger you, you might with one look seal my death-warrant."

"Am I so blood-thirsty? How badly you think of me!"

"Do I?" Reading with the wistful sadness of uncertainty her lovely face. "You know better than that. You know too—do you not?—what it is I would say,—if I dared. Oh, Molly, what have you done to me, what witchery have you used, that, after escaping for twenty-seven long years, I should now fall so hopelessly in——"

"Hush!" says Molly, quickly, and, letting her hand fall lightly on his forehead, brings it slowly, slowly, over his eyes and down his face, until at length it rests upon his lips rebukingly. "Not another word. You have known me but a few days,—but a little short three weeks,—and you would——"

"Yes, I would," eagerly, devouring with fond kisses the snow-flake that would stay his words. "Three weeks,—a year,—ten years,—what does it matter? I think the very first night I saw you here in this garden the mischief was done. My heart left me. You stole the very best of me; and will you give nothing in exchange?"

"I will not listen," says Molly, covering her ears with her hands, but not so closely that she must be deaf. "Do you hear? You are to be silent."

"Do you forbid me to speak?"

"Yes; I am in a hurry; I cannot listen,—*now*," says this born coquette, unable to release her slave so soon.

"Some other time,—when you know me better,—you will listen then: is that what you mean?" Still detaining her with passionate entreaty both in tone and manner. "Molly, give me one word of hope."

"I don't know what I mean," she says, effecting her escape, and moving back to the security of the drawing-room window, which stands open. "I never do know. And I have not got the least bit of memory in the world. Do you know I came out here to tell you tea was to be brought out for us under the trees on the lawn; and when I saw you I forgot everything. Is that a hopeful sign?" With a playful smile.

"I will try to think so; and—don't go yet, Molly." Seeing her about to enter the drawing-room. "Surely, if tea is to be on the lawn, it is there we ought to go."

"I am half afraid of you. If I consent to bestow upon you a little more of my society, will you promise not to talk in—in—that way again to me?"

"But——"

"I will have no 'buts.' Promise what I ask, or I will hide myself from you for the rest of the day."

"I swear, then," says he; and, so protected, Miss Massereene ventures down the balcony steps and accompanies him to the shaded end of the lawn.

By this time it is nearly five o'clock, and as yet oppressively warm. The evening is coming with a determination to rival in dull heat the early part of the day. The sheep in great white snowy patches lie panting in the distant corners of the adjoining fields; the cows, tired of whisking their foolish tails in an unsuccessful war with the insatiable flies, are all huddled together, and give way to mournful lows that reproach the tarrying milkmaid.

Above in the branches a tiny bird essays to sing, but stops half stifled, and, forgetting the tuneful note, contents itself with a lazy "cluck-cluck" that presently degenerates still further into a dying "coo" that is hardly musical, because so full of sleep.

Molly has seated herself upon the soft young grass, beneath the shade of a mighty beech, against the friendly trunk of which she leans her back. Even this short walk from the house to the six stately beeches that are the pride and glory of Brooklyn has told upon her. Her usually merry eyes have subsided into a gentle languor; over them the white lids droop heavily. No little faintest tinge of color adorns her pale cheeks; upon her lap her hands lie idle, their very listlessness betokening the want of energy they feel.

At about two yards' distance from her reclines her guest, full length, his fingers interlaced behind his head, looking longer, slighter than usual, as with eyes upturned he gazes in silence upon the far-off, never-changing blue showing through the net-work of the leaves above him.

"Are you quite used up?" asks Molly, in the slow, indifferent tone that belongs to heat, as the crisp, gay voice belongs to cold. "I never heard you silent for so long before. Do you think you are likely to *die*? Because—don't do it here, please: it would give me such a shock."

"I am far more afraid I shall live," replies her companion. "Oh, how I loathe the summer!"

"You are not so far gone as I feared: you can still use bad language. Now, tell me what sweet thought has held you in thrall so long."

"If I must confess it, I have been thinking of how untold a luxury at this moment would be an iced bath."

"'An iced bath'!" With as much contempt as she can summon. "How prosaic! And I quite flattered myself you were thinking of me." She says this as calmly as though she had supposed him thinking of his dinner.

Tedcastle's lips part in a faint smile, a mere glimmer,—a *laugh* is beyond him,—and he turns his head just so far round as will permit his eyes to fall full upon her face.

"I fancied such thoughts on my part tabooed," he says. "And besides, would they be of any advantage to you?"

"No material advantage, but they would have been only fair. *I* was thinking of *you*."

"Were you? Really!" With such overpowering interest as induces him to raise himself on his elbow, the better to see her. "You were thinking—that——"

"Don't excite yourself. I was wondering whether, when you were a baby, your nose—in proportion, of course—was as lengthy and solemn as it is now."

"Pshaw!" mutters Mr. Luttrell, angrily, and goes back to his original position.

"If it was," pursues Molly, with a ruthless and amused laugh, "you must have been an awfully funny baby to look at." She appears to find infinite amusement in this idea for a full minute, after which follows a disgusted silence that might have lasted until dinner-hour but for the sound of approaching footsteps.

Looking up simultaneously, they perceive Letitia coming toward them, with Sarah behind, carrying a tray, on which are cups, and small round cakes, and plates of strawberries.

"I have brought you your tea at last," cries Letitia, looking like some great fair goddess, with her large figure and stately walk and benign expression, as she bears down upon them. She is still a long way off, yet her voice comes to them clear and distinct, without any suspicion of shouting. She is smiling benevolently, and has a delicious pink color in her cheeks.

"We thought you had forgotten us," says Molly, springing to her feet with a sudden return of animation. "But you have come in excellent time, as we were on the very brink of a quarrel that would have disgraced the Kilkenny cats. And what have you brought us? Tea, and strawberries, and dear little hot cakes! Oh, Letty, how I love you!"

"So do I," says Luttrell. "Mrs. Massereene, may I sit beside you?"

"For protection?" asks she, with a laugh.

In the meantime Molly has arranged the tray before herself, and is busily engaged placing all the worst strawberries and the smallest cake on one plate.

"Before you go any further," says Luttrell, "I won't have that plate. Nothing shall induce me. So you may spare your trouble."

"Then you may go without any, as I myself intend eating all the others."

"Mrs. Massereene, you are my only friend. I appeal to you; is it fair? Just look at all she is keeping for herself. If I die for it, I will get my rights," exclaims Tedcastle, goaded into activity, and springing from his recumbent position, makes straight for the tray. There is a short but decisive battle; and then, victory being decided in favor of Luttrell, he makes a successful raid upon the fruit, and retires covered with glory and a good deal of juice.

"Coward, thief! won't I pay you for this?" cries Molly, viciously.

"I wouldn't use school-boy slang if I were you," returns Luttrell, with provoking coolness, and an evident irritating appreciation of the fruit.

Fortunately for all parties, at this moment John appears upon the scene.

"It *is* warm," says he, sinking on the grass, under the weak impression that he is imparting information.

"I think there is thunder in the air," says Letitia, with a mischievous glance at the late combatants, at which they laugh in spite of themselves.

"Not at all, my dear; you are romancing," says ignorant John. "Well, Molly Bawn, where is my tea? Have you kept me any?"

"As if I would forget *you*! Is it not an extraordinary thing, Letty, that Sarah cannot be induced to bring us a tea-pot? Now, I want more, and must only wait her pleasure."

"Remonstrate with her," says John.

"I am tired of doing so. Only yesterday I had a very lengthy argument with her on the subject, to the effect that as it was I who was having the tea, and not she, surely I might be allowed to have it the way I wished. When I had exhausted my eloquence, and was nearly on the verge of tears, I discovered that she was still at the very point from which we started. 'But the tea is far more genteeler, Miss Molly, when brought up without the tea-pot. It spoils the look of the tray.' I said 'Yes, the *want* of it does,' with much indignation; but I might as well have kept my temper."

"Much *better*," says Luttrell, placidly.

"I do hate having my tea poured out for me," goes on Molly, not deigning to notice him. "I am convinced Sarah lived with a retired tallow-chandler, or something equally horrible, before she came to us. She has one idol to which she sacrifices morning, noon, and night, and I think she calls it 'style.'"

"And what is that?" interposes Luttrell, anxiously.

"I don't know, but I think it has something to do with not putting the tea-pot on the tray, for instance, and taking the pretty fresh covers off the drawing-room chairs when any one is coming, to convince them of the green damask beneath. And once when, during a passing fit of insanity, I dressed my hair into a pyramid, she told me I looked 'stylish.' It took me some time to recover that shock to my vanity."

"I like 'stylish' people myself," says John. "Lady Barton, I am positive, is just what Sarah means by that, and I admire her immensely,—within bounds, of course, my dear Letitia."

"Dreadful, vulgar woman!" says Molly, with a frown. "I'm sure I wouldn't name Letty in the same day with her."

"We all know you are notoriously jealous of her," says John. "Her meridian charms eclipse yours of the dawn."

"How poetical!" laughs Molly. "But the thing to see is Letitia producing the children when her ladyship comes to pay a visit. She always reminds me of the Mother of the Gracchi. Now, confess it, Letty, don't you think Lady Barton's diamonds and rubies and emeralds grow pale and lustreless beside your living jewels?"

"Indeed I do," returns Letitia, with the readiest, most unexpected simplicity.

"Letitia," cries Molly, touched, giving her a little hug, "I do think you are the dearest, sweetest, truest old goose in the world."

"Nonsense, my dear!" says Letitia, with a slow pleased blush that is at once so youthful and so lovely.

"Oh! why won't Sarah come?" says Molly, recurring suddenly to her woes. "I know, even if I went on my knees to Mr. Luttrell, he would not so far trouble himself as to go in and find her; but I think she might remember my weakness for tea."

"There she is!" exclaims John.

To their right rises a hedge, on which it has been customary for ages to dry the household linen, and moving toward it appears Sarah, armed with a basket piled high to the very top.

"Sarah," calls Molly, "Sarah—Sarah!"

Now, Sarah, though an undeniably good servant, and a cleanly one, striking the beholder as a creature born to unlimited caps and spotless aprons, is undoubtedly obtuse. She presents her back hair and heels—that would not have disgraced an elephant—to Miss Massereene's call, and goes on calmly with her occupation of shaking out and hanging up to dry the garments she has just brought.

"Shall I go and call her?" asks Luttrell, with some remains of grace and an air of intense fatigue.

"Not worth your while," says John, with all a man's delicious consideration for a man; "she must turn in a moment, and then she will see us."

For two whole minutes, therefore, they gaze in rapt silence upon the unconscious Sarah. Presently Mr. Massereene breaks the eloquent stillness.

"There is nothing," says he, mildly, "that so clearly declares the sociability—the *bon camaraderie*, so to speak—that ought to exist in every well-brought-up family as the sight of washing done at home. There is such a happy mingling and yet such a thorough disregard of sex about it. It is 'Hail, fellow! well met!' all through. If you will follow Sarah's movements for a minute longer you will better understand what I mean. There! now she is spreading out Molly's pale-green muslin, in which she looked so irresistible last week. And there goes Daisy's pinafore, and Bobby's pantaloons; and now she is pausing to remove a defunct grasshopper from Renee's bonnet! What a charming picture it all makes, so full of life! There go Molly's stock——"

"John," interrupts Molly, indignantly, who has been frowning heavily at him for some time without the smallest result.

"If you say another word," puts in Luttrell, burying his face in the grass, with a deep groan, "if you go one degree further, I shall faint."

"And now comes my shirt," goes on John, in the same even tone, totally unabashed.

"My dear John!" exclaims Letitia, much scandalized, speaking in a very superior tone, which she fondly but erroneously believes to be stern and commanding, "I beg you will pursue the subject no further. We have no desire whatever to learn any particulars about your shirts."

"And why not, my dear?" demands Mr. Massereene, his manner full of mild but firm expostulation. "What theme so worthy of prolonged discussion as a clean shirt? Think of the horrors that encompass all the 'great unwashed,' and then perhaps you will feel as I do. In my opinion it is a topic on which volumes might be written: if I had time I would write them myself. And if you will give yourself the trouble to think, my dear Letitia, you will doubtless be able to bring to mind the fact that once a very distinguished and reasonable person called Hood wrote a song about it. Besides which——"

"She is looking now!" cries Molly, triumphantly. "Sarah—Sa—rah!"

"The 'bells they go ringing for Sarah,'" quotes Mr. Luttrell, irrelevantly. But Sarah has heard, and is hastening toward them, and wrath is for the present averted from his unlucky head.

Smiling, panting, rubicund, comes Sarah, ready for anything.

"Some more tea, Sarah," says Molly, with a smile that would corrupt an archbishop. Molly is a person adored by servants. "That's my cup."

"And that's mine," says Tedcastle, turning his upside down on his saucer. "I am particular about getting my own cup, Sarah, and hope you will not mistake mine for Miss Massereene's. Fill it, and bring it back to me just like this."

"Yes, sir," says Sarah, in perfect good faith.

"And, Sarah—next time we would like the tea-pot," puts in Mr. Massereene, mildly.

CHAPTER VI

"Oh, we fell out,—I know not why,—
And kissed again with tears."
—Tennyson.

They are now drawing toward the close of July. To Luttrell it appears as though the moments are taking to themselves wings to fly away; to more prosaic mortals they drag. Ever since that first day in the garden when he betrayed his love to Molly, he had been silent on the subject, fearful lest he gain a more decided repulse.

Yet this enforced silence is to him a lingering torture; and as a school-boy with money in his pocket burns till he spend it, so he, with his heart brimful of love, is in torment until he can fling its rich treasures at his mistress's feet. Only a very agony of doubt restrains him.

Not that this doubt contains all pain; there is blended with it a deep ecstasy of joy, made to be felt, not spoken; and all the grace and poetry and sweetness of a first great passion,—that thing that in all the chilling after-years never wholly dies,—that earliest, purest dew that falls from the awakening heart.

"O love! young love!
Let saints and cynics cavil as they will,
One throb of yours is worth whole years of ill."

So thinks Luttrell; so think I.

To-day Molly has deserted him, and left him to follow his own devices. John has gone into the next town on some important errand connected with the farm: so perforce our warrior shoulders his gun and sallies forth savagely, bent on slaying aught that comes in his way. As two crows, a dejected rabbit, and an intelligent squirrel are all that present themselves to his notice, he wearies toward three o'clock, and thinks with affection of home. For so far has his air-castle mounted that, were Molly to inhabit a hovel, that hovel to him would be home.

Crossing a stile and a high wall, he finds himself in the middle of the grounds that adjoin the more modest Brooklyn. The shimmer of a small lake makes itself seen through the branches to his right, and as he gains its bank a boat shoots forth from behind the willows, and a gay voice sings:

"There was a little man,

And he had a little gun,

And his bullets they were made of lead, lead, lead;

He went to a brook,

And he saw a little— —"

"Oh, Mr. Luttrell, please, please don't shoot *me*," cries Molly, breaking down in the song with an exaggerated show of feigned terror.

"Do *you* call yourself a 'duck'?" demands Luttrell, with much scorn. "Is there any limit to a woman's conceit? Duck, indeed! say rather— —"

"Swan? Well, yes, I will, if you wish it: I don't mind," says Molly, amiably. "And now tell me, are you not surprised to see me here?"

"I am, indeed. Are you ubiquitous? I thought I left you safe at home."

"So you did. But I never counted on your staying so long away. I was tired of waiting for you. I thought you would *never* come. So in despair I came out here by myself."

"So you absolutely missed me?" says Luttrell, quietly, although his heart is beating rapidly. Too well he knows her words are from the lips alone.

"Oh, didn't I!" exclaims she, heartily. "You should have seen me standing at the gate peering up and down for you and bemoaning my fate, like that silly Mariana in the moated grange. Indeed, if I had been photographed then and there and named 'Forsaken,' I'm positive I would have sold well."

"I don't doubt it."

"Then I grew enraged, and determined to trouble my head no more about you; and then— — It was lucky I came here, wasn't it?"

"Very lucky,—for me. But you never told me you had a boat on the lake."

"Because I hadn't,—at least not for the last two months,—until yesterday. It got broken in the spring, and they have been ever since mending it. They are so slow down here. I kept the news of its return from you a secret all yesterday, meaning to bring you here and show it you as a surprise; and this is how my plan has ended."

"But are you allowed? I thought you did not know the owners of this place."

"Neither do we. He is a retired butcher, I fancy (he doesn't look anything like as respectable as a grocer), with a fine disregard for the Queen's English. We called there one day, Letitia and I (nothing would induce John to accompany us), but Mrs. Butcher was too much for Letitia,—too much for even me," cries Molly, with a laugh, "and I'm not particular: so we never called again. They don't bear malice, however, and rather affect our having our boat here than otherwise. Jump in and row me for a little while."

Over the water, under the hanging branches they glide to the sweet music of the wooing wind, and scarcely care to speak, so perfect is the motion and the stillness.

Luttrell, with his hat off and a cigar between his lips, is far happier than he himself is at all aware. Being of necessity opposite her, he is calmly feasting himself upon the sweet scenery of Molly's face, or else letting his eyes wander to where her slender fingers drag their way through the cool water, leaving small bubbles in their track.

"It is a pity the country is so stupid, is it not?" says Molly, breaking the silence at length, and speaking in a regretful tone. "Because otherwise there is no place like it."

"Some country places are not at all stupid. There are generally too many people about. I think Brooklyn's principal charm is its repose, its complete separation from the world."

"Well, for my own part," seriously, "I think I would excuse the repose and the separation from the world, by which, I suppose, you mean society. I have no admiration for cloisters and convents myself; I like amusement, excitement. If I could, I would live in London all the year round," concludes Molly, with growing animation.

"Oh, horror!" exclaims Luttrell, who, seven years before, thought exactly as she does now, and who occasionally thinks so still. "Who that ever lived for six months among all its grime and smoke and turmoil but would pine for this calmer life?"

"I lived there for more than six months," says Molly, "and I didn't pine for anything. I thought it charming. It is all very well for you"—dejectedly—"who are tired of gayety, to go into raptures over calmness and tranquillity, and that; but if you lived in Brooklyn from summer until winter and from winter back again to summer, and if you could count your balls on one hand,"—holding up five wet open fingers,—"you would think just as I do, and long for change."

"I never knew you had been to London."

"Yes: when I was sixteen I spent a whole year there, with a cousin of my father's, who went to Canada with her husband's regiment afterward. But I didn't go out much, she thought me too young, though I was quite as tall as I am now. She heard me sing once, and insisted on carrying me up with her to get me lessons from Marigny. He took great pains with me: that is why I sing so well," says Molly, modestly.

"I confess I often wondered where your exquisite voice received its cultivation, its finish. Now I know. You were fortunate in securing Marigny. I have known him refuse dozens through want of time; or so he said. More probably he would not trouble himself to teach where there was no certainty of success. Well, and so you dislike the country?"

"No, no. Not so much that. What I dislike is having no one to speak to. When John is away and Letty on the tread-mill—that is, in the nursery—I am rather thrown on my own resources; and they are not much. Your coming was the greatest blessing that ever befell me. When I actually beheld you in your own proper person on the garden path that night, I could have hugged you in the exuberance of my joy."

"Then why on earth didn't you?" says Luttrell, reproachfully, as though he had been done out of something.

"A lingering sense of maiden modesty and a faint idea that perhaps you might not like it alone restrained me. But for that I must have given way to my feelings. Just think, if I had," says Molly, breaking into a merry laugh, "what a horrible fright I would have given you!"

"Not a horrible one, at all events. Molly," bending to examine some imaginary thing in the side of the boat, "have you never—had a—lover?"

"A lover? Oh, yes, I have had any amount of them," says Molly, with an alacrity that makes his heart sink. "I don't believe I could count my adorers: it quite puzzles me to know where to begin. There were the curates,—our rector is not sweet-tempered, so we have a fresh one every year,—and they never fail me. Three months after they come, as regular as clock-work, they ask me to be their wife. Now, I appeal to you,"—clasping her hands and wrinkling up all her pretty forehead,—"do I look like a curate's wife?"

"You do not," replies Luttrell, emphatically, regarding with interest the debonnaire, spirituelle face before him: "no, you most certainly do not."

"Well, I thought not myself; yet each of those deluded young men saw something angelic about me, and would insist on asking me to share his lot. They kept themselves sternly blind to the fact that I detest with equal vigor broth and old women."

"Intolerable presumption!" says Luttrell, parenthetically.

"Was it? I don't think I looked at it in that light. They were all very estimable men, and Mr. Rochfort was positively handsome. You, you may well stare, but some curates, you know, are good-looking, and he was decidedly High Church. In fact, he wasn't half so bad as the generality of them," says Molly, relentingly. "Only—it may be wrong, but the truth is I hate curates. I think nothing of them. They are a mixture of tea and small jokes, and are ever at a stand-still. They are always in the act of budding,—they never bloom; and then they are so afraid of the bishop."

"I thank my stars I'm not a curate," says Luttrell, devoutly.

"However,"—regretfully,—"they were *something*: a proposal is always an excitement. But the present man is married; so that makes it impossible for this present year. There was positively nothing to which to look forward. So you may fancy with what rapture I hailed your coming."

"You are very good," says Luttrell, in an uncertain tone, not being quite sure whether he is intensely amused or outrageously angry, or both. "Had you—any other lovers?"

"Yes. There was the last doctor. He poisoned a poor man afterward by mistake, and had to go away."

"After what?"

"After I declined to assist him in the surgery," says Molly, demurely. "It was a dreadful thing,—the poisoning, I mean,—and caused a great deal of scandal. I don't believe it was anybody's fault, but I certainly did pity the man he killed. And—it might have been me, you know; think of that! He was very much attached to me; and so was the Lefroys' eldest son, and James Warder, and the organist, to say nothing of the baker's boy, who, I am convinced, would cut his throat to oblige me to-morrow morning, if I asked him."

"Well, don't ask him," says Luttrell, imploringly. "He might do it on the door-step, and then think of the horrid mess! Promise me you won't even hint at it until after I am gone."

"I promise," says Molly, laughing.

Onward glides the boat; the oars rise and fall with a tuneful splash. Miss Massereene, throwing her hat with reckless extravagance into the bottom of the punt, bares her white arm to the elbow and essays to catch the grasses as she sweeps by them.

"Look at those lilies," she says, eagerly; "how exquisite, in their broad green frames! Water-sprites! how they elude one!" as she makes a vigorous but unsuccessful grab at some on her right hand.

"Very beautiful," says Luttrell, dreamily, with his eyes on Molly, not on the lilies.

"I want some," says Molly, revengefully; "I always do want what don't want me, and *vice versa*. Oh! look at those beauties near you. Catch them."

"I don't think I can; they are too far off."

"Not if you stoop very much for them. I think if you were to bend over a good deal you might do it."

"I might; I might do something else, too," says Luttrell, calmly, seeing it would be as easy for him to grasp the lilies in question as last night's moon: "I might fall in."

"Oh, never mind that," responds Molly, with charming though premeditated unconcern, a little wicked desire to tease getting the better of her amiability.

Luttrell, hardly sure whether she jests or is in sober earnest, opens his large eyes to their fullest, the better to judge, but, seeing no signs of merriment in his companion, gives way to his feelings a little.

"Well, you *are* cool," he says, slowly.

"I am not, indeed," replies innocent Molly. "How I wish I *were* 'cool,' on such a day as this! Are *you*?"

"No," shortly. "Perhaps that is the reason you recommended me a plunge; or is it for your amusement?"

"You are afraid," asserts Molly, with a little mischievous, scornful laugh, not to be endured for a moment.

"Afraid!" angrily. "Nonsense! I don't care about wetting my clothes, certainly, and I don't want to put out my cigar; but"—throwing away the choice Havana in question—"you shall have your lilies, of course, if you have set your heart on them."

Here, standing up, he strips off his coat with an air that means business.

"I don't want them now," says Molly, in a degree frightened, "at least not those. See, there are others close behind you. But I will pluck them myself, thank you: I hate giving trouble. No, don't put your hands near them. I won't have them if you do."

"Why?"

"Because you are cross, and I detest cross people."

"Because I didn't throw myself into the water head foremost to please you?" with impatient wrath. "They used to call that chivalry long ago. I call it folly. You should be reasonable."

"Oh, don't lose your temper about it," says Molly.

Now, to have a person implore you at any time "not to lose your temper" is simply abominable; but to be so implored when you have lost it is about the most aggravating thing that can occur to any one. So Luttrell finds it.

"I never lose my temper about trifles," he says, loftily.

"Well, I don't know what you call it, but when one puts on a frown, and drags down the corners of one's mouth, and looks as if one was going to devour some one, and makes one's self generally disagreeable, *I* know what *I* call it," says Molly, viciously.

"Would you like to return home?" asks Mr. Luttrell, with prompt solicitude. "You are tired, I think."

"'Tired'? Not in the least, thank you. I should like to stay out here for the next two hours, if— —"

"Yes?"

"If you think you could find amusement for yourself—elsewhere!"

"I'll try," says Tedcastle, quietly taking up the oars and proceeding to row with much appearance of haste toward the landing-place.

By the time they reach it, Miss Massereene's bad temper—not being at any time a lengthened affair—has cooled considerably, though still a very handsome allowance remains. As he steps ashore, with the evident intention of not addressing her again, she feels it incumbent on her to speak just a word or so, if only to convince him that his ill-humor is the worst of the two.

"Are you going home?" asks she, with cold politeness.

"No,"—his eyebrows are raised, and he wears an expression half nonchalant, wholly bored,—"I am going to Grantham."

Now, Grantham is nine miles distant. He must be very angry if he has decided on going to Grantham. It will take him a long, long time to get there, and a long, long time to get back; and in the meantime what is to become of her?

"That is a long way, is it not?" she says, her manner a degree more frigid, lest he mistake the meaning of her words.

"The longer the better," ungraciously.

"And on so hot a day!"

"There are worse things than heat." Getting himself into his coat in such a violent fashion as would make his tailor shed bitter tears over the cruel straining of that garment.

"You will be glad to get away from——" hesitates Molly, who has also stepped ashore, speaking in a tone that would freeze a salamander.

"*Very* glad." With much unnecessary emphasis.

"Go then," cries she, with sudden passion, throwing down the oar she still holds with a decided bang, "and I hope you will *never* come back. There!"

And—will you believe it?—even after this there is no deluge.

So she goes to the right, and he goes to the left, and when too late repent their haste. But pride is ever at hand to tread down tenderness, and obstinacy is always at the heels of pride; and out of this "trivial cause" see what a "pretty quarrel" has been sprung.

"The long and weary day" at length has "passed away." The dinner has come to an unsuccessful end, leaving both Luttrell and his divinity still at daggers drawn. There are no signs of relenting about Molly, no symptoms of weakness about Tedcastle: the war is civil but energetic.

They glower at each other through each course, and are positively devoted in their attentions to John and Letitia. Indeed, they seem bent on bestowing all their conversational outbreaks on these two worthies, to their unmitigated astonishment. As a rule, Mr. and Mrs. Massereene have been accustomed to occupy the background; to-night they are brought to the front with a vehemence that takes away their breath, and is, to say the least of it, embarrassing.

Letitia,—dear soul,—who, though the most charming of women, could hardly be thought to endanger the Thames, understands nothing; John, on the contrary, comprehends fully, and takes a low but exquisite delight in compelling the antagonists to be attentive to each other.

For instance:

"Luttrell, my dear fellow, what is the matter with you this evening? How remiss you are! Why don't you break some walnuts for Molly? I would but I don't wish Letitia to feel slighted."

"No, thank you, John,"—with a touch of asperity from Molly,—"I don't care for walnuts."

"Oh, Molly Bawn! what a tarididdle! Only last night I quite shuddered at the amount of shells you left upon your plate. 'How can that wretched child play such pranks with her digestion?' thought I, and indeed felt thankful it had not occurred to you to swallow the shells also."

"Shall I break you some, Miss Massereene?" asks Luttrell, very coldly.

"No, thank you," ungraciously.

"Luttrell, did you see that apple-tree in the orchard? I never beheld such a show of fruit in my life. The branches will hardly bear the weight when it comes to perfection. It is very worthy of admiration. Molly will show it to you to-morrow: won't you, Molly?"

Luttrell, hastily: "I will go round there myself after breakfast and have a look at it."

John: "You will never find it by yourself. Molly will take you; eh, Molly?"

Molly, cruelly: "I fear I shall be busy all the morning; and in the afternoon I intend going with Letitia to spend the day with the Laytons."

Letitia, agreeably surprised: "Oh, will you, dear? That is very good of you. I thought this morning you said nothing would induce you to come with me. I shall be so glad to have you; they are so intensely dull and difficult."

Molly, still more cruelly: "Well, I have been thinking it over, and it seems, do you know, rather rude my not going. Besides, I hear their brother Maxwell (a few more strawberries, if you please, John) is home from India, and—he used to be *so* good-looking."

John, with much unction: "Oh, has he come at last! I am glad to hear it. (Luttrell, give Molly some strawberries.) You underrate him, I think: he was downright handsome. When Molly Bawn was in short petticoats he used to adore her. I suppose it would be presumptuous to pretend to measure the admiration he will undoubtedly feel for her now. I have a presentiment that fortune is going to favor you in the end, Molly. He must inherit a considerable property."

"Rich and handsome," says Luttrell, with exemplary composure and a growing conviction that he will soon hate with an undying hatred his whilom friend John Massereene. "He must be a favorite of the gods: let us hope he will not die young."

"He can't," says Letitia, comfortably: "he must be forty if he is a day."

"And a good, sensible age, too," remarks John; whereupon Molly, who is too much akin to him in spirit not to fully understand his manœuvering, laughs outright.

Then Letitia rises, and the two women move toward the door; and Molly, coming last, pauses a moment on the threshold, while Luttrell holds the door open for her. His heart beats high. Is she going to speak to him, to throw him even one poor word, to gladden him with a smile, however frozen?

Alas! no. Miss Massereene, with a little curve of her neck, glances back expressively to where an unkind nail has caught the tail of her long soft gown. That miserable nail—not he—has caused her delay. Stooping, he extricates the dress. She bows coldly, without raising her eyes to his. A moment later she is free; still another moment, and she is gone; and Luttrell, with a suppressed but naughty word upon his lips, returns to his despondency and John; while Molly, who, though she has never once looked at him, has read correctly his fond hope and final disappointment, allows a covert smile of pleased malevolence to cross her face as she walks into the drawing-room.

Mr. Massereene is holding a long and very one-sided argument on the subject of the barbarous Mussulman. As Luttrell evinces no faintest desire to disagree with him in his opinions, the subject wears itself out in due course of time; and John, winding up with an amiable wish that every Turk that ever has seen the light or is likely to see the light may be blown into fine dust, finishes his claret and rises, with a yawn.

"I must leave you for awhile," he says: "so get out your cigars, and don't wait for me. I'll join you later. I have had the writing of a letter on my conscience for a week, and I must write it now or never. I really do believe I have grasped my own meaning at last. Did you notice my unusual taciturnity between the fish and the joint?"

"I can't say I did. I imagined you talking the entire time."

"My dear fellow, of what were you thinking. I sincerely trust you are not going to be ill; but altogether your whole manner this evening— — Well, just at that moment a sudden inspiration seized me, and then and there my letter rose up before me, couched in such eloquent language as astonished even myself. If I don't write it down at once I am a lost man."

"But now you have composed it to your satisfaction, why not leave the writing of it until to-morrow?" expostulates Luttrell, trying to look hearty, as he expresses a hypocritical desire for his society.

"I always remark," says John, "that sleeping on those treacherous flights of fancy has the effect of taking the gilt off them. When I rise in the morning they are hardly up to the mark, and appear by no means so brilliant as they did over-night. Something within warns me if I don't do it now I won't do it at all. There is more claret on the sideboard,—or brandy, if you prefer it," says Mr. Massereene, tenderly.

"Thanks,—I want nothing more," replies Luttrell, whose spirits are at zero. As Massereene leaves him, he saunters toward the open window and gazes on the sleeping garden. Outside, the heavens are alive with stars that light the world in a cold, sweet way, although as yet the moon has not risen. All is

"Clear, and bright, and deep;

Soft as love, and calm as death;

Sweet as a summer night without a breath."

Lighting a cigar (by the bye, can any one tell me at what stage of suffering it is a man abandons this unfailing friend as being powerless to soothe?), he walks down the balcony steps, and, still grim and unhappy, makes up his mind to a solitary promenade.

Perhaps he himself is scarcely conscious of the direction he takes, but his footsteps guide him straight over the lawn and down to the very end of it, where a broad stream runs babbling in one corner. It is a veritable love-retreat, hedged in by larches and low-lying evergreens, so as to be completely concealed from view, and a favorite haunt of Molly's,—indeed, such a favorite that now as he enters it he finds himself face to face with her.

An impromptu tableau follows. For a full minute they regard each other unwillingly, too surprised for disdain, and then, with a laudable desire to show how unworthy of consideration either deems the other, they turn slowly away until a shoulder and half a face alone are visible.

Now, Luttrell has the best of it, because he is the happy possessor of the cigar: this gives him something to do, and he smokes on persistently, not to say viciously. Miss Massereene, being without occupation beyond what one's thumbs may afford, is conscious of being at a disadvantage, and wishes she had earlier in life cultivated a passion for tobacco.

Meanwhile, the noisy brook flows on merrily, chattering as it goes, and reflecting the twinkling stars, with their more sedate brethren, the planets. Deep down in the very heart of the water they lie, quivering, changing, gleaming, while the stream whispers their lullaby and dashes its cool soft sides against the banks. A solitary bird drops down to crave a drink, terrifying the other inhabitants of the rushes by the trembling of its wings; a frog creeps in with a dull splash; to all the stream makes kind response; while on its bosom

"Broad water-lilies lay tremulously,

And starry river-buds glimmered by;

And round them the soft stream did glide and dance,

With a motion of sweet sound and radiance."

A little way above, a miniature cataract adds its tiny roar to the many "breathings of the night;" at Molly's feet lie great bunches of blue forget-me-nots.

Stooping, she gathers a handful to fasten at her breast; a few sprays still remain in her hands idle; she has turned so that her full face is to her companion: he has never stirred.

He is still puffing away in a somewhat indignant fashion at the unoffending cigar, looking taller, more unbending in his evening clothes, helped by the dignity of his wrongs. Miss Massereene, having indulged in a long examination of his would-be stern profile, decides on the spot that if there is one thing on earth toward which she bears a rancorous hatred it is an ill-tempered man. What does he mean by standing there without speaking to her? She makes an undying vow that, were he so to stand forever, she would not open her lips to him; and exactly sixty seconds after making that terrible vow she says,—oh, so sweetly!—"Mr. Luttrell!"

He instantly pitches the obnoxious cigar into the water, where it dies away with an angry fizz, and turns to her.

She is standing a few yards distant from him, with her head a little bent and the bunch of forget-me-nots in one hand, moving them slowly, slowly across her lips. There is penitence, coquetry, mischief, a thousand graces in her attitude.

Now, feeling his eyes upon her, she moves the flowers about three inches from her mouth, and, regarding them lovingly, says, "Are not they pretty!" as though her whole soul is wrapt in contemplation of their beauty, and as though no other deeper thought has led her to address him.

"Very. They are like your eyes," replies he, gravely, and with some hesitation, as if the words came reluctantly.

This is a concession, and so she feels it. A compliment to a true woman comes never amiss; and the knowledge that it has been wrung from him against his will, being but a tribute to its truth, adds yet another charm. Without appearing conscious of the fact, she moves a few steps nearer to him, always with her eyes bent upon the flowers, the grass, anywhere but on him: because you will understand how impossible it is for one person to drink in the full beauty of another if checked by that other's watchfulness. Molly, at all events, understands it thoroughly.

When she is quite close to him, so close that if she stirs her dress must touch him, so close that her flower-like face is dangerously near his arm, she whispers, softly:

"I am sorry."

"Are you?" says Luttrell, stupidly, although his heart is throbbing passionately, although every pulse is beating almost to pain. If his life depended upon it, or perhaps because of it, he can frame no more eloquent speech.

"Yes," murmurs Molly, with a thorough comprehension of all he is feeling. "And now we will be friends again, will we not?" Holding out to him a little cool, shy hand.

"Not *friends*," says the young man, in a low, passionate tone, clasping her hand eagerly: "it is too cold a word. I *cannot* be your friend. Your lover, your slave, if you will; only let me feel *near* to you. Molly,"—abandoning her slender fingers for the far sweeter possession of herself, and folding his arms around her with gentle audacity,—"speak to me. Why are you so silent? Why do you not even look at me? You cannot want me to tell you of the love that is consuming me, because you know of it."

"I don't think you ought to speak to me like this at all," says Molly, severely, drawing herself out of his embrace, not hurriedly or angrily, but surely; "I am almost positive you should not; and—and John might not like it."

"I don't care a farthing what John likes," exclaims Luttrell, rather forcibly, giving wings to his manners, as his wrongs of the evening blossom. "What has he or any one to do with it but you and I alone? The question is, do *you* like it?"

"I am not at all sure that I do," says Molly, doubtfully, with a little distracting shake of her head. "You are so vehement, and I——"

"Don't go on," interrupts he, hastily. "You are going to say something unkind, and I won't listen to it. I know it by your eyes. Darling, why are you so cruel to me? Surely you must care for me, be it ever such a little. To think otherwise would—— But I will *not* think it. Molly,"—with increasing fervor,—"say you will marry me."

"But indeed I can't," exclaims Miss Massereene, retreating a step or two, and glancing at him furtively from under her long lashes. "At least"—relenting a little, as she sees his face change and whiten at her words—"not *yet*. It is all so sudden, so unexpected; and you forget I am not accustomed to this sort of thing. Now, the curates"—with an irrepressible smile—"never went on like this: they always behaved modestly and with such propriety."

"'The curates!' What do they know about it?" returns this young man, most unjustly. "Do you suppose I love you like a curate?"

"And yet, when all is told, I suppose a curate is a man," says Molly, uncertainly, as one doubtful of the truth of her assertion, "and a well-behaved one, too. Now, you are quite different; and you have known me such a little time."

"What has time to do with it? The beginning and the ending of the whole matter is this: I love you!"

He is holding her hands and gazing down into her face with all his heart in his eyes, waiting for her next words,—may they not decide his fate?—while she is feeling nothing in the world but a mad desire to break into laughter,—a desire that arises half from nervousness, half from an irrepressible longing to destroy the solemnity of the scene.

"A pinch for stale news," says she, at last, with a frivolity most unworthy of the occasion, but in the softest, merriest whisper.

They are both young. The laugh is contagious. After a moment's struggle with his dignity, he echoes it.

"You can jest," says he: "surely that is a good sign. If you were going to refuse me you would not laugh. Beloved,"—taking her into his fond arms again,—"say one little word to make me happy."

"Will any little word do? Long ago, in the dark ages when I was a child, I remember being asked a riddle *à propos* of short words. I will ask it to you now. What three letters contain everything in the world? Guess."

"No need to guess: I know. YES would contain everything in the world for me."

"You are wrong, then. It is ALL,—all. Absurd, isn't it? I must have been very young when I thought that clever. But to return: would *that* little word do you?"

"Say 'Yes,' Molly."

"And if I say 'No,' what then? Will you throw yourself into this small river? Or perhaps hang yourself to the nearest tree? Or, worse still, refuse to speak to me ever again? Or 'go to skin and bone,' as my old nurse used to say I would when I refused a fifth meal in the day? Tell me which?"

"A greater evil than all those would befall me: I should live with no nearer companion than a perpetual regret. But"—with a shudder—"I will not believe myself so doomed. Molly, say what I ask you."

"Well, 'Yes,' then, since you will have it so. Though why you are so bent on your own destruction puzzles me. Do you know you never spoke to me all this evening? I don't believe you love me as well as you say."

"Don't I?" wistfully. Then, with sudden excitement, "I wish with all my heart I did not," he says, "or at least with only half the strength I do. If I could regulate my affections so, I might have some small chance of happiness; but as it is I doubt—I fear. Molly, do you care for me?"

"At times,"—mischievously—"I do—a *little*."

"And you know I love you?"

"Yes,—it may be,—when it suits you."

"And you,"—tightening his arms round her,—"some time you will love me, my sweet?"

"Yes,—perhaps so,—when it suits me."

"Molly," says Luttrell after a pause, "won't you kiss me?"

As he speaks he stoops, bringing his cheek very close to hers.

"'Kiss you'?" says Molly, shrinking away from him, while flushing and reddening honestly now. "No, I think not. I never in all my life kissed any man but John, and—I don't believe I should like it. No, no; if I cannot be engaged to you without kissing you, I will not be engaged to you at all."

"It shall be as you wish," says Luttrell, very patiently, considering all things.

"You mean it?" Still keeping well away from him, and hesitating about giving the hand he is holding out his to receive.

"Certainly I do."

"And"—anxiously—"you don't *mind*?"

"Mind?" says he, with wrathful reproach. "Of course I mind. Am I a stick or a stone, do you think? You might as well tell me in so many words of your utter indifference to me as refuse to kiss me."

"Do all women kiss the men they promise to marry?"

"All women kiss the men they love."

"What, whether they ask them or not?"

"Of course I mean when they are asked."

"Even if at the time they happen to be married to somebody else?"

"I don't know anything about that," says Luttrell, growing ashamed of himself and his argument beneath the large, horror-stricken eyes of his companion. "I was merely supposing a case where marriage and love went hand in hand."

"Don't suppose," says Miss Massereene; "there is nothing so tiresome. It is like 'fourthly' and 'fifthly' in a sermon: you never know where it may lead you. Am I to understand that all women want to kiss the man they love?"

"Certainly they do," stoutly.

"How very odd!" says Molly.

After which there is a most decided pause.

Presently, as though she had been pondering all things, she says:

"Well, there is one thing: I don't mind your having your arms round me a bit, not in the *least*. That must be something. I would quite as soon they were there as not."

"I suppose that is a step in the right direction," says Luttrell, trying not to see the meaning in her words, because too depressed to accept the comic side of it.

"You are unhappy," says Molly, remorsefully, heaving a quickly suppressed sigh. "Why? Because I won't be good to you? Well,"—coloring crimson and leaning her head back against his shoulder with the air of a martyr, so that her face is upturned,—"you may kiss me once, if you wish,—but only once, mind,—because I can't bear to see you miserable."

"No," returns Luttrell, valiantly, refusing by a supreme effort to allow himself to be tempted by a look at her beauty, "I will not kiss you so. Why should you be made unhappy, and by me? Keep such gifts, Molly, until you can bestow them of your own free will."

But Molly is determined to be generous.

"See, I will give you this one freely," she says, with unwonted sweetness, knowing that she is gaining more than she is giving; and thus persuaded, he presses his lips to the warm tender ones so near his own, while for one mad moment he is absurdly happy.

"You really do love me?" asks Molly, presently, as though just awakening to the fact.

"My darling!—my angel!" whispers he, which is conclusive; because when a man can honestly bring himself to believe a woman an angel he must be very far gone indeed.

"I fancy we ought to go in," says Molly, a little later; "they will be wondering where we are."

"They cannot have missed us yet; it is too soon."

"Soon! Why, it must be hours since we came out here," says Molly, with uplifted brows.

"Have you found it so very long?" asks he, aggrieved.

"No,"—resenting his tone in a degree,—"I have not been bored to death, if you mean that; but I am not so dead to the outer world that I cannot tell whether time has been short or long. And it *is* long," viciously.

"At that rate, I think we had better go in," replies he, somewhat stiffly.

As they draw near the house, so near that the lights from the open drawing-room windows make yellow paths across the grass that runs their points almost to their feet,—Luttrell stops short to say:

"Shall I speak to John to-night or to-morrow morning?"

"Oh! neither to-night nor to-morrow," cries Molly, frightened. "Not for ever so long. Why talk about it at all? Only a few minutes ago nothing was farther from my thoughts, and now you would publish it on the house-tops! Just think what it will be to have every one wondering and whispering about one, and saying, 'Now they have had a quarrel,' and 'Now they have made it up again.' Or, 'See now she is flirting with somebody else.' I could not bear it," says Molly, blind to the growing anger on the young man's face as he listens to and fully takes in the suggestions contained in these imaginary speeches; "it would make me wretched. It might make me hate you!"

"Molly!"

"Yes, it might; and then what would you do? Let us keep it a secret," says Molly, coaxingly, slipping her hand into his, with a little persuasive pressure. "You see, everything about it is so far distant; and perhaps—who knows?—it may never come to anything."

"What do you mean by that?" demands he, passionately, drawing her to him, and bending to examine her face in the uncertain light. "Do you suppose I am a boy or a fool, that you so speak to me? Am I so very happy that you deem it necessary to blast my joy like this? or is it merely to try me? Tell me the truth now, at once: do you mean to throw me over?"

"I do not," with surprise. "What has put such an idea into your head? If I did, why be engaged to you at any time? It is a great deal more likely, when you come to know me better, that you will throw me over."

"Don't build your hopes on that," says Luttrell, grimly, with a rather sad smile. "I am not the sort of fellow likely to commit suicide; and to resign you would be to resign life."

"Well," says Molly, "if I am ever to say anything on the subject I may as well say it now; and I must confess I think you are behaving very foolishly. I may be—I probably am—good to look at; but what is the use of that? You, who have seen so much of the world, have, of course, known people ten times prettier than I am, and—perhaps—fonder of you. And still you come all the way down here to this stupid place to fall in love with me, a girl without a penny! I really think," winds up Molly, growing positively melancholy over his lack of sense, "it is the most absurd thing I ever heard in my life."

"I wish I could argue with your admirable indifference," says he, bitterly.

"If I was indifferent I would not argue," says Molly, offended. "I would not trouble myself to utter a word of warning. You ought to be immensely obliged to me instead of sneering and wrinkling up all your forehead into one big frown. Are you going to be angry again? I do hope," says Molly, anxiously, "you are not naturally ill-tempered, because, if so, on no account would I have anything to do with you."

"I am not," replies he, compelled to laughter by her perturbed face. "Reassure yourself. I seldom forget myself in this way. And you?"

"Oh, I have a fearful temper," says Molly, with a charming smile; "that is why I want to make sure of yours. Because two tyrants in one house would infallibly bring the roof about their ears. Now, Mr. Luttrell, that I have made this confession, will you still tell me you are not frightened?"

"Nothing frightens me," whispers he, holding her to his heart and pressing his lips to her fair, cool cheek, "since you are my own,—my sweet,—my beloved. But call me Tedcastle, won't you?"

"It is too long a name."

"Then alter it, and call me——"

"Teddy? I think I like that best; and perhaps I shall have it all to myself."

"I am afraid not," laughing. "All the fellows in the regiment christened me 'Teddy' before I had been in a week."

"Did they? Well, never mind; it only shows what good taste they had. The name just suits you, you are so fair and young, and handsome," says Molly, patting his cheek with considerable condescension. "Now, one thing more before we go in to receive our scolding: you are not to make love to me again—not even to mention the word—until a whole week has passed: promise."

"I could not."

"You must."

"Well, then, it will be a pie-crust promise."

"No, I forbid you to break it. I can endure a little of it now and again," says Molly, with intense seriousness, "but to be made love to always, every day, would kill me."

CHAPTER VII

"Then they sat down and talked
Of their friends at home ...

And related the wondrous adventure."

—*Courtship of Miles Standish.*

"Do exert yourself," says Molly. "I never saw any one so lazy. You don't pick one to my ten."

"I can't see how you make that out," says her companion in an injured tone. "For the last three minutes you have sat with your hands in your lap arguing about what you don't understand in the least, while I have been conscientiously slaving; and before that you ate two for every one you put in the basket."

"I never heard any one talk so much as you do, when once fairly started," says Molly. "Here, open your mouth until I put in this strawberry; perhaps it will stop you."

"And I find it impossible to do anything with this umbrella," says Luttrell, still ungrateful, eying with much distaste the ancient article he holds aloft: "it is abominably in the way. I wouldn't mind if you wanted it, but you cannot with that gigantic hat you are wearing. May I put it down?"

"Certainly not, unless you wish me to have a sun-stroke. Do you?"

"No, but I really think — —"

"Don't think," says Molly: "it is too fatiguing; and if you get used up now, I don't see what Letitia will do for her jam."

"Why do people make jam?" asks Luttrell, despairingly; "they wouldn't if they had the picking of it: and nobody ever eats it, do they?"

"Yes, I do. I love it. Let that thought cheer you on to victory. Oh! here is another fat one, such a monster. Open your mouth again, wide, and you shall have it, because you really do begin to look weak."

They are sitting on the strawberry bank, close together, with a small square basket between them, and the pretty red and white fruit hanging from its dainty stalks all round them.

Molly, in a huge hat that only partially conceals her face and throws a shadow over her glorious eyes, is intent upon her task, while Luttrell, sitting opposite to her, holds over her head the very largest family umbrella ever built. It is evidently an old and esteemed friend, that has worn itself out in the Massereenes' service, and now shows daylight here and there through its covering where it should not. A troublesome scorching ray comes through one of these impromptu air-holes and alights persistently on his face; at present it is on his nose, and makes that feature appear a good degree larger than Nature, who has been very generous to it, ever intended.

It might strike a keen observer that Mr. Luttrell doesn't like the umbrella; either it or the wicked sunbeams, or the heat generally, is telling on him, slowly but surely; he has a depressed and melancholy air.

"Is it good?" asks Molly, *à propos* of the strawberry. "There, you need not bite my finger. Will you have another? You really do look very badly. You don't think you are going to faint, do you?"

"Molly," taking no notice of her graceful *badinage*, "why don't you get your grandfather to invite you to Herst Royal for the autumn? Could you not manage it in some way? I wish it could be done."

"So do I," returns she, frankly, "but there is not the remotest chance of it. It would be quite as likely that the skies should fall. Why, he does not even acknowledge me as a member of the family."

"Old brute!" says Luttrell from his heart.

"Well, it has always been rather a regret to me, his neglect, I mean," says Molly, thoughtfully, "and besides, though I know it is poor-spirited of me, I confess I have the greatest longing to see my grandfather."

"To '*see*' your grandfather?"

"Exactly."

"Do you mean to tell me," growing absolutely animated through his surprise, "that you have never been face to face with him?"

"Never. I thought you knew that. Why, how amazed you look! Is there anything the matter with him? is he without arms, or legs? or has he had his nose shot off in any campaign? If so, break it to me gently, and spare me the shock I might experience, if ever I make my curtsey to him."

"It isn't that," says Tedcastle: "there's nothing wrong with him beyond old age, and a beastly temper; but it seems so odd that, living all your life in the very next county to his, you should never have met."

"It is not so odd, after all, when you come to think of it," says Molly, "considering he never goes anywhere, as I have heard, and that I lead quite as lively an existence. But is he not a stern old thing, to keep up a quarrel for so many years, especially as it wasn't my fault, you know? I didn't insist on being born. Poor mother! I think she was quite right to run away with papa, when she loved him."

"Quite right," enthusiastically.

"What made her crime so unpardonable was the fact that she was engaged to another man at the time, some rich *parti* chosen by her father, whom she thought she liked well enough until she saw papa, and then she knew, and threw away everything for her love; and she did well," says Molly, with more excitement than would be expected from her on a sentimental subject.

"Still, it was rather hard on the first man, don't you think?" says Luttrell. There is rather less enthusiasm in his tone this time.

"One should go to the wall, you know," argues Molly, calmly, "and I for my part would not hesitate about it. Now, let us suppose I am engaged to you without caring very much about you, you know, and all that, and supposing then I saw another I liked better,—why, then, I honestly confess I would not hold to my engagement with you for an hour!"

Here that wicked sunbeam, with a depravity unlooked for, falling straight through the chink of the umbrella into Mr. Luttrell's eye, maddens him to such a degree that he rises precipitately, shuts the cause of his misfortunes with a bang, and turns on Molly.

"I won't hold it up another instant," he says; "you needn't think it. I wonder Massereene wouldn't keep a decent umbrella in his hall."

"What's the matter with it? I see nothing indecent about it: I think it a very charming umbrella," says Molly, examining the article in question with a critical eye.

"Well, at all events, this orchard is oppressive. If you don't want to kill me, you will leave it, and come to the wood, where we may know what shade means!"

"Nonsense!" returns Molly, unmoved. "It is delicious here, and I won't stir. How can you talk in that wild way about no shade, when you have this beautiful apple-tree right over your head? Come and sit at this side; perhaps," with a smile, "you will feel more comfortable—next to me?"

Thus beguiled, he yields, and seats himself beside her—very much beside her—and reconciles himself to his fate.

"I wish you would remember," she says, presently, "that you have nothing on your head. I would not be rash if I were you. Take my advice and open the umbrella again, or you will assuredly be having a sun-stroke."

This is one for him and two for herself; and—need I say?—the family friend is once more unfurled, and waves to and fro majestically in the soft wind.

"Now, don't you feel better?" asks Molly, placing her two fingers beneath his chin, and turning his still rather angry face toward her.

"I do," replies he; and a smile creeping up into his eyes slays the chagrin that still lingers there, but half *perdu*.

"And—are you happy?"

"Very."

"Intensely happy?"

"Yes."

"So much so that you could not be more so?"

"Yes," replies he again, laughing, and slipping his arm round her waist. "And you?" tenderly.

"Oh, I'm all right!" says Miss Massereene, with much graciousness, but rather disheartening vivacity. "And now begin, Teddy, and tell me all about Herst Royal and its inmates. First, is it a pretty place?"

"It is a magnificent place. But for its attractions, and his twenty thousand pounds a year, I don't believe your grandfather would be known by any one; he is such a regular old bear. Yet he is fond of society, and is never content until he has the house crammed with people, from garret to basement, to whom he makes himself odiously disagreeable whenever occasion offers. I have an invitation there for September and October."

"Will you go?"

"I don't know. I have hardly made up my mind. I have been asked to the Careys, and the Brownes also; and I rather fancy the Brownes. They are the most affording people I ever met: one always puts in such a good time at their place. But for one reason I would go there."

"What reason?"

"That Herst is so much nearer to Brooklyn," with a fond smile. "And, perhaps, if I came over once or twice, you would be glad to see me?"

"Oh, would I not!" cries Molly, her faultless face lighting up at his words. "You may be sure of it. You won't forget, will you? And you will come early, so as to spend the entire day here, and tell me all about the others who will be staying there. Do you know my cousin Marcia?"

"Miss Amherst? Yes. She is very handsome, but too statuesque to please me."

"Am I better-looking?"

"Ten thousand times."

"And Philip Shadwell; he is my cousin also. Do you know him?"

"Very intimately. He is handsome also, but of a dark Moorish sort of beauty. Not a popular man, by any means. Too reserved,—cold,—I don't know what it is. Have you any other cousins?"

"Not on my mother's side. Grandpa had but three children, you know,— my mother, and Philip's mother, and Marcia's father: he married an Italian actress, which must have been a terrible *mésalliance,* and yet Marcia is made much of, while I am not even recognized. Does it not sound unfair?"

"Unaccountable. Especially as I have often heard your mother was his favorite child!"

"Perhaps that explains his harshness. To be deceived by one we love engenders the bitterest hatred of all. And yet how could he hate poor mamma? John says she had the most beautiful, lovable face."

"I can well believe it," replied he, gazing with undisguised admiration upon the perfect profile beside him.

"And Marcia will be an heiress, I suppose?"

"She and Philip will divide everything, people say, the place, of course, going to Philip. Lucky he! Any one might envy him. You know they both live there entirely, although Marcia's mother is alive and resides somewhere abroad. Philip was in some dragoon regiment, but sold out about two years ago: debt, I fancy, was the cause, or something like it."

"Marcia is the girl you ought to have fallen in love with, Ted."

"No, thank you; I very much prefer her cousin. Besides, I should have no chance, as she and Philip are engaged to each other: they thought it a pity to divide the twenty thousand pounds a year. Do you know, Molly, I never knew what it was to covet my neighbor's goods until I met you? so you have that to answer for; but it does seem hard that one man should be so rich, and another so poor."

"Are you poor, Teddy?"

"Very. Will that make you like me less?"

"Probably it will make me like you more," replies she, with a bewitching smile, stroking down the hand that supports the obnoxious umbrella (the other is supporting herself) almost tenderly. "It is only the very nicest men that haven't a farthing in the world. I have no money either, and if I had I could not keep it: so we are well met."

"But think what a bad match you are making," says he, regarding her curiously. "Did you never ask yourself whether I was well off, or otherwise?"

"Never!" with a gay laugh. "If I were going to marry you next week or so, it might occur to me to ask the question; but everything is so far away, what does it signify? If you had the mines of Golconda, I should not like you a bit better than I do."

"My own darling! Oh, Molly, how you differ from most girls one meets. Now, in London, once they find out I am only the third son, they throw me over without warning, and generally manage to forget the extra dance they had promised, while their mothers look upon me, and such as me, as a pestilence. And you, sweetheart, you never once asked me how much a year I had!"

"You have your pay, I suppose?" says Molly, doubtfully. "Is that much?"

"Very handsome," replies he, laughing; "a lieutenant's pay generally is. But I have something besides that; about as much as most fellows would spend on their stabling. I have precisely five hundred and fifty pounds a year, neither more nor less, and I owe two hundred pounds. Does not that sound tempting? The two hundred pounds I owe don't count, because the governor will pay up that; he always does in the long run; and I haven't asked him for anything out of the way now for fully eight months." He says this with a full consciousness of his own virtue.

"I call five hundred and fifty pounds a year a great deal," says Molly, with a faint ring of disappointment in her tone. "I fancied you downright poor from what you said. Why, you might marry to-morrow morning on that."

"So I might," agrees he, eagerly; "and so I will. That is, not to-morrow, exactly, but as soon as ever I can."

"Perhaps you will," says Molly, slowly; "but, if so, it will not be me you will marry. Bear that in mind. No, we won't argue the matter: as far as I am concerned it doesn't admit of argument." Then recurring to the former topic: "Why, John has only seven hundred pounds, and he has all the children and Letitia and me to provide for, and he keeps Lovat—that is the eldest boy—at a very good school as well. How *could* you call yourself poor, with five hundred pounds a year?"

"It ought to be six hundred and fifty pounds; but I thought it a pity to burden myself with superfluous wealth in my palmy days, so I got rid of it," says he, laughing.

"Gambling?"

"Well, yes, I suppose so."

"Cards?"

"No, horses. It was in India,—stupid part, you know, and nothing to do. Potts suggested military races, and we all caught at it. And—and I didn't have much luck, you know," winds up Luttrell, ingenuously.

"I don't like that young man," says Molly, severely. "You are always talking of him, and he is my idea of a ne'er-do-weel. Your Mr. Potts seems never to be out of mischief. He is the head and front of every offense."

"Are you talking of Potts?" says her lover, in grieved amazement. "A better fellow never stepped. Nothing underhand about Potts. When you see him you will agree with me."

"I will not. I can see him in my mind's eye already. I know he is tall, and dark, and insinuating, and, in fact, a Mephistopheles."

Luttrell roars.

"Oh, if you could but see Potts!" he says. "He is the best fellow in the world, but—— He ought to be called Rufus: his hair is red, his face is red, his nose is red, he is all red," finishes Tedcastle, with a keen enjoyment of his friend's misfortunes.

"Poor man," kindly; "I forgive him his small sins; he must be sufficiently punished by his ugliness. Did you like being in India?"

"Pretty well. At times it was rather slow, and our regiment has somehow gone to the dogs of late. No end of underbred fellows have joined, with quite too much the linen-draper about them to be tolerated."

"How sad! Your candor amazes me. I thought every soldier made it a point to be enthusiastic over his brother soldiers, whether by being so he lied or not."

"Then look upon me as an exception. The fact is, I grew rather discontented about three years ago when my greatest chum sold out and got married. You have no idea how lost a fellow feels when that happens. But for Potts I might have succumbed."

"Potts! what a sweet name it is!" says Molly, mischievously.

"What's in a name?" with a laugh. "He was generally called Mrs. Luttrell, we were so much together: so his own didn't matter. But I missed Penthony Stafford awfully."

"And Mrs. Penthony, did you like her?"

"Lady Stafford, you mean? Penthony is a baronet. Yes, I like her immensely, and the whole affair was so peculiar. You won't believe me when I tell you that, though they have now been married for three years, her husband has never seen her."

"But that would be impossible."

"It is a fact for all that. Shall I tell you the story? Most people know it by this, I think: so I am breaking no faith by telling it to you."

"Never mind whether you are or not," says Molly: "I must and will hear it now."

"Well, to begin with, you must understand that she and her husband are first cousins. Have you mastered that fact?"

"Though not particularly gifted, I think I have. I rather flatter myself I could master more than that," says Molly, significantly, giving his ear a pinch, short but sharp.

"She is also a cousin of mine, though not so near. Well, about three years ago, when she was only Cecil Hargrave, and extremely poor, an uncle of theirs died, leaving his entire property, which was very considerable, between them, on the condition that they should marry each other. If they refused, it was to go to a lunatic asylum, or a refuge for dogs, or something equally uninteresting."

"He would have made a very successful lunatic himself, it seems to me. What a terrible condition!"

"Now, up to this they had been utter strangers to each other, had never even been face to face, and being told they must marry whether they liked it or not, or lose the money, they of course on the spot conceived an undying hatred for each other. Penthony even refused to see his possible wife, when urged to do so, and Cecil, on her part, quite as strenuously opposed a meeting. Still, they could not make up their minds to let such a good property slip through their fingers."

"It *was* hard."

"Things dragged on so for three months, and then, Cecil, being a woman, was naturally the one to see a way out of it. She wrote to Sir

Penthony saying, if he would sign a deed giving her a third of the money, and promising never to claim her as his wife, or interfere with her in any way, beyond having the marriage ceremony read between them, she would marry him."

"And he?" asks Molly, eagerly, bending forward in her excitement.

"Why, he agreed, of course. What was it to him? he had never seen her, and had no wish to make her acquaintance. The document was signed, the license was procured. On the morning of the wedding, he looked up a best man, and went down to the country, saw nothing of his bride until a few minutes before the service began, when she entered the room covered with so thick a veil that he saw quite as little of her then, was married, made his best bow to the new Lady Stafford, and immediately returning to town, set out a few days later for a foreign tour, which has lasted ever since. Now, is not that a thrilling romance, and have I not described it graphically?"

"The 'Polite Story-teller' sinks into insignificance beside you: such a flow of language deserves a better audience. But really, Teddy, I never heard so extraordinary a story. To marry a woman, and never have the curiosity to raise her veil to see whether she was ugly or pretty! It is inconceivable! He must be made of ice."

"He is warm-hearted, and one of the jolliest fellows you could meet. Curiously enough, from a letter he wrote me just before starting he gave me the impression that he believed his wife to be not only plain, but vulgar in appearance."

"And is she?"

"She is positively lovely. Rather small, perhaps, but exquisitely fair, with large laughing blue eyes, and the most fetching manner. If he had raised her veil, I don't believe he would ever have gone abroad to cultivate the dusky nigger."

"What became of her,—'poor maid forlorn?'"

"She gave up 'milking the cow with the crumpled horn,' and the country generally, and came up to London, where she took a house, went into society, and was the rage all last season."

"Why did you not tell him how pretty she was?" impatiently.

"Because I was in Ireland at the time on leave, and heard nothing of it until I received that letter telling of the marriage and his departure. I was thunderstruck, you may be sure, but it was too late then to interfere. Some one told me the other day he is on his way home."

"'When Greek meets Greek' we know what happens," says Molly. "I think *their* meeting will be awkward."

"Rather. She is to be at Herst this autumn: she was a ward of your grandfather's."

"Don't fall in love with her, Teddy."

"How can I, when you have put it out of my power? There is no room in my heart for any one but Molly Bawn. Besides, it would be energy wasted, as she is encased in steel. A woman in her equivocal position, and possessed of so much beauty, might be supposed to find it difficult to steer her bark safely through all the temptations of a London season; yet the flattery she received, and all the devotion that was laid at her feet, touched her no more than if she was ninety, instead of twenty-three."

"Yet what a risk it is! How will it be some day if she falls in love? as they say all people do once in their lives."

"Why, then, she will have her *mauvais quart-d'heure*, like the rest of us. Up to the present she has enjoyed her life to the utmost, and finds everything *couleur de rose*."

"Would it not be charming," says Molly, with much *empressement*, "if, when Sir Penthony comes home and sees her, they should both fall in love with each other?"

"Charming, but highly improbable. The fates are seldom so propitious. It is far more likely they will fall madly in love with two other people, and be unhappy ever after."

"Oh, cease such raven's croaking," says Molly, laying her hand upon his lips. "I will not listen to it. Whatever the Fates may be, Love, I know, is kind."

"Is it?" asks he, wistfully. "You are my love—are you kind?"

"And you are my lover," returns Molly. "And you most certainly are not kind, for that is the third time you have all but run that horrid umbrella into my left eye. Surely, because you hold it up for your own personal convenience is no reason why you should make it an instrument of torture to every one else. Now you may finish picking those strawberries without me, for I shall not stay here another instant in deadly fear of being blinded for life."

With this speech—so flagrantly unjust as to render her companion dumb—she rises, and catching up her gown, runs swiftly away from him down the garden-path, and under the wealthy trees, until at last the garden-gate receives her in its embrace and hides her from his view.

CHAPTER VIII

"Thine eyes I love, and they as pitying me,
Knowing thy heart, torment me with disdain."
—Shakespeare.

All round one side of Brooklyn, and edging on to the retired butcher's country residence, or rather what he is pleased to term, with a knowing jerk of the thumb over his right shoulder, his "little villar in the south," stretches a belt of trees, named by courtesy "the wood." It is a charming spot, widening and thickening toward one corner, which has been well named the "Fairies' Glen," where crowd together all the "living grasses" and wild flowers that thrive and bloom so bravely when nursed on the earth's bosom.

On one side rise gray rocks, cold and dead, save for the little happy life that, springing up above, flows over them, leaping, laughing from crag to crag, bedewing leaf and blossom, and dashing its gem-like spray over all the lichens and velvet mosses and feathery ferns that grow luxuriantly to hide the rugged jags of stone.

Here, at night, the owls delight to hoot, the bats go whirring past, the moonbeams surely cast their kindest rays; by day the pigeons coo from the topmost boughs their tales of love, while squirrels sit blinking merrily, or run their Silvios on their Derby days.

Just now it is neither night nor garish day, but a soft, early twilight, and on the sward that glows as green as Erin's, sit Molly and her attendant slave.

"The reason I like you," says Molly, reverting to something that has gone before, and tilting back her hat so that all her pretty face is laid bare to the envious sunshine, while the soft rippling locks on her forehead make advances to each other through the breeze, "the reason I like you,—no,"—seeing a tendency on his part to creep nearer, "no, stay where you are. I only said I liked you. If I had mentioned the word love, then indeed—but, as it is, it is far too warm to admit of any endearments."

"You are right,—as you always are," says Luttrell, with suspicious amiability, being piqued.

"You interrupted me," says Miss Massereene, leaning back comfortably and raising her exquisite eyes in lazy admiration of the green and leafy tangle far above her. "I was going to say that the reason I like you so much is because you look so young, quite as young as I do,—more so, indeed, I think."

"It is a poor case," says Luttrell, "when a girl of nineteen looks older than a man of twenty-seven."

"That is not the way to put it. It is a charming and novel case when a man of twenty-seven looks younger than a girl of nineteen."

"How much younger?" asks Luttrell, who is still sufficiently youthful to have a hankering after mature age. "Am I fourteen or nine years old in your estimation?"

"Don't let us dispute the point," says Molly, "and don't get cross. I see you are on for a hot argument, and I never could follow even a mild one. I think you young, and you should be glad of it, as it is the one good thing I see about you. As a rule I prefer dark men,—but for their unhappy knack of looking old from their cradles,—and have a perfect passion for black eyes, black skin, black locks, and a general appearance of fierceness! Indeed, I have always thought, up to this, that there was something about a fair man almost ridiculous. Have not you?"

Here she brings her eyes back to the earth again, and fastens them upon him with the most engaging frankness.

"No. I confess it never occurred to me before," returns Luttrell, coloring slightly through his Saxon skin.

Silence. If there is any silent moment in the throbbing summer. Above them the faint music of the leaves, below the breathing of the flowers, the hum of insects. All the air is full of the sweet warblings of innumerable songsters. Mingling with these is the pleasant drip, drip of the falling water.

A great lazy bee falls, as though no longer able to sustain its mighty frame, right into Miss Massereene's lap, and lies there humming. With a little start she shakes it off, almost fearing to touch it with her dainty rose-white fingers.

Thus rudely roused, she speaks:

"Are you asleep?" she asks, not turning her head in her companion's direction.

"No," coldly; "are you?"

"Yes, almost, and dreaming."

"Dreams are the children of an idle brain," quotes he, somewhat maliciously.

"Yes?" sweetly. "And so you really have read your Shakespeare? And can actually apply it every now and then with effect, to the utter confusion of your friends? But I think you might have spared *me*. Teddy!" bending forward and casting upon him a bewitching, tormenting, adorable glance from under her dark lashes, "if you bite your moustache any harder it will come off, and then what will become of me?"

With a laugh Luttrell flings away the fern he has been reducing to ruin, and rising, throws himself upon the grass at her feet.

"Why don't I hate you?" he says, vehemently. "Why cannot I feel even decently angry with you? You torment and charm in the same breath. At times I say to myself, 'She is cold, heartless, unfeeling,' and then a word, a look—Molly," seizing her cool, slim little hand as it lies passive in her lap, "tell me, do you think you will ever—I do not mean to-morrow, or in a week, or a month, but in all the long years to come, do you think you will ever love me?" As he finishes speaking, he presses his lips with passionate tenderness to her hand.

"Now, who gave you leave to do that?" asks Molly, *à propos* of the kissing.

"Never mind: answer me."

"But I do mind very much indeed. I mind dreadfully."

"Well, then, I apologize, and I am very sorry, and I won't do it again: is that enough?"

"No, the fact still remains," gazing at her hand with a little pout, as though the offending kiss were distinctly visible; "and I don't want it."

"But what can be done?"

"I think—you had better—take it back again," says she, the pretended pout dissolving into an irresistible smile, as she slips her fingers with a sudden unexpected movement into his; after which she breaks into a merry laugh." "And now tell me," he persists, holding them close prisoners, and bestowing a loving caress upon each separately.

"Whether I love you? How can I, when I don't know myself? Perhaps at the end I may be sure. When I lie a-dying you must come to me, and bend over me, and say, 'Molly Bawn, do you love me?' And I shall whisper back with my last breath, 'yes' or 'no,' as the case may be."

"Don't talk of dying," he says, with a shudder, tightening his clasp.

"Why not? as we must die."

"But not now, not while we are young and happy. Afterward, when old age creeps on us and we look on love as weariness, it will not matter."

"To me, that is the horror of it," with a quick distasteful shiver, leaning forward in her earnestness, "to feel that sooner or later there will be no hope; that we *must* go, whether with or without our own will,—and it is never with it, is it?"

"Never, I suppose."

"It does not frighten me so much to think that in a month, or perhaps next year, or at any moment, I may die,—there is a blessed uncertainty about that,—but to know that, no matter how long I linger, the time will surely come when no prayers, no entreaties, will avail. They say of one who has cheated death for seventy years, that he has had a good long life: taking that, then, as an average, I have just fifty-one years to live, only half that to enjoy. Next year it will be fifty, then forty-nine, and so on until it comes down to one. What shall I do then?"

"My own darling, how fanciful you are! your hands have grown cold as ice. Probably when you are seventy you will consider yourself a still fascinating person of middle age, and look upon these thoughts of to-day as the sickly fancies of an infant. Do not let us talk about it any more. Your face is white."

"Yes," says Molly, recovering herself with a sigh, "it is the one thing that horrifies me. John is religious, so is Letty, while I—oh, that I could find pleasure in it! You see," speaking after a slight pause, with a smile, "I am at heart a rebel, and hate to obey. Mind you never give me an order! How good it would be to be young, and gay, and full of easy laughter, always,—to have lovers at command, to have some one at my feet forever!"

"'Some one,'" sadly. "Would any one do? Oh, Molly, can you not be satisfied with me?"

"How can I be sure? At present—yes," running her fingers lightly down the earnest, handsome face upraised to hers, apparently quite forgetful of her late emotion.

"Well, at all events," says the young man, with the air of one who is determined to make the best of a bad bargain, "there is no man you like better than me."

"At present,—no," says the incorrigible Molly.

"You are the greatest flirt I ever met in my life," exclaims he, with sudden anger.

"Who? I?"

"Yes,—you," vehemently.

A pause. They are much farther apart by this time, and are looking anywhere but at each other. Molly has her lap full of daisies, and is stringing them into a chain in rather an absent fashion; while Luttrell, who is too angry to pretend indifference, is sitting with gloom on his brow and a straw in his mouth, which latter he is biting vindictively.

"I don't believe I quite understand you," says Molly at length.

"Do you not? I cannot remember saying anything very difficult of comprehension."

"I must be growing stupid, then. You have accused me of flirting; and how am I to understand that, I who never flirted? How should I? I would not know how."

"You must allow me to differ with you; or, at all events, let me say your imitation of it is highly successful."

"But," with anxious hesitation, "what is flirting?"

"Pshaw!" wrathfully, "have you been waiting for me to tell you? It is trying to make a fool of a fellow, neither more nor less. You are pretending to love me, when you know in your heart you don't care *that* for me." The "that" is both forcible and expressive, and has reference to an indignant sound made by his thumb and his second finger.

"I was not aware that I ever 'pretended to love' you," replies Molly, in a tone that makes him wince.

"Well, let us say no more about it," cries he, springing to his feet, as though unable longer to endure his enforced quietude. "If you don't care for me, you don't, you know, and that is all about it. I dare say I shall get over it; and if not, why, I shall not be the only man in the world made miserable for a woman's amusement."

Molly has also risen, and, with her long daisy chain hanging from both her hands, is looking a perfect picture of injured innocence; although in truth she is honestly sorry for her cruel speech.

"I don't believe you know how unkind you are," she says, with a suspicion of tears in her voice, whether feigned or real he hardly dares conjecture. Feeling herself in the wrong, she seeks meanly to free herself from the false position by placing him there in her stead.

"Do not let us speak about unkindness, or anything else," says the young man, impatiently. "Of what use is it? It is the same thing always: I am obnoxious to you; we cannot put together two sentences without coming to open war."

"But whose fault was it this time? Think of what you accuse me! I did not believe you could be so rude to me!" with reproachful emphasis.

Here she directs a slow lingering glance at him from her violet eyes. There are visible signs of relenting about her companion. He colors, and persistently refuses, after the first involuntary glance, to allow his gaze to meet hers again; which is, of all others, the surest symptom of a coming rout. There are some eyes that can do almost anything with a man. Molly's eyes are of this order. They are her strongest point; and were they her sole charm, were she deaf and dumb, I believe it would be possible to her, by the power of their expressive beauty alone, to draw most hearts into her keeping.

"Did you mean what you said just now, that you had no love for me?" he asks, with a last vain effort to be stern and unforgiving. "Am I to believe that I am no more to you than any other man?"

"Believe nothing," murmurs she, coming nearer to lay a timid hand upon his arm, and raising her face to his, "except this, that I am your own Molly."

"Are you?" cries he, in a subdued tone, straining her to his heart, and speaking with an emotional indrawing of the breath that betrays more than his words how deeply he is feeling, "my very own? Nay, more than that, Molly, you are my all, my world, my life: if ever you forget me, or give me up for another, you will kill me: remember that."

"I will remember it. I will never do it," replies she, soothingly, the touch of motherhood that is in all good women coming to the front as she sees his agitation. "Why should I, when you are such a dear old boy? Now come and sit down again, and be reasonable. See, I will tie you up with my flowery chain as punishment for your behavior, and"—with a demure smile—"the kiss you stole in the *melée* without my permission."

"This is the chain by which I hold you," he says, rather sadly, surveying his wrists, round which the daisies cling. "The links that bind *me* to *you* are made of sterner stuff. Sweetheart," turning his handsome, singularly youthful face to hers, and speaking with an entreaty that savors strongly of despair, "do not let your beauty be my curse!"

"Why, who is fanciful now?" says Molly, making a little grimace at him. "And truly, to hear you speak, one must believe love is blind. Is it Venus," saucily, "or Helen of Troy, I most closely resemble? or am I 'something more exquisite still'? It puzzles me why you should think so very highly of my personal charms. Ted," leaning forward to look into her lover's eyes, "tell me this. Have you been much away? Abroad, I mean, on the Continent and that?"

"Well, yes, pretty much so."

"Have you been to Paris?"

"Oh, yes, several times."

"Brussels?"

"Yes."

"Vienna?"

"No. I wait to go there with you."

"Rome?"

"Yes, twice. The governor was fond of sending us abroad between the ages of seventeen and twenty-five,—to enlarge our minds, he said; to get rid of us, he meant."

"Are there many of you?"

"An awful lot. I would be ashamed to say how many. Ours was indeed a 'numerous father.'"

"He isn't dead?" asks Molly, in a low tone befitting the occasion in case he should be.

"Oh no: he is alive and kicking," replies Mr. Luttrell, with more force than elegance. "And I hope he will keep on so for years to come. He is about the best friend I have, or am likely to have."

"I hope he won't keep up the kicking part of it," says Molly, with a delicious laugh that ripples through the air and shows her utter enjoyment of her own wit. Not to laugh when Molly laughs, is impossible; so Luttrell joins her, and they both make merry over his vulgarity. In all the world, what is there sweeter than the happy, penetrating, satisfying laughter of unhurt youth?

"Lucky you, to have seen so much already," says Molly, presently, with an envious sigh; "and yet," with a view to self-support, "what good has it done you? Not one atom. After all your traveling you can do nothing greater than fall absurdly in love with a village maiden. Will your father call that enlarging your mind?"

"I hope so," concealing his misgivings on the point. "But why put it so badly? Instead of village maiden, say the loveliest girl I ever met."

"What!" cries Molly, the most naïve delight and satisfaction animating her tone; "after going through France, Germany, Italy, and India, you can honestly say I am the loveliest woman you ever met?"

"You put it too mildly," says Luttrell, raising himself on his elbow to gaze with admiration at the charming face above him, "I can say more. You are ten thousand times the loveliest woman I ever met."

Molly smiles, nay, more, she fairly dimples. Try as she will and does, she cannot conceal the pleasure it gives her to hear her praises sung.

"Why, then I am a 'belle,' a 'toast,'" she says, endeavoring unsuccessfully to see her image in the little basin of water that has gathered at the foot of the rocks; "while you," turning to run five white fingers over his hair caressingly, and then all down his face, "you are the most delightful person I ever met. It is so easy to believe what you tell one, and so pleasant. I have half a mind to—kiss you!"

"Don't stop there: have a whole mind," says Luttrell, eagerly. "Kiss me at once, before the fancy evaporates."

"No," holding him back with one lazy finger (he is easy to be repulsed), "on second thought I will reserve my caress. Some other time, when you are good,—perhaps. By the bye, Ted, did you really mean you would take me to Vienna?"

"Yes, if you would care to go there."

"Care? that is not the question. It will cost a great deal of money to get there, won't it? Shall we be able to afford it?"

"No doubt the governor will stand to me, and give a check for the occasion," says Luttrell, warming to the subject. "Anyhow, you shall go, if you wish it."

"Wait until your father hears you have wedded a pauper, and then you will see what a check you will get," says Miss Massereene, with a contemptible attempt at a joke.

"A pun!" says Luttrell, springing to his feet with a groan; "that means a pinch. So prepare."

"I forbid you," cries she, inwardly quaking, and, rising hurriedly, stands well away from him, with her petticoats caught together in one hand ready for flight. "I won't allow you. Don't attempt to touch me."

"It is the law of the land," declares he, advancing on her, while she as steadily retreats.

"Dear Teddy, good Teddy," cries she, "spare me this time, and I will never do it again—no, not though it should tremble forever on the tip of my tongue. As you are strong, be merciful. Do forgive me this once."

"Impossible."

"Then I defy you," retorts Miss Massereene, who, having manœuvred until she has placed a good distance between herself and the foe, now turns, and flies through the trees, making very successful running for the open beyond. Not until they are within full view of the house does he manage to come up with her. And then the presence of John sunning himself on the hall-door step, surrounded by his family, effectually prevents her ever obtaining that richly-deserved punishment.

CHAPTER IX

"After long years."

It is raining, not only raining, but pouring. All the gracious sunshine of yesterday is obliterated, forgotten, while in its place the sullen raindrops dash themselves with suppressed fury against the window-panes. Huge drops they are, swollen with the hidden rage of many days, that fall, and burst heavily, and make the casements tremble.

Outside, the flowers droop and hang their pretty heads in sad wonder at this undeserved Nemesis that has overtaken them. Along the sides of the graveled paths small rivulets run frightened. There is no song of birds in all the air. Only the young short grass uprears itself, and, drinking in with eager greediness the welcome but angry shower, refuses to bend its neck beneath the yoke.

"How I hate a wet day!" says Luttrell, moodily, for the twentieth time, staring blankly out of the deserted school-room window, where he and Molly have been yawning, moping for the last half-hour.

"Do you? I love it," replies she, out of a sheer spirit of contradiction; as, if there is one thing she utterly abhors it is the idea of rain.

"If I said I loved it, *you* would say the reverse," says he, laughing, not feeling equal to the excitement of a quarrel.

"Without doubt," replies she, laughing too: so that a very successful opening is rashly neglected. "Surely it cannot keep on like this all day," she says, presently, in a dismal tone, betraying by her manner the falsity of her former admiration: "we shall have a dry winter if it continues much longer. Has any wise man yet discovered how much rain the clouds are capable of containing at one time? It would be such a blessing if they had: then we might know the worst, and make up our minds to it."

"Drop a line to the clerk of the weather office; he might make it his business to find out if you asked him."

"Is that a joke?" with languid disgust. "And you professed yourself indignant with me yesterday when I perpetrated a really superior one! You ought to be ashamed of yourself. I would not condescend to anything so feeble."

"That reminds me I have never yet paid you off for that misdemeanor. Now, when time is hanging so heavily on my hands, is a most favorable opportunity to pay the debt. I embrace it. And you too. So 'prepare for cavalry.'"

"A fig for all the hussars in Europe," cries Molly, with indomitable courage.

Meantime, Letitia and John in the morning room—that in a grander house would have been designated a boudoir—are holding a hot discussion.

Lovat, the eldest son, being the handsomest and by far the most scampish of the children, is of course his mother's idol. His master, however, having written to say that up to this, in spite of all the trouble that has been taken with him, he has evinced a far greater disposition for cricket and punching his companions' heads than for his Greek and Latin, Lovat's father had given it as his opinion that Lovat deserves a right good flogging; while Lovat's mother maintains that all noble, high-spirited boys are "just like that," and asks Mr. Massereene, with the air of a Q. C., whether he never felt a distaste for the dead languages.

Mr. Massereene replying that he never did, that he was always a model boy, and never anywhere but at the head of his class, his wife instantly declares she doesn't believe a word of it, and most unfairly rakes up a dead-and-gone story, in which Mr. Massereene figures as the principal feature, and is discovered during school hours on the top of a neighbor's apple-tree, with a long-suffering but irate usher at the foot of it, armed with his indignation and a birch rod.

"And for three mortal hours he stood there, while I sat up aloft grinning at him," says Mr. Massereene, with (considering his years) a disgraceful appreciation of his past immoral conduct; "and when at last the gardener was induced to mount the tree and drag me ignominiously to the ground, I got such a flogging as made a chair for some time assume the character of a rack."

"And you deserved it, too," says Letitia, with unwonted severity.

"I did, indeed, my dear," John confesses, heartily, "richly. I am glad to see that at last you begin to take a sensible view of the subject. If I deserved a flogging because I once shirked my tasks, what does not Lovat deserve for a long course of such conduct?"

"He is not accused of stealing apples, at all events; and, besides, Lovat is quite different," says Letitia, vaguely. Whereupon John tells her her heart is running away with her head, and that her partiality is so apparent that he must cease from further argument, and goes on with his reading.

Presently, however, he rises, and, crossing the room, stands over her, watching her white shapely fingers as they deftly fill up the holes in the little socks that lie in the basket beside her. She is so far *en rapport* with him as to know that his manner betokens a desire for confidence.

"Have you anything to say to me, dear?" she asks, looking up and suspending her employment for the time being.

"Letitia," begins he, thoughtfully, not to say solemnly, "it is quite two months since Luttrell first put in an appearance in this house. Now, I don't wish to seem inhospitable,—far be it from me: a thirst for knowledge alone induces me to put the question,—but, *do* you think he means to reside here permanently?"

"It is certainly very strange," says Letitia, unmoved by his eloquence to even the faintest glimmer of a smile, so deep is her interest in the subject,— "the very oddest thing. If, now, it were a place where a young man could find any amusement, I would say nothing; but here! Do you know, John,"— mysteriously,—"I have my suspicions."

"No!" exclaims Mr. Massereene, betraying the wildest curiosity in voice and gesture,—so wild as to hint at the possibility of its not being genuine. "You don't say so!"

"It has once or twice occurred to me— —"

"Yes?"

"I have certainly thought— —"

"Letitia,"—with authority,—"don't think, or suspect, or let it occur to you any more: *say* it."

"Well, then, I think he is in love with Molly."

John breaks into a heavy laugh.

"What it is to be a woman of penetration," says he. "So you have found that out. Now, that is where we men fail. But are you certain? Why do you think it?"

"I am almost convinced of it," Letitia says, with much solemnity. "Last night I happened to be looking out of one of the windows that overhang the garden, and there in the moonlight (it was quite ten o'clock) I saw Molly give him a red rose; and he took it, and gazed at it as though he were going to devour it; and then he kissed it; and after that he kissed Molly's hand! Now, I don't think, John, unless a young man was—you know—eh?"

"I altogether agree with you. Unless a young man *was*, you know, why, he wouldn't—that's all. I am glad, however, he had the grace to stop at the hand,—that it was not Molly's lips he chose instead."

"My *dear* John!"

"My darling Letty! have I said anything so very *outre*? Were you never kissed by a young man?"

"Only by you," returns Mrs. Massereene, laughing apologetically, and blushing a rare delicate pink that would not have disgraced her at eighteen.

"Ah, you may well be excused, considering how you were tempted. It is not every day one meets—— By the bye, Letty, did you cease your eavesdropping at that point?"

"Yes; I did not like to remain longer."

"Then depend upon it, my dear, you did not see the last act in that drama."

"You surely do not think Molly——"

"I seldom trouble to think. I only know Luttrell is an uncommonly good-looking fellow, and that the moon is a white witch."

"He *is* good-looking," says Letitia, rising and growing troubled; "he is more than that,—he is charming. Oh, John! if our Molly were to fall in love with him, and grow unhappy about it, what would we do? I don't believe he has anything beyond his pay."

"He has something more than that, I know, but not much. The Luttrells have a good deal of spare cash throwing about among them."

"But what of that? And a poor man would be wretched for Molly. Remember what an expensive regiment he is in. Why, I suppose as it is he can hardly keep himself. And how would it be with a wife and a large family?"

"Oh, Letitia! let us have the marriage ceremony first. Why on earth will you saddle the miserable man with a large family so soon? And wouldn't a small one do? Of what use to pile up the agony to such a height?"

"I think of no one but Molly. There is nothing so terrible as a long engagement, and that is what it will come to. Do you remember Sarah Annesley? She grew thinner and thinner day by day, and her complexion became positively yellow when Perceval went away. And her mother said it was suspense preying upon her."

"So they *said*, my dear; but we all *know* it was indigestion."

"John,"—austerely,—"what is the exact amount of Mr. Luttrell's income?"

"About six hundred a year, I think."

"As much as that?" Slightly relieved. "And will his father allow him anything more?"

"Unless you insist upon my writing to Sir William, I could not tell you that."

"Six hundred a year is far too little."

"It is almost as much as we have."

"But you are not in the army, and you are not a fashionable young man."

"If you say that again I shall sue for a divorce. But seriously, Letty, perhaps you are exciting yourself about nothing. Who knows but they are indifferent to each other?"

"I fear they are not. And I will not have poor Molly made unhappy."

"Why not 'poor Luttrell'? It is far more likely as I see it."

"I don't want any one to be unhappy. And something must be done."

"Exactly." After a pause, with ill-concealed cowardice: "Will you do it?"

"Do what?"

"That awful 'something' that is to be done."

"Certainly not. It is your duty to—to—find out everything, and ask them both what they mean."

"Then I won't," declares John, throwing out his arms decisively. "I would not be bribed to do it. What! ask a man his intentions! I couldn't bring myself to do such a thing. How could I look him in the face again? They must fight the best battle they can for themselves, like every one else. I won't interfere."

"Very good. I shall speak to Molly. And I really think we ought to go and look them up. I have seen neither of them since breakfast time."

"The rain has ceased. Let us go out by the balcony," says Mr. Massereene, stepping through the open window. "I heard them in the school-room as I passed."

Now, this balcony, as I have told you, runs along all one side of the house, and on it the drawing-room, school-room, and one of the parlor windows open. Thick curtains hang from them and conceal in part the outer world; so that when John and Letty stand before the school-room window to look in they do so without being themselves seen. And this, I regret to say, is what they see:

In the centre of the room a square table, and flying round and round it, with the tail of her white gown twisted over her right arm, is Miss Massereene, with Mr. Luttrell in full chase after her.

"Well, upon my word!" says Mr. Massereene, unable through bewilderment to think of any remark more brilliant.

Round and round goes Molly, round and round follows her pursuer; until Luttrell, finding his prey to be quite as fleet if not fleeter than himself, resorts to a mean expedient, and, catching hold of one side of the table, pushes it, and Molly behind it, slowly but surely into the opposite corner.

There is no hope. Steadily, certainly, she approaches her doom, and with flushed cheeks and eyes gleaming with laughter, makes a vain protest.

"Now I have you," says Luttrell, drawing an elaborate penknife from his pocket, in which all the tools that usually go to adorn a carpenter's shop fight for room. "Prepare for death, or—I give you your choice: I shall either cut your jugular vein or kiss you. Don't hurry. Say which you prefer. It is a matter of indifference to me."

"Cut every vein in my body first," cries Molly, breathless but defiant.

["Letitia," whispers John, "I feel I am going to laugh. What shall I do?"

"Don't," says Letitia, with stern promptitude. "That is what you will do. It is no laughing matter. I hope you are not going to make a jest of it, John."

"But, my dear, supposing I can't help it?" suggests he, mildly. "Our risible faculties are not always under our control."

"On an occasion such as this they should be."

"Letitia," says Mr. Massereene, regarding her with severity, "you are going to laugh yourself; don't deny it."

"No,—no, indeed," protests Letitia, foolishly, considering her handsome face is one broad smile, and that her plump shoulders are visibly shaking.]

"It is mean! it is shameful!" says Molly, from within, seeing no chance of escape. Whichever way she rushes can be only into his arms.

"All that you can say shan't prevent me," decides Luttrell, moving toward her with fell determination in his eye.

"Perhaps a little that I can say may have the desired effect," breaks in Mr. Massereene, advancing into the middle of the room, with Letitia, looking rather nervous, behind him.

Tableau.

There is a sudden, rather undignified, cessation of hostilities on the part of Mr. Luttrell, who beats a hasty retreat to the wall, where he stands as though glad of the support. He bears a sneaky rather than a distinguished appearance, and altogether has the grace to betray a considerable amount of shame.

Molly, dropping her gown, turns a rich crimson, but is, I need hardly say, by far the least upset of the two delinquents. She remains where she is, hedged in by the table, and is conscious of feeling a wild desire to laugh.

Determined to break the silence, which is proving oppressive, she says, demurely:

"How fortunate, John, that you happened to be on the spot! Mr. Luttrell was behaving *so* badly!"

"I don't need to be told that."

"But how did you come here?" asks Molly, making a brave but unsuccessful effort to turn the tables upon the enemy. "And Letitia, too! I do hate people who turn up when they are least expected. What were you doing on the balcony?"

"Watching you—and—your friend," says John, very gravely for him. He addresses himself entirely to Molly, her "friend" being in the last stage of confusion and utterly incapable of speech. At this, however, he can support the situation no longer, and, coming forward, says eagerly:

"John, let me explain. The fact is, I asked Miss Massereene to marry me, a little time ago, and she has promised to do so—if you—don't object." After this bit of eloquence he draws himself up, with a little shake, as though he had rid himself of something disagreeable, and becomes once more his usual self.

Letitia puts on a "didn't I tell you?" sort of air, and John says:

"Is that so?" looking at Molly for confirmation.

"Yes, if it is your wish," cries she, forsaking her retreat, and coming forward to lay her hand upon her brother's arm entreatingly, and with a gesture full of tenderness. "But if you do object, if it vexes you in the very slightest degree, John, I——"

"But you will give your consent, Massereene," interrupts her lover, hastily, as though dreading the remainder of the sentence, "won't you?" He too has come close up to John, and stands on one side, opposite Molly. Almost, from the troubled expression of his face as he looks at the girl, one might imagine him trying to combat her apparent lukewarmness more then her brother's objections.

"Things seem to have progressed very favorably without my consent," says John, glancing at the unlucky table, which has come in for a most unfair share of the blame. "But before giving you my blessing I acknowledge— now we are on the subject—I would like to know on what sum you intend setting up housekeeping." Here Letitia, who has preserved a strict neutrality throughout, comes more to the front. "It is inconvenient, and anything but romantic, I know, but people must eat, and those who indulge in *violent exercise* are generally possessed of healthy appetites."

"I have over five hundred a year," says Luttrell, coloring, and feeling as if he had said fifty and was going to be called presumptuous. He also feels that John has by some sudden means become very many years older than he really is.

"That includes everything?"

"Everything. When my uncle—Maxwell Luttrell—hops the—that is, drops off—I mean dies," says Luttrell whose slang is extensive and rather confusing, "I shall come in for five thousand pounds more."

"How can you speak in such a cold-blooded way of your uncle's death?" says Molly, who is not so much impressed by the occasion as she should be.

"Why not? There is no love lost between us. If he could leave it away from me he would; but that is out of his power."

"That makes it seven hundred," says Letitia, softly, *à propos* of the income.

"Nearer eight," says he, brightening at her tone.

"Molly, you wish to marry Tedcastle?" John asks his sister, gazing at her earnestly.

"Ye—es; but I'm not in a hurry, you know," replies she, with a little nod.

Massereene regards her curiously for a moment or two; then he says:

"She is young, Luttrell; she has seen little of the world. You must give her time. I know no man I would prefer to you as a brother; but—give her time. Be satisfied with the engagement; do not let us speak of marriage just yet."

"Not unless she wishes it," says the young man bravely, and perhaps a little proudly.

"In a year," says John, still with his eyes on his beautiful sister, and speaking with marked hesitation, as though waiting for her to make some sign by which he shall know how to best forward her secret wishes; "then we may begin to talk about it."

"Yes, then we may talk about it," echoes Molly, cheerfully.

"But a year!—it is a lifetime," says Luttrell, with some excitement, turning his eyes, full of a mute desire for help, upon Letitia. And when did Letitia ever fail any one?

"I certainly think it is too long," she says, truthfully and kindly.

"No," cries Molly, pettishly, "it shall be as John wishes. Why, it is nothing! Think of all the long years to come afterward, when we shall not be able to get rid of each other, no matter how earnestly we may desire it; and then see how small in comparison is this one year."

Luttrell, who has grown a little pale, goes over to her and takes her hand in both his. His face is grave, fuller of purpose than they have ever seen it. To him the scene is a betrothal, almost a marriage.

"You will be true to me?" he says, with suppressed emotion. "Swear that you will, before your brother."

"Of course I will," with a quick, nervous laugh. "Why should I be otherwise? You frighten me with your solemn ways. Am I more to you than I was yesterday? Why, how should I be untrue to you, even if I wished it? I shall see no one from the day you leave until you come again."

At this moment the noise of the door-handle being turned makes him drop her hand, and they all fall simultaneously into what they hope is an easy attitude. And then Sarah appears upon the threshold with a letter and a small packet between her first finger and thumb. She is a very genteel girl, is Sarah, and would scorn to take a firm grasp of anything.

"This 'ere is for you, sir," she says, delivering the packet to Luttrell, who consigns it hastily to his coat-pocket; "and this for you, Miss Molly," giving the letter. "The postman says, sir, as 'ow they only come by the afternoon, but I am of the rooted opinion that he forgot 'm this morning."

Thus Sarah, who is loquacious though trustworthy, and bears an undying grudge to the postman, in that he has expressed himself less enamored of her waning charms than of those of the more buxom Jane, who queens it over the stewpans and the cold joints.

"Most improper of the postman," replies Mr. Massereene, soothingly.

Meantime, Molly is standing staring curiously at her missive.

"I don't know the writing," she says in a vague tone. "I do hope it isn't a bill."

"A bill, with that monogram!" exclaims Luttrell. "Not likely. I would swear to a dunning epistle at twenty yards' distance."

"Who can it be from?" wonders Molly, still dallying with one finger inserted beneath the flap of the envelope.

"Perhaps, if you look within you may find out," suggests John, meekly; and thus encouraged she opens the letter and reads.

At first her face betrays mere indifference, then surprise, then a sudden awakening to intense interest, and lastly unmitigated astonishment.

"It is the most extraordinary thing," she says, at last, looking up, and addressing them in an awestruck whisper, "the most unexpected. After all these years,—I can scarcely believe it to be true."

"But what is it, darling?" asks Letty, actually tingling with excitement.

"An invitation to Herst Royal!"

"I don't believe you," cries Luttrell, who means no rudeness at all, but is merely declaring in a modern fashion how delighted beyond measure he is.

"Look: is not that Marcia's writing? I suppose she wrote it, though it is dictated by grandpapa."

All four heads were instantly bent over the clear, bold calligraphy to read the cold but courteous invitation it contains.

"Dear Eleanor" is given to understand that her grandfather will be pleased to make her acquaintance, if she will be pleased to transfer herself and her maid to Herst Royal on the twenty-seventh of the present month. There are a few hints about suitable trains, a request that a speedy reply in the affirmative will be sent, and then "dear Eleanor" is desired to look upon Mr. Amherst as her "affectionate grandfather." Not one word about all the neglect that has been showered upon her for nineteen years.

"Well?" says Luttrell, who is naturally the first to recover himself.

"Had you anything to do with this?" asks John, turning almost fiercely to him.

"Nothing, on my honor."

"He must be near death," says Letitia. Molly is silent, her eyes still fixed upon the letter. "I think, John—she ought to go."

"Of course she shall go," returns John, a kind of savage jealousy pricking him. "I can't provide for her after my death. That old man may be softened by her face or terrified by the near approach of dissolution into doing her justice. He has neither watched her, nor tended her, nor loved her; but now that she has come to perfection he claims her."

"John," cries Molly, with sudden passion, flinging herself into his arms, "I will not go. No, not one step. What is he to me, that stern old tyrant, who has refused for nineteen years to acknowledge me? While you, my dear, my darling, you are my all."

"Nonsense, child!" speaking roughly, although consoled and strengthened by her caress and loving words. "It is what I have been wishing for all these years. Of course you must go. It is only right you should be recognized by your relations, even though it is so late in the day. Perhaps he will leave you a legacy; and"—smiling—"I think I may console myself with the reflection that old Amherst will scarcely be able to cut me out."

"You may, without flattering yourself," says Luttrell.

"Letitia, do you too want to get rid of me?" asks Molly, still half crying.

"You are a hypocrite," says Letitia; "you know you are dying to go. I should, were I in your place. Instead of lamenting, you ought to be thanking your stars for this lucky chance that has befallen you; and you should be doubly grateful to us for letting you go, as we shall miss you horribly."

"I shan't stay any time," says Molly, reviving. "I shall be back before you realize the fact that I have gone. I know in polite society no one is expected to outstay a month at the very longest."

"You cover me with confusion," says Luttrell, laughing. "Consider what unmentionable form I have displayed. How long have I outstayed my time? It is uncommonly good of you, Mrs. Massereene, not to have given me my *congé* long ago; but my only excuse is that I have been so utterly happy. Perhaps you will forgive me when you learn that I must tear myself away on Thursday."

"Oh! must you?" says Letitia, honestly sorry. Now that the engagement is *un fait accompli*, and the bridegroom-elect has declared himself not altogether so insolvent as she had feared, she drops precautionary measures and gives way to the affection with which she has begun to regard him. "You are going to Herst also. Why cannot you stay here to accompany Molly? Her going is barely three weeks distant."

"If I could I would not require much pressing, you can readily believe that. But duty is imperative, and go I must."

"You did not tell me you were going," says Molly, looking aggrieved. "How long have you known it?"

"For a week. I could not bear to think about leaving, much less to speak of it, so full of charms has Brooklyn proved itself," — with a smile at Mrs. Massereene, — "but it is an indisputable fact for all that."

"Well, in spite of Lindley Murray I maintain that life is long," says Massereene, who has been silent for the past few minutes. "And I need hardly tell you, Luttrell, you are welcome here whenever you please to come."

"Thank you, old boy," says Luttrell.

"Come out," whispers Molly, slipping her hand into her lover's (she minds John and Letitia about as much as she minds the tables and chairs); "the rain has ceased; and see what a beautiful sun. I have any amount of things to say to you, and a whole volume of questions to ask about my detested *grand-père*. So freshen your wits. But first before we go" — mischievously, and with a little nod full of reproof — "I really think you ought to apologize to John for your scandalous behavior of this morning."

"Molly, I predict this glorious future for you," says her brother: "that you will be returned to me from Herst Royal in disgrace."

When they have reached the summer-house in the garden, whither they have wended their way, with a view to shade (as the sun, having been debarred from shining for so many hours, is now exerting itself to the utmost to make up for lost time), Luttrell draws from his pocket the identical parcel delivered to him by Sarah, and, holding it out to Molly, says, somewhat shamefacedly:

"Here is something for you."

"For me?" coloring with surprise and pleasant expectation. She is a being so unmistakably delighted with anything she receives, be it small or great, that it is an absolute joy to give to her. "What is it?"

"Open it and see. I have not seen it myself yet, but I hope it will please you."

Off comes the wrapper; a little leather case is disclosed, a mysterious fastener undone, and there inside, in its velvet shelter, lies an exquisite diamond ring that glistens and flashes up into her enchanted eyes.

"Oh, Teddy! it cannot be for me," she says, with a little gasp that speaks volumes; "it is too beautiful. Oh, how good of you to think of it! And how did you know that if there is one thing on earth which I love it is a ring? And *such* a ring! You wicked boy, I do believe you have spent a fortune on it." Yet in reality she hardly guesses the full amount of the generous sum that has been so willingly expended on that glittering hoop.

"I am glad you like it," he says, radiant at her praise. "I think it is pretty."

"'Pretty' is a poor word. It is far too handsome. I would scold you for your extravagance, but I have lost the power just now. And do you know," raising her soft, flushed face to her lover,—"I never had a ring before in my life, except a very old-fashioned one of my mother's, an ancient square, you know, with hair in the centre, and all around it big pearls, that are anything but pearly now, as they have grown quite black. Thank you a thousand times."

She slips her arm around his neck and presses her lips warmly, unbashfully to his cheek. Be it ever so cold, so wanting in the shyness that belongs to conscious tenderness, it is still the very first caress she has ever given him of her own accord. A little thrill runs through him, and a mad longing to catch her in his arms, as he feels the sweet, cool touch; yet he restrains himself. Some innate sense of honor, born on the occasion, a shrinking lest she should deem him capable of claiming even so natural a return for his gift, compels him to forego his desire. It is noticeable, too, that he does not even place the ring upon her engaged finger, as most men would have done. It is a bauble meant to gratify her: why make it a fetter, be it ever so light a one?

"I am amply repaid," he says, gently. "Was there ever such luck as your getting that invitation this morning? I wonder what could have put it into the old fellow's head to invite you? Are you glad you are going?"

"I am. I almost think it is mean of me to be so glad, but I can't help it. Is my grandfather so very terrific?"

"He is all of that," says Luttrell, "and a good deal more. If I were an American I would have no scruples about calling him a 'darned old cuss': as it is, I will smother my feelings, and let you discover his failings for yourself."

"If he is as bad as you say, I wonder he gets any one to visit him."

"He does, however. We all go,—generally the same lot every year; though I have been rather out of it for a time, on account of my short stay in India. He has first-class shooting; and when he is not in the way, it is pretty jolly. He hates old people, and never allows a chaperon inside his doors,—I mean elderly chaperons. The young ones don't count: they, as a rule, are backward in the art of talking at one and making things disagreeable all round."

"But he is old himself."

"That's just it. It is all jealousy. He finds every old person he meets, no matter how unpleasant, a decided improvement on himself; whereas he can always hope the young ones may turn out his counterparts."

"Really, if you say much more, I shall be afraid to go to Herst."

"Oh, well"—temporizing—"perhaps I exaggerate slightly. He has a wretched temper, and he takes snuff, you know, but I dare say there are worse."

"I have heard of damning praise," says Molly, laughing. "You are an adept at it."

"Am I? I didn't know. Well, do you know, in spite of all my uncivil remarks, there is a certain charm about Herst that other country-houses lack? We all understand our host's little weaknesses, in the first place, and are, therefore, never caught sleeping. We feel as if we were at school again, united by a common cause, with all the excitement of a conspiracy on foot that has a master for its victim; though, to confess the truth, the master in our case has generally the best of it, as he has a perfect talent for hitting on one's sore point. Then, too, we know to a nicety when the dear old man is in a particularly vicious mood, which is usually at dinner-time, and we keep looking at each other through every course, wondering on whose devoted head the shell of his wrath will first burst; and when that is over we wonder again whose turn it will be next."

"It must keep you very lively."

"It does; and, what is better, it prevents formality, and puts an end to the earlier stages of etiquette. We feel a sort of relationship, a clanship among us; and, indeed, for the most part, we are related, as Mr. Amherst prefers entertaining his family to any others,—it is so much easier to be unpleasant to them than to strangers. I am connected with him very distantly through my mother; so is Cecil Stafford; so is Potts in some undefined way."

"Now, don't tell me you are my cousin," says Molly, "because I wouldn't like it."

"I am not proud; if you will let me be your husband, I won't ask anything more. Oh, Molly, how I wish this year was at an end!"

"Do you? I don't. I am absolutely dying to go to Herst." Then, turning eyes that are rather wistful upon him, she says, earnestly, "Do they—the women, I mean—wear very lovely clothes? To be like them must I—be very well dressed?"

"You always are very well dressed, are you not?" asks her lover, in return, casting a loving, satisfied glance over the fresh, inexpensive Holland gown she wears, with a charming but strictly masculine disregard of the fact that muslin is not silk, nor cotton cashmere.

"Am I? You stupid boy!" says Molly; but she laughs in a little pleased way and pats his hand. Next to being praised herself, the sweetest thing to a woman is to have her dress praised. "Not I. Well, no matter; they may crush me if they please with their designs by Worth, but I defy them to have a prettier ring than mine," smiling at her new toy as it still lies in the middle of her hand. "Is Herst very large, Teddy? How shall I remember my own room? It will be so awkward to be forever running into somebody else's, won't it?"

"Your maid will manage all that for you."

"My maid?" coloring slowly, but still with her eyes on his. "And—supposing I have no maid?"

"Well, then," says Tedcastle, who has been bred in the belief that a woman without her maid is as lost as a babe without its mother, "why, then, I suppose, you would borrow one from your nearest neighbor. Cecil Stafford would lend you hers. I know my sisters were only allowed one maid between each two; and when they spent the autumn in different houses they used to toss up which should have her."

"What does a maid do for one, I wonder?" muses independent Molly.

"I should fancy you could better answer that than I."

"No,—because I never had one."

"Well, neither had I," says Luttrell; at which they both laugh.

"I am afraid," says Molly, in a rather dispirited tone, "I shall feel rather strange at Herst. I wish you could manage to be there the very day I arrive,—could you, Teddy? I would not be so lonely if I knew for certain you would be on the spot to welcome me. It is horrible going there for—that is—to be inspected."

"I will surely be there a day or two after, but I doubt if I could be there on the twenty-seventh. You may trust me to do my best."

"I suppose it is—a very grand place," questions Molly, growing more and more depressed, "with dinner-parties every day, and butlers, and footmen, and all the rest of it? And I shall be there, a stranger, with no one to care whether I enjoy myself or not."

"You forget me," says Luttrell, quietly.

"True," returns she, brightening; "and whenever you see me sitting by myself, Teddy, you are to come over to me, no matter how engaged you may be, and sit down beside me. If I have any one else with me, of course you need not mind it."

"I see." Rather dryly. "Two is company, three is trumpery."

"Have I vexed you? How foolish you are! Why, if you are jealous in imagination, how will it be in reality? There will be many men at Herst; and perhaps—who knows——"

"What?"

"I may fall in love with some of them."

"Very likely." With studied coolness.

"Philip Shadwell, for instance?"

"It may be."

"Or your Mr. Potts?"

"There is no accounting for tastes."

"Or any one else that may happen to please me?"

"I see nothing to prevent it."

"And what then?"

"Why, then you will forget me, and like him,—until you like some one else better."

"Now, if I were a dignified young lady," says Molly, "I should feel insulted; but, being only Molly Bawn, I don't. I forgive you; and I won't fall in love with any one; so you may take that thunder-cloud off your brow as soon as it may please your royal highness."

"What do you gain by making me unhappy?" asks he, impetuously seizing the hand she has extended to him with all the air of an offended but gracious queen.

"Everything." Laughing. "I delight in teasing you, you look so deliciously miserable all through; it is never time thrown away upon you. Now, if you could only manage to laugh at my sallies or tease me back again, I dare say I should give in in a week and let you rest in peace ever after. Why don't you?"

"Perhaps because I can't. All people are not gifted with your fertile imagination. Or because it would give *me* no pleasure to see *you* 'deliciously miserable.'"

"Oh, you *wouldn't* see that," says Molly, airily. "All you could say would not suffice to bring even the faintest touch of misery into my face. Angry I might be, but 'miserable,' never!"

"Be assured, Molly, I shall never put your words to the test. Your happiness means mine."

"See how the diamonds flash!" says Molly, presently, recurring to her treasure. "Is this the engagement-finger? But I will not let it stay there, lest it might betray me."

"But every one knows it now."

"Are John and Letty every one? At Herst they are still in blissful ignorance. Let them remain so. I insist on our engagement being kept secret."

"But why?"

"Because if it was known it would spoil all my fun. I have noticed that men avoid a *fiancée* as they would a—a rattlesnake."

"I cannot see why being engaged should spoil your fun."

"But it would for all that. Come now, Ted, be candid: how often were you in love before you met me?"

"Never." With the vehemence of a thousand oaths.

"Well, then, to put it differently, how many girls did you like?"

"Like?" Reluctantly. "Oh, as for that, I suppose I did fancy I liked a few girls."

"Just so; and I should like to like a few men," says Miss Massereene, triumphantly.

"You don't know what you are talking about," says Tedcastle, hotly.

"Indeed I do. That is just one of the great points which the defenders of women's rights forget to expatiate upon. A man may love as often as he chooses, while a woman must only love once, or he considers himself very badly used. Why not be on an equal footing? Not that I want to love any one," says Molly; "only it is the injustice of the thing I abhor."

"Love any one you choose," says Tedcastle, passionately, springing to his feet, "Shadwell or any other fellow that comes in your way, I shan't interfere. It is hardly necessary for you to say you don't 'want to love one.' Your heart is as cold as ice. It is high time this engagement—this farce— should come to an end."

"If you wish it," says Molly, quietly, in a subdued tone, yet as she says it she moves one step—no more—closer to him.

"But I do not wish it; that is my cruel fate!" cries the young man, taking both her hands and laying them over his heart with a despairing tenderness. "There are none happy save those incapable of knowing a lasting affection. Oh, Molly!"—remorsefully—"forgive me. I am speaking to you as I ought not. It is all my beastly temper; though I used not to be ill-tempered," says he, with sad wonder. "At home and among our fellows I was always considered rather easy-going than otherwise. I think the knowledge that I must part from you on Thursday (though only for a short time) is embittering me."

"Then you are really sorry to leave me?" questions Molly, peering up at him from under her straw hat.

"You know I am."

"But very sorry,—desperately so?"

"Yes." Gravely, and with something that is almost tears in his eyes. "Why do you ask me, Molly? Is it not palpable enough?"

"It is not. You look just the same as ever,—quite as 'easy-going'"—with a malicious pout—"as either your 'home' or your 'fellows' could desire. I quite buoyed myself up with the hope that I should see you reduced to a skeleton as the last week crept to its close, and here you are robust and well to do as usual. I call it unfeeling," says Miss Massereene, reproachfully, "and I don't believe you care a pin about me."

"Would you like to see me 'reduced to a skeleton'?" asks Luttrell, reproachfully. "You talk as though you had been done out of something; but a man may be horribly cut up about a thing without letting all the world know of it."

"You conceal it with great skill," says Molly, placing her hand beneath his chin, under a pretense of studying his features, but in reality to compel him to look at her; and, as it is impossible for any one to gaze into another's eyes for any length of time without showing emotion of some kind, presently he laughs.

"Ah!" cries she, well pleased, "now I have made you laugh, your little attack of the spleens will possibly take to itself wings and fly away."

All through the remainder of this day and the whole of the next—which is his last—she is sweetness itself to him. Whatever powers of tormenting she possesses are kept well in the background, while she betrays nothing but a very successful desire to please.

She wanders with him contentedly through garden and lawn; she sits beside him; at dinner she directs swift, surreptitious smiles at him across the flowers; later on she sings to him his favorite songs; and why she scarcely knows. Perhaps through a coquettish desire to make the parting harder; perhaps to make his chains still stronger; perhaps to soothe his evident regret; perhaps (who can say?) because she too feels that same regret.

And surely to-night some new spirit is awake within her. Never has she sung so sweetly. As her glorious voice floats through the dimly-lighted room and out into the more brilliant night beyond, Luttrell, and Letitia, and John sit entranced and wonder secretly at the great gift that has been given her.

"If ever words are sweet, what, what is song

When lips we love the melody prolong!"

Molly in every-day life is one thing; Molly singing divinely is another. One wonders curiously, when hearing her, how anything so gay, so *debonnaire* as she, can throw such passion into words, such thrilling tenderness, such wild and mournful longing.

"Molly," cries John impatiently from the balcony, "I cannot bear to hear you sing like that. One would think your heart was broken. Don't do it, child."

And Molly laughs lightly, and bursts into a barcarolle that utterly precludes the idea of any deep feeling; after which she gives them her own "Molly Bawn," and then, shutting down the piano, declares she is tired, and that evidently John doesn't appreciate her, and so she will sing no more.

Then comes the last morning,—the cruel moment when farewell must be said.

The dog-cart is at the door; John is good-naturedly busy about the harness; and, Letitia having suddenly and with suspicious haste recollected important commands for the kitchen, whither she withdraws herself, the lovers find themselves alone.

"Hurry, man, you will barely catch it," cries John, from outside, meaning the train; having calculated to a nicety how long it would take him to give and receive a kiss, now that he has been married for more years than he cares to count.

Luttrell, starting at his voice, seizes both Molly's hands.

"Keep thinking of me always," he says, in a low tone, "always, lest at any moment you forget."

Molly makes him no answer, but slowly raises to him eyes wet with unshed tears. It is more than he has hoped for.

"Molly," he cries, hurriedly, only too ready to grasp this small bud of a longed-for affection, "you will be sorry for me? There are tears in your eyes,—you will *miss* me? You love me, surely,—a little?"

Once more the lovely dewy eyes meet his; she nods at him and smiles faintly.

"A little," he repeats, wistfully. (Perhaps he has been assuring himself of some more open encouragement,—has dreamed of spoken tenderness, and feels the disappointment.) "Some men," he goes on, softly, "can lay claim to all the great treasure of their love's heart, while I—see how eagerly I accept the bare crumbs. Yet, darling, believe me, your sweet coldness is dearer to me than another woman's warmest assertion. And later—who knows?—perhaps— —"

"Yes, perhaps," says Molly, stirred by his emotion or by some other stronger sentiment lying deep at the bottom of her heart, "by and by I may perhaps bore you to death by the violence of my devotion. Meantime"— standing on tiptoe, and blushing just enough to make her even more adorable than before, and placing two white hands on his shoulders—"you shall have one small, wee kiss to carry away with you."

Half in doubt he waits until of her own sweet accord her lips do verily meet his; and then, catching her in his arms, he strains her to him, forgetful for the moment of the great fact that neither time nor tide waits for any man.

"You are not going, I suppose?" calls John, his voice breaking in rudely upon the harrowing scene. "Shall I send the horse back to the stables? Here, James,"—to the stable boy,—"take round Rufus; Mr. Luttrell is going to stay another month or two."

"Remember," says Luttrell, earnestly, still holding her as though loath to let her go.

"You remind me of Charles the First," murmurs she, smiling through her tears. "Yes, I will remember *you*, and all you have *said*, and—*everything*. And more, I shall be longing to see you again. Now go." Giving him a little push.

Presently—he hardly knows how—he finds himself in the dog-cart, with John, oppressively cheerful, beside him, and, looking back as they drive briskly up the avenue, takes a last glance at Brooklyn, with Molly on the steps, waving her hand to him, and watching his retreating form with such a regretful countenance as gives him renewed courage.

In an upper window is Letitia, more than equal to the occasion, armed with one of John's largest handkerchiefs, that bears a strong resemblance to a young sheet as it flutters frantically hither and thither in the breeze; while below the two children, Daisy and Renee,—under a mistaken impression that the hour is festive,—throw after him a choice collection of old boots much the worse for wear, which they have purloined with praiseworthy adroitness from under their nurse's nose.

"Oh, Letty, I do feel so honestly lonely," says Molly, half an hour later, meeting her sister-in-law on the stairs.

"Do you, dearest?" admiringly. "That is very nice of you. Never mind; you know you will soon see him again. And let us come and consult about the dresses you ought to wear at Herst."

"Yes, do let us," returns Miss Massereene, brightening with suspicious alacrity, and drawing herself up as straight as a young tree out of the despondent attitude she has been wearing. "That will pass the time better than anything."

Whereupon Letitia chuckles with ill-suppressed amusement and gives it as her opinion that "dear Molly isn't as bad as she thinks herself."

John has done his duty, has driven the melancholy young man to the station, and very nearly out of his wits—by insisting on carrying on a long and tedious argument that lasts the entire way, waiting pertinaciously for a reply to every one of his questions.

This has taken some time, more especially as the train was late and the back drive hilly; yet when at length he reaches his home he finds his wife and Molly still deep in the mysteries of the toilet.

"Well?" says his sister, as he stands in the doorway regarding them silently. As she speaks she allows the dejected expression of two hours ago to return to her features, her lids droop a little over her eyes, her forehead goes up, the corners of her mouth go down. She is in one instant a very afflicted Molly. "Well?" she says.

"He isn't well at all," replies John, with a dismal shake of the head and as near an imitation of Molly's rueful countenance as he can manage at so short a notice; "he is very bad. I never saw a worse case in my life. I doubt if he will last out the day. I don't know how you regard it, but I call it cruelty to animals."

"You need not be unfeeling," says Molly, reproachfully, "and I won't listen to you making fun of him behind his back. You wouldn't before his face."

"How do you know?" As though weighing the point. "I never saw him funny until to-day. He was on the verge of tears the entire way. It was lucky I was beside him, or he would have drenched the new cushions. For shame's sake he refrained before me, but I know he is in floods by this."

"He is not," says Molly, indignantly. "Crying, indeed! What an idea! He is far too much of a man for that."

"I am a man too," says John, who seems to find a rich harvest of delight in the contemplation of Luttrell's misery. "And once, before we were married, when Letitia treated me with disdain, I gave way to my feelings to such an extent that— —"

"Really, John," interposes his wife, "I wish you would keep your stupid stories to yourself, or else go away. We are very busy settling about Molly's things."

"What things? Her tea-things,—her playthings? Ah! poor little Molly! her last nice new one is gone."

"Letty, I hope you don't mind, dear," says Molly, lifting a dainty china bowl from the table near her. "Let us trust it won't break; but, whether it does or not, I must and will throw it at John."

"She should at all events have one pretty new silk dress," murmurs Letitia, vaguely, whose thoughts "are with her heart, and that is far away," literally buried, so to speak, in the depths of her wardrobe. "She could not well do without it. Molly,"—with sudden inspiration,—"you shall have mine. That dove-color always looks pretty on a girl, and I have only worn it once. It can easily be made to fit you."

"I wish, Letitia, you would not speak to me like that," says Molly, almost angrily, though there are tears in her eyes. "Do you suppose I want to rob you? I have no doubt you would give me every gown you possess, if I so willed it, and leave yourself nothing. Do remember I am going to Herst more out of spite and curiosity than anything else, and don't care in the least how I look. It is very unkind of you to say such things."

"You are the kindest soul in the world, Letty," says John from the doorway; "but keep your silk. Molly shall have one too." After which he decamps.

"That is very good of John," says Molly. "The fact is, I haven't a penny of my own,—I never have a week after I receive my allowance,—so I must only do the best I can. If I don't like it, you know, I can come home. It is a great thing to know, Letty, that *you* will be glad to have me, whether I am well dressed or very much the reverse."

"Exactly. And there is this one comfort also, that you look well in anything. By the bye, you must have a maid. You shall take Sarah, and we can get some one in until you come back to us. That"—with a smile—"will prevent your leaving us too long to our own devices. You will understand without telling what a loss the fair Sarah will be."

"You are determined I shall make my absence felt," says Molly, with a half-smile. "Really, Letty, I don't like— —"

"But I do," says Letty. "I don't choose you to be one whit behind any one else at Herst. Without doubt they will beat you in the matter of clothes;

but what of that? I have known many titled people have a fine disregard of apparel."

"So have I," returns Molly, gayly. "Indeed, were I a man, possessed with a desire to be mistaken for a lord, I would go to the meanest 'old clo' shop and purchase there the seediest garments and the most dilapidated hat (with a tendency toward greenness), and a pair of boots with a patch on the left side, and, having equipped myself in them, saunter down the 'shady side of Pall Mall' with a sure and certain conviction that I was 'quite the thing.' Should my ambitious longings soar as high as a dukedom, I would add to the above costume a patch on the right boot as well, and— questionable linen."

"Well," says Letitia, with a sigh, "I hope Marcia is a nice girl, and that she will be kind to you."

"So do I,"—with a shrug,—"but from her writing I am almost sure she isn't."

tale. Had he no prospects, and were you penniless, I wonder how far 'love' would guide you?"

"To the end," says Marcia, quickly. "What has money to do with it? It can neither be bought nor sold. It is a poor affection that would wither under poverty; at least it would have no fears for us."

"Us,—us," returns this detestable old pagan, with a malicious chuckle. "How sure we are! how positive! ready to risk our all upon our lover's truth! Yet, were I to question this faithful lover upon the same subject, I fear me that I should receive a widely different answer."

"I hope not, dear," says Marcia, gently, speaking in her usual soft, low tone. Yet a small cold finger has been laid upon her heart. A dim foreboding crushes her. Only a little pallor, so slight as to be imperceptible to her tormentor, falls across the upper part of her face and tells how blood has been drawn. Yet it is hardly the mere piercing of the skin that hurts us most; it is in the dark night hours when the wound rankles that our agony comes home to us.

"When is this girl coming?" asks the old man, presently, in a peevish tone, vexed that, as far as he can tell, his arrow has overshot the mark. "I might have known she would have caught at the invitation."

"On the twenty-seventh,—the day you mentioned. She must be anxious to make your acquaintance, as she has not lost an hour," says Marcia, in a tone that might mean anything. "But"—sweetly—"why distress yourself, dear, by having her at all? If it disturbs your peace in the very least, why not write to put her off, at all events until you feel stronger? Why upset yourself, now you are getting on so nicely?" As she speaks she lets her clear, calm eyes rest fully upon the hopeless wreck of what once was strong before her. No faintest tinge of insincerity mars the perfect kindliness of her tone. "Why not let us three remain as we are, alone together?"

"What!" cries Mr. Amherst, angrily, and with excitement, raising himself in his chair, "am I to shut myself up within these four walls with nothing to interest me from day to day beyond your inane twaddle? No, I thank you. I will have the house full,—full—do you hear, Marcia?—and that without delay? Do you want me to die of *ennui* in this bare barrack of a place?"

"Well, do not make yourself ill, dear," says Marcia, with an admirably executed sigh. "It shall be as you wish, of course. I only spoke for your good,—because—I suppose (being the only near relative I have on earth besides my mother), I—love you."

"You are very good," replies the old man, grimly, utterly untouched by all this sweetness, "but I will have my own way. And don't you 'dear' me again. Do you hear, Marcia? I won't have it: it reminds me of my wife. Pah!"

The days fade, the light wanes, and night's cold dewy mantle falls thickly on the longing earth.

Marcia, throwing wide her casements, stretches out her arms to the moonlight and bathes her white face and whiter neck in the cool flood that drenches all the quiet garden.

There is peace everywhere, and rest, and happy sleep, but not for Marcia; for days, for weeks, she has been haunted by the fear that Philip's affection for her is but a momentary joy, that, swiftly as the minutes fly, so it dwindles. To-night this fear is strong upon her.

Not by his word, not by his actions, but by the subtle nothings that, having no name, yet are, and go to make up the dreaded whole, has this thought been forced upon her. The cooling glance, the suppressed restlessness, the sudden lack of conversation, the kind but unloving touch, the total absence of a lover's jealousy,—all go to prove the hateful truth. And now her grandfather's sneer of the morning comes back to torture her and make assurance doubly sure. Yet hardly three months have passed since Philip Shadwell asked her to be his wife.

"Already his love wanes," she murmurs, turning up her troubled face and eyes, too sad for tears, to the starry vault above her, where the small luminous bodies blink and tremble and take no heed of a ridiculous love-tale, more or less. Her tone is low and despairing; and as she speaks she beats her hands together slowly, noiselessly, yet none the less passionately.

In vain she tries to convince herself her doubts are groundless, to compel herself to believe her arms are full, when in her heart she knows she but presses to her bosom an empty, fleeting shadow. The night's dull vapors have closed upon her, and, while exaggerating her misery, still open her eyes with kind cruelty to the end that surely awaits her.

So she sits hugging her fears until the day breaks, and early morning, peeping in at her, wafts her a kiss as it flies over the lawn and field and brooklet. Then, wearied by her watching, she flings herself upon her bed, and, gaining a short but dreamless sleep, wakens refreshed, to laugh at her misgivings of the night before,—at her grandfather's hints,—at aught that speaks to her of Philip's falseness.

Despair follows closely upon night. Hope comes in the train of day. And Marcia, standing erect before her glass, with her beautiful figure drawn to its full height and her handsome head erect, gazes long and earnestly at the reflection therein. At last the deep flush of satisfaction dyes her cheeks; all her natural self-reliance and determination return to her; with a little laugh at her own image (on which she builds her hopes), she defies fate, and, running down the staircase with winged feet, finds herself on the last step, almost in Philip's arms.

"Abroad so early!" he says, with a smile; and the kindliness of his tone, the more than kindness of his glance, confirm her hopes of the morning. She is looking very pretty, and Philip likes pretty women, hence the kindly smile. And yet, though he might have done so without rebuke (perhaps because of that), he forgot to kiss her. "You are the early bird, and you have caught me," he says. "I can only hope you will not make your breakfast off me. See,"—holding out to her an unclosed letter,—"the deed is done. I have written to my solicitor to get me the money from Lazarus and Harty."

"Oh, Philip! I have been thinking," she says, following him into the library, "and now it seems to me a risk. You know his horror of Jews,—you know how he speaks of your own father and his unfortunate dealings with them. Yesterday I felt brave, and advised you, as I fear, wrongly; to-day——"

"I have been thinking it over too,"—lighting the taper on the table, and applying the sealing-wax to the flame,—"and now it seems to me the only course left open. And yet"—speaking gayly, but pausing as the wax falls upon the envelope—"perhaps—who knows?—I may be sealing my own fate."

"You make me superstitious. Why imagine horrors? Yet if you have any doubts, Philip,"—laying one shapely white finger upon the letter,—"do not send it. Something tells me to warn you. And, besides, are you quite sure they will lend you the money?"

"They will hardly refuse a paltry two thousand to the heir of Herst Royal."

"But you are not the heir."

"In the eyes of the world I am."

"And yet they know it can be left to any one else."

"To you, for instance."

"That would hardly alter your position, except that you would be then, not heir, but master," she says, smiling sweetly at him. "No, I was supposing myself also disinherited. This cousin that is coming,—Eleanor Massereene,—she, too, is his grandchild."

As a rule, when speaking of those we hate, quite as much as when speaking of those we love, we use the pronoun alone. Mr. Amherst is "he" always to his relatives.

"What! Can you believe it possible a little uneducated country girl, with probably a snub nose, thick boots, and no manners to speak of, can cut you out? Marcia, you grow modest. Why, even I, a man, can see her in my mind's eye, with a freckled complexion (he hates freckles), and a frightened gasp between each word, and a wholesome horror of wine, and a general air of hoping the earth will open presently to swallow her up."

"But how if she is totally different from all this?"

"She won't be different. Her father was a wild Irishman. Besides, I have seen her sort over and over again, and it is positive cruelty to animals to drag the poor creatures from their dull homes into the very centre of life and gayety. They never can make up their minds whether the butler that announces dinner is or is not the latest arrival; and they invariably say, 'No, thank you,' when asked to have anything. To them the fish-knife is a thing unknown and afternoon tea the wildest dissipation."

"Well, I can only hope and trust she will turn out just what you say," says Marcia, laughing.

Four days later, meeting her on his way to the stables, he throws her a letter from his solicitor.

"It is all right," he says, and goes on a step or two, as though hurried, while she hastily runs her eyes over it.

"Well, and now your mind is at rest," she calls after him, as she sees the distance widening between them.

"For the present, yes."

"Well, here, take your letter."

"Tear it up; I don't want it," he returns, and disappears round the angle of the house.

Her fingers form themselves as though about to obey him and tear the note in two. Then she pauses.

"He may want it," she says to herself, hesitating. "Business letters are sometimes useful afterward. I will keep it for him."

She slips it into her pocket, and for the time being thinks no more of it. That night, as she undresses, finding it again, she throws it carelessly into a drawer, where it lies for many days forgotten.

It is the twentieth of August: in seven days more the "little country girl with freckles and a snub nose" will be at Herst Royal, longing "for the earth to open and swallow her up."

To Philip her coming is a matter of the most perfect indifference. To Marcia it is an event,—and an unpleasant one.

When, some three years previously, Marcia Amherst consented to leave the mother she so sincerely loved to tend an old and odious man, she did so at his request and with her mother's full sanction, through desire of the gold that was to be (it was tacitly understood) the reward of her devotion. There was, however, another condition imposed upon her before she might come to Herst and take up permanent quarters there. This was the entire forsaking of her mother, her people, and the land of her birth.

To this also there was open agreement made: which agreement was in private broken. She was quite clever enough to manage a clandestine correspondence without fear of discovery; but letters, however frequent, hardly make up for enforced absence from those we love, and Marcia's affection for her Italian mother was the one pure sentiment in her rather scheming disposition. Yet the love of riches, that is innate in all, was sufficiently strong in her to bear her through with her task.

But now the fear that this new-comer, this interloper, may, after all her detested labor, by some fell chance become a recipient of the spoil (no matter in how small a degree), causes her trouble.

Of late, too, she has not been happy. Philip's coldness has been on the increase. He himself, perhaps, is hardly aware of the change. But what woman loving but feels the want of love? And at times her heart is racked with passionate grief.

Now, as she and her lip-love stand side by side in the oriel window that overlooks the graveled path leading into the gardens, the dislike to her cousin's coming burns hotly within her.

Outside, in his bath chair, wheeled up and down by a long-suffering attendant, goes Mr. Amherst, in happy ignorance of the four eyes that watch his coming and going with such distaste.

Up and down, up and down he goes, his weakly head bent upon his chest, his fierce eyes roving restlessly to and fro. He is still invalid enough to prefer the chair to the more treacherous aid of his stick.

"He reminds me of nothing so much as an Egyptian mummy," says Philip, presently: "he looks so hard, and shriveled, and unreal. Toothless, too."

"He ought to die," says Marcia, with perfect calmness, as though she had suggested the advisability of his going for a longer drive.

"Die!" With a slight start, turning to look at her. "Ah! yes, of course. But"—with a rather forced laugh—"he *won't*, take my word for it. Old gentlemen with unlimited means and hungry heirs live forever."

"He has lived long enough," says Marcia, still in the same slow, calculating tone. "Of what use is he? Who cares for him? What good does he do in each twenty-four hours? He is merely taking up valuable room,—keeping what should by right be yours and mine. And, Philip," laying her hand upon his arm to insure his attention,—"I understand the mother of this girl who is coming was his favorite daughter."

"Well," surprised at her look and tone, which have both grown intense,—"that is not my fault. You need not cast such an upbraiding glance on me."

"What if he should alter his will in her favor? More unlikely things have happened. I cannot divest myself of fear when I think of her. Should he at this late hour repent him of his injustice toward his dead daughter, he might——" She pauses. "But rather than that——" Here she pauses again; and her lids falling somewhat over her eyes, leave them small but wonderfully deep.

"What, Marcia?" asks Philip, with a sudden anxiety he would willingly suppress, were it not for his strong desire to learn what her thoughts may be.

For a full minute she makes him no reply, and then, as though hardly aware of his question, goes on meditatively.

"Philip, how frail he is!" she says, almost in a whisper, as the chair goes creaking beneath the window. "Yet what a hold he has on life! And it is *I* give him that hold,—*I* am the rope to which he clings. At night, when sleep is on him and lethargy succeeds to sleep, mine is the duty to rouse him and minister such medicines as charm him back to life. Should I chance to forget, his dreams might end in death. Last night, as I sat by his bedside, I thought, were I to forget,—what then?"

"Ay, what then? Of what are you thinking?" cries her companion, in a tone of suppressed horror, resisting by a passionate movement the spell she had almost cast upon him by the power of her low voice and deep, dark eyes. "Would you kill the old man?"

"Nay, it is but to forget," replies she, dreamily, her whole mind absorbed in her subject, unconscious of the effect she is producing. She has not turned her eyes upon him (else surely the terrible fear and shrinking in his must have warned her to go no further), but has her gaze fixed rather on the hills and woods and goodly plains for which she is not only willing but eager to sell all that is best of her. "To remain passive, and then"—straightening her hand in the direction of the glorious view that spreads itself before them—"all this would be ours."

"Murderess!" cries the young man, in a low, concentrated tone, his voice vibrating with disgust and loathing as he falls back from her a step or two.

The word thrills her. With a start she brings herself back to the present moment, turns to look at him, and, looking slowly, learns the truth. The final crash has come, her fears are realized; she has lost him forever.

"What is it, Philip? what word have you used?" she asks, with nervous vehemence, as though only half comprehending; "why do you look at me so strangely? I have said nothing,—nothing that should make you shrink from me."

"You have said enough,"—with a shiver, "too much; and your face said more. I desire you never to speak to me on the subject again."

"What! you will not even hear me?"

"No; I am only thankful I have found you out in time."

"Say rather for this lucky chance I have afforded you of breaking off a detested engagement," cries she, with sudden bitterness. "Hypocrite! how long have you been awaiting it?"

"You are talking folly, Marcia. What reason have I ever given you that you should make me such a speech? But for what has just now happened,—but for your insinuations——"

"Ay,"—slowly,—"you shrink from hearing your thoughts put into words."

"Not *my* thoughts," protests he, vehemently.

"No?" searchingly, drawing a step nearer him. "Are you *sure*? Have you never wished our grandfather dead?"

"I may have wished it," confesses he, reluctantly, as though compelled to frankness, "but to compass my wish—to——"

"If you have wished it you have murdered," returns she, with conviction. "You have craved his death: what is that but unuttered crime? There is little difference; it is but one step the more in the same direction. And I,—in what way am I the greater sinner? I have but said aloud what you whisper to your heart."

"Be silent," cries he, fiercely. "All your sophistry fails to make me a partner in your guilt."

"I am the honester of the two," she goes on, rapidly, unheeding his anger. "As long as the accursed thing is unspoken, you see no harm in it; once it makes itself heard, you start and sicken, because it hurts your tender susceptibilities. Yet hear me, Philip." Suddenly changing her tone of passionate scorn to one of entreaty as passionate, "Do not cast me off for a few idle words. They have done no harm. Let us be as we were."

"Impossible," replies he coldly, unloosing her fingers from his arm, all the dislike and loathing of which he is capable compressed into the word. "You have destroyed my trust in you."

A light that means despair flashes across Marcia's face as she stands in all her dark but rather evil beauty before him; then suddenly she falls upon her knees.

"Philip, have pity on me!" she cries painfully. "I love you,—I have only you. Here in this house I am alone, a stranger in my own land. Do not you too turn from me. Ah! you should be the last to condemn, for if I dreamed of sin it was for your sake. And after all, what did I say? The thought that this girl's coming might upset the dream of years agitated me, and I spoke—I—but I meant nothing—nothing." She drags herself on her knees nearer to him and attempts to take his hand. "Darling, do not be so stern. Forgive me. If you cast me off, Philip, you will kill not only my body, but all that is good in me."

"Do not touch me," returns he, harshly, the vein of brutality in him coming to the surface as he pushes her from him and with slight violence unclasps her clinging fingers.

The action is in itself sufficient, but the look that accompanies it— betraying as it does even more disgust than hatred—stings her to self-control. Slowly she rises to her feet. As she does so, a spasm, a contraction near her heart, causes her to place her hand involuntarily against her side, while a dull gray shadow covers her face.

"You mean," she says, speaking with the utmost difficulty, "that all—is at an end—between us."

"I do mean that," he answers, very white, but determined.

"Then beware!" she murmurs, in a low, choked voice.

CHAPTER XI

"You stood before me like a thought,
A dream remembered in a dream."

—Coleridge.

It is five o'clock in the afternoon, and Herst is the richer by one more inmate. Molly has arrived, has been received by Marcia, has pressed cheeks with her, has been told she is welcome in a palpably lying tone, and finally has been conducted to her bedroom. Such a wonder of a bedroom compared with Molly's snug but modest sanctum at home,—a very marvel of white and blue, and cloudy virginal muslins, and filled with innumerable luxuries.

Molly, standing in the centre of it,—unaware that she is putting all its other beauties to shame—gazes round her in silent admiration, appreciates each pretty trifle to its fullest, and finally feels a vague surprise at the curious sense of discontent that pervades her.

Her reception so far has not been cordial. Marcia's cold unloving eyes have pierced her and left a little cold frozen spot within her heart. She is chilled and puzzled, and with all her strength is wishing herself home again at Brooklyn, with John and Letty, and all the merry, tormenting, kindly children.

"What shall I do for you now, Miss Molly?" asks Sarah, presently breaking in upon these dismal broodings. This antiquated but devoted maiden has stationed herself at the farthest end of the big room close to Molly's solitary trunk (as though suspicious of lurking thieves), and bears upon her countenance a depressed, not to say dejected, expression. "Like mistress, like maid," she, too, is filled with the gloomiest forebodings.

"Open my trunk and take out my clothes," says Molly, making no effort at disrobing, beyond a melancholy attempt at pulling off her gloves, finger by finger.

Sarah does as she is bidden.

"'Tis a tremenjous house, Miss Molly."

"Very. It is a castle, not a house."

"There's a deal of servants in it."

"Yes," absently.

"Leastways as far as I could judge with looking through the corners of my eyes as I came along them big passages. From every door a'most there popped a head bedizened with gaudy ribbons, and I suppose the bodies was behind 'em."

"Let us hope so, Sarah." Rising, and laughing rather hysterically. "The bare idea that those mysterious heads should lack a decent finish fills me with the liveliest horror." Then, in a brighter tone, "Why, what is the matter with you, Sarah? You look as if you had fallen into the very lowest depths of despair."

"Not so much that as lonesome, miss; they all seem so rich and grand that I feel myself out of place."

Molly smiles a little. After all, in spite of the difference in their positions, it is clear to her that she and her maid share pretty much the same fears.

"There was a very proud look about the set of their caps," says Sarah, waxing more and more dismal. "Suppose they were to be uncivil to me, Miss Molly, on account of my being country-reared and my gowns not being, as it were, in the height of the fashion, what should I do? It is all this, miss, that is weighing me down."

"Suppose, on the contrary," says her mistress, with a little defiant ring in her tone, stepping to the glass and surveying her beautiful face with eager scrutiny, "you were to make a sensation, and cut out all these supercilious dames in your hall, how would it be then? Come, Sarah, let me teach you your new duties. First take my hat, now my jacket, now— —"

"Shall I do your hair, Miss Molly?"

"No," with a laugh,—"I think not. I had one trial of you in that respect; it was enough."

"But all maids do their young ladies' hair, don't they, miss? I doubt they will altogether look down upon me when they find I can't do even that."

"I shall ring for you every day when I come to dress for dinner. Once in my room, who shall know whether you do my hair or not? And I faithfully promise you, Sarah, to take such pains with the performance myself as shall compel every one in the house to admire it and envy me my excellent maid. 'See Miss Massereene's hair!' they will say, in tearful whispers. 'Oh, that I too could have a Sarah!' By the bye, call me Miss Massereene for the future, not Miss Molly,—at least until we get home again."

"Yes, Miss—Massereene. Law! it do sound odd," says Sarah, with a little respectful laugh, "but high-sounding too, I think. I do hope I shan't forget it, Miss Molly. Perhaps you will be good enough to remind me when I go wrong?"

A knock at the door prevents reply. Molly cries out, "Come in," and, turning, finds herself face to face with a fine old woman, who stands erect, and firm, in spite of her many years, in the doorway. She is clad in a sombre gown of brown silk, and has an old-fashioned chain round her neck that hangs far below her waist, which is by no means the most contemptible portion of her.

"I beg your pardon, Miss Massereene; I could not resist coming to see if you were quite comfortable," she says, respectfully.

"Quite, thank you," replies Molly, in a degree puzzled. "You are"— smiling—"the housekeeper?"

"I am. And you, my dear,"—regarding her anxiously,—"are every inch an Amherst, in spite of your bonny blue eyes. You will forgive the freedom of my speech," says this old dame, with an air that would not have disgraced a duchess, "when I tell you I nursed your mother."

"Ah! did you?" says Molly, flushing a little, and coming up to her eagerly, with both hands extended, to kiss the fair old face that is smiling so kindly on her. "But how could one think it? You are yet so fresh, so good to look at."

"Tut, my dear," says the old lady, mightily pleased nevertheless. "I am old enough to have nursed your grandmother. And now can I do anything for you?"

"You can," replies Molly, turning toward Sarah, who is regarding them with an expression that might at any moment mean either approval or displeasure. "This is my maid. We are both strangers here. Will you see that she is made happy?"

"Come with me, Sarah, and I will make you acquainted with our household," says Mrs. Nesbitt, promptly.

As the door closes behind them, leaving her to her own society, a rather unhappy shade falls across Molly's face.

A sensation of isolation—loneliness—oppresses her. Indeed, her discouraging reception has wounded her more than she cares to confess even to her own heart. If they did not want her at Herst, why had they invited her? If they did want her, surely they might have met her with more civility; and on this her first visit her grandfather at least might have been present to bid her welcome.

Oh, that this hateful day were at an end! Oh, for some way of making the slow hours run hurriedly!

With careful fingers she unfastens and pulls down all her lovely hair until it falls in rippling masses to her waist. As carefully, as lingeringly, she rolls it up again into its usual artistic knot at the back of her head. With still loitering movements she bathes the dust of travel from her face and hands, adjusts her soft gray gown, puts straight the pale-blue ribbon at her throat, and now tells herself, with a triumphant smile, that she has got the better of at least half an hour of this detested day.

Alas! alas! the little ormolu ornament that ticks with such provoking *empressement* upon the chimney-piece assures her that her robing has occupied exactly ten minutes from start to finish.

This will never do. She cannot well spend her evening in her own room, no matter how eagerly she may desire to do so; so, taking heart of grace, she makes a wicked *moue* at her own rueful countenance in the looking-glass, and, opening her door hastily, lest her courage fail her, runs down the broad oak staircase into the hall beneath.

Quick-witted, as women of her temperament always are, she remembers the situation of the room she had first entered, and, passing by all the other closed doors, goes into it, to find herself once more in Marcia's presence.

"Ah! you have come," says Miss Amherst, looking up languidly from her *macrame*, with a frozen smile that owes its one charm to its brevity. "You have made a quick toilet." With a supercilious glance at Molly's Quakerish gown, that somehow fits her and suits her to perfection. "You are not fatigued?"

"Fatigued?" Smiling, with a view to conciliation. "Oh, no; it is such a little journey."

"So it is. How strange this should be our first meeting, living so close to each other as we have done! My grandfather's peculiar disposition of course accounts for it: he has quite a morbid horror of aliens."

"Is one's granddaughter to be considered an alien?" asks Molly, with a laugh. "The suggestion opens an enormous field for reflection. If so, what are one's nephews, and one's nieces, and cousins, first, second, and third? Poor third-cousins! it makes one sad to think of them."

"I think perhaps Mr. Amherst's incivility toward you arose from his dislike to your mother's marriage. You don't mind my speaking, do you? It was more than good of you to come here at all, considering the circumstances,—I don't believe I could have been so forgiving,—but I know he felt very bitterly on the subject, and does so still."

"Does he? How very absurd! Amhersts cannot always marry Amhersts, nor would it be a good thing if they could. I suppose, however, even he can be forgiving at times. Now, for instance, how did he get over your father's marriage?"

Marcia raises her head quickly. Her color deepens. She turns a glance full of displeased suspicion upon her companion, who meets it calmly, and with such an amount of innocence in hers as might have disarmed a Machiavelli. Not a shadow of intention mars her expression; her widely-opened blue eyes contain only a desire to know; and Marcia, angry, disconcerted, and puzzled, lets her gaze return to her work. A dim idea that it will not be so easy to ride rough-shod over this country-bred girl as she had hoped oppresses her, while a still more unpleasant doubt that her intended snubbing has recoiled upon her own head adds to her discontent. Partly through policy and partly with a view to showing this recreant Molly the rudeness of her ways, she refuses an answer to her question and starts a different topic in a still more freezing tone.

"You found your room comfortable, I hope, and—all that?"

"Quite all that, thank you," cordially. "And such a pretty room too!" (She is unaware as she speaks that it is one of the plainest the house contains.) "How large everything seems! When coming down through all those corridors and halls I very nearly lost my way. Stupid of me was it not? But it is an enormous house, I can see."

"Is it? Perhaps so. Very much the size of most country houses, I should say. And yet, no doubt, to a stranger it would seem large. Your own home is not so?"

"Oh, no. If you could only see poor Brooklyn in comparison! It is the prettiest little place in all the world, I think; but then it *is* little. It would require a tremendous amount of genius to lose one's self in Brooklyn."

"How late it grows!" says Marcia, looking at the clock and rising. "The first bell ought to ring soon. Which would you prefer,—your tea here or in your own room? I always adopt the latter plan when the house is empty, and take it while dressing. By the bye, you have not seen—Mr. Amherst?"

"My grandfather? No."

"Perhaps he had better be told you are here."

"Has he not yet heard of my arrival?" asks Molly, impulsively, some faint indignation stirring in her breast.

"He knew you were coming, of course; I am not sure if he remembered the exact hour. If you will come with me, I will take you to the library."

Across the hall in nervous silence Molly follows her guide until they reach a small anteroom, beyond which lies the "chamber of horrors," as, in spite of all her efforts to be indifferent, Molly cannot help regarding it.

Marcia knocking softly at the door, a feeble but rasping voice bids them enter; and, throwing it widely open, Miss Amherst beckons her cousin to follow her into the presence of her dreaded grandfather.

Although looking old, and worn, and decrepit, he is still evidently in much better health than when last we saw him, trundling up and down the terraced walk, endeavoring to catch some faint warmth from the burning sun.

His eyes are darker and fiercer, his nose a shade sharper, his temper evidently in an uncorked condition; although he may be safely said to be on the mend, and, with regard to his bodily strength, in a very promising condition.

Before him is a table covered with papers, from which he looks up ungraciously, as the girls enter.

"I have brought you Eleanor Massereene," says Marcia, without preamble, in a tone so kind and gentle as makes Molly even at this awful moment marvel at the change.

If it could be possible for the old man's ghastly skin to assume a paler hue, at this announcement, it certainly does so. With suppressed but apparent eagerness he fixes his eyes upon the new grandchild, and as he does so his hand closes involuntarily upon the paper beneath it; his mouth twitches; a shrinking pain contracts his face. Yes, she is very like her dead mother.

"How long has she been in my house?" he asks, presently, after a pause that to Molly has been hours, still with his gaze upon her, though beyond this prolonged examination of her features he has vouchsafed her no welcome.

"She came by the half-past four train. Williams met her with the brougham."

"And it is nearly six. Pray why have I been kept so long in ignorance of her arrival?" Not once as he speaks does he look at Marcia, or at anything but Molly's pale, pretty, disturbed face.

"Dear grandpapa, you have forgotten. Yesterday I told you the hour we expected her. But no doubt, with so many important matters upon your mind," with a glance at the littered table, "you forgot this one."

"I did," slowly, "so effectually as to make me doubt having ever heard it. No, Marcia, no more excuses, no more lies: you need not explain. Be satisfied that whatever plans you formed to prevent my bidding your cousin welcome to my house were highly successful. At intrigue you are a proficient. I admire proficiency in all things,—but—for the future—be so good as to remember that I *never* forget."

"Dear grandpapa," with a pathetic but very distinct sigh, "it is very hard to be misjudged!"

"Granted. Though at times one must own it has its advantages. Now, if for instance I could only bring myself, now and again, to misjudge you, how very much more conducive to the accomplishment of your aims it would be! Leave the room. I wish to speak to your cousin."

Reluctant, but not daring to disobey, and always with the same aggrieved expression upon her face, Marcia withdraws.

As the door closes behind her, Mr. Amherst rises, and holds out one hand to Molly.

"You are welcome," he says, quietly, but coldly, and evidently speaking with an effort.

Molly, coming slowly up to him, lays her hand in his, while entertaining an earnest hope that she will not be called upon to seal the interview with a kiss.

"Thank you," she says, faintly, not knowing what else to say, and feeling thoroughly embarrassed by the fixity and duration of his regard.

"Yes," speaking again, slowly, and absently. "You are welcome— Eleanor. I am glad I have seen you before—my death. Yes—you are very like— — Go!" with sudden vehemence, "leave me; I wish to be alone."

Sinking back heavily into his arm-chair, he motions her from him, and Molly, finding herself a moment later once more in the anteroom, breathes a sigh of thankfulness that this her first strange interview with her host is at an end.

"Dress me quickly, Sarah," she says, as she gains her own room about half an hour later, and finds that damsel awaiting her. "And make me look as beautiful as possible; I have yet another cousin to investigate, and something tells me the third will be the charm, and that I shall get on with him. Young men"—ingenuously, and forgetting she is expressing her thoughts aloud— "are certainly a decided improvement on young women. If, however, there is really any understanding between Philip and Marcia, it will rather spoil my amusement and—still I need not torment myself beforehand, as that is a matter I shall learn in five minutes."

"There's a very nice young man down-stairs, miss," breaks in Sarah, at this juncture, with a simper that has the pleasing effect of making one side of her face quite an inch shorter than the other.

"What! you have seen him, then?" cries Molly, full of her own idea, and oblivious of dignity. "Is he handsome, Sarah? Young? Describe him to me."

"He is short, miss, and stoutish, and—and——"

"Yes! Do go on, Sarah, and take that smile off your face: it makes you look downright imbecile. 'Short!' 'Stout!' Good gracious! of what on earth could Teddy have been thinking."

"His manners is most agreeable, miss, and altogether he is a most gentleman-like young man."

"Well, of course he is all that, or he isn't anything; but stout!——"

"Not a bit stiffish, or uppish, as one might expect, considering where he come from. And indeed, Miss Molly," with an irrepressible giggle, "he did say as how——"

"What!" icily.

"As how I had a very bewidging look about the eyes."

"Sarah," exclaims Miss Massereene, sinking weakly into a chair, "do you mean to tell me my cousin Philip—Captain Shadwell—told you—had the impertinence to speak to you about——"

"Law, Miss Molly, whatever are you thinking about?—Captain Shadwell! why, I haven't so much as laid eyes on him! I was only speaking of his young man, what goes by the name of Peters."

"Ridiculous!" cries Molly, impatiently; then bursting into a merry laugh, she laughs so heartily and so long that the somewhat puzzled Sarah feels compelled to join.

"'Short, and stout, and gentlemanly'—ha, ha, ha! And so Peters said you were bewidging, Sarah? Ah! take care, and do not let him turn your head: if you *do*, you will lose all your fun, and gain little for it. Is that a bell? Oh, Sarah! come, dispatch, dispatch, or I shall be late, and eternally disgraced."

The robing proceeds, and when finished leaves Molly standing before her maid with (it must be confessed) a very self-satisfied smirk upon her countenance.

"How am I looking, Sarah? I want a candid opinion; but on no account say anything disparaging."

"Lovely!" says Sarah, with comfortable haste. "There's no denying it, Miss Molly. Miss Amherst below, for all her dark hair and eyes (and I don't say but that she is handsome), could not hold a candle to you, as the saying is—and that's a fact."

"Is there anything in all the world," says Miss Massereene, "so sweet as sincere praise? Sarah, you are a charming creature. Good-bye; I go—let us hope—to victory. But if not,—if I find the amiable relatives refuse to acknowledge my charms I shall at least know where to come to receive the admiration I feel I so justly deserve!"

So saying, with a little tragic flourish, she once more wends her way down-stairs, trailing behind her her pretty white muslin gown, with its flecks of coloring, blue as her eyes, into the drawing-room.

The close of autumn brings to us a breath of winter. Already the daylight has taken to itself wings and flown partially away; and though, as yet, a good deal of it through compassion lingers, it is but a half-hearted dallying that speaks of hurry to be gone.

The footman, a young person, of a highly morbid and sensitive disposition, abhorrent of twilights, has pulled down all the blinds in the sitting-rooms, and drawn the curtains closely, has lit the lamps, and poked into a blaze the fire, that Mr. Amherst has the wisdom to keep burning all the year round in the long chilly room.

Before the fire, with one arm on the mantel-piece, and one foot upon the fender, stands a young man, in an attitude suggestive of melancholy. Hearing the rustling of a woman's garments, he looks up, and, seeing Molly, stares at her, first lazily, then curiously, then amazedly, then——

She is quite close to him; she can almost touch him; indeed, no farther can she go without putting him to one side; and still he has not stirred. The situation grows embarrassing, so embarrassing that, what with the ludicrous silence and Philip Shadwell's eyes which betray a charmed astonishment, Molly feels an overpowering desire to laugh. She compromises matters by smiling, and lowering her eyelids just half an inch.

"You do not want all the fire, do you?" she asks, demurely, in a low tone.

"I beg your pardon," exclaims Philip, in his abstraction, moving in a direction closer to the fire, rather than from it. "I had no idea I was. I"— doubtfully, "am I speaking to Miss Massereene?"

"You are. And I—I know I am speaking to Captain Shadwell."

"Yes," slowly. "That is my name,—Philip Shadwell."

"We are cousins, then," says Molly, kindly, as though desirous of putting him at his ease. "I hope we shall be, what is far better, friends."

"We must be; we are friends," returns he, hastily, so full of surprise and self-reproach as to be almost unconscious of his words.

Is this the country cousin full of freckles and *mauvaise honte*, who was to be pitied, and lectured, and taught generally how to behave?—whose ignorance was to draw forth groans from pit and gallery and boxes? A hot blush at his own unmeant impertinence thrills him from head to foot. Were she ever, by any chance, to hear what he had said. Oh, perish the thought!—it is too horrible!

A little laugh from Molly somewhat restores his senses.

"You should not stare so," she says, severely, with an adorable attempt at a frown. "And you need not look at me all at once, you know, because, as I am going to stay here a whole month, you will have plenty of time to do it by degrees, without fatiguing yourself. By the bye," reproachfully, "I have come a journey to-day, and am dreadfully tired, and you have never even offered me a chair; must I get one for myself?"

"You have driven any manners I may possess out of my head," replies he, laughing, too, and pushing toward her the coziest chair the room contains. "Your sudden entrance bewildered me; you came upon me like an apparition; more especially as people in this house never get to the drawing-room until exactly one minute before dinner is announced."

"Why?"

"Lest we should bore each other past forgiveness. Being together as we are every day, and all day long, one can easily imagine how a very little more pressure would smash the chains of politeness. You may have heard of the last straw and its disastrous consequences?"

"I have. I am sorry I frightened you. To-morrow night I shall know better, and shall leave you to your silent musings in peace."

"No; don't do that!" says her companion, earnestly. "On no account do that. I think the half-hour before dinner, sitting by the fire, alone, as we are now, the best of the whole day; that is, of course, if one spends it with a congenial companion."

"Are you a congenial companion?"

"I don't know," smiling. "If you will let me, I can at least try to be."

"Try, then, by all means." In a moment or two,—"I should like to fathom your thoughts," says Molly. "When I came in, there was more than bewilderment in your face; it showed—how shall I express it? You looked as though you had expected something else?"

"Will you forgive me if I say I did?"

"What, then? A creature tall, gaunt, weird——?"

"No."

"Fat, red, uncomfortable?"

This touches so nearly on the truth as to be unpleasant. He winces.

"I will tell you what I did not expect," he says, hastily, coloring a little. "How should I? It is so seldom one has the good luck to discover in autumn a rose belonging to June."

His voice falls.

"Am I one?" asks she, looking with dangerous frankness into the dark eyes above her, that are telling her silently, eloquently, she is the fairest, freshest, sweetest queen of flowers in all the world.

The door opens, and Mr. Amherst enters, then Marcia. Philip straightens himself, and puts on his usual bored, rather sulky expression. Molly smiles upon her grumpy old host. He offers her his arm, Philip does the same to Marcia, and together they gain the dining-room.

It is an old, heavily wainscoted apartment, gloomy beyond words, so immense that the four who dine in it tonight appear utterly lost in its vast centre.

Marcia, in an evening toilet of black and ivory, sits at the head of the table, her grandfather opposite to her. Philip and Molly are *vis-à-vis* at the sides. Behind stand the footmen, as sleek and well-to-do, and imbecile, as one can desire.

There is a solemnity about the repast that strikes but fails to subdue Molly. It has a contrary effect, making her spirits rise, and creating in her a very mistaken desire for laughter. She is hungry too, and succeeds in eating a good dinner, while altogether she comes to the conclusion that it may not be wholly impossible to put in a very good time at Herst.

Never does she raise her eyes without encountering Philip's dark ones regarding her with the friendliest attention. This also helps to reassure her. A friend in need is a friend indeed, and this friend is handsome as well as kind, although there is a little something or other, a suppressed vindictiveness, about his expression, that repels her.

She compares him unfavorably with Luttrell, and presently lets her thoughts wander on to the glad fact that to-morrow will see the latter by her side, when indeed she will be in a position to defy fate,—and Marcia. Already she has learned to regard that dark-browed lady with distrust.

"Is any one coming to-morrow?" asks Mr. Amherst, *à propos* of Molly's reverie."

"Tedcastle, and Maud Darley."

"Her husband?"

"I suppose so. Though she did not mention him when writing."

"Poor Darley!" with a sneer: "she never does mention him. Any one else?"

"Not to-morrow."

"I wonder if Luttrell will be much altered," says Philip; "browned, I suppose, by India, although his stay there was of the shortest."

"He is not at all bronzed," breaks in Molly, quietly.

"You know him?" Marcia asks, in a rather surprised tone, turning toward her.

"Oh, yes, very well," coloring a little. "That is, he was staying with us for a short time at Brooklyn."

"Staying with you?" her grandfather repeats, curiously. It is evidently a matter of wonder with them, her friendship with Tedcastle.

"Yes, he and John, my brother, are old friends. They were at school together, although John is much older, and he says——"

Mr. Amherst coughs, which means he is displeased, and turns his head away. Marcia gives an order to one of the servants in a very distinct tone. Philip smiles at Molly, and Molly, unconscious of offense, is about to return to the charge, and give a lengthened account of her tabooed brother, when luckily she is prevented by a voice from behind her chair, which says:

"Champagne, or Moselle?"

"Champagne," replies Molly, and forgets her brother for the moment.

"I thought all women were prejudiced in favor of Moselle," says Philip, addressing her hastily, more from a view to hinder a recurrence to the forbidden topic than from any overweening curiosity to learn her taste in wines. "Are not you?"

"I am hardly in a position to judge," frankly, "as I have never tasted Moselle, and champagne only once. Have I shocked you? Is that a very lowering admission?"

Mr. Amherst coughs again. The corners of Marcia's mouth take a disgusted droop. Philip laughs out loud.

"On the contrary, it is a very refreshing one," he says, in an interested and deeply amused tone, "more especially in these degenerate days when most young ladies can tell one to a turn the precise age, price, and retailer of one's wines. May I ask when was this memorable 'once'?"

"At the races at Loaminster. Were you ever there? I persuaded my brother to take me there the spring before last, and he went."

"We were there that year, with a large party," says Marcia. "I do not remember seeing you on the stand."

"We were not on it. We drove over, John and I and Letty, in the little trap, a Norwegian, and dreadfully shaky it was, but we did not care, and we sat in it all day, and saw everything very well. Then a friend of John's, a man in the Sixty-second, came up, and asked to be introduced to me, and afterward others came, and persuaded us to have luncheon with them in their marquee. It was there," nodding at Philip, "I got the champagne. We had great fun, I remember, and altogether it was quite the pleasantest day I ever spent in my life."

As she speaks, she dimples, and blushes, and beams all over her pretty face as she recalls that day's past glories.

"The Sixty-second?" says Marcia. "I recollect. A very second-rate regiment I thought it. There was a Captain Milburd in it, I remember."

"That was John's friend," says Molly, promptly; "he was so kind to me that day. Did you like him?"

"Like him! A man all broad plaid and red tie. No, I certainly did not like him."

"His tie!" says Molly, laughing gayly at the vision she has conjured up,—"it certainly *was* red. As red as that rose," pointing to a blood-colored flower in the centre of a huge china bowl of priceless cost, that ornaments the middle of the table, and round which, being opposite to him, she has to peer to catch a glimpse of Philip. "It was the reddest thing I ever saw, except his complexion. But I forgave him, he was so good-natured."

"Does good-nature make up for everything?" asks Philip, dodging the bowl in his turn to meet her eyes.

"For most things. Grandpapa," pointing to a family portrait over the chimney-piece that has attracted her attention ever since her entrance, "whose is that picture?"

"Your grandmother's. It is like you, but," says the old man with his usual gracefulness, "it is ten times handsomer."

"*Very* like you," thinks the young man, gazing with ever increasing admiration at the exquisite tints and shades and changes in the living face before him, "only you are ten thousand times more beautiful!"

Slowly, and with much unnecessary delay, the dinner drags to an end, only to be followed by a still slower hour in the drawing-room.

Mr. Amherst challenges Philip to a game of chess, that most wearisome of games to the on-looker, and so arranges himself that his antagonist cannot, without risking his neck, bestow so much as a glance in Miss Massereene's direction.

Marcia gets successfully through two elaborate fantasies upon the piano, that require rather more than the correct brilliancy of her touch to make up for the incoherency of their composition; while Molly sits apart, dear soul, and wishes with much devoutness that the inventor of chess had been strangled at his birth.

At ten o'clock precisely Mr. Amherst rises, having lost his game, and a good deal of his temper, and expresses his intention of retiring without delay to his virtuous slumbers. Marcia asks Molly whether she too would not wish to go to her room after the day's fatigue; at which proposition Molly grasps with eagerness. Philip lights her candle,—they are in the hall together,—and then holds out his hand.

"Do you know we have not yet gone through the ceremony of shaking hands?" he says, with a kindly smile, and a still more kindly pressure; which I am afraid met with some faint return. Then he wishes her a good night's rest, and she wends her way up-stairs again, and knows the long-thought-of, hoped-for, much-dreaded day is at an end.

CHAPTER XII

"The guests are met, the feast is set;
May'st hear the merry din."

—*Ancient Mariner.*

"Teddy is coming to-day," is Molly's first thought next morning, as, springing from her bed, she patters across the floor in her bare feet to the window, to see how the weather is going to greet her lover.

"He is coming." The idea sends through her whole frame a little thrill of protective gladness. How happy, how independent she will feel with her champion always near her! A sneer loses half its bitterness when resented by two instead of one, and Luttrell will be a sure partisan. Apart from all which, she is honestly glad at the prospect of so soon meeting him face to face.

Therefore it is that with shining eyes and uplifted head she takes her place at the breakfast-table, which gives the pleasantest meal at Herst—old Amherst being ever conspicuous by his absence at it.

Philip, too, is nowhere to be seen.

"It will be a *tête-à-tête* breakfast," says Marcia, with a view to explanation. "Grandpapa never appears at this hour, nor—of late—does Philip."

"How unsociable!" says Molly, rather disappointed at the latter's defection. "Do they never come? All the year round?"

"Grandpapa never. But Philip, I presume, will return to his usual habits once the house begins to fill,—I mean, when the guests arrive."

"This poor little guest is evidently of small account," thinks Molly, rather piqued, and, as the thought crosses her mind, the door opens and Philip comes toward her.

"Good-morning," he says, cheerfully.

"You have breakfasted?" Marcia asks, coldly, in a rather surprised tone.

"Long since. But I will take a cup of coffee from you now, if you will allow me."

"I hardly think you deserve it," remarks Molly, turning luminous, laughing eyes upon him. "Marcia has just been telling me of your bad habits. Fancy your preferring your breakfast all alone to having it with——"

"You?" interrupts he, quickly. "I admit your argument; it was bearish; but I was particularly engaged this morning. You shall not have to complain of my conduct in the future, however, as I am resolved to mend my ways. See how you have improved me already."

"Too sudden a reformation, I fear, to be lasting."

"No. It all hinges on the fact that the iron was hot. There is no knowing what you may not do with me before you leave, if you will only take the trouble to teach me. Some more toast?"

"No, thank you."

Marcia grows a shade paler, and lets one cup rattle awkwardly against another. Have they forgotten her very presence?

"I have not much fancy for the *rôle* of teacher," goes on Molly, archly: "I have heard it is an arduous and thankless one. Besides, I believe you to be so idle that you would disgrace my best efforts."

"Do you? Then you wrong me. On the contrary, you would find me a very apt pupil,—ambitious, too, and anxious to improve under your tuition."

"Suppose," breaks in Marcia, with deadly civility, "you finish your *tête-à-tête* in the drawing-room. We have quite done breakfast, I think, and one wearies of staring at the very prettiest china after a bit. Will you be good enough to ring the bell, Philip?"

"Our *tête-à-tête*, as you call it, must be postponed," says Philip, smiling, rising to obey her order; "I am still busy, and must return to my work. Indeed, I only left it to pay you a flying visit."

Although his tone includes both women, his eyes rest alone on Molly.

"Then you do actually work, sometimes?" says that young lady, with exaggerated surprise and uplifted lids.

"Now and then,—occasionally—as little as I can help."

"What a speech, coming from an ambitious pupil!" cries she, gayly. "Ah! did I not judge you rightly a moment ago when I accused you of idleness?"

Philip laughs, and disappears, while Molly follows Marcia into a small drawing-room, a sort of general boudoir, where the ladies of the household are in the habit of assembling after breakfast, and into which, sooner or later, the men are sure to find their way.

Marcia settles down to the everlasting macrame work on which she seems perpetually engaged, while indolent Molly sits calmly, and it must be confessed very contentedly, with her hands before her.

After a considerable silence, Marcia says, icily:

"I fear you will find Herst Royal dull. There is so little to amuse one in a house where the host is an invalid. Do you read?"

"Sometimes," says Molly, studying her companion curiously, and putting on the air of ignorance so evidently expected.

"Yes? that is well. Reading is about the one thing we have to occupy our time here. In the library you will probably be able to suit yourself. What will you prefer? an English work? or"—superciliously—"perhaps French? You are without doubt a French scholar."

"If you mean that I consider myself complete mistress of the French language," says Molly, meekly, "I must say no."

"Ah! of course not. The remote country parts in which you live afford, I dare say, few opportunities of acquiring accomplishments."

"We have a National School," says Molly, with increasing mildness, and an impassive countenance.

"Ah!" says Marcia again. Her look—her tone—say volumes.

"You are very accomplished, I suppose," says Molly, presently, her voice full of resigned melancholy. "You can paint and draw?"

"Yes, a little."

"And play, and sing?"

"Well, yes," modestly; "I don't sing much, because my chest is delicate."

"Thin voice," thinks Molly to herself.

"How fortunate you are!" she says aloud. "How I envy you! Why, there is positively *nothing* you cannot do! Even that macrame, which seems to me more difficult than all the other things I have mentioned, you have entirely mastered. Now, I could not remember all those different knots to save my life. How clever you are! How attractive men must find you!" Molly sighs.

A shade crosses Marcia's face. Her eyelids quiver. Although the shaft (be it said to Molly's praise) was innocently shot, still it reached her cousin's heart, for has she not failed in attracting the one man she so passionately loves?

"I really hardly know," Miss Amherst says, coldly. "I—don't go in for that sort of thing. And you,—do you paint?"

"Oh, no."

"You play the piano, perhaps?"

"I try to, now and then."

("'The Annen Polka,' and on memorable occasions 'The Battle of Prague,'" thinks Marcia, comfortably.) "You sing," she says.

"I do," with hesitation.

("'Rosalie the Prairie Flower,' and the 'Christy Minstrels' generally," concludes Marcia, inwardly.) "That is charming," she says out loud: "it is so long since we have had any one here with a talent for music."

"Oh," says Molly, biting a little bit off her nail, and then examining her finger in an embarrassed fashion, "you must not use the word talented, that implies so much, and I—really you know I—— Why," starting to her feet, and regaining all her usual impulsive gayety, "that is surely Philip walking across the lawn, and he said he was so busy. Can we not go out, Marcia? The day is so lovely."

"If you want Philip, I dare say one of the servants will bring him to you," says Marcia, insolently.

Just before luncheon the Darleys arrive. Henry Darley, tall, refined, undemonstrative; Mrs. Darley, small and silly, with flaxen hair, blue eyes, pink and white complexion, and a general wax-dollyness about her; and just such a tiny, foolishly obstinate mouth as usually goes with a face like hers. She is vain, but never ill-natured, unless it suits her purpose; frivolous, but in the main harmless; and, although indifferent to her husband,—of whom she is utterly unworthy,—takes care to be thoroughly respectable. Full of the desire, but without the pluck, to go altogether wrong, she skirts around the edges of her pet sins, yet having a care that all those who pass by shall see her garments free of stain.

"I understand my husband, and my husband understands me," she is in the habit of saying to those who will take the trouble to listen; which is strictly true as regards the latter part of the speech, though perhaps the former is not so wise an assertion.

With her she brings her only child, a beautiful little boy of six.

She greets Marcia with effusion, and gushes over Molly.

"So glad, dear, so charmed to make your acquaintance. Have always felt such a deep interest in your poor dear mother's sad but romantic story. So out of the common as it was, you know, and delightfully odd, and—and—all that. Of course you are aware there is a sort of cousinship between us. My father married your——" and so on, and on, and on.

She talks straight through lunch to any one and every one without partiality; although afterward no one can remember what it was she was so eloquent about.

"Tedcastle not come?" she says, presently, catching Marcia's eye. "I quite thought he was here. What an adorable boy he was! I do hope he is not changed. If India has altered him, it will be quite too bad."

"He may come yet," replies Marcia; "though I now think it unlikely. When writing he said to-day, or to-morrow; and with him that always means to-morrow. He is fond of putting off; his second thoughts are always his best."

"Always," thinks Molly, angrily, feeling suddenly a keen sense of sure disappointment. What does she know about him? After all he said on parting he must, he *will* come to-day.

Yet somehow, spite of this comforting conclusion, her spirits sink, her smile becomes less ready, her luncheon grows flavorless. Something within compels her to believe that not until the morrow shall she see her lover.

When they leave the dining-room she creeps away unnoticed, and, donning her hat, sallies forth alone into the pleasant wood that surrounds the house.

For a mile or two she walks steadily on, crunching beneath her feet with a certain sense of vicious enjoyment those early leaves that already have reached death. How very monotonous all through is a big wood! Trees, grass, sky overhead! Sky, grass, trees.

She pulls a few late wild flowers that smile up at her coaxingly, and turns them round and round within her fingers, not altogether tenderly.

What a fuss poets, and painters, and such-like, make about flowers, wild ones especially! When all is said, there is a terrible sameness about them; the same little pink ones here, the same little blue ones there; here the inevitable pale yellow, there the pure warm violet. Well, no doubt there is certainly a wonderful variety—but still——

Looking up suddenly from her weak criticism, she sees coming quickly toward her—very close to her—Teddy Luttrell.

With a glad little cry, she flings the ill-treated flowers from her and runs to him with hands outstretched.

"You have come," she cries, "after all! I *knew* you would; although she said you wouldn't. Oh, Teddy, I had *quite* given you up."

Luttrell takes no notice of this contradictory speech. With his arms round her, he is too full of the intense happiness of meeting after separation the beloved, to heed mere words. His eyes are fastened on her perfect face.

How more than fair she is! how in his absence he has misjudged her beauty! or is it that she grows in excellence day by day? Not in all his lover's silent raptures has he imagined her half as lovely as she now appears standing before him, her hands clasped in his, her face flushed with unmistakable joy at seeing him again.

"Darling, darling!" he says, with such earnest delight in his tones that she returns one of his many kisses, out of sheer sympathy. For though glad as she is to welcome him as a sure ally at Herst, she hardly feels the same longing for the embrace that he (with his heart full of her alone) naturally does.

"You look as if you were going to tell me I have grown tall," she says, amused at his prolonged examination of her features. "John always does, when he returns from London, with the wild hope of keeping me down. Have I?"

"How can I tell? I have not taken my eyes from your face yet."

"Silly boy, and I have seen all the disimprovements in you long ago. I have also seen that you are wearing an entirely new suit of clothes. Such reckless extravagance! but they are very becoming, and I am fond of light gray, so you are forgiven. Why did you not come sooner? I have been *longing* for you. Oh, Teddy, I don't like Marcia or grandpapa a bit; and Philip has been absent nearly all the time; you said you would come early."

"So I did, by the earliest train; you could hardly have left the house when I arrived, and then I started instantly to find you. My own dear darling," with a sigh of content, "how good it is to see you again, and how well you are looking!"

"Am I?" laughing. "So are you, disgracefully well. You haven't a particle of feeling, or you would be emaciated by this time. Now confess you did not miss me at all."

"Were I to speak forever, I could not tell you how much. Are you not 'the very eyes of me'?" says the young man, fondly.

"That is a very nonsensical quotation," says Molly, gayly. "Were you to see with my eyes, just consider how different everything would appear. Now, for instance, *I* would never have so far forgotten myself as to fall so idiotically and ridiculously in love, as you did, with beautiful Molly Massereene!"

At this little touch of impertinence they both laugh merrily. After which, with some hesitation, and a rather heightened color, Tedcastle draws a case from his pocket, and presents it to her.

"I brought you a—a present," he says, "because I know you are fond of pretty things."

As she opens the case and sees within it, lying on its purple velvet bed, a large dull gold locket, with a wreath of raised forget-me-nots in turquoises and enamel on one side, she forms her lips into a round "Oh!" of admiration and delight, more satisfactory than any words.

"Do you like it? I am so glad! I saw it one day, quite accidentally, in a window, and at once it reminded me of you. I thought it would exactly suit you. Do you remember down by the river-side that night, after our first important quarrel, when I asked you to marry me?"

"I remember," softly.

"You had forget-me-nots in your hands then, and in your dress. I can never forget you, as you looked at that moment; and those flowers will ever be associated with you in my mind. Surely they are the prettiest that grow. I call them 'my sweet love's flower.'"

"How fond you are of me!" she says, wistfully, something like moisture in her eyes, "and," turning her gaze again upon his gift, "you are too good: you are always thinking how to please me. There is only one thing wanting to make this locket perfect," raising her liquid eyes to his again, "and that is your face inside it."

At which words, you may be sure, Luttrell is repaid over and over again all the thought and care he has expended on the choosing of the trinket.

"And so you are not in love with Herst?" he says, presently, as they move on through the sweet wood, his arm around her.

"With Herst? No, I have no fault to find with Herst; the place is beautiful. But I confess I do not care about my grandfather or Marcia: of the two I prefer my grandfather, but that is saying very little. Philip alone has been very nice to me,—indeed, more than kind."

"More! What does Marcia say to that?"

"Oh, there is nothing between them; I am sure of that. They either hate each other or else familiarity has bred contempt between them, and they avoid each other all they can, and never speak unless compelled. For instance, she says to him, 'Tea or coffee, Philip?' and he makes her a polite reply; or he says to her, 'Shall I stir the fire for you?' and she makes *him* a polite reply. But it can hardly be called a frantic attachment."

"Like ours?" laughing and bending his tall slight figure to look into her face.

"In our case you have all the franticness to yourself," she says; but as she says it she puts her own soft little hand over the one that encircles her waist, to take the sting out of her words; though why she said it puzzles even herself: nevertheless there is great truth, in her remark, and he knows it.

"Then Philip is handsome," she says: "it is quite a pleasure to look at him. And I admire him very much."

"He *is* a good-looking fellow," reluctantly, and as though it were a matter of surprise nature's having bestowed beauty upon Philip Shadwell, "but surly."

"'Surly!' not to me."

"Oh, of course not to you! A man must be a brute to be uncivil to a woman. And I don't say he is that," slowly, and as though it were yet an undecided point whether Philip should be classed with the lower creation or not. "Do not let your admiration for him go too far, darling; remember——"

"About that," interrupts she, hurriedly, "you have something to remember also. Your promise to keep our engagement a dead secret. You will not break it?"

"I never," a little stiffly, "break a promise. You need not have reminded me of this one."

Silence.

Glancing up at her companion stealthily, Molly can see his lips are in a degree compressed, and that for the first time since their reunion his eyes are turned determinedly from her. Her heart smites her. So good as he is to her, she has already hurt and wounded him.

With a little caressing, tender movement, she rubs her cheek up and down against his sleeve for a moment or two, and then says, softly:

"Are you cross with me, Teddy? Don't then. I am so glad, so happy, to have you with me again. Do not spoil this one good hour by putting a nasty unbecoming little frown upon your forehead. Come, turn your face to me again: when you look at me, I know you will smile, for my sake."

"My own darling," says Luttrell, passionately.

The morrow brings new faces, and Herst is still further enlivened by the arrival of two men from some distant barracks,—one so tall, and the other so diminutive, as to call for an immediate joke about "the long and the short of it."

Captain Mottie is a jolly, genial little soul, with a perpetual look on all occasions as though he couldn't help it, and just one fault, a fatal tendency toward punning of the weakest description with which he hopes in vain to excite the risibility of his intimates. Having a mind above disappointment, however, he feels no depression on marking the invariable silence that follows his best efforts, and, with a perseverance worthy of a better cause, only nerves himself for fresh failures.

Nature, having been unprodigal to him in the matter of height, makes up for it generously in the matter of breadth, with such lavish generosity, indeed, that he feels the time has come when, with tears in his eyes, he must say "no" to his bitter beer.

His chum, Mr. Longshanks (commonly called "Daddy Longlegs," on account of the length of his lower limbs), is his exact counterpart, being as silent as the other is talkative; seldom exerting himself, indeed, to shine in conversation, or break the mysterious quiet that envelops him, except when he faithfully (though unsmilingly) helps out his friend's endeavors at wit, by saying "ha! ha!" when occasion calls for it. He has a red nose that is rather striking and suggests expense. He has also a weakness for gaudy garments, and gets himself up like a showy commercial traveler.

They are both related in some far-off manner to their host, though how, I believe, both he and they would be puzzled to explain. Still, the relationship beyond dispute is there, which is everything. *Enfin* they are harmless beings, such as come in useful for padding purposes in country houses during the winter and autumn seasons, being, according to their friends' account, crack shots, "A1 at billiards," and "beggars to ride."

It is four o'clock. The house is almost deserted. All the men have been shooting since early morning. Only Molly and Marcia remain in possession of the sitting-room that overlooks the graveled walk, Mrs. Darley having accompanied Mr. Amherst in his customary drive.

The sound of wheels coming quickly down the avenue compels Molly to glance up from the book she is enjoying.

"Somebody is coming," she says to Marcia; and Marcia, rising with more alacrity than is her wont, says, "It must be Lady Stafford," and goes into the hall to receive her guest. Molly, full of eager curiosity to see this cousin of Tedcastle's whose story has so filled her with interest, rises also, and cranes her neck desperately round the corner of the window to try and catch a glimpse of her, but in vain, the unfriendly porch prevents her, and, sinking back into her seat, she is fain to content herself by listening to the conversation that is going on in the hall between Marcia and the new arrival.

"Oh, Marcia, is that you?" says a high, sweet voice, with a little complaining note running through it, and then there is a pause, evidently filled up by an osculatory movement. "How odiously cool and fresh you do look! while I—what a journey it has been! and how out of the way! I really don't believe it was nearly so far the last time. Have the roads lengthened, or have they pushed the house farther on? I never felt so done up in my life."

"You do look tired, dear. Better go to your room at once, and let me send you up some tea."

"Not tea," says the sweet voice; "anything but *that*. I am quite too far gone for *tea*. Say sherry, Marcia, or—no,—Moselle. I think it is Moselle that does me good when I am fatigued to death."

"You shall have it directly. Matthews, show Lady Stafford her room."

"One moment, Marcia. Many people come yet? Tedcastle?"

"Yes, and Captain Mottie, with his devoted attendant, and the Darleys."

"Maudie? Is she as fascinating as ever? I do hope, Marcia, you have got her young man for her this time, as she was simply unbearable last year."

"I have not," laughing: "it is a dead secret, but the fact is, he *wouldn't come*."

"I like that young man; though I consider he has sold us shamefully. Any one else?"

"My cousin, Eleanor Massereene."

"*The* cousin! I am so glad. Anything new is such a relief. And I have heard she is beautiful: is she?"

"Beauty is in the eye of the beholder," quotes Marcia, in a low tone, and with a motion of her hand toward the open door inside which sits Molly, that sends Lady Stafford up-stairs without further parley.

"Is it Lady Stafford?" asks Molly, as Marcia re-enters the room.

"Yes."

"She seems very tired."

"I don't know, really. She thinks she is,—which amounts to the same thing. You will see her in half an hour or so as fresh as though fatigue were a thing unknown."

"How does she do it?" asks Molly, curiously, who has imagined Lady Stafford by her tone to be in the last stage of exhaustion.

"How can I say? I suppose her maid knows."

"Why? Does she—paint?" asks Molly, with hesitation, who has been taught to believe that all London women are a mixture of false hair, rouge, pearl powder, and belladonna.

"Paint!" with a polite disgust, "I should hope not. If you are a judge in that matter you will be able to see for yourself. I know nothing of such things, but I don't think respectable women paint."

"But," says Molly, who feels a sudden anger at her tone, and as sudden a desire to punish her for her insolence, opening her blue eyes innocently wide, "*you* are respectable, Marcia?"

"What do you mean by that?" growing pale with anger, even through that delicate *soupçon* of color that of late she has been compelled to use to conceal her pallor. "Do you mean to insinuate that *I* paint?"

"I certainly thought you did," still innocent, still full of wonder: "you said——"

"I would advise you for the future to restrain such thoughts: experience will teach you they show want of breeding. In the meantime, I beg you to understand that I do *not* paint."

"Oh, Marcia!"

"You are either extremely impertinent or excessively ignorant, or both!" says Marcia, rising to her full height, and turning flashing eyes upon her cousin, who is regarding her with the liveliest reproach. "I insist on knowing what you mean by your remarks."

"Why, have you forgotten all about those charming water-color sketches in the small gallery up-stairs?" exclaims Molly, with an airy irrepressible laugh. "There, don't be angry: I was only jesting; no one would for a moment suspect you of such a disreputable habit."

"Pray reserve your jests for those who may appreciate them," says Miss Amherst, in a low angry tone: "I do not. They are as vulgar as they are ill-timed."

"But I took a good rise out of her all the same," says Molly to herself, as she slips from the room full of malicious laughter.

Before dinner—not sooner—Lady Stafford makes her appearance, and quite dazzles Molly with her beauty and the sweetness of her manner. She seems in the gayest spirits, and quite corroborates all Marcia has said about her exhibiting no symptoms of fatigue. Her voice, indeed, still retains its sad tone, but it is habitual to her, and does not interfere with the attractive liveliness of her demeanor, but only adds another charm to the many she already possesses.

She is taller than Tedcastle has led Molly to believe, and looks even smaller than she really is. Her eyelids droop at the corners, and give her a pensive expression that softens the laughter of her blue eyes. Her nose is small and clever, her mouth very merry, her skin exquisite, though devoid of the blue veins that usually go with so delicate a white, and her hair is a bright, rich gold. She is extremely lovely, and, what is far better, very pleasing to the eye.

"I am much better," she says, gayly, addressing Marcia, and then, turning to Molly, holds out to her a friendly hand.

"Miss Massereene, I know," she smiles, looking at her, and letting a pleased expression overspread her features as she does so. "Marcia told me of your arrival; I have heard of you also from other people; but their opinion I must reserve until I have become your friend. At all events, they did not lie in their description. No, you must not cross-examine me; I will not tell what they said."

She is a decided addition to the household; they all find her so. Even Mr. Longshanks brightens up, and makes a solitary remark at dinner; but, as nobody catches it, he is hardly as unhappy as otherwise assuredly he would have been.

After dinner she proves herself as agreeable in the drawing-room (during that wretched half-hour devoid of men) as she had been when surrounded by them, and chatters on to Marcia and Molly of all things possible and impossible.

Presently, however, the conversation drifting toward people of whose existence Molly has hitherto been unaware, she moves a little apart from the other two, and amuses herself by turning over a book of Byron's beauties; while wishing heartily those stupid men would weary of their wine,—vain wish!

By degrees the voices on the other sofa wax fainter and fainter, then rise with sudden boldness, as Marcia, secure in her French—says in that language, evidently in answer to some remark, "No; just conceive it,—she is totally uneducated, that is, in the accepted meaning of the word. The very morning after her arrival she confessed to me she knew nothing of French, nothing to signify of music, nothing, in fact, of anything."

"But her air, her whole bearing,—it is inconceivable," says Lady Stafford. "She must have had some education surely."

"She spoke of a National School! Consider the horror of it! I expect her brother must be a very low sort of person. If she can read and write it is as much as we need hope for. That is the worst of living in one of those petty villages, completely out of society."

"What a pity, with her charming face and figure!" says Lady Stafford, also (I regret to say) so far forgetting herself as to speak in the language she believes falsely to be unknown to Molly.

"Yes, she is rather pretty," admits Marcia, against her will; "but beauty when attached to ignorance is only a matter of regret, as it seems to me."

"True," says Lady Stafford, pityingly, letting her eyes fall on Molly.

The latter, whose own eyes have been fixed vacantly on some distant and invisible object outside in the dark garden, now rises, humming softly, and going toward the window presses her forehead against one of the cool panes. So stationed, she is out of sight and hearing.

The door opens, and the men come in by twos. Luttrell makes straight for Molly, and as an excuse for doing so says out loud:

"Miss Massereene, will you sing us something?"

"I don't sing," returns Molly, in a distinct and audible tone,—audible enough to make Marcia raise her shoulders and cast an "I told you so" glance at Cecil Stafford.

Luttrell, bewildered, gazes at Molly.

"But——" he commences, rashly.

"I tell you I don't sing," she says, again, in a lower, more imperative tone, although even now she repents her of the ill-humor that has balked her of a revenge so ready to her hand. To sing a French song, with her divine voice, before Marcia! A triumph indeed!

All night long the conversation between her cousin and Lady Stafford rankles in her mind. What a foolish freak it was her ever permitting Marcia to think of her as one altogether without education! Instinct might have told that her cousin would not scruple about applying such knowledge to her disadvantage. And yet why is Marcia her enemy? How has she ever injured her? With what purpose does she seek to make her visit unpleasant to her?

And to speak contemptuously of her to Lady Stafford, of all people, whom already she likes well enough to covet her regard in return,—it is too bad. Not for worlds would she have had her think so poorly of her.

At all events she will lose no time in explaining, on the morrow; and with this determination full upon her she retires to rest, with some small comfort at her heart.

CHAPTER XIII

"Music hath charms."

"May I come in?" says Molly, next day, knocking softly at Lady Stafford's door.

"By all means," returns the plaintive voice from within; and Molly, opening the door, finds Cecil has risen, and is coming forward eagerly to meet her.

"I knew your voice," says the blonde, gayly. "Come in and sit down, do. I am *ennuyée* to the last degree, and will accept it as a positive charity if you will devote half an hour to my society."

"But you are sure I am not in the way?" asks Molly, hesitating; "you are not—busy?"

"Busy! Oh, what a stranger I am to you, my dear," exclaims Cecil, elevating her brows: "it is three long years since last I was busy. I am sure I wish I were: perhaps it might help me to get through the time. I have spent the last hour wondering what on earth brought me to this benighted spot, and I really don't know yet."

"Grandpapa's invitation, I suppose," says Molly, laughing.

"Well, yes, perhaps so; and something else,—something that I verily believe brings us all!—the fact that he has untold money, and can leave it where he pleases. There lies the secret of our yearly visitations. We outsiders don't of course hope to be the heir,—Philip is that, or Marcia, or perhaps both; but still there is a good deal of ready money going, and we all hope to be 'kindly remembered.' Each time we sacrifice ourselves by coming down here, we console ourselves by the reflection that it is at least another hundred tacked on to our legacy."

"What if you are disappointed?"

"I often think of that," says her ladyship, going off into a perfect peal of laughter. "Oh, the fun it would be! Think of our expressions. I assure you I spend whole hours picturing Maud Darley's face under the circumstances; you know she takes those long drives with him every day in the fond hope of cutting us all out and getting the lion's share."

"Poor woman! it is sad if she has all her trouble for nothing. I do not think I should like driving with grandpapa."

"I share your sentiments: neither should I. Still, there is a charm in money. Every night before going to bed I tot up on my fingers the amount of the bequest I feel I ought to receive. It has reached two thousand pounds by this. Next visit will commence a fresh thousand."

"You are sanguine," says Molly. "I wonder if I shall go on hoping like you, year after year."

"I request you will not even insinuate such a thing," cries Lady Stafford in pretended horror. "'Year after year!' Why, how long do you mean him to live? If he doesn't die soon, I shall certainly throw up my chance and cut his acquaintance." Then, with sudden self-reproach, "Poor old fellow," she says, "it is a shame to speak of him like this even in jest. He may live forever, as far as I am concerned. Now tell me something about yourself, and do take a more comfortable chair: you don't look half cozy."

"Don't make me too comfortable, or perhaps I shall bore you to death with the frequency of my visits. You will have me again to-morrow if you don't take care."

"Well, I hope so. Remember you have *carte blanche* to come here whenever you choose. I was fast falling into the blues when I heard you knock, so you may fancy how welcome you were, almost as welcome as my cousin."

"Marcia?" asks Molly, feeling slightly disappointed at the "almost."

"Oh, dear, no,—not Marcia; she and I don't get on a bit too well together, and she was excessively disagreeable all this morning: she is her grandfather's own child. I am sure she need not visit Philip's defection on me; but she has a horrible temper, and that's the truth. No, I meant Tedcastle; he is my cousin also. I do so like Tedcastle: don't you?"

"Very much indeed," coloring faintly. "But," hastily, "I have not yet told you what brought me here to-day."

"Do you mean to tell me you had an object in coming?" cries her ladyship, throwing up her little white jeweled hands in affected reproach. "That something keener than a desire for my society has brought you to my boudoir? You reduce me to despair! I did for one short quarter of an hour believe you 'loved me for myself alone.'"

"No," laughing, and blushing, too, all through her pale clear skin, "I confess to the object. I—the fact is—I have felt a little deceitful ever since last night. Because—in spite of Marcia's superior information on the subject, I have had some slight education, and I *do* know a little French!"

"Ah!" cries Lady Stafford, rising and blushing herself, a vivid crimson: "you heard, you understood all. Well," with a sudden revival, and a happy remembrance of her own words, "I didn't say anything bad, did I?"

"No, no: I would not have come here if you had. You said all there was of the kindest. You were *so* kind. I could not bear to deceive you or let you retain a false opinion of me. Marcia, indeed, outdid herself, though I am guiltless of offense toward her. She is evidently not aware of the fact that one part of my life was spent in London with my aunt, my father's sister, and that while with her I had the best masters to be found. I am sorry for Marcia, but I could not bring myself to speak just then."

Cecil burst into a merry, irresistible laugh.

"It is delicious!" cries she, wickedly. "A very comedy of errors. If we could but manage some effective way of showing Marcia her mistake. Can you," with sudden inspiration, "sing?"

"I can," says Molly, calmly.

"You can. That sounds promising. I wonder you don't say 'a little,' as all young ladies do, more especially when they sing a good deal more than any one wants them to! Come here, and let me see what you mean by that uncompromising 'can.'"

Opening a small cottage piano at the other end of her pretty sitting-room, she motions Molly to the instrument.

"Play for me," Molly says, bent on doing her very best. "I can sing better standing."

"What, then?"

"This," taking up a song of Sullivan's, after a rapid survey of the pile of music lying on one side.

She sings, her lovely voice thrilling and sobbing through the room, sings with a passionate desire to prove her powers, and well succeeds. For a minute after she has finished, Cecil does not speak, and then goes into raptures, as "is her nature to."

"Oh that I had your voice!" cries she, with genuine tears in her eyes. "I would have the world at my feet. What a gift! a voice for a goddess! Molly—may I call you so?—I absolutely pity Marcia when I think of her consternation."

"She deserves it," says Molly, who feels her cousin's conduct deeply. "I will sing to-night, if you will get Marcia to ask me."

So the two conspirators arrange their little plan, Cecil Stafford being quite mischievous enough to enjoy the thought of Miss Amherst's approaching discomfiture, while Molly feels all a woman's desire to restore her hurt vanity.

Dinner is half over; and so far it has been highly successful. Mr. Amherst's temper has taken this satisfactory turn,—he absolutely refuses to speak to any of his guests.

Under these circumstances every one feels it will be the better part of valor not to address him,—all, that is, except Mrs. Darley, who, believing herself irresistible, goes in for the doubtful task of soothing the bear and coaxing him from his den.

"I am afraid you have a headache, dear Mr. Amherst," she says, beaming sweetly upon him.

"Are you, madam? Even if I were a victim to that foolish disorder, I hardly see why the fact should arouse a feeling of terror in your breast. Only weak-minded girls have headaches."

A faint pause. Conversation is languishing, dying, among the other guests; they smell the fight afar, and pause in hungry expectation of what is surely coming.

"I pity any one so afflicted," says Mrs. Darley, going valiantly to her death: "I am a perfect martyr to them myself." Here she gives way to a little sympathetic sigh, being still evidently bent on believing him weighed down with pain heroically borne.

"Are you?" says Mr. Amherst, with elaborate politeness. "You astonish me. I should never have thought it. Rheumatism, now, I might. But how old are you, madam?"

"Well, really," says Mrs. Darley, with a pretty childish laugh which she rather cultivates, being under the impression that it is fascinating to the last degree, "asking me so suddenly puts the precise day I was born out of my head. I hardly remember—exactly—when——"

Conversation has died. Every one's attention is fixed; by experience they know the end is nigh.

"Just so; I don't suppose you could, it happened such a long time ago!" says this terrible old man, with an audible chuckle, that falls upon a silent and (must it be said?) appreciative audience.

Mrs. Darley says no more; what is there left to say? and conversation is once more taken up, and flows on as smoothly as it can, when everybody else is talking for a purpose.

"*Is* she old?" Molly asks Philip, presently, in a low tone, when the buzz is at its highest; "very old, I mean? She looks so babyish."

"How old would you say?" speaking in the same guarded tone as her own, which has the effect of making Luttrell and Marcia believe them deep in a growing flirtation.

"About twenty-two or three."

"She does it uncommonly well then," says Philip, regarding Mrs. Darley with much admiration,—"uncommonly well; her maid must be a treasure."

"But why? Is she older than that?"

"I don't know, I am sure," says Philip, unkindly, with an amused smile. "She used to be my age, but I haven't the faintest idea in the world what she is—now!"

After one or two more playful sallies on the part of their host,—for having once found his tongue he takes very good care to use it, and appears fatally bent on making his hearers well aware of its restoration,—the ladies adjourn to the drawing-room, where Mrs. Darley instantly retires behind her handkerchief and gives way to a gentle sob.

"That detestable old man!" she says, viciously; "how I hate him! What have I done, that he should treat me with such exceeding rudeness? One would think I was as old as—as—Methuselah! Not that his mentioning my age puts me out in the least,—why should it?—only his manner is so offensive!"

And as she finishes she rolls up the corners of her handkerchief into a little point, and carefully picks out, one by one, the two tears that adorn her eyes, lest by any chance they should escape, and, running down her cheeks, destroy the evening's painting.

"Don't distress yourself about it, Maud," says Lady Stafford, kindly, although strongly divided between pity for the angry Maud and a growing desire to laugh; "nobody minds him: you know we all suffer in turn. Something tells me it will be my turn next, and then you will indeed see a noble example of fortitude under affliction."

There is no time for more; the door opens and the men come in, more speedily to-night than is their wont, no doubt driven thereto by the amiability of Mr. Amherst.

Maud suppresses the tell-tale handkerchief, and puts on such a sweet smile as utterly precludes the idea of chagrin. The men, with the usual amount of bungling, fall into their places, and Cecil seizes the opportunity to say to Marcia, in a low tone:

"You say Miss Massereene sings. Ask her to give us something now. It is so slow doing nothing all the evening, and I feel Mr. Amherst is bent on mischief. Besides, it is hard on you, expecting you to play all the night through."

"I will ask her if you wish it," Marcia says, indifferently, "but remember, you need not look for a musical treat. I detest bad singing myself."

"Oh, anything, anything," says Cecil, languidly sinking back into her chair.

Thus instigated, Marcia does ask Molly to sing.

"If you will care to hear me," Molly answers, coldly rather than diffidently, and rising, goes to the piano.

"Perhaps there may be something of mine here that you may know," Marcia says, superciliously, pointing to the stand; but Molly, declaring that she can manage without music, sits down and plays the opening chords of Gounod's "Berceuse."

A moment later, and her glorious voice, rarely soft, and sweet as a child's, yet powerful withal, rings through the room, swells, faints, every note a separate delight, falling like rounded pearls from her lips.

A silence—truest praise of all—follows. One by one the talkers cease their chatter; the last word remains a last word; they forget the thought of a moment before.

A dead calm reigns, while Molly sings on, until the final note drops from her with lingering tenderness.

Even then they seem in no hurry to thank her; almost half a minute elapses before any one congratulates her on the exquisite gift that has been given her.

"You have been days in the house, and never until now have let us hear you," Philip says, leaning on the top of the piano; he is an enthusiast where music is concerned. "How selfish! how unkind! I could hardly have believed it of you."

"Was I ever asked before?" Molly says, raising her eyes to his, while her fingers still run lightly over the notes.

"I don't know. I suppose it never occurred to us, and, as you may have noticed, there is a dearth of graciousness among us. But for you to keep such a possession a secret was more than cruel. Sing again."

"I must not monopolize the piano: other people can sing too."

"Not like you." He pauses, and then says, slowly, "I used to think nature was impartial in the distribution of her gifts,—that, as a rule, we all received pretty much the same amount of good at her hands; to one beauty, to another talent, and so on; but I was wrong: she has her favorites, it appears. Surely already you had had more than your share, without throwing in your perfect voice."

Molly lowers her eyes, but makes no reply; experience has taught her that this is one of the occasions on which "silence is golden."

"You sing yourself, perhaps?" she says, presently, when she has tired of waiting for him to start a subject.

"Occasionally. Will you sing this with me?" taking up a celebrated duet and placing it before her. "Do you know it?"

"Yes, Mr. Luttrell and I used to sing it often at Brooklyn: it was a great favorite of ours."

"Oh, that! Indeed!" laying it aside with suspicious haste. "Shall we try something else?"

"And why something else?" composedly. "Does that not suit your voice? If it does, I will sing it with you with pleasure."

"Really?" regarding her closely, with what is decidedly more than admiration in his gaze. "Are there no recollections hidden in that song?"

"How can I tell? I never saw that particular edition before. Open it, and let us see," returns Molly, with a merry laugh. "Who knows what we may find between the pages?"

"If I might only believe you," he says, earnestly, still only half convinced. "Do you mean to tell me Luttrell spent an entire month with you, and left you heart-whole? I cannot believe it."

"Then don't," still laughing.

At this instant, Luttrell, who has with moody eyes been watching Philip's eager face from the other end of the room, saunters up, and seeing the old well-remembered duet lying open before Molly, suddenly thinks it may be there for him, and cheering up, says pleasantly:

"Are you going to sing it with me?"

"Not to-night," Molly replies, kindly; "Philip has just asked me to sing it with him. Some other time."

"Ah!" says Luttrell, more wounded than he cares to confess; for is not that very song endeared to him by a thousand memories? and turning on his heel, he walks away.

With a little impulsive gesture Molly rises from the piano-stool, and, without again looking at Philip, moves across the room to the seat she had originally vacated. As she does so she passes close by Marcia, who, ever since her cousin's voice first sounded in her ears, has been sitting silent, now pale, now red.

She stays Molly by a slight movement of the hand, and says, coldly:

"I thought you told me you could neither sing nor understand French?"

"I don't think I could have said quite that," Molly replies, quietly; "I told you I sang a little; it is not customary to laud one's own performances."

"You are a clever actress," says Marcia, so low as to be unheard by all but Molly: "with such a voice as yours, and such masterly command of all emotion and expression, you should make the stage your home."

"Perhaps I shall find your hint useful in the future," says Molly, with a slight shrug of her shoulders: "when one is poor it is always well to know there is something one can put one's hand to when things come to the worst; but at present I feel sufficiently at home where I am. I am glad," calmly, "my singing pleased you,—if, indeed, it did."

"You sing magnificently," Marcia says, aloud, giving her meed of praise justly, but unwillingly.

"And such a charming song as that is!" breaks in Mrs. Darley: "I remember hearing it for the first time, just after my marriage; indeed, while we were yet enjoying our wedding tour. Do you remember it, dearest?" As she murmurs the tender words, she turns upon her lord two azure eyes so limpid and full of trust and love that any man ignorant of the truth would have sworn by all his gods her desire was with her husband, whereas every inch of heart she possesses has long since been handed over to a man in the Horse Guards Blue.

"Humph!" says Henry Darley, eloquently; and without further rejoinder goes on with the game of chess he is playing with Mr. Amherst.

"Let us have something else, Eleanor," her grandfather says, looking up for an instant from his beloved queens and kings and castles; "another song."

This is such a wonderful request coming from Mr. Amherst, who is known to abhor Marcia's attempts, that every one looks surprised.

"Willingly, grandpapa," says Molly, and, going once more to the piano, gladly puts the obnoxious duet away, feeling sure its appearance has caused Tedcastle's annoyance. "Though if he is going to be jealous so early in the game as this," thinks she, "I don't fancy I shall have an altogether festive time of it."

"What shall it be?" she asks, aloud.

"Nothing Italian, at all events," says Mr. Amherst (all Marcia's endeavors are in that language); "I like something I can understand, and I hate your runs and trills."

"I will sing you my own song," says Molly, gayly, and gives them "Molly Bawn" deliciously.

"How pretty that is!" says Lady Stafford; "and so wild,—quite Irish! But your name, after all, is Eleanor, is it not?"

"There is, I believe, a tradition in the family to that effect," says Molly, smiling, "but it is used up, and no one now pays to it the least attention. I myself much prefer Molly. I am always called Molly Bawn at home."

Her voice lingers on the word "home." In an instant, amidst all the luxuries and charms of this beautiful drawing-room at Herst, her mind goes back to the old, homely, beloved sanctum at Brooklyn, where she sees John, and Letty, and all the happy, merry, good-hearted children, harmoniously mixed up together.

"It is a pity," says Mr. Amherst, purposely, seeing an opening for one of his cheerful remarks, "that everything about Ireland should be so wretchedly low."

"It *is* swampy," replies Miss Molly, promptly.

At this dangerous moment the door is thrown wide open, and a servant announces "Mr. Potts."

The effect is electric. Everybody looks up, and pleased, and glad; while the owner of this euphonious name comes forward, and, having shaken hands with Marcia, turns to old Amherst.

"How d'ye do, sir?" he says, heartily. "I hope you are better."

"Do you?" says Mr. Amherst, unamiably, feeling still a keen regret that the neat retort intended for Molly must wait another occasion. "I would believe you if I could, but it isn't in human nature. Yes, I am better, thank you; much better. I dare say with care I shall last this winter, and probably the next, and perhaps outlive a good many of you." He chuckles odiously as he winds up this pleasing speech.

Mr. Potts, rather taken aback, mutters something inaudible, and turns to Lady Stafford, who receives him warmly.

He is a young man of about twenty-four (though he might, in appearance, be any age from that to forty-four), and is short rather than tall. His eyes are gray, small, and bright, and full of fun, bespeaking imperturbable good humor.

His hair is red. It is hair that admits of no compromise; it is neither auburn, golden, nor light brown—it is a distinct and fiery red. His nose is "poor, but honest," and he has a thorough and most apparent appreciation of himself.

As I said before, Lady Stafford greets him warmly; he is one of her special pets.

"How are you getting on?" he asks, mysteriously, when the first questions and answers have been gone through. "Old boy evidently worse than ever. The wine theory would not suit his case; age does anything but improve him. He has gone to the bad altogether. I suppose you've been putting in an awful bad time of it?"

"We have, indeed," says Lady Stafford; "he has been unbearable all through dinner, though he was pretty well yesterday. I think myself it must be gout; every twinge brings forth a caustic speech."

By this time every one had shaken hands with the newcomer, and welcomed him heartily. He seems specially pleased to see Tedcastle.

"Luttrell! you here? Never had a hint of it. So glad to see you, old man! Why, you're looking as fit as even your best friend could wish you."

"Meaning yourself," says Luttrell. "Now, let's have a look at you. Why, Planty, what an exquisite get up! New coat and—etc. latest tie, and diamonds *ad lib*. Quite coquettish, upon my word. Who gave you the diamonds, Potts? Your mother?"

"No; I got tired of hinting there," says Potts, ingenuously, "so gave it up, and bought 'em myself. They are fetching, I take it. Luttrell, who is the girl at the piano? Never saw anything so lovely in all my life."

"Miss Massereene."

"Indeed! Been received, and all that? Well, there's been nothing this season to touch on her. Introduce me, Ted, do!"

He is introduced. And Molly, smiling up at him one of her own brightest, kindliest smiles, makes him then and there her slave forever. On the spot, without a second's delay, he falls head over ears in love with her.

By degrees he gets back to Lady Stafford, and sinks upon the sofa beside her. I say "sinks" unadvisedly; he drops upon the sofa, and very nearly makes havoc of the springs in doing so.

"I want to tell you who I saw in town the day before I left—a week ago," he says, cautiously.

"A week ago! And have you been ever since getting here?"

"No; I did it by degrees. First, I went down to the Maplesons', and spent two days there—very slow, indeed; then I got on to the Blouts', and found it much slower there; finally, I drove to Talbot Lowry's night before last, and stayed there until this evening. You know he lives only three miles from here."

"He is at home now, then?"

"Yes. He always *is* at home, I notice, when—you are here!"

"No!" says Cecil, with a little faint laugh. "You don't say so! what a remarkable coincidence!"

"An annual coincidence. But you don't ask me who it was I saw in London. Guess."

"The Christy Minstrels, without doubt. They never perform out of London, so I suppose are the only people in it now."

"Wrong. There was one other person—Sir Penthony Stafford!"

"Really!" says Cecil, coloring warmly, and sitting in a more upright position. "He has returned, then? I thought he was in Egypt."

"So he was, but he has come back, looking uncommon well, too—as brown as a berry. To my thinking, as good a fellow to look at as there is in England, and a capital fellow all round into the bargain!"

"Dear me!" says Cecil. "What a loss Egypt has sustained! And what a partisan you have become! May I ask," suppressing a pretended yawn behind her perfumed fan, "where your *rara avis* is at present hiding?"

"I asked him," says Mr. Potts, "but he rather evaded the question."

"And is *that* your Mr. Potts?" asks Molly, finding herself close to Tedcastle, speaking with heavy and suspicious emphasis.

"Yes," Tedcastle admits, coloring slightly as he remembers the glowing terms in which he has described his friend. "Don't you—eh, don't you like him?"

"Oh! like him? I cannot answer that yet; but," laughing, "I certainly don't admire him."

And indeed Mr. Potts's beauty is not of the sort to call forth raptures at first sight.

"I have seen many different shades of red in people's hair," says Molly, "but I have never seen it rosy until now. Is it dyed? It is the most curious thing I ever looked at."

As indeed it is. When introduced to poor Potts, when covering him with a first dispassionate glance, one thinks not of his pale gray orbs, his large good-humored mouth, his freckles, or his enormous nose, but only of his hair. Molly is struck by it at once.

"He is a right good fellow," says Luttrell, rather indignantly, being scarcely in the mood to laugh at Molly's sarcasms.

"He may be," is her calm reply, "but if I were he, rather than go through life with that complexion and that unhappy head, I would commit suicide."

Then there is a little more music. Marcia plays brilliantly enough, but it is almost impossible to forget during her playing that she has had an excellent master. It is not genuine, or from the heart. It is clever, but it is acquired, and falls very flatly after Molly's perfect singing, and no one in the room feels this more acutely than Marcia herself.

Then Luttrell, who has a charming voice, sings for them something pathetic and reproachful, you may be sure, as it is meant for Molly's ears; and then the evening is at an end, and they all go to their own rooms.

What a haven of rest and security is one's own room! How instinctively in grief or joy one turns to it, to hide from prying eyes one's inmost thoughts, one's hopes, and despairs!

To-night there are two sad hearts at Herst; Marcia's, perhaps, the saddest, for it is full of that most maddening, most intolerable of all pains, jealousy.

For hours she sits by her casement, pondering on the cruelty of her fate, while the unsympathetic moon pours its white rays upon her.

"Already his love is dead," she murmurs, leaning naked arms upon the window-sill, and turning her lustrous southern eyes up to the skies above her. "Already. In two short months. And how have I fallen short? how have I lost him? By over-loving, perhaps. While she, who does not value it, has gained my all."

A little groan escapes her, and she lets her dark head sink upon her outstretched arms. For there is something in Philip's eyes as they rest on Molly, something undefined, hardly formed, but surely there, that betrays to Marcia the secret feeling, of which he himself is scarcely yet aware.

One hardly knows how it is, but Molly, with a glance, a gesture, three little words pointed by a smile from the liquid eyes, can draw him to her side. And when a man of his cold, reserved nature truly loves, be sure it is a passion that will last him his life.

Tedcastle, too, is thoroughly unhappy to-night. His honest, unprying mind, made sharp by "love's conflict," has seen through Philip's infatuation, and over his last cigar before turning in (a cigar that to-night has somehow lost half its soothing properties) makes out with a sinking of the heart what it all means.

He thinks, too, yet upbraids himself for so thinking, that Miss Massereene must see that Philip Shadwell, heir to Herst and twenty thousand pounds a year, is a better catch than Teddy Luttrell, with only his great love for her, and a paltry six hundred pounds a year.

Is it not selfish of him to seek to keep her from what is so evidently to her advantage? Perhaps he ought to throw up his engagement, and, passing out of her life, leave her to reap the "good the gods provide."

In vain he tries to argue himself into this heroic frame of mind. The more he tries, the more obnoxious grows the idea. He cannot, he will not give her up.

"Faint heart," says Teddy, flinging the remnant of his cigar with fierce determination into the grate, "never won fair lady; she is mine, so far, the fairest darling that ever breathed, and be it selfish or otherwise, keep her I will if I can."

But he sighs as he utters the word "can," and finds his couch, when at length he does seek it, by no means a bed of roses.

While Molly, the pretty cause of all this heart-burning, lies in slumber, soft and sweet, and happy as can be, with her "red, red" lips apart and smiling, her breathing pure and regular as a little child's, and all her "nut-brown" hair like a silken garment round her.

Cecil Stafford, walking leisurely up and down her apartment, is feeling half frightened, half amused, at the news conveyed to her by Mr. Potts, of her husband's arrival in England. Now, at last, after these three years, she may meet him at any moment face to face.

Surely never was a story so odd, so strange as hers! A bride unknown, a wife whose face has never yet been seen!

"Well," thinks Cecil, as she seats herself while her maid binds up her long fair hair, "no use troubling about it beforehand. What must be must be. And at all events the dreaded interview cannot be too soon, as until my return to town I believe I am pretty safe from him here."

But in saying this she reckons without her host in every sense of the word.

CHAPTER XIV

"Oh, beware, my lord, of jealousy;
It is the green-eyed monster who doth mock
The meat it feeds on."
—*Othello.*

Next day at luncheon Mr. Amherst, having carefully mapped out one of his agreeable little surprises, and having selected a moment when every one is present, says to her, with a wicked gleam of anticipative amusement in his cunning old eyes:

"Sir Penthony is in England."

Although she has neither hint nor warning of what is coming, Lady Stafford is a match for him. Mr. Potts's intelligence of the evening before stands her now in good stead.

"Indeed!" she says, without betraying any former knowledge, turning eyes of the calmest upon him; "you surprise me. Tired so soon of Egyptian sphinxes! I always knew he had no taste. I hope he is quite well. I suppose you heard from him?"

"Yes. He is well, but evidently pines for home quarters and old friends. Thinking you would like to see him after so long a separation, I have invited him here. You—you don't object?"

"I?" says her ladyship, promptly, reddening, but laughing too very successfully. "Now, why should I object? On the contrary, I shall be charmed; he will be quite an acquisition. If I remember rightly,"—with a little affected drooping of the lids,—"he is a very handsome man, and, I hear, amusing."

Mr. Amherst, foiled in his amiable intention of drawing confusion on the head of somebody, subsides into a grunt and his easy-chair. To have gone to all this trouble for nothing, to have invited secretly this man, who interests him not at all, in hopes of a little excitement, and to have those hopes frustrated, disgusts him.

Yet, after all, there will, there must be some amusement in store for him, in watching the meeting between this strange pair. He at least may not prove as cool and indifferent as his pretty wife.

"He will be here to dinner to-day," he says, grumpishly, knowing that all around him are inwardly rejoicing at his defeat.

This is a thunder-bolt, though he is too much disheartened by his first defeat to notice it. Lady Stafford grows several shades paler, and—luncheon being at an end—rises hurriedly. Going toward the door, she glances back, and draws Molly by a look to her side.

"Come with me," she says; "I must speak to some one, and to you before any of the others."

When they have reached Cecil's pretty sitting-room, off which her bedroom opens, the first thing her ladyship does is to subside into a seat and laugh a little.

"It is like a play," she says, "the idea of his coming down here, to find *me* before him. It will be a surprise; for I would swear that horrible old man never told him of my being in the house, or he would not have come. Am I talking Greek to you, Molly? You know my story, surely?"

"I have heard something of it—not much—from Mr. Luttrell," says Molly, truthfully.

"It is a curious one, is it not? and one not easily matched. It all came of that horrible will. Could there be anything more stupid than for an old man to depart this life and leave behind him a document binding two young people in such a way as makes it 'do or die' with them? I had never seen my cousin in all my life, and he had never seen me; yet we were compelled at a moment's notice to marry each other or forfeit a dazzling fortune."

"Why could you not divide it?"

"Because the lawyers said we couldn't. Lawyers are always aggressive. My great-uncle had particularly declared it should not be divided. It was to be all or none, and whichever of us refused to marry the other got nothing. And there was so much!" says her ladyship, with an expressive sigh.

"It was a hard case," Molly says, with deep sympathy.

"It was. Yet, as I managed it, it wasn't half so bad. Now, I dare say many women would have gone into violent hysterics, would have driven their relations to the verge of despair and the shivering bridegroom to the brink of delirious joy, and then given in,—married the man, lived with him, and been miserable ever after. But not I."

Here she pauses, charmed at her own superior wisdom, and, leaning back in her chair, with a contented smile, puts the tips of her fingers together daintily.

"Well, and you?" says Molly, feeling intensely interested.

"I? I just reviewed the case calmly. I saw it was a great deal of money,—too much to hesitate about,—too much also to make it likely a man would dream of resigning it for the sake of a woman more or less. So I wrote to my cousin explaining that, as we had never known each other, there could be very little love lost between us, and that I saw no necessity why we ever *should* know each other,—and that I was quite willing to marry him, and take a third of the money, if he would allow me to be as little to him in the future as I was in the present, by drawing up a formal deed of separation, to be put in force at the church-door, or the door of any room where the marriage ceremony should be performed."

"Well?"

"Well, I don't know how it would have been but that, to aid my request, I inclosed a photograph of our parlormaid (one of the ugliest women it has ever been my misfortune to see), got up in her best black silk, minus the cap, and with a flaming gold chain round her neck,—you know the sort of thing,—and I never said who it was."

"Oh, Cecil, how could you?"

"How couldn't I? you mean. And, after all, my crime was of the passive order; I merely sent the picture, without saying anything. How could I help it if he mistook me for Mary Jane? Besides, I was fighting for dear life, and all is fair in love and war. I could not put up with the whims and caprices of a man to whom I was indifferent."

"Did you know he had whims and caprices?"

"Molly," says Lady Stafford, slowly, with a fine show of pity, "you are disgracefully young: cure yourself, my dear, as fast as ever you can, and as a first lesson take this to heart: if ever there was a mortal man born upon this earth without caprices it must have been in the year one, because no one that I have met knows anything about him."

"Well, for the matter of that," says Molly, laughing, "I don't suppose I should like a perfect man, even if I did chance to meet him. By all accounts they are stilted, disagreeable people, with a talent for making everybody else seem small. But go on with your story. What was his reply?"

"He agreed cordially to all my suggestions, named a very handsome sum as my portion, swore by all that was honorable he would never interfere with me in any way, was evidently ready to promise anything, and—sent me back my parlor-maid. Was not that insulting?"

"But when he came to marry you he must have seen you?"

"Scarcely. I decided on having the wedding in our drawing-room, and wrote again to say it would greatly convenience my cousin and myself (I lived with an old cousin) if he would not come down until the very morning of the wedding. Need I say he grasped at this proposition also? I was dressed and ready for my wedding by the time he arrived, and shook hands with him with my veil down. You may be sure I had secured a very thick one."

"Do you mean to tell me," says Molly, rising in her excitement, "that he never asked you to raise your veil?"

"Never, my dear. I assure you the 'best man' he brought down with him was by far the more curious of the two. But then, you must remember, Sir Penthony had seen my picture." Here Cecil goes off into a hearty burst of laughter. "If you had seen that maid once, my dear, you would not have been ambitious of a second view."

"Still I never heard of anything so cold, so unnatural," says Miss Massereene, in high disgust. "I declare I would have broken off with him then and there, had it been me."

"Not if you lived with my cousin Amelia, feeling yourself a dependent on her bounty. She was a startling instance of how a woman *can* worry and torment. The very thought of her makes my heart sore in my body and chills my blood to this day. I rejoice to say she is no more."

"Well, you got married?"

"Yes, in Amelia's drawing-room. I had a little gold band put on my third finger, I had a cold shake-hands from my husband, a sympathetic one from his groomsman, and then found myself once more alone, with a title and plenty of money, and—that's all."

"What was his friend's name?"

"Talbot Lowry. He lives about three miles from here, and"—with an airy laugh—"is rather too fond of me."

"What a strange story!" says Molly, regarding her wistfully. "Do you never wish you had married some one you loved?"

"I never do," gayly. "Don't look to me for sentiment, Molly, because I am utterly devoid of it. I know I suffer in your estimation by this confession, but it is the simple truth. I don't wish for anything. And yet"—pausing suddenly—"I do. I have been wishing for something ever since that old person down-stairs tried to take me back this morning, and failed so egregiously."

"And your wish is——"

"That I could make my husband fall madly in love with me. Oh, Molly, what a revenge that would be! And why should he not, indeed?" Going over to a glass and gazing earnestly at herself. "I am pretty,—very pretty, I think. Speak, Molly, and encourage me."

"You know you are lovely," says Molly, in such good faith that Cecil kisses her on the spot. "But what if you should fall in love with him?"

"Perhaps I have done so long ago," her ladyship replies, in a tone impossible to translate, being still intent on the contemplation of her many charms. Then, quickly, "No, no, Molly, I am fire-proof."

"Yet any day you may meet some one to whom you must give your love."

"Not a bit of it. I should despise myself forever if I once found myself letting my pulse beat half a second faster for one man than for another."

"Do you mean to tell me you have never loved?"

"Never, never, never. And, indeed, to give myself due credit, I believe the fact that I have a husband somewhere would utterly prevent anything of the sort."

"That is a good thing, if the idea lasts. But won't you feel awkward in meeting him this evening?"

"I? No, but I dare say he will; and I hope so too," says her ladyship, maliciously. "For three long years he has never been to see whether I were well or ill—or pining for him," laughing. "And yet, Molly, I do feel nervous, awfully, ridiculously nervous, at the bare idea of our so soon coming face to face.

"Is he handsome?"

"Ye—es, pretty well. Lanky sort of man, with a good deal of nose, you know, and very little whisker. On my word, now I think of it, I don't think he had any at all."

"Nose?"

"No, whisker. He was clean-shaven, all but the moustache. I suppose you know he was in Ted's regiment for some time?"

"So he told me."

"I wonder what he *hasn't* told you? Shall I confess, Molly, that I know your secret, and that it was I chose that diamond ring upon your finger? There, do not grudge me your confidence; I have given you mine and anything I have heard is safe with me. Oh, what a lovely blush, and what a shame to waste such a charming bit of color upon me! Keep it for dessert."

"How will Sir Penthony like Mr. Lowry's close proximity?" Molly asks, presently, when she has confessed a few interesting little facts to her friend.

"I hope he won't like it. If I thought I could make him jealous I would flirt with poor Talbot under his nose," says Cecil, with eloquent vulgarity. "I feel spitefully toward him somehow, although our separation was my own contrivance."

"Have you a headache, dear?" Seeing her put her hand to her head.

"A slight one,—I suppose from the nerves. I think I will lie down for an hour or two before commencing the important task of arming for conquest. And—are you going out, Molly? Will you gather me a few fresh flowers—anything white—for my hair and the bosom of my dress?"

"I will," says Molly, and, having made her comfortable with pillows and perfumes, leaves her to her siesta.

"Anything white." Molly travels the gardens up and down in search of all there is of the loveliest. Little rosebuds, fresh though late, and dainty bells, with sweet-scented geraniums and drooping heaths,—a pure and innocent bouquet.

Yet surely it lacks something,—a little fleck of green, to throw out its virgin fairness. Above, high over her head, a creeping rosebush grows, bedecked with palest, juiciest leaves.

Reaching up her hand to gather one of the taller branches, a mote, a bit of bark—some hateful thing—falls into Molly's right eye. Instant agony is the result. Tears stream from the offended pupil; the other eye joins in the general tribulation; and Molly, standing in the centre of the grass-plot, with her handkerchief pressed frantically to her face, and her lithe body swaying slightly to and fro through force of pain, looks the very personification of woe.

So thinks Philip Shadwell as, coming round the corner, he unperceived approaches.

"What is it?" he asks, trying to see her face, his tones absolutely trembling from agitation on her behalf. "Molly, you are in trouble. Can I do anything for you?"

"You can," replies Miss Massereene, in a lugubrious voice; though, in spite of her pain, she can with difficulty repress an inclination to laugh, so dismal is his manner. "Oh! you *can*."

"Tell me what. There is nothing—*Speak*, Molly."

"Well, I'm not exactly weeping," says Miss Massereene, slowly withdrawing one hand from her face, so as to let the best eye rest upon him;

"it is hardly mental anguish I'm enduring. But if you can get this awful thing that is in my eye out of it I shall be intensely grateful."

"Is that all?" asks Philip, much relieved.

"And plenty, too, I think. Here, do try if you can see anything."

"Poor eye!"—pathetically—"how inflamed it is! Let me see—there—don't blink—I won't be able to get at it if you do. Now, turn your eye to the right. No. Now to the left. Yes, there is," excitedly. "No, it isn't," disappointedly. "Now let me look below; it *must* be there."

Just at this delicate moment who should turn the corner but Luttrell! Oh, those unlucky corners that will occur in life, bringing people upon the scene, without a word of warning, at the very time when they are least wanted!

Luttrell, coming briskly onward in search of his ladylove, sees, marks, and comes to a dead stop. And this is what he sees.

Molly in Philip's—well, if not exactly in his embrace, something very near it; Philip looking with wild anxiety into the very depths of Molly's lovely eyes, while the lovely eyes look back at Philip full of deep entreaty. Tableau!

It is too much. Luttrell, stung cruelly, turns as if to withdraw, but after a step or two finds himself unable to carry out the dignified intention, and pauses irresolutely. His back being turned, however, he is not in at the closing act, when Philip produces triumphantly on the tip of his finger such a mere atom of matter as makes one wonder how it could ever have caused so much annoyance.

"Are you better now?" he asks, anxiously, yet with pardonable pride.

"I—am—thank you." Blinking thoughtfully, as though not yet assured of the relief. "I am so much obliged to you. And—yes, I *am* better. Quite well, I think. What should I have done without you?"

"Ah, that I could believe myself necessary to you at any time!" Philip is beginning, with fluent sentimentality, when, catching sight of Tedcastle, he stops abruptly. "Here is Luttrell," he says, in an injured tone, and seeing no further prospect of a *tête-à-tête*, takes his departure.

Molly is still petting her wounded member when Luttrell reaches her side.

"What is the matter with you?" he asks, with odious want of sympathy. "Have you been crying?"

"No," replies Molly, indignant at his tone,—so unlike Shadwell's. "Why should you think so?"

"Why? Because your eyes are red; and certainly as I came up, Shadwell appeared to be doing his utmost to console you."

"Anything the matter with you, Teddy?" asks Miss Massereene, with suspicious sweetness. "You seem put out."

"Yes,"—sternly,—"and with cause. I do not relish coming upon you suddenly and finding you in Shadwell's arms."

"Where?"

"Well, if not exactly in his arms, very nearly there," says Tedcastle, vehemently.

"You are forgetting yourself." Coldly. "If you are jealous of Philip, say so, but do not disgrace yourself by using coarse language. There was a bit of bark in my eyes. I suppose you think it would have been better for me to endure torments than allow Philip—who was very kind—to take it out? If you do, I differ from you."

"I am not speaking alone of this particular instance in which you seem to favor Shadwell," says the young man, moodily, his eyes fixed upon the sward beneath him. "Every day it grows more palpable. You scarcely care to hide your sentiments now."

"You mean"—impatiently—"you would wish me to speak to no one except you. You don't take into account how slow this would be for me." She says this cruelly. "I care no more for Philip than I do for any other man."

"Just so. I am the other man, no doubt. I have never been blind to the fact that you do not care for me. Why take the trouble of acting a part any longer?"

"'Acting a part'! Nonsense!" says Molly. "I always think that the most absurd phrase in the world. Who does not act a part? The thing is to act a good one."

"Is yours a good part?" Bitterly.

"You are the best judge of that," returns she, haughtily. "If you do not think so, why keep to our engagement? If you wish to break it, you need fear no opposition from me." So saying, she sweeps past him and enters the house.

Yet in spite of her anger and offended pride, her eyes are wet and her hands trembling as she reaches Cecil's room and lays the snow-white flowers upon her table.

Cecil is still lying comfortably ensconced among her pillows, but has sufficient wakefulness about her to notice Molly's agitation.

"You have been quarreling, *ma belle*," she says, raising herself on her elbow; "don't deny it. Was it with Marcia or Tedcastle?"

"Tedcastle," Molly replies, laughing against her will at the other's shrewdness, and in consequence wiping away a few tears directly afterward. "It is nothing; but he is really intolerably jealous, and I can't and won't put up with it."

"Oh, that some one was jealous about me!" says Cecil, with a prolonged sigh. "Go on."

"It was nothing, I tell you. All because Philip kindly picked a little bit of dust out of my eye."

"How good of Philip! considering all the dust you have thrown into his of late. And Ted objected?"

"Yes, and was very rude into the bargain. I wouldn't have believed it of him."

"Well, you know yourself you have been going on anyhow with Philip during the past few days."

"Oh, Cecil, how can you say so? Am I to turn my back on him when he comes to speak to me? And even supposing I had flirted egregiously with him (which is not the case), is that a reason why one is to be scolded and abused and have all sorts of the most dreadful things said to one?" (I leave my readers to deplore the glaring exaggeration of this speech.) "He looked, too, as if he could have eaten me then and there. I know this, I shan't forgive him in a hurry."

"Poor Ted! I expect he doesn't have much of a time with you," says Cecil, shaking her head.

"Are you laughing at me?" cries Molly, wrathfully. "Then make ready for death." And, taking the smaller Cecil in her arms, she most unkindly lifts her from among her cozy cushions and deposits her upon the floor. "There! Now will you repent? But come, Cecil, get up, and prepare for your husband's reception. I will be your maid to-night, if you will let me. What will you wear?"

"Pale blue. It suits me best. See, that is my dress." Pointing to a light-blue silk, trimmed with white lace, that lies upon the bed. "Will you really help me to dress? But you cannot do my hair?"

"Try me."

She does try, and proves so highly satisfactory that Cecil is tempted to offer splendid wages if she will consent to come and live with her.

The hair is a marvel of artistic softness. Every fresh jewel lends a grace; and when at length Cecil is attired in her blue gown, she is all that any one could possibly desire.

"Now, honestly, how do I look?" she asks, turning round to face Molly. "Anything like a housemaid?" With a faint laugh that has something tremulous about it.

"I never saw you half so charming," Molly answers, deliberately. "Oh, Cecil! what will he say when he finds out—when he discovers how you have deceived him?"

"Anything he likes, my dear!" exclaims Cecil, gayly giving a last touch to the little soft fair locks near her temples. "He ought to be pleased. It would be a different thing altogether, and a real grievance, if, being like the housemaid, I had sent him a photo of Venus. He might justly complain then; but now— — There, I can do no more!" says her ladyship, with a sigh, half pleased, half fearful. "If I weren't so shamefully nervous I would do very well."

"I don't believe you are half as frightened for yourself at this moment as I am for you. If I were in your shoes I should faint. It is to me an awful ordeal."

"I am so white, too," says Cecil, impatiently. "You haven't—I suppose, Molly—but of course you haven't— —"

"What, dear?"

"Rouge. After all, Therese was right. When leaving town she asked me should she get some; and, when I rejected the idea with scorn, said there was no knowing when one might require it. Perhaps afterward she did put it in. Let us ring and ask her."

"Never mind it. You are no comparison prettier without it. Cecil,"— doubtingly,—"I hope when it comes to the last moment you will have nerve."

"Be happy," says Cecil. "I am always quite composed at last moments; that is one of my principal charms. I never create sensations through vulgar excitement. I shall probably astonish you (and myself also) by my extreme coolness. In the meantime I"—smiling—"I own I should like a glass of sherry. What o'clock is it, Molly?"

"Just seven."

"Ah! he must be here now. How I wish it was over!" says Lady Stafford, with a little sinking of the heart.

"And I am not yet dressed. I must run," exclaims Molly. "Good-bye, Cecil. Keep up your spirits, and remember above all things how well your dress becomes you."

Two or three minutes elapse,—five,—and still Cecil cannot bring herself to descend. She is more nervous about this inevitable meeting than she cares to own. Will he be openly cold, or anxious to conciliate, or annoyed? The latter she greatly fears. What if he should suspect her of having asked Mr. Amherst to invite him? This idea torments her more than all the others, and chains her to her room.

She takes up another bracelet and tries it on. Disliking the effect, she takes it off again. So she trifles, in fond hope of cheating time, and would probably be trifling now had not the handle of her door been boldly turned, the door opened, and a young man come confidently forward.

His confidence comes to an untimely end as his astonished eyes rest on Cecil.

"I beg your pardon, I'm sure," he says, beating a hasty retreat back to the landing outside. "I had no idea—I'm awfully sorry—but this room used to be mine."

"It is mine now," says Cecil, accepting the situation at a glance, recognizing Sir Penthony without hesitation.

He is a tall young man,—"lanky," as she has herself expressed him,—with thick brown hair, closely cropped. He has handsome dark eyes, with a rather mocking expression in them, and has a trick of shutting them slightly if puzzled or annoyed. His voice is extremely charming, though it has a distinct croak (that can hardly be called husky or hoarse) that is rather fascinating. His short upper lip is covered by a heavy brown moustache that hides a laughing mouth. He is aristocratic and good-looking, without being able to lay claim to actual beauty.

Just now he is overwhelmed with confusion, as Cecil, feeling compelled thereto, steps forward, smiling, to reassure him.

"You have made a mistake,—you have lost your way," she says, in a tone that trembles ever such a little in spite of her efforts to be calm.

"To my shame I confess it," he says, laughing, gazing with ill-concealed admiration at this charming azure vision standing before him. "Foolishly I forgot to ask for my room, and ran up the stairs, feeling certain that the one that used to be mine long ago must be so still. Can you forgive me?"

"I think I can. Meantime, if you are Sir Penthony Stafford, your room lies there," pointing to the last door opening on the corridor.

"Thank you," yet making no haste to reach the discovered shelter. "May I not know to whom I am indebted for so much kindness?"

"I dare say you will be introduced in proper form by and by," says Cecil, demurely, making a movement as though to leave him. "When you are dressed you shall be formally presented."

"At least," he asks, hastily, with a view to detaining her, "do me one more service before you go. If you know me so well, perhaps you can tell me if any of my friends are staying here at present?"

"Several. Teddy Luttrell for one."

"Indeed! And— —"

"The Darleys. You know them?"

"Little woman,—dolly,—bizarre in manner and dress?"

"A most accurate description. And there is another friend,—one who ought to be your dearest: I allude to Lady Stafford."

"Lady Stafford!"

"Yes, your wife. You don't seem over and above pleased at my news."

"Is a man always pleased at his wife's unexpected appearance?" asks Sir Penthony, recovering himself with a rather forced laugh. "I had no idea she was here. I— — Is she a friend of yours?"

"The dearest friend I have. I know no one," declares her ladyship, fervently, "I love so fondly."

"Happy Lady Stafford! I almost think I would change places with her this moment. At all events, whatever faults she may possess, she has rare taste in friends."

"You speak disparagingly. Has she a fault?"

"The greatest a woman can have: she lacks that one quality that would make her a 'joy forever.'"

"Your severity makes you unkind. And yet, do you know she is greatly liked. Nay, she has been *loved*. Perhaps when you come to know her a little better (I do not conceal from you that I have heard something of your story), you will think more tenderly of her. Remember, 'beauty is only skin deep.'"

"Yes,"—with a light laugh,—"But 'ugliness goes to the bone.'"

"That is the retort discourteous. I see it is time wasted to plead my friend's cause. Although, perhaps,"—reproachfully,—"not blessed with actual beauty, still——"

"No, there's *not* much beauty about her," says Sir Penthony, with something akin to a groan. Then, "I beg your pardon," he murmurs; "pray excuse me. Why should I trouble a stranger with my affairs?" He stands aside, with a slight bow, to let her pass. "And you won't tell me your name?" he cannot resist saying before losing sight of her.

"Make haste with your dressing; you shall know then," glancing back at him, with a bewitching smile.

"Be sure I shall waste no time. If, in my hurry, I appear to less advantage than usual to-night, you must not be the one to blame me."

"A very fair beginning," says Cecil, as she slips away. "Now I must be firm. But, oh dear, oh dear! he is much handsomer even than I thought."

CHAPTER XV

"If I am not worth the wooing,
I surely am not worth the winning."

—*Miles Standish.*

The minutes, selfishly thoughtless of all but themselves, fly rapidly. Cecil makes her way to the drawing-room, where she is followed presently by Molly, then by Luttrell; but, as these two latter refuse to converse with each other, conversation is rather one-sided.

Mr. Amherst, contrary to his usual custom, appears very early on the field, evidently desirous of enjoying the fray to its utmost. He looks quite jubilant and fresh for him, and his nose is in a degree sharper than its wont. He opens an animated discourse with Cecil; but Lady Stafford, although *distrait* and with her mind on the stretch, listening for every sound outside, replies brilliantly, and, woman-like, conceals her anxiety with her tongue.

At length the dreaded moment comes. There is a sound of footfalls, nearer—nearer still—then, "clearer, deadlier than before," and the door opens, to discover Sir Penthony upon the threshold.

Lady Stafford is sitting within the embrasure of the window.

"Fortune favors me," she says hurriedly to Molly, alluding to the other guests' non-appearance.

"Your wife is staying with me," Mr. Amherst begins, complacently; and, pointing to Cecil, "Allow me to introduce you to——"

"Lady Stafford," Cecil interrupts, coming forward while a good deal of rich crimson mantles in her cheeks. She is looking lovely from excitement; and her pretty, rounded, graceful figure is shown off to the best advantage by the heavy fall of the red draperies behind her.

Sir Penthony gazes, spell-bound, at the gracious creature before him; the color recedes from his lips and brow; his eyes grow darker. Luttrell with difficulty suppresses a smile. Mr. Amherst is almost satisfied.

"You are welcome," Cecil says, with perfect self-possession, putting out her hand and absolutely taking his; for so stunned is he by her words that he even forgets to offer it.

Drawing him into a recess of the window, she says, reproachfully, "Why do you look so astonished? Do you not know that you are gratifying that abominable old man? And will you not say you are glad to see me after all these long three years?"

"I don't understand," Sir Penthony says, vaguely. "Are there two Lady Staffords? And whose wife are you?"

"Yours! Although you don't seem in a hurry to claim me," she says, with a rarely pretty pout.

"Impossible!"

"I am sorry to undeceive you, but it is indeed the truth I speak."

"And whose picture did I get?" he asks, a faint glimmer of the real facts breaking in upon him.

"The parlor-maid's," says Cecil, now the strain is off her, laughing heartily and naturally,—so much so that the other occupants of the room turn to wonder enviously what is going on behind the curtains. "The parlor-maid! And such a girl as she was! Do you remember her nose? It was celestial. When that deed on which we agreed was sealed, signed, and delivered, without hope of change, I meant to send you my real photo, but somehow I didn't. I waited until we should meet; and now we have met and— — Why do you look so disconsolate? Surely, surely, I am an improvement on Mary Jane?"

"It isn't that," he says, "but—what a fool I have been!"

"You have indeed," quickly. "The idea of letting that odious old man see your discomfiture! By the bye, does my 'ugliness go to the bone,' Sir Penthony?"

"Don't! When I realize my position I hate myself."

"Could you not even see my hair was yellow, whilst Mary Jane's was black,—a sooty black?"

"How could I see anything? Your veil was so thick, and, besides, I never doubted the truth of— —"

"Oh, that veil! What trouble I had with it!" laughs Cecil. "First I doubled it, and then nearly died with fright lest you should imagine me the Pig-faced Lady, and insist on seeing me."

"Well, and if I had?"

"Without doubt you would have fallen in love with me," coquettishly.

"Would not that have been desirable? Is it not a good thing for a man to fall in love with the woman he is going to marry?"

"Not unless the woman falls in love with him," with a little expressive nod that speaks volumes.

"Ah! true," says Sir Penthony, rather nettled.

"However, you showed no vulgar curiosity on the occasion, although I think Mr. Lowry, who supported you at the last moment, suggested the advisability of seeing your bride. Ah, that reminds me he lives near here. You will be glad to renew acquaintance with so particular a friend."

"There was nothing particular about our friendship; I met him by chance in London at the time, and—er—he did as well as any other fellow."

"Better, I should say. He is a particular friend of mine."

"Indeed! I shouldn't have thought him your style. Like Cassius, he used to have a 'lean and hungry look.'"

"Used he? I think him quite good-looking."

"He must have developed, then, in body as in intellect. Three years ago he was a very gaunt youth indeed."

"Of course, Stafford," breaks in Mr. Amherst's rasping voice, "we can all make allowances for your joy on seeing your wife again after such a long absence. But you must not monopolize her. Remember she is the life of our party."

"Thank you, Mr. Amherst. What a delightful compliment!" says Cecil, with considerable *empressement*. "Sir Penthony was just telling me what an enjoyable voyage he had; and I was congratulating him. There is nothing on earth so depressing or so humiliating as sea-sickness. Don't you agree with me?"

Mr. Amherst mutters something in which the word "brazen" is distinctly heard; while Cecil, turning to her companion, says hastily, holding out her hand, with a soft, graceful movement:

"We are friends?"

"Forever, I trust," he replies, taking the little plump white hand within his own, and giving it a hearty squeeze.

To some the evening is a long one,—to Luttrell and Molly, for instance, who are at daggers drawn and maintain a dignified silence toward each other.

Tedcastle, indeed, holds his head so high that if by chance his gaze should rest in Molly's direction, it must perforce pass over her without fear of descending to her face. (This is wise, because to look at Molly is to find one's self disarmed.) There is an air of settled hostility about him that angers her beyond all words.

"What does he mean by glowering like that, and looking as though he could devour somebody? How different he used to be in dear old Brooklyn! Who could have thought he would turn out such a Tartar? Well, there is no knowing any man; and yet— — It is a pity not to give him something to glower about," thinks Miss Massereene, in an access of rage, and forthwith deliberately sets herself out to encourage Shadwell and Mr. Potts.

She has a brilliant success, and, although secretly sore at heart, manages to pass her time agreeably, and, let us hope, profitably.

Marcia, whose hatred toward her rival grows with every glance cast at her from Philip's eyes, turns to Tedcastle and takes him in hand. Her voice is low, her manner subdued, but designing. Whatever she may be saying is hardly likely to act as cure to Teddy's heart-ache; at least so thinks Cecil, and, coming to the rescue, sends Sir Penthony across to talk to him, and drawing him from Marcia's side, leads him into a lengthened history of all those who have come and gone in the old regiment since he sold out.

The *ruse* is successful, but leaves Cecil still indignant with Molly. "What a wretched little flirt she is!" She turns an enraged glance upon where Miss Massereene is sitting deep in a discussion with Mr. Potts.

"Have you any Christian name?" Molly is asking, with a beaming smile, fixing her liquid Irish eyes upon the enslaved Potts. "I hear you addressed as Mr. Potts,—as Potts even—but never by anything that might be mistaken for a first name."

"Yes," replies Mr. Potts, proudly. "I was christened Plantagenet. Good sound, hasn't it? Something to do with the Dark Ages and Pinnock, only I never remember clearly what. Our fellows have rather a low way of abbreviating it and bringing it down to 'Planty.' And—would you believe it?—on one or two occasions they have so far forgotten themselves as to call me 'the regular Plant.'"

"What a shame!" says Miss Massereene, with deep sympathy.

"Let 'em," says Mr. Potts, heroic, if vulgar, shaking his crimson head. "It's fun to them, and it's by no means 'death' to me. It does no harm. But it's a nuisance to have one's mother put to the trouble of concocting a fine name, if one doesn't get the benefit of it."

"I agree with you. Were I a man, and rejoiced in such a name as Plantagenet, I would insist upon having every syllable of it distinctly sounded, or I'd know the reason why. 'All or nothing' should be my motto."

"I never think of it, I don't see my wife's cards," says Mr. Potts, who has had a good deal of champagne, and is rather moist about the eyes. "'Mrs. Plantagenet Potts' would look well, wouldn't it?"

"Very aristocratic," says false Molly, with an admiring nod. "I almost think,—I am not quite sure,—but I almost think I would marry a man to bear a name like that."

"Would you?" cries Mr. Potts, his tongue growing freer, while enthusiasm sparkles in every feature. "If I only thought that, Miss Molly——"

"How pretty Mrs. Darley is looking to-night!" interrupts Molly, adroitly; "what a clear complexion she has!—just like a child's."

"Not a bit of it," says Mr. Potts. "Children don't require 'cream of roses' and 'Hebe bloom' and—and all that sort of thing, you know—to get 'emselves up."

"Ah! my principal pity for her is that she doesn't seem to have anything to say."

"Englishwomen never have, as a rule; they are dull to the last degree. Now, you are a singular exception."

"English! I am not English," says Molly, with exaggerated disgust. "Do not offend me. I am Irish—altogether, thoroughly Irish,—heart and mind a Paddy."

"No! are you, by Jove?" says Mr. Potts. "So am I—at least, partly so. My mother is Irish."

So she had been English, Welsh, and Scotch on various occasions; there is scarcely anything Mrs. Potts had *not* been. There was even one memorable occasion on which she had had Spanish blood in her veins, and (according to Plantagenet's account) never went out without a lace mantilla flowing from her foxy head. It would, indeed, be rash to fix on any nationality to which the venerable lady might not lay claim, when her son's interests so willed it.

"She came from—er—Galway," he says now; "good old family too— but—out at elbows and—and—that."

"Yes?" Molly says, interested. "And her name?"

"Blake," replies he, unblushingly, knowing there never was a Blake that did not come out of Galway.

"I feel quite as though I had known you forever," says Molly, much pleased. "You know my principal crime is my Hibernian extraction, which perhaps makes me cling to the fact more and more. Mr. Amherst cannot forgive me—my father."

"Yet he was of good family, I believe, and all that?" questioningly.

"Beyond all doubt. What a question for you to ask! Did you ever hear of an Irishman who wasn't of good family? My father"—with a mischievous smile—"was a direct descendant of King O'Toole or Brian Boru,—I don't know which; and if the king had only got his own, my dear brother would at this moment be dispensing hospitality in a palace."

"You terrify me," said Mr. Potts, profoundly serious. "Why, the blood of all the Howards would be weak as water next to yours. Not that there is anything to be surprised at; for if over there was any one in the world who ought to be a princess it is——"

"Molly, will you sing us something?" Lady Stafford breaks in, impatiently, at this juncture, putting a stop to Mr. Potts's half-finished compliment.

"Molly, I want to speak to you for a moment," Luttrell says next day, coming upon her suddenly in the garden.

"Yes?" coldly. "Well, hurry, then; they are waiting for me in the tennis-ground."

"It seems to me that some one is always waiting for you now when I want to speak to you," says the young man, bitterly.

"For me?" with a would-be-astonished uplifting of her straight brows. "Oh, no, I am not in such request at Herst. I am ready to listen to you at any time; although I must confess I do not take kindly to lecturing."

"Do I lecture you?"

"Do not let us waste time going into details: ask me this all-important question and let me be gone."

"I want to know"—severely, yet anxiously—"whether you really meant all you said yesterday morning?"

"Yesterday morning!" says Miss Massereene, running all her ten little white fingers through her rebellious locks, and glancing up at him despairingly. "Do you really expect me to remember all I may have said yesterday morning? Think how long ago it is."

"Shall I refresh your memory? You gave me to understand that if our engagement came to an end you would be rather relieved than otherwise."

"Did I? How very odd! Yes, by the bye, I do recollect something of the kind. And you led up to it, did you not?—almost asked me to say it, I think, by your unkind remarks."

"Let us keep to the truth," says Luttrell, sternly. "You know such an idea would never cross my mind. While you—I hardly know what to think. All last night you devoted yourself to Shadwell."

"That is wrong; he devoted himself to me. Besides, I spoke a little to Mr. Potts."

"Yes, I suppose you could not be satisfied to let even an idiot like Potts go free."

"Idiot! Good gracious! are you talking of your friend Mr. Potts? Why, I was tired to death of hearing his praises sung in my ears morning, noon, and night at Brooklyn; and now, because I am barely civil to him, he must be called an idiot! That is rather severe on him, is it not?"

"Never mind Potts. I am thinking principally of Shadwell. Of course, you are quite at liberty to spend your time with whom you choose, but at all events I have the right to know what you mean seriously to do. You have to decide between Shadwell and me."

"I shall certainly not be rude to Philip," Molly says, decisively, leaning against the trunk of a flowering tree, and raising defiant, beautiful violet eyes to his. "You seem to pass your time very agreeably with Marcia. I do not complain, mind, but I like fairness in all things."

"I thought little country girls like you were all sweetness, and freshness, and simplicity," says Luttrell, with sudden vehemence. "What lies one hears in one's lifetime! Why, you might give lessons in coquetry and cruelty to many a town-bred woman."

"Might I? I am glad you appraise me so highly. I am glad I have escaped all the 'sweetness, and freshness,' and general imbecility the orthodox village maiden is supposed to possess. Though why a girl must necessarily be devoid of wit simply because she has spent her time in good, healthy air, is a thing that puzzles me. Have you delayed me only to say this?"

"No, Molly," cries Luttrell, desperately, while Molly, with cool fingers and a calm face, plucks a flower to pieces, "it is impossible you can have so soon forgotten. Think of all the happy days at Brooklyn, all the vows we interchanged. Is there inconstancy in the very air at Herst?"

His words are full of entreaty, his manner is not. There is an acidity about the latter that irritates Molly.

"All Irish people are fickle," she says recklessly, "and I am essentially Irish."

"All Irish people are kind-hearted, and you are not so," retorts he. "Every hour yields me an additional pang. For the last two days you have avoided me,—you do not care to speak to me,—you——"

"How can I, when you spend your entire time upbraiding me and accusing me of things of which I am innocent?"

"I neither accuse nor upbraid; I only say that——"

"Well, I don't think you can say much more,"—maliciously,—"because—I see Philip coming."

He has taken her hand, but now, stung by her words and her evident delight at Shadwell's proximity, flings it furiously from him.

"If so, it is time I went," he says, and turning abruptly from her, walks toward the corner that must conceal him from view.

A passing madness seizes Molly. Fully conscious that Luttrell is still within hearing, fatally conscious that it is within her power to wound him and gain a swift revenge for all the hard words she chooses to believe he has showered down on her, she sings,—slightly altering the ideas of the poet to suit her own taste,—she sings, as though to the approaching Philip:

> "He is coming, my love, my sweet!
>
> Was it ever so airy a tread,
>
> My heart would know it and beat,
>
> Had it lain for a century dead."

She smiles coquettishly, and glances at Shadwell from under her long dark lashes. He is near enough to hear and understand; so is Luttrell. With a suppressed curse the latter grinds his heel into the innocent gravel and departs.

CHAPTER XVI

"Love is hurt with jar and fret,

Love is made a vague regret,

Eyes with idle tears are wet."

—*The Miller's Daughter.*

It is evening; the shadows are swiftly gathering. Already the dusk—sure herald of night—is here. Above in the trees the birds are crooning their last faint songs and ruffling their feathers on their night-perches.

How short the days have grown! Even into the very morning of sweet September there has fallen a breath of winter,—a chill, cold breath that tells us summer lies behind.

Luttrell, with downcast eyes and embittered heart, tramples through the same green wood (now, alas, fuller of fallen leaves) where first, at Herst, he and Molly re-met.

With a temperament as warm but less hopeful than hers, he sees the imaginary end that lies before him and his beloved. She has forsaken him, she is the bride of another,—that other is Shadwell. She is happy with him. This last thought, strange to say, is the unkindest cut of all.

He has within his hand a stout stick he took from a tree as he walked along; at this point of the proceeding he breaks it in two and flings it to one side. Happy! away from him, with perhaps only a jesting recollection of all the sweet words, the tender thoughts he has bestowed upon her! The thought is agony; and, if so, what will the reality be?

At all events he need not witness it. He will throw up his commission, and go abroad,—that universal refuge for broken hearts; though why we must intrude our griefs and low spirits and general unpleasantnesses upon our foreign neighbors is a subject not yet sufficiently canvassed. It seems so unkind toward our foreign neighbors.

A rather shaky but consequently picturesque bridge stretches across a little stream that slowly, lovingly babbles through this part of the wood. Leaning upon its parapet, Luttrell gives himself up a prey to gloomiest forebodings, and with the utmost industry calls up before him all the most miserable possibilities. He has reached the verge of suicide,—in a moment more (in his "mind's eye") he will be over, when a delicious voice behind him says, demurely:

"May I pass, please?"

It is Molly: such a lovely Molly!—such a naughty unrepentant, winsome Molly, with the daintiest and widest of straw hats, twined with wild flowers, thrown somewhat recklessly toward the back of her head.

"I am sorry to disturb you," says this apparition, gazing at him unflinchingly with big, innocent eyes, "but I do not think there is room on this bridge for two to pass."

Luttrell instantly draws his tall, slight, handsome figure to its fullest height, and, without looking at her, literally crushes himself against the frail railing behind him, lest by any means he should touch her as she passes. But she seems in no hurry to pass.

"It is my opinion," she says, in a matter-of-fact tone of warning, "that those wooden railings have seen their best days; and if you try them much harder you will find, if not a watery grave, at all events an exceedingly moist coat."

There is so much truth in this remark that Luttrell sees the wisdom of abstaining from further trial of their strength, and, falling into an easier position, makes as though he too would leave the bridge by the side from which she came on it. This brings them nearly face to face.

Now, dear reader, were you ever in the middle of a crossing, eager to reach the other side of the street? And did you ever meet anybody coming toward you on that crossing, also anxious to reach his other side of the street? And did you ever find yourself and that person politely dancing before each other for a minute or so, debarring each other's progress, because, unhappily, both your thoughts led you in the same direction? And did you ever feel an irresistible desire to stop short and laugh aloud in that person's face? Because now all this happens to Molly and Luttrell.

Each appears full of a dignified haste to quit the other's society. Molly steps to the right, so does Luttrell to the left, at the very same instant; Luttrell, with angry correction of his first movement, steps again to his first position, and so, without pausing, does Molly. Each essay only leaves them as they began, looking fair into each other's eyes. When this has happened three times, Molly stops short and bursts into a hearty laugh.

"Do try to stay still for one second," she says, with a smile, "and then perhaps we shall manage it. Thank you."

Then, being angry with herself, for her mistaken merriment, like a true woman she vents her displeasure upon him.

"I suppose you knew I was coming here this evening," she exclaims, with ridiculous injustice, "and followed to spoil any little peace I might have?"

"I did not know you were coming here. Had I known it——"

A pause.

"Well,"—imperiously,—"why do you hesitate? Say the unkind thing. I hate innuendoes. Had you known it——"

"I should certainly have gone the other way." Coldly: "Meanly as you may think of me, I have not fallen so low that I should seek to annoy you by my presence."

"Then without doubt you have come to this quiet place searching for solitude, in which to think out all your hard thoughts of me."

"I never think hardly of you, Molly."

"You certainly were not thinking kindly."

Now, he might easily have abashed her at this point by asking "where was the necessity to think of her at all?" but there is an innate courtesy, a natural gentleness about Luttrell that utterly forbids him.

"And," goes on his tormentor, the more angry that she cannot induce him to revile her, "I do not wish you to call me 'Molly' any more. Only those who—who love me call me by that name. Marcia and my grandfather (two people I detest) call me Eleanor. You can follow their example for the future."

"There will not be any future. I have been making up my mind, and—I shall sell out and go abroad immediately."

"Indeed!" There was a slight, a very slight, tremble in her saucy tones. "What a sudden determination! Well, I hope you will enjoy yourself. It is charming weather for a pleasure-trip."

"It is."

"You shouldn't lose much more time, however. Winter will soon be here; and it must be dismal in the extreme traveling in frost and snow."

"I assure you"—bitterly—"there is no occasion to hurry me. I am as anxious to go as ever you could desire."

"May I ask when you are going, and where?"

"No, you may not," cries he, at length fiercely goaded past endurance; "only, be assured of this: I am going as far from you as steam can take me; I am going where your fatal beauty and heartlessness cannot touch me; where I shall not be maddened day by day by your coquetry, and where perhaps—in time—I may learn to forget you."

His indignation has made him appear at least two inches taller than his ordinary six feet. His face is white as death, his lips are compressed beneath his blonde moustache, his dark blue eyes—not unlike Molly's own—are flashing fire.

"Thank you," says his companion, with exaggerated emphasis and a graceful curtsey; "thank you very much, Mr. Luttrell. I had no idea, when I lingered here for one little moment, I was going to hear so many home truths. I certainly do not want to hear any more."

"Then why don't you go?" puts in Luttrell, savagely.

"I would—only—perhaps you may not be aware of it, but you have your foot exactly on the very end of my gown."

Luttrell raises his foot and replaces it upon the shaking planks with something that strongly resembles a stamp,—so strongly as to make the treacherous bridge quake and tremble; while Molly moves slowly away from him until she reaches the very edge of their uncertain resting-place.

Here she pauses, glances backward, and takes another step, only to pause again,—this time with decision.

"Teddy," she says, softly.

No answer.

"Dear Teddy," more softly still.

No answer.

"*Dearest* Teddy."

Still no answer.

"Teddy—*darling!*" murmurs Molly, in the faintest, fondest tone, using toward him for the first time this tenderest of all tender love words.

In another moment his arms are around her, her head is on his breast. He is vanquished,—routed with slaughter.

In the heart of this weak-minded, infatuated young man there lingers not the slightest thought of bitterness toward this girl who has caused him so many hours of torment, and whose cool, soft cheek now rests contentedly against his.

"My love,—my own,—you do care for me a little?" he asks, in tones that tremble with gladness and sorrow, and disbelief.

"Of course, foolish boy." With a bright smile that revives him. "That is, at times, when you do not speak to me as though I were the fell destroyer of your peace or the veriest shrew that ever walked the earth. Sometimes, you know,"—with a sigh,—"you are a very uncomfortable Teddy."

She slips a fond warm arm around his shoulder and caresses the back of his neck with her soft fingers. Coquette she may be, flirt she is to her finger-tips, but nothing can take away from her lovableness. To Luttrell she is at this moment the most charming thing on which the sun ever shone.

"How can you be so unkind to me," he says, "so cold? Don't you know it breaks my heart?"

"*I* cold!" With reproachful wonder. "*I* unkind! Oh, Teddy! and what are you? Think of all you said to me yesterday and this morning; and now, now you called me a coquette! What could be worse than that? To say it of me, of all people! Ted,"—with much solemnity,—"stare at me,—stare *hard*,—and see do I look the *very least bit* in the world like a coquette?"

He does stare hard, and doing so forgets the question in hand, remembering only that her eyes, her lips, her hair are all the most perfect of their kind.

"My beloved," he whispers, caressingly.

"It is all your own fault," goes on Circe, strong in argument. "When I provoke you I care nothing for Philip Shadwell, or your Mr. Potts, or any of them: but when you are uncivil to me, what am I to do? I am driven into speaking to some one, although I don't in the least care for general admiration, as you well know."

He does not know; common sense forbids him to know; but she is telling her fibs with so much grace of feature and voice that he refuses to see her sin. He tries, therefore, to look as if he agreed with her, and succeeds very fairly.

"Then you did not mean anything you said?" he asks, eagerly.

"Not a syllable," says Molly. "Though even if I did you will forgive me, won't you? You always do forgive me, don't you?"

It would be impossible to describe the amount of pleading, sauciness, coaxing she throws into the "won't you?" and "don't you?" holding up her face, too, and looking at him out of half-shut, laughing, violet eyes.

"I suppose so," he says, smiling. "So abject a subject have I become that I can no longer conceal even from myself the fact that you can wind me round your little finger."

He tightens his arm about her, and considering, I dare say, she owes him some return for so humble a speech—stoops as though to put his lips to hers.

"Not yet," she says, pressing her fingers against his mouth. "I have many things to say to you yet before—— For one, I am not a coquette?"

"No."

"And you are not going abroad to—forget me? Oh, Teddy!"

"If I went to the world's end I could not compass that. No, I shall not go abroad now."

"And"—half removing the barring fingers—"I am the dearest, sweetest, best Molly to be found anywhere?"

"Oh, darling! don't you know I think so?" says Luttrell, with passionate fondness.

"And you will never forgive yourself for making me so unhappy?"

"Never."

"Very well,"—taking away her hand, with a contented sigh,—"now you may kiss me."

So their quarrel ends, as all her quarrels do, by every one being in the wrong except herself. It is their first bad quarrel; and although we are told "the falling out of faithful friends is but the renewal of love," still, believe me, each angry word creates a gap in the chain of love,—a gap that widens and ever widens more and more, until at length comes the terrible day when the cherished chain falls quite asunder. A second coldness is so much easier than a first!

CHAPTER XVII

"One silly cross

Wrought all my loss.

O frowning fortune!"

—The Passionate Pilgrim.

It was an unfortunate thing,—nay, more, it was an unheard-of thing (because for a man to fall in love with his own wife has in it all the elements of absurdity, and makes one lose faith in the wise saws and settled convictions of centuries),—but the fact remained. From the moment Sir Penthony Stafford came face to face with his wife in the corridor at Herst he lost his heart to her.

There only rested one thing more to make the catastrophe complete, and that also came to pass: Cecil was fully and entirely aware of his sentiments with regard to her.

What woman but knows when a man loves her? What woman but knows (in spite of all the lies she may utter to her own heart) when a man has ceased to love her? In dark moments, in the cruel quiet of midnight, has not the terrible certainty of her loss made her youth grow dead within her?

Cecil's revenge has come, and I hardly think she spares it. Scrupulously, carefully, she adheres to her *rôle* of friend, never for an instant permitting him to break through the cold barricade of mere good-fellowship she has raised between them.

Should he in an imprudent moment seek to undermine this barrier, by a word, a smile, sweet but chilling, she expresses either astonishment or amusement at his presumption (the latter being perhaps the more murderous weapon of the two, as ridicule is death to love), and so checks him.

To her Sir Penthony is an acquaintance,—a rather amusing one, but still an acquaintance only,—and so she gives him to understand; while he chafes and curses his luck a good deal at times, and—grows desperately jealous.

The development of this last quality delights Cecil. Her flirtation with Talbot Lowry,—not that it can be called a flirtation, being a very one-sided affair, the affection Talbot entertains for her being the only affection about it,—carefully as he seeks to hide it, irritates Sir Penthony beyond endurance, and, together with her marked coldness and apparent want of desire for his society, renders him thoroughly unhappy.

All this gratifies Cecil, who is much too real a woman not to find pleasure in seeing a man made miserable for love of her.

"I wish you could bring yourself to speak to me now and then without putting that odious 'Sir' before my name," he says to her one day. "Anybody would say we were utter strangers."

"Well, and so we are," Cecil replies, opening wide her eyes in affected astonishment. "How can you dispute it? Why, you never even saw me until a few days ago."

"You are my wife at all events," says the young man, slightly discomfited.

"Ay, more's the pity," murmurs her ladyship, with such a sudden, bewitching, aggravating smile as entirely condones the incivility of her speech. Sir Penthony smiles too.

"Cecil—Cis,—a pretty name.—It rhymes with kiss," he says, rather sentimentally.

"So it does. And Penthony,—what does that rhyme with? Tony— money. Ah! that was our stumbling block."

"It might have been a worse one. There are more disagreeable things than money. There was once upon a time a stubborn mare, and even she was made to go by this same much-abused money. By the bye,"— thoughtfully,—"you don't object to your share of it, do you?"

"By no means. I purchased it so dearly I have quite a veneration for it."

"I see. I don't think my remark called for so ungracious a reply. To look at you one could hardly imagine a cruel sentiment coming from your lips."

"That shows how deceitful appearances can be. Had you troubled yourself to raise my veil upon your wedding-day you might have made yourself miserable for life. Really, Sir Penthony, I think you owe me a debt of gratitude."

"Do you? Then I confess myself *un*grateful. Oh, Cecil, had I only known——" Here he pauses, warned by the superciliousness of her bearing, and goes on rather lamely. "Are you cold? Shall I get you a shawl?" They are standing on the veranda, and the evening is closing in.

"Cold? No. Who could feel cold on so divine an evening? It reminds one of the very heart of summer, and—— Ah!" with a little start and a pleased smile, "here is Mr. Lowry coming across the grass."

"Lowry! It seems to me he always is coming across the grass." Testily. "Has he no servants, no cook, no roof over his head? Or what on earth brings him here, morning, noon, and night?"

"I really think he must come to see me," says Lady Stafford, with modest hesitation. "He was so much with me in town, off and on, that I dare say he misses me now. He was very attentive about bringing me flowers and—and that."

"No doubt. It is amazing how thoughtful men can be on occasions. You like him very much?"

"Very much indeed. He is amiable, good-natured, and has such kind brown eyes."

"Has he?" With exaggerated surprise. "Is he indeed all that you say? It is strange how blind a man can be to his neighbor's virtues, whatever he may be to his faults. Now, if I had been asked my opinion of Talbot Lowry, I would have said he was the greatest bore and about the ugliest fellow I ever met in my life."

"Well, of course, strictly speaking, no one could call him handsome," Cecil says, feeling apologetic on the score of Mr. Lowry; "but he has excellent points; and, after all, with me, good looks count for very little." She takes a calm survey of her companion's patrician features as she speaks; but Sir Penthony takes no notice of her examination, as he is looking straight before him at nothing in the world, as far as she can judge.

"I never meet him without thinking of Master Shallow," he says, rather witheringly. "May I ask how he managed to make himself so endurable to you?"

"In many ways. Strange as it may appear to you, he can read poetry really charmingly. Byron, Tennyson, even Shakespeare, he has read to me until," says Cecil, with enthusiasm, "he has actually brought the tears into my eyes."

"I can fancy it," says Sir Penthony, with much disgust, adjusting his eyeglass with great care in his right eye, the better to contemplate the approach of this modern hero. "I can readily believe it. He seems to me the very personification of a 'lady's man,'—a thorough-paced carpet knight. When," says Sir Penthony, with careful criticism, "I take into consideration the elegant slimness of his lower limbs and the cadaverous leanness of his under-jaw, I can almost see him writing sonnets to his mistress's eyebrow."

"If"—severely—"there is one thing that absolutely repels me, it is sarcasm. Don't you be sarcastic. It doesn't suit you. I merely said Mr. Lowry probably feels at a loss, now his mornings are unoccupied, as he generally spent them with me in town."

"Happy he. Were those mornings equally agreeable to you?"

"They were indeed. But, as you evidently don't admire Talbot, you can hardly be expected to sympathize with my enjoyment."

"I merely hinted I thought him a conceited coxcomb; and so I do. Ah, Lowry, how d'ye do? Charmed to see you. Warm evening, is it not?"

"You are come at last, Mr. Lowry," Cecil says, with sweet meaning in her tone, smiling up at him as he stands beside her, with no eyes but for her. "What a glorious day we have had! It makes one sad to think it cannot continue. I do so hate winter."

"Poor winter!" says Lowry, rather insipidly. "It has my most sincere sympathy. As for the day, I hardly noticed its beauties: I found it long."

"The sign of an idler. Did you find it *very* long?"

"Very," says Lowry, with a look that implies his absence from her side was the sole cause of its tedium, and such an amount of emphasis as awakens in Sir Penthony a mad desire to horsewhip him. Though how, in these degenerate days, *can* one man horsewhip another because he makes use of that mild word "very"?

It certainly is a delicious evening. Five o'clock has crept on them almost insensibly, and tea has been brought out to the veranda. Within, from the drawing-room, a roaring fire throws upon the group outside white arms of flame, as though petitioning them to enter and accept its warm invitation.

Marcia, bending over the tea-tray, is looking tall and handsome, and perhaps a degree less gloomy than usual. Philip, too, is present, also tall and handsome; only he, by way of contrast, is looking rather more moody than usual. Molly is absent; so is Luttrell.

Mr. Potts, hovering round the tea-table, like an over-grown clumsy bee, is doing all that mortal man can do in the way of carrying cups and upsetting spoons. There are few things more irritating than the clatter of falling spoons, but Mr. Potts is above irritation, whatever his friends may be, and meets each fresh mishap with laudable equanimity. He is evidently enjoying himself, and is also taking very kindly to such good things in the shape of cake as the morbid footman has been pleased to bring.

Sir Penthony, who has sturdily declined to quit the battle-field, stands holding his wife's cup on one side, while Mr. Lowry is supplying her with cake on the other. There is a good deal of obstinacy mingled with their devotion.

"I wonder where Molly can be?" Lady Stafford says, at length. "I always know by instinct when tea is going on in a house. She will be sorry if she misses hers. Why don't somebody go and fetch her? You, for instance," she says, turning her face to Sir Penthony.

"I would fly to her," replies he, unmoved, "but I unfortunately don't know where she is. Besides, I dare say if I knew and went I would find myself unwelcome. I hate looking people up."

"I haven't seen her all day," says Mr. Potts, in an aggrieved tone, having finished the last piece of plum-cake, and being much exercised in his mind as to whether it is the seed or the sponge he will attack next. "She has been out walking, or writing letters, or something, since breakfast. I hope nothing has happened to her. Perhaps if we instituted a search——"

At this moment, Molly, smiling, *gracieuse*, appears at the open window and steps on the veranda. She is dressed in a soft blue clinging gown, and has a flower, fresh-gathered, in her hair, another at her throat, another held loosely in her slender fingers.

"Talk of an angel!" says Philip, softly, but audibly.

"*Were* you talking of me?" asks modest Molly, turning toward him.

"Well, if ever I heard such a disgracefully conceited speech!" says Lady Stafford, laughing. But Philip says, "We were," still with his eyes on Molly.

"Evidently you have all been pining for me," says Molly, gayly. "It is useless your denying it. Mr. Potts,"—sweetly,—"leave me a little cake, will you? Don't eat it *all* up. Knowing as you do my weakness for seed-cake, I consider it mean of you to behave as you are now doing."

"You shall have it all," says Mr. Potts, magnanimously. "I devoted myself to the plum-cake so as to leave this for you; so you see I don't deserve your sneer."

Philip straightens himself, and his moodiness flies from him. Marcia, on the contrary, grows *distrait* and anxious. Molly, with the air of a little *gourmand*, makes her white teeth meet in her sweet cake, and, with a sigh of deep content, seats herself on the window-sill.

Mr. Potts essays to do likewise. In fact, so great is his haste to secure the coveted position that he trips, loses balance, and crash goes tea, cup, and all—with which he meant to regale his idol—on to the stone at his feet.

"You seem determined to outdo yourself this evening, Potts," Sir Penthony says, mildly, turning his eyeglass upon the delinquent. "First you did all you knew in the way of battering the silver, and now you have turned your kind attention on the china. I really think, too, that it is the very best china,—Wedgwood, is it not? Only yesterday I heard Mr. Amherst explaining to Lady Elizabeth Eyre, who is rather a connoisseur in china, how blessed he was in possessing an entire set of Wedgwood unbroken. I heard him asking her to name a day to come and see it."

"I don't think you need pile up the agony any higher," Philip interposes, laughing, coming to the rescue in his grandfather's absence. "He will never find it out."

"I'm so awfully sorry!" Mr. Potts says, addressing Marcia, his skin having by this time borrowed largely of his hair in coloring. "It was unpardonably awkward. I don't know how it happened. But I'll mend it again for you, Miss Amherst; I've the best cement you ever knew up-stairs; I always carry it about with me."

"You do right," says Molly, laughing.

"The hot tea won't affect it afterward," goes on Potts triumphantly.

"He is evidently in the habit of going about breaking people's pet china and mending it again,—knows all about it," murmurs Sir Penthony, *sotto voce*, with much interest. "It isn't a concoction of your own, Potts, is it?"

"No; a fellow gave it to me. The least little touch mends, and it never gives way again."

"That's what's-*meant* to do," Captain Mottie has the audacity to say, very unwisely. Of course no one takes the faintest notice. They all with one consent refuse indignantly to see it; and Longshank's inevitable "Ha, ha!" falls horribly flat. Only Molly, after a wild struggle with her better feelings, gives way, and bursts into an irrepressible fit of laughter, for which the poor captain is intensely grateful.

Mrs. Darley, who is doing a little mild running with this would-be Joe Miller, encouraged by Molly, laughs too, and gives the captain to understand that she thinks it a joke, which is even more than could be expected of her.

A sound of footsteps upon the gravel beneath redeems any further awkwardness. They all simultaneously crane their necks over the iron railings, and all at a glance see Mr. Amherst slowly, but surely, advancing on them.

He is not alone. Beside him, affording him the support of one arm, walks a short, stout, pudgy little man, dressed with elaborate care, and bearing all the distinguishing marks of the lowest breeding in his face and figure.

It is Mr. Buscarlet, the attorney, without whose advice Mr. Amherst rarely takes a step in business matters, and for whom—could he be guilty of such a thing—he has a decided weakness. Mr. Amherst is frigid and cutting.

Mr. Buscarlet is vulgar and gushing. They say extremes meet. In this case they certainly do, for perhaps he is the only person in the wide world with whom old Amherst gets on.

With Marcia he is a bugbear,—a *bête noire*. She does not even trouble herself to tolerate him, which is the one unwise step the wise Marcia took on her entrance into Herst.

Now, as he comes puffing and panting up the steps to the veranda, she deliberately turns her back on him.

"Pick up the ghastly remains, Potts," Sir Penthony says, hurriedly, alluding to the shattered china. Mr. Amherst is still on the lowest step, having discarded Mr. Buscarlet's arm. "If there is one thing mine host abhors more than another, it is broken china. If he catches you red-handed, I shudder for the consequences."

"What an ogre you make him out!" says Molly. "Has he, then, a private Bastile, or a poisoned dagger, this terrible old man?"

"Neither. He clings to the traditions of the 'good old times.' Skinning alive, which was a favorite pastime in the dark ages, is the sort of thing he affects. Dear old gentleman, he cannot bear to see ancient usages sink into oblivion. Here he is."

Mr. Potts, having carefully removed all traces of his handiness, gazes with recovered courage on the coming foe.

"Have some tea, grandpapa," says Marcia, attentively, ignoring Mr. Buscarlet.

"No, thank you. Mr. Buscarlet will probably have some, if he is asked," says grandpapa, severely.

"Ah, thank you; thank you. I will take a little tea from Miss Amherst's fair hands," says the man of law, rubbing his own ecstatically as he speaks.

"Mr. Longshanks, give this to Mr. Buscarlet," says Marcia, turning to Longshanks with a cup of tea, although Mr. Buscarlet is at her other elbow, ready to receive it from her "fair hands."

Mr. Longshanks does as he is bidden; and the attorney, having received it, walks away discomfited, a fresh score against this haughty hostess printed on his heart. He has the good luck to come face to face with pretty Molly, who is never unkind to any one but the man who loves her. They have met before, so he has no difficulty about addressing her, though, after his rebuff from Marcia, he feels some faint pangs of diffidence.

"Is it not a glorious evening?" he says, with hesitation, hardly knowing how he will be received; "what *should* we all do but for the weather?"

"Is it not?" says Molly, with the utmost cheerfulness, smiling on him. She is so sorry for his defeat, which she witnessed, that her smile is one of her kindest. "If this weather might only continue, how happy we should be. Even the flowers would remain with us." She holds up the white rose in her hand for his admiration.

"A lovely flower, but not so lovely as its possessor," says this insufferable old lawyer, with a smirk.

"Oh, Mr. Buscarlet! I doubt you are a sad flirt," says Miss Molly, with an amused glance. "What would Mrs. Buscarlet say if she knew you were going about paying compliments all round?"

"Not all round, Miss Massereene, pardon me. There is a power about beauty stronger than any other,—a charm that draws one out of one's self." With a fat obeisance he says this, and a smile he means to be fascinating.

Molly laughs. In her place Marcia would have shown disgust; but Molly only laughs—a delicious laugh, rich with the very sweetest, merriest music. She admits even to herself she is excessively amused.

"Thank you," she says. "Positively you deserve anything for so pretty a speech. I am sorry I have nothing better to offer, but—you shall have my rose."

Still smiling, she goes close to him, and with her own white fingers places the rose in the old gentleman's coat; while he stands as infatuated by her grace and beauty as though he still could call himself twenty-four with a clear conscience, and had no buxom partner at home ready to devour him at a moment's notice.

Oh, lucky, sweetly-perfumed, pale white rose! Oh, fortunate, kindly, tender manner! You little guess your influence over the future.

Old Mr. Amherst, who has been watching Molly from afar, now comes grumbling toward her and leads Mr. Buscarlet away.

"Grandpa is in a bad temper," says Marcia, generally, when they have quite gone.

"No, you don't say so? What a remarkable occurrence!" exclaims Cecil. "Now, what *can* have happened to ruffle so serene a nature as his?"

"I didn't notice it; I was making a fresh and more lengthened examination of his features. Yet, I still adhere to my original conviction: his nose is his strong point." Mr. Potts says this as one would who had given to the subject years of mature study.

"It *is* thin," says Lady Stafford.

"It is. Considering his antiquity, his features are really quite handsome. But his nose—his nose," says Mr. Potts, "is especially fine. That's a joke: do you see it? Fine! Why, it is sharper than an awl. 'Score two on the shovel for that, Mary Ann.'"

For want of something better to do, they all laugh at Mr. Potts's rather lame sally. Even Mr. Longshanks so far forgets himself and his allegiance to his friend as to say "Ha-ha-ha!" out loud—a proceeding so totally unexpected on the part of Longshanks that they all laugh again, this time the more heartily that they cannot well explain the cause of their merriment.

Captain Mottie is justly vexed. The friend of his soul has turned traitor, and actually expended a valuable laugh upon an outsider.

Mrs. Darley, seeing his vexation, says, quietly, "I do not think it is good form, or even kind, to speak so of poor Mr. Amherst behind his back. I cannot bear to hear him abused."

"It is only his nose, dear," says Cecil; "and even you cannot call it fat without belying your conscience."

Mrs. Darley accepts the apology, and goes back to her mild flirtation.

"How silly that woman is!" Cecil says, somewhat indignantly. She and Molly and one or two of the men are rather apart. "To hear her going in for simple sentiments is quite too much for me. When one looks at her, one cannot help— —" She pauses, and taps her foot upon the ground, impatiently.

"She is rather pretty," says Lowry, glancing carelessly at the powdered doll's face, with its wealth of dyed hair.

"There was a young lady named Maud,"

says Sir Penthony, addressing his toes,

"Who had recently come from abroad,

Her bloom and her curls,

Which astonished the girls,

Were both an ingenious fraud.

"Ah! here is Tedcastle coming across to us."

Tedcastle, with the boy Darley mounted high on his shoulder, comes leisurely over the lawn and up the steps.

"There, my little man, now you may run to your mother," he says to the child, who shows a morbid dislike to leave his side (all children adore Luttrell). "What! not tired of me yet? Well, stay, then."

"Tea, Tedcastle?"

"No, thank you."

"Let me get you some more, Miss Massereene," says Plantagenet. "You came late, and have been neglected."

"I think I will take a very little more. But," says Molly, who is in a tender mood, "you have been going about on duty all the evening. I will ask Mr. Luttrell to get me some this time, if he will be so kind." She accompanies this with a glance that sets Luttrell's fond heart beating.

"Ah, Molly, why did you not come with Teddy and me this day, as usual?" says little Lucien Darley, patting her hand. "It was so nice. Only there was no regular sun this evening, like yesterday. It was hot, but I could see no dear little dancing sunbeams; and I asked Teddy why, and he said there could be no sun where Molly was not. What did he mean by that?"

"Yes, what *could* he have meant by that?" asks Sir Penthony, in a perplexed tone, while Molly blushes one of her rare, sweet blushes, and lowers her eyes. "It was a wild remark. I can see no sense in it. But perhaps he will kindly explain. I say, Luttrell, you shouldn't spend your time telling this child fairy tales; you will make him a visionary. He says you declared Miss Massereene had entire control over the sun, moon, and stars, and that they were never known to shine except where she was."

"I have heard of the '*enfant terrible*,'" says Luttrell, laughing, to cover some confusion; "I rejoice to say I have at last met with one. Lucien, I shall tell you no more fantastic stories."

CHAPTER XVIII

"These violet delights have violet ends,
And in their triumph die, like fire and powder."

—*Romeo and Juliet.*

"That is the way with you men; you don't understand us,—
you *cannot*."

—*Courtship of Miles Standish.*

Whether it is because of Marcia's demeanor toward Mr. Buscarlet, or the unusual excellence of the weather, no one can tell, but to-night Mr. Amherst is in one of his choicest moods.

Each of his remarks outdoes the last in brilliancy of conception, whilst all tend in one direction, and show a laudable desire to touch on open wounds. Even the presence of his chosen intimate, the lawyer, who remains to dinner and an uncomfortable evening afterward, has not the power to stop him, though Mr. Buscarlet does all in his knowledge to conciliate him, and fags on wearily through his gossiping conversations with an ardor and such an amount of staying power as raises admiration even in the breast of Marcia.

All in vain. The little black dog has settled down on the old gentleman's shoulders with a vengeance and a determination to see it out with the guests not to be shaken.

Poor Mr. Potts is the victim of the hour. Though why, because he is enraged with Marcia, Mr. Amherst should expend his violence upon the wretched Plantagenet is a matter for speculation. He leaves no stone unturned to bring down condemnation on the head of this poor youth and destroy his peace of mind; but fortunately, Plantagenet has learned the happy knack of "ducking" mentally and so letting all hostile missiles fly harmless over his rosy head.

After dinner Mr. Darley good-naturedly suggests a game of besique with his host, but is snubbed, to the great grief of those assembled in the drawing-room. Thereupon Darley, with an air of relief, takes up a book and retires within himself, leaving Mr. Buscarlet to come once more to the front.

"You have heard, of course, about the Wyburns?" he says, addressing Mr. Amherst. "They are very much cut up about that second boy. He has turned out such a failure! He missed his examination again last week."

"I see no cause for wonder. What does Wyburn expect? At sixty-five he weds a silly chit of nineteen without an earthly idea in her head, and then dreams of giving a genius to the world! When," says Mr. Amherst, turning his gaze freely upon the devoted Potts, "men marry late in life they always beget fools."

"That's me," says Mr. Potts, addressing Molly in an undertone, utterly unabashed. "My father married at sixty and my mother at twenty-five. In me you behold the fatal result."

"Well, well," goes on Mr. Buscarlet, hastily, with a view to checking the storm, "I think in this case it was more idleness than want of brain."

"My dear Buscarlet, did you ever yet hear of a dunce whose mother did not go about impressing upon people how idle the dear boy was? Idle? Pooh! lack of intellect!"

"At all events, the Wyburns are to be pitied. The eldest son's marriage with one so much beneath him was also a sad blow."

"Was it? Others endure like blows and make no complaint. It is quite the common and regular thing for the child you have nurtured, to grow up and embitter your life in every possible way by marrying against your wishes, or otherwise bringing down disgrace upon your head. I have been especially blessed in my children and grandchildren."

"Just so, no doubt,—no doubt," says Mr. Buscarlet, nervously. There is a meaning sneer about the old man's lips.

"Specially blessed," he repeats. "I had reason to be proud of them. Each child as he or she married gave me fresh cause for joy. Marcia's mother was an Italian dancer."

"She was an actress," Marcia interposes, calmly, not a line of displeasure, not the faintest trace of anger, discernible in her pale face. "I do not recollect having ever heard she danced."

"Probably she suppressed that fact. It hardly adds to one's respectability. Philip's father was a spendthrift. His son develops day by day a very dutiful desire to follow in his footsteps."

"Perhaps I might do worse," Shadwell replies, with a little aggravating laugh. "At all events, he was *beloved*."

"So he was,—while his money lasted. Eleanor's father——"

With a sudden, irrepressible start Molly rises to her feet and, with a rather white face, turns to her grandfather.

"I will thank you, grandpapa, to say nothing against *my* father," she says, in tones so low, yet so full of dignity and indignation, that the old man actually pauses.

"High tragedy," says he, with a sneer. "Why, you are all wrongly assorted. The actress should have been your mother, Eleanor."

Yet it is noticeable that he makes no further attempt to slight the memory of the dead Massereene.

"I shan't be able to stand much more of this," says Mr. Potts, presently, coming behind the lounge on which sit Lady Stafford and Molly. "I shall infallibly blow out at that obnoxious old person, or else do something equally reprehensible."

"He is a perfect bear," says Cecil angrily.

"He is a wicked old man," says Molly, still trembling with indignation.

"He is a jolly old snook," says Mr. Potts. But as neither of his listeners know what he means, they do not respond.

"Let us do something," says Plantagenet, briskly.

"But what? Will you sing for us, Molly? 'Music hath charms to soothe the savage breast.'"

"It would take a good deal of music to soothe our *bête noire*," says Potts. "Besides—I confess it,—music is not what Artemus Ward would call my 'forte.' I don't understand it. I am like the man who said he only knew two tunes in the world: one was 'God save the Queen,' and the other wasn't. No, let us do something active,—something unusual, something wicked."

"If you can suggest anything likely to answer to your description, you will make me your friend for life," says Cecil, with solemnity. "I feel bad."

"Did you ever see a devil?" asks Mr. Potts, in a sepulchral tone.

"A what?" exclaim Cecil and Molly, in a breath.

"A devil," repeats he, unmoved. "I don't mean our own particular old gentleman, who has been behaving so sweetly to-night, but a regular *bona fide* one."

"Are you a spiritualist?" Cecil asks with awe.

"Nothing half so paltry. There is no deception about my performance. It is simplicity itself. There is no rapping, but a great deal of powder. Have you ever seen one?"

"A devil? Never."

"Should you like to?"

"Shouldn't I!" says Cecil, with enthusiasm.

"Then you shall. It won't be much, you know, but it has a pretty effect, and anything will be less deadly than sitting here listening to the honeyed speeches of our host. I will go and prepare my work, and call you when it is ready."

In twenty minutes he returns and beckons them to come; and, rising, both girls quit the drawing-room.

With much glee Mr. Potts conducts them across the hall into the library, where they find all the chairs and the centre table pushed into a corner, as though to make room for one soup-plate which occupies the middle of the floor.

On this plate stands a miniature hill, broad at the base and tapering at the summit, composed of blended powder and water, which Mr. Potts has been carefully heating in an oven during his absence until, according to his lights, it has reached a proper dryness.

"Good gracious! what is it?" asks Molly.

"Powder," says Potts.

"I hope it won't go off and blow us all to bits," says Cecil, anxiously.

"It will go off, certainly, but it won't do any damage," replies their showman, with confidence; "and really it is very pretty while burning. I used to make 'em by hundreds when I was a boy, and nothing ever happened except once, when I blew the ear off my father's coachman."

This is not reassuring. Molly gets a little closer to Cecil, and Cecil gets a little nearer to Molly. They both sensibly increase the distance between them and the "devil."

"Now I am going to put out the lamp," says Plantagenet, suiting the action to the word and suddenly placing them in darkness. "It don't look anything if there is light to overpower its own brilliancy."

Striking a match, he applies it to the little black mountain, and in a second it turns into a burning one. The sparks fly rapidly upward. It seems to be pouring its fire in little liquid streams all down its sides.

Cecil and Molly are in raptures.

"It is Vesuvius," says the former.

"It is Mount Etna," says the latter, "except much better, because they don't seem to have any volcanoes nowadays. Mr. Potts, you deserve a prize medal for giving us such a treat."

"Plantagenet, my dear, I didn't believe it was in you," says Cecil. "Permit me to compliment you on your unprecedented success."

Presently, however, they slightly alter their sentiments. Every schoolboy knows how overpowering is the smell of burnt powder.

"What an intolerable smell!" says Molly, when the little mound is half burned down, putting her dainty handkerchief up to her nose. "Oh! what is it? Gunpowder? Brimstone? *Sulphur?*"

"And extremely appropriate, too, dear," says Cecil, who has also got her nose buried in her cambric; "entirely carries out the character of the entertainment. You surely don't expect to be regaled with incense or attar of roses. By the bye, Plantagenet, is there going to be much more of it,—the smell, I mean?"

"Not much," replies he. "And, after all, what is it? If you went out shooting every day you would think nothing of it. For my part I almost like the smell. It is wholesome, and—er— — Oh, by Jove!"

There is a loud report,—a crash,—two terrified screams,—and then utter darkness. The base of the hill, being too dry, has treacherously gone off without warning: hence the explosion.

"You aren't hurt, are you?" asks Mr. Potts, a minute later, in a terrified whisper, being unable to see whether his companions are dead or alive.

"Not much," replies Cecil, in a trembling tone; "but, oh! what has happened? Molly, speak."

"I am quite safe," says Molly, "but horribly frightened. Mr. Potts, are you all right?"

"I am." He is ignorant of the fact that one of his cheeks is black as any nigger's, and that both his hands resemble it. "I really thought it was all up when I heard you scream. It was that wretched powder that got too dry at the end. However, it doesn't matter."

"Have you both your ears, Molly?" asks Cecil, with a laugh; but a sudden commotion in the hall outside, and the rapid advance of footsteps in their direction, check her merriment.

"I hear Mr. Amherst's voice," says Mr. Potts, tragically. "If he finds us here we are ruined."

"Let us get behind the curtains at the other end of the room," whispers Cecil, hurriedly; "they may not find us there,—and—throw the plate out of the window."

No sooner said than done: Plantagenet with a quick movement precipitates the soup-plate—or rather what remains of it—into the courtyard beneath, where it falls with a horrible clatter, and hastily follows his two companions into their uncertain hiding-place.

It stands in a remote corner, rather hidden by a bookcase, and consists of a broad wooden pedestal, hung round with curtains, that once supported a choice statue. The statue having been promoted some time since, the three conspirators now take its place, and find themselves completely concealed by its falling draperies.

This recess, having been originally intended for one, can with difficulty conceal two, so I leave it to your imagination to consider how badly three fare for room inside it.

Mr. Potts, finding himself in the middle, begins to wish he had been born without arms, as he now knows not how to dispose of them. He stirs the right one, and Cecil instantly declares in an agonized whisper that she is falling off the pedestal. He moves the left, and Molly murmurs frantically in another instant she will be through the curtains at her side. Driven to distraction, poor Potts, with many apologies, solves the difficulty by placing an arm round each complainant, and so supports them on their treacherous footing.

They have scarcely brought themselves into a retainable position when the door opens and Mr. Amherst enters the room, followed by Sir Penthony Stafford and Luttrell.

With one candlestick only are they armed, which Sir Penthony holds, having naturally expected to find the library lighted.

"What is the meaning of this smell?" exclaims Mr. Amherst, in an awful voice, that makes our three friends shiver in their shoes. "Has any one been trying to blow up the house? I insist on learning the meaning of this disgraceful affair."

"There doesn't seem to be anything," says Tedcastle, "except gunpowder, or rather the unpleasant remains of it. The burglar has evidently flown."

"If you intend turning the matter into a joke," retorts Mr. Amherst, "you had better leave the room."

"Nothing shall induce me to quit the post of danger," replies Luttrell, unruffled.

Meantime, Sir Penthony, who is of a more suspicious nature, is making a more elaborate search. Slowly, methodically he commences a tour round the room, until presently he comes to a stand-still before the curtains that conceal the trembling trio.

Mr. Amherst, in the middle of the floor, is busily engaged examining the chips of china that remain after their *fiasco*,—and that ought to tell the tale of a soup-plate.

Tedcastle comes to Sir Penthony's side.

Together they withdraw the curtains; together they view what rests behind them.

Grand tableau!

Mr. Potts, with half his face blackened beyond recognition, glares out at them with the courage of despair. On one side of him is Lady Stafford, on the other Miss Massereene; from behind each of their waists protrudes a huge and sooty hand. That hand belongs to Potts.

Three pairs of eyes gleam at the discoverers, silently, entreatingly, yet with what different expressions! Molly is frightened, but evidently braced for action; Mr. Potts is defiant; Lady Stafford is absolutely convulsed with laughter. Already filled with a keen sense of the comicality of the situation, it only wanted her husband's face of indignant surprise to utterly unsettle her. Therefore it is that the one embarrassment she suffers from is a difficulty in refraining from an outburst of merriment.

There is a dead silence. Only the grating of Mr. Amherst's bits of china mars the stillness. Plantagenet, staring at his judges, defies them, without a word, to betray their retreat. The judges—although angry—stare back at him, and acknowledge their inability to play the sneak. Sir Penthony drops the curtain,—and the candle. Instantly darkness covers them. Luttrell scrapes a heavy chair along the waxed borders of the floor; there is some faint confusion, a rustle of petticoats, a few more footsteps than ought to be in the room, an uncivil remark from old Amherst about some people's fingers being all thumbs, and then once more silence.

When, after a pause, Sir Penthony relights his candle, the search is at an end.

Now that they are well out of the library, though still in the gloomy little anteroom that leads to it, Molly and Cecil pause to recover breath. For a few moments they keep an unbroken quiet. Lady Stafford is the first to speak,—as might be expected.

"I am bitterly disappointed," she says, in a tone of intense disgust. "It is a downright swindle. In spite of a belief that has lasted for years, that nose of his is a failure. I think *nothing* of it. With all its length and all its sharpness, it never found us out!"

"Let us be thankful for that same," returns Molly, devoutly.

By this time they have reached the outer hall, where the lamps are shining vigorously. They now shine down with unkind brilliancy on Mr. Potts's disfigured countenance. A heavy veil of black spreads from his nose to his left ear, rather spoiling the effect of his unique ugliness.

It is impossible to resist; Lady Stafford instantly breaks down, and gives way to the laughter that has been oppressing her for the last half-hour, Molly chimes in, and together they laugh with such hearty delight that Mr. Potts burns to know the cause of their mirth, that he may join in.

He grins, however, in sympathy, whilst waiting impatiently an explanation. His utter ignorance of the real reason only enhances the absurdity of his appearance and prolongs the delight of his companions.

When two minutes have elapsed, and still neither of them offers any information, he grows grave, and whispers rather to himself than them, the one word, "Hysterics?"

"You are right," cries Cecil: "I was never nearer hysterics in my life. Oh, Plantagenet! your face is as black as—as——"

"Your hat!" supplies Molly, as well as she can speak. "And your hands,—you look demoniacal. Do run away and wash yourself and—— I hear somebody coming."

Whereupon Potts scampers up-stairs, while the other two gain the drawing-room, just as Mr. Amherst appears in the hall.

Seeing them, half an hour later, seated in all quietude and sobriety, discussing the war and the last new marvel in bonnets, who would have supposed them guilty of their impromptu game of "hide and seek"?

Tedcastle and Sir Penthony, indeed, look much more like the real culprits, being justly annoyed, and consequently rather cloudy about the brows. Yet, with a sense of dignified pride, the two gentlemen abstain from giving voice to their disapprobation, and make no comment on the event of the evening.

Mr. Potts is serenity itself, and is apparently ignorant of having given offense to any one. His face has regained its pristine fairness, and is scrupulously clean; so is his conscience. He looks incapable of harm.

Bed-hour arrives, and Tedcastle retires to his pipe without betraying his inmost feelings. Sir Penthony is determined to follow his lead; Cecil is equally determined he shall not. To have it out with him without further loss of time is her fixed intention, and with that design she says, a little imperiously:

"Sir Penthony, get me my candle."

She has lingered, before saying this, until almost all the others have disappeared. The last of the men is vanishing round the corner that leads to the smoking-room; the last of the women has gone beyond sight of the staircase in search of her bedroom fire. Cecil and her husband stand alone in the vast hall.

"I fear you are annoyed about something," she says, in a maddening tone of commiseration, regarding him keenly, while he gravely lights her candle.

"Why should you suppose so?"

"Because of your gravity and unusual silence."

"I was never a great talker, and I do not think I am in the habit of laughing more than other people."

"But you have not laughed at all,—all this evening, at least,"—with a smile,—"not since you discovered us in durance vile."

"Did you find the situation so unpleasant? I fancied it rather amused you,—so much so that you even appeared to forget the dignity that, as a married woman, ought to belong to you."

"Well, but!"—provokingly—"you forget how very *little* married I am."

"At all events you are my wife,"—rather angrily; "I must beg you to remember that. And for the future I shall ask you to refrain from such amusements as call for concealment and necessitate the support of a young man's arm."

"I really do not see by what right you interfere with either me or my amusements," says Cecil, hotly, after a decided pause. Never has he addressed her with so much sternness. She raised her eyes to his and colors richly all through her creamy skin. "Recollect our bargain."

"I do. I recollect also that you have my name."

"And you have my money. That makes us quits."

"I do not see how you intend carrying out that argument. The money was quite as much mine as yours."

"But you could not have had it without me."

"Nor you without me."

"Which is to be regretted. At least I should have had a clear half, which I haven't; so you have the best of it. And—I will not be followed about, and pried after, and made generally uncomfortable by any one."

"Who is prying after you?"

"You are."

"What do you mean, Cecil?" Haughtily.

"Just what I say. And, as I never so far forget myself as to call *you* by your Christian name without its prefix, I think you might have the courtesy to address *me* as Lady Stafford."

"Certainly, if you wish it."

"I do. Have you anything more to say?"

"Yes, more than— —"

"Then pray defer it until to-morrow, as"—with a bare-faced attempt at a yawn—"I really cannot sit up any longer. Good-night, Sir Penthony."

Sir Penthony puts the end of his long moustache into his mouth,—a sure sign of irritation,—and declines to answer.

"Good-night," repeats her ladyship, blandly, going up the staircase, with a suspicion of a smile at the corners of her lips, and feeling no surprise that her polite little adieu receives no reply.

When she has reached the centre of the broad staircase she pauses, and, leaning her white arms upon the banisters, looks down upon her husband, standing irresolute and angry in the hall beneath.

"Sir Penthony," murmurs she; "Sir— —" Here she hesitates for so long a time that when at last the "Penthony" does come it sounds more familiar and almost unconnected with the preceding word.

Stafford turns, and glances quickly up at her. She is dressed in some soft-flowing gown of black, caught here and there with heavy bows and bands of cream-color, that contrast admirably with her hair, soft skin, her laughing eyes, and her pouting, rosy lips. In her hair, which she wears low on her neck, is a black comb studded with pearls; there are a few pearls round her neck, a few more in her small ears; she wears no bracelets, only two narrow bands of black velvet caught with pearls, that make her arms seem even rounder and whiter than they are.

"Good-night," she says, for the third time, nodding at him in a slow, sweet fashion that has some grace or charm about it all its own, and makes her at the instant ten times lovelier than she was before.

Stafford, coming forward until he stands right under her, gazes up at her entranced like some modern Romeo. Indeed, there is something almost theatrical about them as they linger, each waiting for the other to speak,— he fond and impassioned, yet half angry too, she calm and smiling, yet mutinous.

For a full minute they thus hesitate, looking into each other's eyes; then the anger fades from Stafford's face, and he whispers, eagerly, tenderly:

"Good-night, my——"

"Friend," murmurs back her ladyship, decisively, leaning yet a little farther over the banisters.

Then she kisses her hand to him and drops at his feet the rose that has lain on her bosom all the evening, and, with a last backward glance and smile, flits away from him up the darkened staircase and vanishes.

"I shall positively lose my heart to her if I don't take care," thinks the young man, ruefully, and very foolishly, considering how long ago it is since that misfortune has befallen him. But we are ever slow to acknowledge our own defeats. His eyes are fixed upon the flower at his feet.

"No, I do not want her flowers," he says, with a slight frown, pushing it away from him disdainfully. "It was a mere chance my getting it. Any other fellow in my place at the moment would have been quite as favored,—nay, beyond doubt more so. I will not stoop for it."

With his dignity thus forced to the front, he walks the entire length of the hall, his arms folded determinedly behind him, until he reaches a door at the upper end.

Here he pauses and glances back almost guiltily. Yes, it is still there, the poor, pretty yellow blossom that has been so close to her, now sending forth its neglected perfume to an ungrateful world.

It is cruel to leave it there alone all night, to be trodden on, perhaps, in the morning by an unappreciative John or Thomas, or, worse still, to be worn by an appreciative James. Desecration!

"'Who hesitates is lost,'" quotes Stafford, aloud, with an angry laugh at his own folly, and, walking deliberately back again, picks up the flower and presses it to his lips.

"I thought that little speech applied only to us poor women," says a soft voice above him, as, to his everlasting chagrin, Cecil's mischievous, lovable face peers down at him from the gallery overhead. "Have another flower, Sir Penthony? You seem fond of them."

She throws a twin-blossom to the one he holds on to his shoulder as she speaks with very accurate aim.

"It was yours," stammers Sir Penthony, utterly taken aback.

"*So* it was,"—with an accent of affected surprise,—"which makes your behavior all the more astonishing. Well, do not stand there kissing it all night, or you will catch cold, and then—what *should* I do?"

"What?"

"Die of grief, most probably." With a little mocking laugh.

"Very probably. Yet you should pity me too, in that I have fallen so low as to have nothing better given me to kiss. I am wasting my sweetness on——"

"Is it sweetness?" asks she, wickedly.

At this they both laugh,—a low, a soft laugh, born of the hour and a fear of interruption, and perhaps a dread of being so discovered, that adds a certain zest to their meeting. Then he says, still laughing, in answer to her words, "Try."

"No, thank you." With a little *moue*. "Curiosity is not my besetting sin, although I could not resist seeing how you would treat my parting gift a moment ago. Ah!"—with a little suppressed laugh of the very fullest enjoyment,—"you cannot think what an interesting picture you made,—almost tragic. First you stalked away from my unoffending rose with all the dignity of a thousand Spaniards; and then, when you had gone sufficiently far to make your return effective, you relented, and, seizing upon the flower as though it were—let us say, for convenience sake—*myself*, devoured it with kisses. I assure you it was better than a play. Well,"—with a sigh,—"I won't detain you any longer. I'm off to my slumbers."

"Don't go yet, Cecil. Wait one moment. I—have something to say to you."

"No doubt. A short time since you said the same thing. Were I to stay now you might, perhaps, finish that scolding; instinct told me it was hanging over me; and—I hate being taken to task."

"I will not, I swear I will never again attempt to scold you about anything, experience having taught me the futility of such a course. Cecil, stay."

"Lady Stafford, if you please, Sir Penthony." With a tormenting smile.

"Lady Stafford then,—anything, if you will only stay."

"I can't, then. Where should I be without my beauty sleep? The bare idea fills me with horror. Why, I should lose my empire. Sweet as parting is, I protest I, for one, would not lengthen it until to-morrow. Till then—farewell. And—Sir Penthony—be sure you dream of me. I like being dreamed of by my——"

"By whom?"

"My slaves," returns this coquette of all coquettes, with a last lingering glance and smile. After which she finally disappears.

"There is no use disguising the fact any longer,—I *have* lost my heart," groans Sir Penthony, in despair, as he straightway carries off both himself and his cherished flowers to the shelter of his own room.

CHAPTER XIX

"I'll tell thee a part,
Of the thoughts that start
To being when thou art nigh."

—Shelley.

The next day is Sunday, and a very muggy, disagreeable one it proves. There is an indecision about it truly irritating. A few drops of rain here and there, a threatening of storm, but nothing positive. Finally, at eleven o'clock, just as they have given up all hope of seeing any improvement, it clears up in a degree,—against its will,—and allows two or three depressed and tearful sunbeams to struggle forth, rather with a view to dishearten the world than to brighten it.

Sunday at Herst is much the same as any other day. There are no rules, no restrictions. In the library may be found volumes of sermons waiting for those who may wish for them. The covers of those sermons are as clean and fresh to-day as when they were placed on their shelves, now many years ago, showing how amiably they *have* waited. You may play billiards if you like; you need not go to church if you don't like. Yet, somehow, when at Herst, people always do go,—perhaps because they needn't, or perhaps because there is such a dearth of amusements.

Molly, who as yet has escaped all explanation with Tedcastle, coming down-stairs, dressed for church, and looking unusually lovely, finds almost all the others assembled before her in the hall, ready to start.

Laying her prayer-books upon a table, while with one hand she gathers up the tail of her long gown, she turns to say a word or two to Lady Stafford.

At this moment both Luttrell and Shadwell move toward the books. Shadwell, reaching them first, lays his hand upon them.

"You will carry them for me?" says Molly, with a bright smile to him; and Luttrell, with a slight contraction of the brow, falls back again, and takes his place beside Lady Stafford.

As the church lies at the end of a pleasant pathway through the woods, they elect to walk it; and so in twos and threes they make their way under the still beautiful trees.

"It is cold, is it not?" Molly says to Mrs. Darley once, when they come to an open part of the wood, where they can travel in a body; "wonderfully so for September."

"Is it? I never mind the cold, or—or anything," rejoins Mrs. Darley, affectedly, talking for the benefit of the devoted Mottie, who walks beside her, "laden with golden grain," in the shape of prayer-books and hymnals of all sorts and sizes, "if I have any one with me that suits me; that is, a sympathetic person."

"A lover you mean?" asks uncompromising Molly. "Well, I don't know; I think that is about the time, of all others, when I should object to feeling cold. One's nose has such an unpleasant habit of getting beyond one's control in the way of redness; and to feel that one's cheeks are pinched and one's lips blue is maddening. At such times I like my own society best."

"And at other times, too," said Philip, disagreeably; "this morning, for instance." He and Molly have been having a passage of arms, and he has come off second best.

"I won't contradict you," says Molly, calmly; "it would be rude, and, considering how near we are to church, unchristian."

"A pity you cannot recollect your Christianity on other occasions," says he, sneeringly.

"You speak with feeling. How have I failed toward *you* in Christian charity?"

"Is it charitable, is it kind to scorn a fellow-creature as you do, only because he loves you?" Philip says, in a low tone.

Miss Massereene is first honestly surprised, then angry. That Philip has made love to her now and again when opportunity occurred is a fact she does not seek to deny, but it has been hitherto in the careless, half-earnest manner young men of the present day affect when in the society of a pretty woman, and has caused her no annoyance.

That he should now, without a word of warning (beyond the slight sparring-match during their walk, and which is one of a series), break forth with so much vehemence and apparent sense of injury, not only alarms but displeases her; whilst some faint idea of treachery on her own part toward her betrothed, in listening to such words, fills her with distress.

There is a depth, an earnestness, about Philip not to be mistaken. His sombre face has paled, his eyes do not meet hers, his thin nostrils are dilated, as though breathing were a matter of difficulty; all prove him genuinely disturbed.

To a man of his jealous, passionate nature, to love is a calamity. No return, however perfect, can quite compensate him for all the pains and fears his passion must afford. Already Philip's torture has begun; already the pangs of unrequited love have seized upon him.

"I wish you would not speak to me like—as—in such a tone," Molly says, pettishly and uneasily. "Latterly, I hate going anywhere with you, you are so ill-tempered; and now to-day—— Why cannot you be pleasant and friendly, as you used to be when I first came to Herst?"

"Ah, why indeed?" returns he, bitterly.

At this inauspicious moment a small rough terrier of Luttrell's rushes across their path, almost under their feet, bent on some mad chase after a mocking squirrel; and Philip, maddened just then by doubts and the coldness of her he loves, with the stick he carries strikes him a quick and sudden blow; not heavy, perhaps, but so unexpected as to draw from the pretty brute a sharp cry of pain.

Hearing a sound of distress from his favorite, Luttrell turns, and, seeing him shrinking away from Molly's side, casts upon her a glance full of the liveliest reproach, that reduces her very nearly to the verge of tears. To be so misunderstood, and all through this tiresome Philip, it is too bad! As, under the circumstances, she cannot well indulge her grief, she does the next best thing, and gives way to temper.

"Don't do that again," she says, with eyes that flash a little through their forbidden tears.

"Why?" surprised in his turn at her vehemence; "it isn't your dog; it's Luttrell's."

"No matter whose dog it is; don't do it again. I detest seeing a poor brute hurt, and for no cause, but merely as a means to try and rid yourself of some of your ill-temper."

"There is more ill-temper going than mine. I beg your pardon, however. I had no idea you were a member of the Humane Society. You should study the bearing-rein question, and vivisection, and—that," with a sullen laugh.

"Nothing annoys me so much as wanton cruelty to dumb animals."

"There are other—perhaps mistakenly termed—superior animals on whom even *you* can inflict torture," he says, with a sneer. "All your tenderness must be reserved for the lower creation. You talk of brutality: what is there in all the earth so cruel as a woman? A lover's pain is her joy."

"You are getting out of your depth,—I cannot follow you," says Molly, coldly. "Why should you and I discuss such a subject as lovers? What have we in common with them? And it is a pity, Philip, you should allow your anger to get so much the better of you. When you look savage, as you do now, you remind me of no one so much as grandpapa. And *do* recollect what an odious old man he makes."

This finishes the conversation. He vouchsafes her no reply. To be considered like Mr. Amherst, no matter in how far-off a degree, is a bitter insult. In silence they continue their walk; in silence reach the church and enter it.

It is a gloomy, antiquated building, primitive in size, and form, and service. The rector is well-meaning, but decidedly Low. The curate is unmeaning, and abominably slow. The clerk does a great part of the duty.

He is an old man, and regarded rather in the light of an institution in this part of the county. Being stone deaf, he puts in the responses anyhow, always in the wrong place, and never finds out his mistake until he sees the clergyman's lips set firm, and on his face a look of patient expectation, when he coughs apologetically, and says them all over again.

There is an "Amen" in the middle of every prayer, and then one at the end. This gives him double trouble, and makes him draw his salary with a clear conscience. It also creates a lively time for the school-children, who once at least on every Sunday give way to a loud burst of merriment, and are only restored to a sense of duty by a severe blow administered by the sandy-haired teacher.

It is a good old-fashioned church too, where the sides of the pews are so high that one can with difficulty look over them, and where the affluent man can have a real fire-place all to himself, with a real poker and tongs and shovel to incite it to a blaze every now and again.

Here, too, without rebuke the neighbors can seize the opportunity of conversing with each other across the pews, by standing on tiptoe, when occasion offers during the service, as, for instance, when the poor-box is going round. And it *is* a poor-box, and no mistake,—flat, broad, and undeniable pewter, at which the dainty bags of a city chapel would have blushed with shame.

When the clergyman goes into the pulpit every one instantly blows his or her nose, and coughs his or her loudest before the text is given out, under a mistaken impression that they can get it all over at once, and not have to do it at intervals further on. This is a compliment to the clergyman, expressing their intention of hearing him undisturbed to the end, and, I suppose, is received as such.

It is an attentive congregation,—dangerously so, for what man but blunders in his sermon now and then? And who likes being twitted on week-days for opinions expressed on Sundays, more especially if he has not altogether acted up to them! It is a suspicious congregation too (though perhaps not singularly so, for I have perceived others do the same), because whenever their priest names a chapter and verse for any text he may choose to insert in his discourse, instantly and with avidity each and all turn over the leaves of their Bibles, to see if it be really in the identical spot mentioned, or whether their pastor has been lying. This action may not be altogether suspicion; it may be also thought of as a safety-valve for their *ennui*, the rector never letting them off until they have had sixty good minutes of his valuable doctrine.

All the Herst party conduct themselves with due discretion save Mr. Potts, who, being overcome by the novelty of the situation and the length of the sermon, falls fast asleep, and presently, at some denunciatory passage, pronounced in a rather distinct tone by the rector, rousing himself with a precipitate jerk, sends all the fire-irons with a fine clatter to the ground, he having been most unhappily placed nearest the grate.

"The ruling passion strong in death," says Luttrell, with a despairing glance at the culprit; whereupon Molly nearly laughs outright, while the school-children do so quite.

Beyond this small *contre-temps*, however, nothing of note occurs; and, service being over, they all file decorously out of the church into the picturesque porch outside, where they stand for a few minutes interchanging greetings with such of the county families as come within their knowledge.

With a few others too, who scarcely come within that aristocratic pale, notably Mrs. Buscarlet. She is a tremendously stout, distressingly healthy woman, quite capable of putting her husband in a corner of her capacious pocket, which, by the bye, she insists on wearing outside her gown, in a fashion beloved of our great-grandmothers, and which, in a modified form, last year was much affected by our own generation.

This alarming personage greets Marcia with the utmost *bonhommie*, being apparently blind to the coldness of her reception. She greets Lady Stafford also, who is likewise at freezing-point, and then gets introduced to Molly. Mrs. Darley, who even to the uninitiated Mrs. Buscarlet appears a person unworthy of notice, she lets go free, for which favor Mrs. Darley is devoutly grateful.

Little Buscarlet himself, who has a weakness for birth, in that he lacks it, comes rambling up to them at this juncture, and tells them, with many a smirk, he hopes to have the pleasure of lunching with them at Herst, Mr. Amherst having sent him a special invitation, as he has something particular to say to him; whereupon Molly, who is nearest to him, laughs, and tells him she had no idea such luck was in store for her.

"You are the greatest hypocrite I ever met in my life," Sir Penthony says in her ear, when Buscarlet, smiling, bowing, radiant, has moved on.

"I am not indeed; you altogether mistake me," Molly answers. "If you only knew how his anxiety to please, and Marcia's determination *not* to be pleased, amuse me, you would understand how thoroughly I enjoy his visits."

"I ask your pardon. I had no idea we had a student of human nature among us. Don't study *me*, Miss Massereene, or it will unfit you for further exertions; I am a living mass of errors."

"Alas that I cannot contradict you!" says Cecil, with a woful sigh, who is standing near them.

Mr. Amherst, who never by any chance darkens the doors of a church, receives them in the drawing-room on their return. He is in an amiable mood and pleased to be gracious. Seizing upon Mr. Buscarlet, he carries him off with him to his private den, so that for the time being there is an end of them.

"For all small mercies," begins Mr. Potts, solemnly, when the door has closed on them; but he is interrupted by Lady Stafford.

"'Small,' indeed," grumbles she. "What do you mean? I shan't be able to eat my lunch If that odious little man remains, with his 'Yes, Lady Stafford;' 'No, Lady Stafford;' 'I quite agree with your ladyship,' and so on. Oh, that I could drop my title!"—this with a glance at Sir Penthony;—"at all events while he is present." This with another and more gracious glance at Stafford. "Positively I feel my appetite going already, and that is a pity, as it was an uncommonly good one."

"Cheer up, dear," says Molly; "and remember there will be dinner later on. Poor Mr. Buscarlet! There must be something wrong with me, because I cannot bring myself to think so disparagingly of him as you all do."

"I am sorry for you. Not to know Mr. Buscarlet's little peculiarities of behavior argues yourself unknown," Marcia says, with a good deal of intention. "And I presume they cannot have struck you, or you would scarcely be so tolerant."

"He certainly sneezes very incessantly and very objectionably," Molly says, thoughtfully. "I hate a man who sneezes publicly; and his sneeze is so unpleasant,—so exactly like that of a cat. A little wriggle of the entire body, and then a little soft—splash!"

"My *dear* Molly!" expostulates Lady Stafford.

"But is it not?" protests she; "is it not an accurate description?"

"Yes, its accuracy is its fault. I almost thought the man was in the room."

"And then there is Mrs. Buscarlet: I never saw any one like Mrs. Buscarlet," Maud Darley says, plaintively; "did you? There is so much of her, and it is all so nasty. And, oh! her voice! it is like wind whistling through a key-hole."

"Poor woman," says Luttrell, regretfully, "I think I could have forgiven her had she not worn that very verdant gown."

"My dear fellow, I thought the contrast between it and her cheeks the most perfect thing I ever saw. It is evident you have not got the eye of an artist," Sir Penthony says, rather unfeelingly.

"I never saw any one so distressingly healthy," says Maud, still plaintively. "Fat people are my aversion. I don't mind a comfortable-looking body, but she is much too stout."

"Let us alter that last remark and say she has had too much stout, and perhaps we shall define her," remarks Tedcastle. "I hate a woman who shows her food."

"The way she traduced those Sedleys rather amused me," Molly says, laughing. "I certainly thought her opinion of her neighbors very pronounced."

"She shouldn't have any opinion," says Lady Stafford, with decision. "You, my dear Molly, take an entirely wrong view of it. Such people as the Buscarlets, sprung from nobody knows where, or cares to know, should be kept in their proper place, and be sat upon the very instant they develop a desire to progress."

"How can you be so illiberal?" exclaims Molly, aghast at so much misplaced vehemence. "Why should they not rise with the rest of the world?"

"Eleanor has quite a *penchant* for the Buscarlets," says Marcia, with a sneer; "she has quite adopted them, and either will not, or perhaps does not, see their enormities."

Nobody cares to notice this impertinence, and Mr. Potts says, gravely:

"Lady Stafford has never forgiven Mrs. Buscarlet because once, at a ball here, she told her she was looking very '*distangy.*' Is that not true?"

Cecil laughs.

"Why should not every one have an opinion?" Molly persists. "I agree with the old song that 'Britons never shall be slaves:' therefore, why should they not assert themselves? In a hundred years hence they will have all the manners and airs of we others."

"Then they should be locked up during the intermediate stage," says Cecil, with an uncompromising nod of her blonde head. "I call them insufferable; and if Mr. Buscarlet when he comes in again makes himself agreeable to me—me!—I shall insult him,—that's all! No use arguing with me, Molly,—I shall indeed." She softens this awful threat by a merry sweet-tempered little laugh.

"Let us forget the little lawyer and talk of something we all enjoy,—to-day's sermon, for instance. You admired it, Potts, didn't you? I never saw any one so attentive in my life," says Sir Penthony.

Potts tries to look as if he had never succumbed during service to "Nature's sweet restorer;" and Molly says, apologetically:

"How could he help it? The sermon was so long."

"Yes, wasn't it?" agrees Plantagenet, eagerly. "The longest I ever heard. That man deserves to be suppressed or excommunicated; and the parishioners ought to send him a round robin to that effect. Odd, too, how much at sea one feels with a strange prayer-book. One looks for one's prayer at the top of the page, where it always used to be in one's own particular edition, and, lo! one finds it at the bottom. Whatever you may do for the future, Lady Stafford, don't lend me your prayer-book. But for the incessant trouble it caused me, between losing my place and finding it again, I don't believe I should have dropped into that gentle doze."

"Had you ever a prayer-book of your own?" asks Cecil, unkindly. "Because if so it is a pity you don't air it now and again. I have known you a great many years,—more than I care to count,—and never, never have I seen you with the vestige of one. I shall send you a pocket edition as a Christmas-box."

"Thanks awfully. I shall value it for the giver's sake. And I promise you that when next we meet—such care shall it receive—even *you* will be unable to discover a scratch on it."

"Plantagenet, you are a bad boy," says Cecil.

"I thought the choir rather good," Molly is saying; "but why must a man read the service in a long, slow, tearful tone? Surely there is no good to be gained by it; and to find one's self at 'Amen' when he is only in the middle of the prayer has something intolerably irritating about it. I could have shaken that curate."

"Why didn't you?" says Sir Penthony. "I would have backed you up with the greatest pleasure. The person I liked best was the old gentleman with the lint-white locks who said 'Yamen' so persistently in the wrong place all through; I grew quite interested at last, and knew the exact spot where it was likely to come in. I must say I admire consistency."

"How hard it is to keep one's attention fixed," Molly says, meditatively, "and to preserve a properly dismal expression of countenance! To look solemn always means to look severe, as far as I can judge. And did you ever notice when a rather lively and secular set of bars occur in the voluntary, how people cheer up and rouse themselves, and give way to a little sigh or two? I hope it isn't a sigh of relief. We feel it's wicked, but we always do it."

"Still studying poor human nature," exclaims Sir Penthony. "Miss Massereene, I begin to think you a terrible person, and to tremble when I meet your gaze."

"Well, at all events no one can accuse them of being High Church," says Mrs. Darley, alluding to her pastors and masters for the time being. "The service was wretchedly conducted; hardly any music, and not a flower to speak of."

"My dear! High Church! How could you expect it? Only fancy that curate intoning!" says Cecil, with a laugh.

"I couldn't," declares Sir Penthony; "so much exertion would kill me."

"That's why he *isn't* High Church," says Mr. Potts of the curate, speaking with a rather sweeping air of criticism. "He ain't musical; he can't intone. Take my word for it, half the clergy are Anglicans merely because they think they have voices, and feel what a loss the world will sustain if it don't hear them."

"Oh, what a malicious remark!" says Molly, much disgusted.

Here the scene is further enlivened by the reappearance of Mr. Amherst and the lawyer, which effectually ends the conversation and turns their thoughts toward the dining-room.

CHAPTER XX

"Trifles light as air."

—*Othello.*

When luncheon is over, Sir Penthony Stafford retires to write a letter or two, and half an hour afterward, returning to the drawing-room, finds himself in the presence of Mr. Buscarlet, unsupported.

The little lawyer smiles benignly; Sir Penthony responds, and, throwing himself into a lounging-chair, makes up his mind to be agreeable.

"Well, Mr. Buscarlet, and what did you think of the sermon?" he says, briskly, being rather at a loss for a congenial topic. "Tedious, eh? I saw you talking to Lady Elizabeth after service was over. She is a fine woman, all things considered."

"She is indeed,—remarkably so: a very fine presence for her time of life."

"Well, there certainly is not much to choose between her and the hills in point of age," allows Sir Penthony, absently—he is inwardly wondering where Cecil can have gone to,—"still she is a nice old lady."

"Quite so,—quite so; very elegant in manner, and in appearance decidedly high-bred."

"Hybrid!" exclaims Sir Penthony, purposely misunderstanding the word. "Oh, by Jove, I didn't think you so severe. You allude, of course, to her ladyship's mother, who, if report speaks truly, was a good cook spoiled by matrimony. 'Hybrid!' Give you my word, Buscarlet, I didn't believe you capable of anything half so clever. I must remember to tell it at dinner to the others. It is just the sort of thing to delight Mr. Amherst."

Now, this lawyer has a passion for the aristocracy. To be noticed by a lord,—to press "her ladyship's" hand,—to hold sweet converse with the smallest scion of a noble house,—is as honey to his lips; therefore to be thought guilty of an impertinence to one of this sacred community, to have uttered a word that, if repeated, would effectually close to him the doors of Lady Elizabeth's house, fills him with horror.

"My dear Sir Penthony, pardon me," he says, hastily, divided between the fear of offending the baronet and a desire to set himself straight in his own eyes, "you quite mistake me. 'Hybrid!'—such a word, such a thought, never occurred to me in connection with Lady Elizabeth Eyre, whom I hold in much reverence. Highly bred I meant. I assure you you altogether misunderstand. I—I never made a joke in my life."

"Then let me congratulate you on your maiden effort; you have every reason to be proud of it," laughs Sir Penthony, who is highly delighted at the success of his own manœuvre. "Don't be modest. You have made a decided hit: it is as good a thing as ever I heard. But how about Lady Elizabeth, eh? should *she* hear it? Really, you will have to suppress your wit, or it will lead you into trouble."

"But—but—if you will only allow me to explain—I protest I——"

"Ah! here come Lady Stafford and Miss Massereene. Positively you must allow me to tell them——" And, refusing to listen to Mr. Buscarlet's vehement protestations, he relates to the new-comers his version of the lawyer's harmless remark, accompanying the story with an expressive glance—that closely resembles a wink—at Lady Stafford. "I must go," he says, when he has finished, moving toward the door, "though I hardly think I do wisely, leaving, you alone with so dangerous a companion."

"I assure you, my dear Lady Stafford," declares Mr. Buscarlet, with tears in his eyes and dew on his brow, "it is all a horrible, an unaccountable mistake, a mere connection of ideas by your husband,—no more, no more, I give you my most sacred honor."

"Oh, sly Mr. Buscarlet!" cries her ladyship, lightly, "cruel Mr. Buscarlet! Who would have thought it of you? And we all imagined you such an ally of poor dear Lady Elizabeth. To make a joke about her parentage, and such a good one too! And Sir Penthony found you out? Clever Sir Penthony."

"I swear, my dear lady, I——"

"Ah, ha! wait till she hears of it. How she *will* enjoy it! With all her faults, she is good-tempered. It will amuse her. Molly, my dear, is not Mr. Buscarlet terribly severe?"

"Naughty Mr. Buscarlet!" says Molly, shaking a reproachful dainty-white finger at him. "And I believed you so harmless."

At this they both laugh so immoderately that presently the lawyer loses all patience, and, taking up his hat, rushes from the room in a greater rage than he could have thought possible, considering that one of his provocators bears a title.

They are still laughing when the others enter the room, and insist on learning the secret of their mirth. Tedcastle alone fails to enjoy it. He is *distrait*, and evidently oppressed with care. Seeing this, Molly takes heart of grace, and, crossing to his side, says, sweetly:

"Do you see how the day has cleared? That lovely sun is tempting me to go out. Will you take me for a walk?"

"Certainly,—if you want to go." Very coldly.

"But of course I do; and nobody has asked me to accompany them; so I am obliged to thrust myself on you. If"—with a bewitching smile—"you won't mind the trouble just this once, I will promise not to torment you again."

Through the gardens, and out into the shrubberies beyond, they go in silence, until they reach the open; then Molly says, laughing: "I know you are going to scold me about Mr. Potts. Begin at once, and let us get it over."

Her manner is so sweet, and she looks so gay, so fresh, so harmless, that his anger melts as dew beneath the sun.

"You need not have let him place his arm around you," he says, jealously.

"If I hadn't I should have slipped off the pedestal; and what did his arm signify in comparison with that? Think of my grandfather's face; think of mine; think of all the horrible consequences. I should have been sent home in disgrace, perhaps—who knows?—put in prison, and you might 'never, never, see your darling any more.'"

She laughs.

"What a jealous fellow you are, Ted!"

"Am I?"—ruefully. "I don't think I used to be. I never remember being jealous before."

"No? I am glad to hear it."

"Why?"

"Because"—with an adorable glance and a faint pressure of his arm—"it proves to me you have never *loved* before."

This tender insinuation blots out all remaining vapors, leaving the atmosphere clear and free of clouds for the rest of their walk, which lasts till almost evening. Just before they reach the house, Luttrell says, with hesitation:

"I have something to say to you, but I am afraid if I do say it you will be angry."

"Then *don't* say it," says Miss Massereene, equably. "That is about the most foolish thing one can do. To make a person angry unintentionally is bad enough, but to know you are going to do it, and to say so, has something about it rash, not to say impertinent. If you are fortunate enough to know the point in the conversation that is sure to rouse me to wrath, why not carefully skirt round it?"

"Because I lose a chance if I leave it unsaid; and you differ so widely from most girls—it may not provoke *you*."

"Now you compel me to it," says Molly, laughing. "What! do you think I could suffer myself to be considered a thing apart? Impossible. No one likes to be thought odd or eccentric except rich old men, and Bohemians, and poets; therefore I insist on following closely in my sisters' footsteps, and warn you I shall be in a furious passion the moment you speak, whether or not I am really annoyed. Now go on if you dare?"

"Well, look here," begins Luttrell, in a conciliating tone.

"There is not the slightest use in your beating about the bush, Teddy," says Miss Massereene, calmly. "I am going to be angry, so do not waste time in diplomacy."

"Molly, how provoking you are!"

"No! Am I? Because I wish to be like other women?"

"A hopeless wish, and a very unwise one."

"'Hopeless!' And why, pray?" With a little uplifting of the straight brows and a little gleam from under the long curled lashes.

"Because," says her lover, with fond conviction, "you are so infinitely superior to them, that they would have to be born all over again before you could bring yourself to fall into their ways."

"What! every woman in the known world?"

"Every one of them, I am eternally convinced."

"Teddy," says Molly, rubbing her cheek in her old caressing fashion against his sleeve, and slipping her fingers into his, "you may go on. Say anything you like,—call me any name you choose,—and I promise not to be one bit angry. There!"

When Luttrell has allowed himself time to let his own strong brown fingers close upon hers, and has solaced himself still further by pressing his lips to them, he takes courage and goes on, with a slightly accelerated color:

"Well, you see, Molly, you have made the subject a forbidden one, and—er—it is about our engagement I want to speak. Now, remember your promise, darling, and don't be vexed with me if I ask you to shorten it. Many people marry and are quite comfortable on five hundred pounds a year; why should not we? I know a lot of fellows who are doing uncommonly well on less."

"Poor fellows!" says Molly, full of sympathy.

"I know I am asking you a great deal,"—rather nervously,—"but won't you think of it, Molly?"

"I am afraid I won't, just yet," replies that lady, suavely. "Be sensible, Teddy; remember all we said to John, and think how foolish we should look going back of it all. Why should things not go on safely and secretly, as at present, and let us put marriage out of our heads until something turns up? I am like Mr. Micawber; I have an almost religious belief in the power things have of turning up."

"*I* haven't," says Luttrell, with terse melancholy.

"So much the worse for you. And besides, Teddy, instinct tells me you are much nicer as a lover than you will be as a husband. Once you attain to that position, I doubt I shall be able to order you about as I do at present."

"Try me."

"Not for a while. There, don't look so dismal, Ted; are we not perfectly happy as we are?"

"You may be, perhaps."

"Don't say, 'perhaps;' you may be certain of it," says she, gayly. "I haven't a doubt on the subject. Come, do look cheerful again. Men as fair as you should cultivate a perpetual smile."

"I wish I was a nigger," says Luttrell, impatiently. "You have such an admiration for blackamoors, that then, perhaps, you might learn to care for me a degree more than you do just now. Shadwell is dark enough for you."

"Yes; isn't he handsome?" With much innocent enthusiasm. "I thought last night at dinner, when——"

"I don't in the least want to know what you thought last night of Shadwell's personal appearance," Luttrell interrupts her, angrily.

"And I don't in the least want you to hold my hand a moment longer," replies Miss Massereene, with saucy retaliation, drawing her fingers from his with a sudden movement, and running away from him up the stone steps of the balcony into the house.

All through the night, both when waking and in dreams, the remembrance of the slight cast upon her absent mother by Mr. Amherst, and her own silent acceptance of it, has disturbed the mind of Marcia. "A dancer!" The word enrages her.

Molly's little passionate movement and outspoken determination to hear no ill spoken of her dead father showed Marcia even more forcibly her own cowardice and mean policy of action. And be sure she likes Molly none the more in that she was the one to show it. Yet Molly cannot possibly entertain the same affection for a mere memory that she feels for the mother on whom she has expended all the really pure and true love of which she is capable.

It is not, therefore, toward her grandfather, whose evil tongue has ever been his own undoing, she cherishes the greatest bitterness, but toward herself, together with a certain scorn that, through moneyed motives, she has tutored herself to sit by and hear the one she loves lightly mentioned.

Now, looking back upon it, it appears to her grossest treachery to the mother whose every thought she knows is hers, and who, in her foreign home, lives waiting, hoping, for the word that shall restore her to her arms.

A kind of anxiety to communicate with the injured one, and to pour out on paper the love she bears her, but dares not breathe at Herst, fills Marcia. So that when the house is silent on this Sunday afternoon,—when all the others have wandered into the open air,—she makes her way to the library, and, sitting down, commences one of the lengthy, secret, forbidden missives that always find their way to Italy, in spite of prying eyes and all the untold evils that so surely wait upon discovery.

To any one acquainted with Marcia, her manner of commencing her letter would be a revelation. To one so cold, so self-contained, the weaker symptoms of affection are disallowed; yet this is how she begins:

> "My own Beloved,—As yet I have no good news to send you, and little that I can say,—though ever as I write to you my heart is full. The old man grows daily more wearisome, more detestable, more inhuman, yet shows no sign of death. He is even, as it seems to me, stronger and more full of life than when last I wrote to you, now three weeks ago. At times I feel dispirited, almost despairing, and wonder if the day will ever come when we two shall be reunited,—when I shall be able to welcome you to my English home, where, in spite of prejudices, you will be happy, because you will be with me."

Here, unluckily, because of the trembling of her fingers, a large spot of ink falls heavily from her pen upon the half-written page beneath, destroying it.

With an exclamation expressive of impatience, Marcia pushes the sheet to one side and hastily commences again upon another. This time she is more successful, and has reached almost the last word in her final tender message, when a footstep approaching disturbs her. Gathering up her papers, she quits the library by its second door, and, gaining her own room, finishes and seals her packet.

Not until then does she perceive that the blotted sheet is no longer in her possession,—that by some untoward accident she must have forgotten it behind her in her flight.

Consternation seizes her. Whose were the footsteps that broke in upon her quietude? Why had she not stood her ground? With a beating heart she runs down-stairs, enters the library once more with cautious steps, only to find it empty. But, search as she may, the missing paper is not to be found.

What if it has fallen into her grandfather's keeping! A cold horror falls upon her. After all these weary years of hated servitude to be undone! It is impossible even fickle fortune should play her such a deadly trick!

Yet the horror continues until she finds herself again face to face with her grandfather. He is more than usually gracious,—indeed, almost marked in his attentions to her,—and once more Marcia breathes freely. No; probably the paper was destroyed; even she herself in a fit of abstraction may have torn it up before leaving the library.

The evening, being Sunday, proves even duller than usual. Mr. Amherst, with an amount of consideration not to be expected, retires to rest early. The others fall insensibly into the silent, dozy state. Mr. Darley gives way to a gentle snore. It is the gentlest thing imaginable, but effectual. Tedcastle starts to his feet and gives the fire a vigorous poke. He also trips very successfully over the footstool, that goes far to make poor Darley's slumbers blest, and brings that gentleman into a sitting posture.

"This will never do," Luttrell says, when he has apologized profusely to his awakened friend. "We are all growing sleepy. Potts, exert your energies and tell us a story."

"Yes, do, Plantagenet," says Lady Stafford, rousing herself resolutely, and shutting up her fan with a lively snap.

"I will," says Potts, obligingly, without a moment's hesitation.

"Potts is always equal to the occasion," Sir Penthony remarks, admiringly. "As a penny showman he would have been invaluable and died worth any money. Such energy, such unflagging zeal is rare. That pretty gunpowder plot he showed his friends the other night would fetch a large audience."

"Don't ask me to be the audience a second time," Lady Stafford says, unkindly. "To be blown to bits once in a lifetime is, I consider, quite sufficient."

"'Well, if ever I do a ky-ind action again,'" says Mr. Potts,—who is brimful of odd quotations, chiefly derived from low comedies,—posing after Toole. "It is the most mistaken thing in the world to do anything for anybody. You never know where it will end. I once knew a fellow who saved another fellow from drowning, and hanged if the other fellow didn't cling on him ever after and make him support him for life."

"I'm sure that's an edifying tale" says Sir Penthony, with a deep show of interest. "But—stop one moment, Potts. I confess I can't get any further for a minute or two. *How* many fellows were there? There was your fellow, and the other fellow, and the other fellow's fellow; was that three fellows or four? I can't make it out. I apologize all round for my stupidity, but would you say it all over again, Potts, and very slowly this time, please, to see if I can grasp it?"

"Give you my honor I thought it was a conundrum," says Henry Darley.

Plantagenet laughs as heartily as any one, and evidently thinks it a capital joke.

"You remind me of no one so much as Sothern," goes on Sir Penthony, warming to his theme. "If you went on the stage you would make your fortune. But don't dream of acting, you know; go in for being yourself, pure and simple,—plain, unvarnished Plantagenet Potts,—and I venture to say you will take London by storm. The British public would go down before you like corn before the reaper."

"Well, but your story,—your story, Plantagenet," Lady Stafford cries, impatiently.

"Did you hear the story about my mother and——"

"Potts," interrupts Stafford, mildly but firmly, "if you are going to tell the story about your mother and the auctioneer I shall leave the room. It will be the twenty-fifth time I have heard it already, and human patience has a limit. One must draw the line somewhere."

"What auctioneer?" demands Potts, indignant. "I am going to tell them about my mother and the auction; I never said a word about an auctioneer; there mightn't have been one, for all I know."

"There generally *is* at an auction," ventures Luttrell, mildly. "Go on, Potts; I like your stories immensely, they are so full of wit and spirit. I know this one, about your mother's bonnet, well; it is an old favorite,—quite an heirloom—the story, I mean, not the bonnet. I remember so distinctly the first time you told it to us at mess: how we did laugh, to be sure! Don't forget any of the details. The last time but four you made the bonnet pink, and it must have been so awfully unbecoming to your mother! Make it blue to-night."

"Now do go on, Mr. Potts; I am dying to hear all about it," declares Molly.

"Well, when my uncle died," begins Potts, "all his furniture was sold by auction. And there was a mirror in the drawing-room my mother had always had a tremendous fancy for——"

"'And my mother was always in the habit of wearing a black bonnet,'" quotes Sir Penthony, gravely. "I know it by heart."

"If you do you may as well tell it yourself," says Potts, much offended.

"Never mind him, Plantagenet; do go on," exclaims Cecil, impatiently.

"Well, she was in the habit of wearing a black bonnet, as it *happens*," says Mr. Potts, with suppressed ire; "but just before the auction she bought a new one, and it was pink."

"Oh, why on earth don't you say blue?" expostulates Luttrell, with a groan.

"Because it was pink. I suppose I know my mother's bonnet better than you?"

"But, my dear fellow, think of her complexion! And at first, I assure you, you always used to make it blue."

"I differ with you," puts in Sir Penthony, politely. "I always understood it was a sea-green."

"It was *pink*," reiterates Plantagenet, firmly. "Well, we had a cook who was very fond of my mother——"

"I thought it was a footman. And it really *was* a footman, you know," says Luttrell, reproachfully.

"The butler, you mean, Luttrell," exclaims Sir Penthony, with exaggerated astonishment at his friend's want of memory.

"And she, having most unluckily heard my mother say she feared she could not attend the auction, made up her mind to go herself and at all hazards secure the coveted mirror for her— —"

"And she didn't know my mother had on the new sea-green bonnet,'" Sir Penthony breaks in, with growing excitement.

"No, she didn't," says Mr. Potts, growing excited too. "So she started for my uncle's,—the cook, I mean,—and as soon as the mirror was put up began bidding away for it like a steam-engine. And presently some one in a pink bonnet began bidding too, and there they were bidding away against each other, the cook not knowing the bonnet, and my mother not being able to see the cook, she was so hemmed in by the crowd, until presently it was knocked down to my mother,—who is a sort of person who would die rather than give in,—and, would you believe it?" winds up Mr. Potts, nearly choking with delight over the misfortunes of his maternal relative, "she had given exactly five pounds more for that mirror than she need have done!"

They all laugh, Sir Penthony and Luttrell with a very suspicious mirth.

"Poor Mrs. Potts!" says Molly.

"Oh, *she* didn't mind. When she had relieved herself by blowing up the cook she laughed more than any of us. But it was a long time before the 'governor' could be brought to see the joke. You know he paid for it," says Plantagenet, naively.

"Moral: never buy a new bonnet," says Sir Penthony.

"Or keep an affectionate cook," says Luttrell.

"Or go to an auction," says Philip. "It is a very instructive tale: it is all moral."

"The reason I so much admire it. I know no one such an adept at pointing a moral and adorning a tale as our Plantagenet."

Mr. Potts smiles superior.

"I think the adornment rested with you and Luttrell," he says, with cutting sarcasm, answering Sir Penthony.

"Potts, you aren't half a one. Tell us another. Your splendid resources can't be yet exhausted," says Philip.

"Yes, do, Potts, and wake me when you come to the point," seconds Sir Penthony, warmly, sinking into an arm-chair and gracefully disposing an antimacassar over his head.

"A capital idea," murmurs Luttrell. "It will give us all a hint when we are expected to laugh."

"Oh, you can chaff as you like," exclaims Mr. Potts, much aggrieved; "but I wonder, if *I* went to sleep in an arm-chair, which of *you* would carry on the conversation?"

"Not one of them," declares Cecil, with conviction: "we should all die of mere inanition were it not for you."

"I really think they're all jealous of me," goes on Plantagenet, greatly fortified. "I consider myself by far the most interesting of them all, and the most—er——"

"Say it, Potts; don't be shy," says Sir Penthony, raising a corner of the antimacassar, so as to give his friends the full encouragement of one whole eye. "'Fascinating,' I feel sure, will be the right word in the right place here."

"It would indeed. I know nobody so really entertaining as Plantagenet," says Cecil, warmly.

"Your ladyship's judgment is always sound. I submit to it," returns Sir Penthony, rising to make her a profound bow.

CHAPTER XXI

> "'Why come you drest like a village maid
> That are the flower of the earth?'
> 'If I come drest like a village maid
> I am but as my fortunes are.'"
> —*Lady Clare.*

It is close on October. Already the grass has assumed its sober garb of brown; a general earthiness is everywhere. The leaves are falling,—not now in careful couples or one by one, but in whole showers,—slowly, sorrowfully, as though loath to quit the sighing branches, their last faint rustling making their death-song.

Molly's visit has drawn to an end. Her joyous month is over. To-day a letter from her brother reminding her of her promise to return is within her hand, recalling all the tender sweets of home life, all the calm pleasure she will gain, yet bringing with it a little sting, as she remembers all the gay and laughing hours that she must lose. For indeed her time at Herst has proved a good time.

"I have had a letter from my brother, grandpapa: he thinks it is time I should return," she says, accosting the old man as he takes his solitary walk up and down one of the shaded paths.

"Do you find it so dull here?" asks he, sharply, turning to read her face.

"Dull? No, indeed. How should I? I shall always remember my visit to you as one of the happy events of my life."

"Then remain a little longer," he growls, ungraciously. "The others have consented to prolong their stay; why should not you? Write to your— to Mr. Massereene to that effect. I cannot breathe in an empty house. It is my wish, my desire that you shall stay," he finishes, irritably, this being one of his painful days.

So it is settled. She will obey this crabbed veteran's behest and enjoy a little more of the good the gods have provided for her before returning to her quiet home.

"You will not desert us in our increased calamities, Molly, will you?" asks Cecil, half an hour later, as Molly enters the common boudoir where Lady Stafford and Marcia sit alone, the men being absent with their guns, and Mrs. Darley consequently in the blues. "Where have you been? We quite fancied you had taken a lesson out of poor dear Maudie's book and retired to your couch. Do you stay on at Herst?" She glances up anxiously from her painting as she speaks.

"Yes. Grandpapa has asked me to put off my departure for a while. So I shall. I have just written to John to say so, and to ask him if I may accept this second invitation."

"Do you think it likely he will refuse?" Marcia asks, unpleasantly.

"He may. But when I represent to him how terribly his obduracy will distress you all, should he insist on my return, I feel sure he will relent," retorts Molly, nonchalantly.

"Now that Mr. Amherst has induced us all to stay, don't you think he might do something to vary the entertainment?" says Cecil, in a faintly injured tone. "Shooting is all very well, of course, for those who like it; and so is tennis; and so are early hours; but *toujours perdrix*. I confess I hate my bed until the small hours are upon me. Now, if he would only give a ball, for instance! Do you think he would, Marcia, if he was asked?"

"How can I say?"

"Would *you* ask him, dear?"

"Well, I don't think I would," replies Marcia, with a rather forced laugh; "for this reason, that it would not be of the slightest use. I might as well ask him for the moon. If there is one thing he distinctly abhors, it is a ball."

"But he might go to bed early, if he wished," persists Cecil; "none of us would interfere or find fault with that arrangement. We would try and spare him, dear old thing. I don't see why our enjoyment should put him out in the least, if he would only be reasonable. I declare I have a great mind to ask him myself."

"Do," says Molly, eagerly, who is struck with admiration at the entire idea, having never yet been to a really large ball.

"I would rather somebody else tried it first," confesses Cecil, with a frank laugh. "A hundred times I have made up my mind to ask a favor of him, but when I found myself face to face with him, and he fixed me with his eagle eye, I quailed. Molly, you are a new importation; try your luck."

"Well, I don't mind if I do," says Molly, valiantly. "He can't say worse than 'No.' And here he is, coming slowly along under the balcony. Shall I seize the present opportunity and storm the citadel out of hand? I am sure if I wait I shall be like Bob Acres and find my courage oozing out through my fingers."

"Then don't," says Cecil. "If he molests you badly, I promise to interfere."

Molly steps on to the balcony, and, looking down, awaits the slow and languid approach of her grandfather. Just as he arrives beneath her she bends over until he, attracted by her presence, looks up.

She is laughing down upon him, bent on conquest, and has a blood-red rose in one hand. She waves it slightly to and fro, as though uncertain, as though dallying about giving utterance to some thought that pines for freedom.

The old man, pausing, looks up at her, and, looking, sighs,—perhaps for his dead youth, perhaps because she so much resembles her mother, disowned and forgotten.

"Have a rose, grandpapa?" says Molly, stooping still farther over the iron railings, her voice sweet and fresh as the dead and gone Eleanor's. As she speaks she drops the flower, and he dexterously, by some fortuitous chance, catches it.

"Well done!" cries she, with a gay laugh, clapping her hands, feeling half surprised, wholly amused, at his nimbleness. "Yet stay, grandpapa, do not go so soon. I—have a favor to ask of you."

"Well?"

"We have been discussing something delightful for the past five minutes,—something downright delicious; but we can do nothing without you. Will you help us, grandpapa? will you?" She asks all this with the prettiest grace, gazing down undaunted into the sour old face raised to hers.

"Why are you spokeswoman?" demands he, in a tone that makes the deeply attentive Cecil within groan aloud.

"Well—because—I really don't believe I know why, except that I chose to be so. But grant me this, my first request. Ah! do, now, grandpapa."

The sweet coaxing of the Irish "Ah!" penetrates even this withered old heart.

"What is this wonderful thing you would have me do?" asks he, some of the accumulated verjuice of years disappearing from his face; while Lady Stafford, from behind the curtain, looks on trembling with fear for the success of her scheme, and Marcia listens and watches with envious rage.

"We want you to—give a ball," says Molly, boldly, with a little gasp, keeping her large eyes fixed in eager anxiety upon his face, while her pretty parted lips seem still to entreat. "Say 'yes' to me, grandpapa."

How to refuse so tender a pleading? How bring the blank that a "No" must cause upon her *riante*, lovely face?

"Suppose I say I cannot?" asks he; but his tone has altered wonderfully, and there is an expression that is almost amiable upon his face. The utter absence of constraint, of fear, she displays in his presence has charmed him, being so unlike the studied manner of all those with whom he comes in contact.

"Then I shall cry my eyes out," says Molly, still lightly, though secretly her heart is sinking.

There is a perceptible pause. Then Mr. Amherst says, slowly, regretfully:

"Crying will come too soon, child. None escape. Keep your eyes dry as long as your heart will let you. No, you shall not fret because of me. You shall have your ball, I promise you, and as soon as ever you please."

So saying, and with a quick movement of the hand that declines all thanks, he moves away, leaving Molly to return to the boudoir triumphant, though somewhat struck and saddened by his words and manner.

"Let me embrace you," cries Cecil, tragically, flinging herself into her arms. "Molly, Molly, you are a siren!"

Without a word or a look, Marcia rises slowly and quits the room.

The invitations are issued, and unanimously accepted. A ball at Herst is such a novelty, that the county to a man declare their intention of being present at it. It therefore promises to be a great success.

As for the house itself, it is in a state of delicious unrest. There is a good deal of noise, but very little performance, and every one gives voice now and then to the most startling opinions. One might, indeed, imagine that all these people—who, when in town during the season, yawn systematically through their two or three balls of a night—had never seen one, so eager and anxious are they for the success of this solitary bit of dissipation.

Lady Stafford is in great form, and becomes even more *debonnaire* and saucy than is her wont. Even Marcia seems to take some interest in it, and lets a little vein of excitement crop up here and there through all the frozen placidity of her manner; while Molly, who has never yet been at a really large affair of the kind, loses her head and finds herself unable to think or converse on any other subject.

Yet in all this beautiful but unhappy world where is the pleasure that contains no sting of pain? Molly's is a sharp little sting that pricks her constantly and brings an uneasy sigh to her lips. Perhaps in a man's eyes the cause would be considered small, but surely in a woman's overwhelming. It is a question of dress, and poor Molly's mind is much exercised thereon.

When all the others sit and talk complacently of their silks and satins, floating tulles and laces, she, with a pang, remembers that all she has to wear is a plain white muslin. It is hard. No doubt she will look pretty—perhaps prettier and fairer than most—in the despised muslin; but as surely she will look poorly attired, and the thought is not inspiring.

No one but a woman can know what a woman thinks on such a subject; and although she faces the situation philosophically enough, and by no means despises herself for the pangs of envy she endures when listening to Maud Darley's account of the triumph in robes to be sent by Worth for the Herst ball, she still shrinks from the cross-examination she will surely have to undergo at the hands of Cecil Stafford as to her costume for the coming event.

One day, a fortnight before the ball, Cecil does seize on her, and, carrying her off to her own room and placing her in her favorite chair, says, abruptly:

"What about your dress, Molly?"

"I don't know that there is anything to say about it," says Molly, who is in low spirits. "The only thing I have is a new white muslin, and that will scarcely astonish the natives."

"Muslin! Oh, Molly! Not but that it is pretty always,—I know nothing more so,—but for a ball-dress—terribly *rococo*. I have set my heart on seeing you resplendent; and if you are not more gorgeous than Marcia I shall break down. Muslin won't do at all."

"But I'm afraid it must."

"What a pity it is I am so much shorter than you!" says Cecil, regretfully. "Now, if I was taller we might make one of my dresses suit you."

"Yes, it is a pity,—a dreadful pity," says Molly, mournfully. "I should like to be really well dressed. Marcia, I suppose, will be in satin, or something else equally desirable."

"No doubt she will deck herself out in Oriental splendor, if she discovers you can't," says Cecil, angrily.

There is a pause,—a decided one. Cecil sits frowning and staring at Molly, who has sunk into an attitude expressive of the deepest dejection. The little ormolu clock, regardless of emotion, ticks on undisturbed until three full minutes vanish into the past. Then Cecil, as though suddenly inspired, says, eagerly:

"Molly, why not ask your grandfather to give you a dress?"

"Not for all the world! Nothing would induce me. If I never was to see a ball I would not ask him for sixpence. How could you think it of me, Cecil?"

"Why didn't I think of it long ago, you mean? I only wish he was *my* grandfather, and I would never cease persecuting him, morning, noon, and night. What is the use of a grandfather if it isn't to tip one every now and then?"

"You forget the circumstances of my case."

"I do not indeed. Of course, beyond all doubt, he behaved badly; still— —I really think," says Cecil, in a highly moralizing tone, "there is nothing on earth so mistaken as pride. I am free from it. I don't know the meaning of it, and I know I am all the happier in consequence."

"Perhaps I am more angry than proud."

"It is the same thing, and I wish you weren't. Oh, Molly! do ask him. What can it signify what he thinks?"

"Nothing; but a great deal what John thinks. It would be casting a slight upon him, as though he stinted me in clothes or money, and I will not do it."

"It would be such a simple way," says Cecil, with a melancholy sigh,— dear Molly is so obstinate and old-fashioned; then follows another pause, longer and more decided than the last. Molly, with her back turned to her friend, commences such a dismal tattoo upon the window-pane as would be sufficient to depress any one without further cause. Her friend is pondering deeply.

"Molly," she says, presently, with a fine amount of indifference in her tone,—rather suspicious, to say the least of it,—"I feel sure you are right,— quite right. I like you all the better for—your pride, or whatever you may wish to call it. But what a pity it is your grandfather would not offer you a dress or a check to buy it! I suppose"—quietly—-"if he did, you would take it?"

"What a chance there is of that!" says Molly, still gloomy. "Yes, if he *offered* it I do not think I could bring myself to refuse it. I am not adamant. You see"—with a faint laugh—"my pride would not carry me very far."

"Far enough. Let us go down to the others," says Cecil, rising and yawning slightly. "They will think we are planning high treason if we absent ourselves any longer."

Together they go down-stairs and into the drawing-room, which they find empty.

As they reach the centre of it, Cecil stops abruptly, and, saying carelessly, "I will be back in one moment," turns and leaves the room.

The apartment is deserted. No sound penetrates to it. Even the very fire, in a fit of pique, has degenerated into a dull glow.

Molly, with a shiver, rouses it, throws on a fresh log, and amuses herself trying to induce the tardy flames to climb and lick it until Lady Stafford returns. So busy has she been, it seems to her as though only a minute has elapsed since her departure.

"This does look cozy," Cecil says, easily sinking into a lounging-chair. "Now, if those tiresome men had not gone shooting we should not be able to cuddle into our fire as we are doing at present. After all, it is a positive relief to get them out of the way,—sometimes."

"You don't seem very hearty about that sentiment."

"I am, for all that. With a good novel I would now be utterly content for an hour or two. By the bye, I left my book on the library table. If you were good-natured, Molly, I know what you would do."

"So do I: I would get it for you. Well, taking into consideration all things, your age and growing infirmities among them, I will accept your hint." And, rising, she goes in search of the missing volume.

Opening the library door with a little bang and a good deal of reckless unconsciousness, she finds herself in Mr. Amherst's presence.

"Oh!" cries she, with a surprised start. "I beg your pardon, grandpapa. If"—pausing on the threshold—"I had known you were here, I would not have disturbed you."

"You don't disturb me," replies he, without looking up; and, picking up the required book, Molly commences a hasty retreat.

But just as she gains the door her grandfather's voice once more arrests her.

"Wait," he says; "I want to ask you a question that—that has been on my mind for a considerable time."

To the commonest observer it would occur that from the break to the finish of this little sentence is one clumsy invention.

"Yes?" says Molly.

"Have you a dress for this ball,—this senseless rout that is coming off?" says Mr. Amherst, without looking at her.

"Yes, grandpapa." In a tone a degree harder.

"You are my granddaughter. I desire to see you dressed as such. Is"— with an effort—"your gown a handsome one?"

"Well, that greatly depends upon taste," returns Molly, who, though angry, finds a grim amusement in watching the flounderings of this tactless old person. "If we are to believe that beauty unadorned is adorned the most, I may certainly flatter myself I shall be the best dressed woman in the room. But there *may* be some who will not call white muslin 'handsome.'"

"White muslin up to sixteen is very charming," Mr. Amherst says, in a slow tone of a connoisseur in such matters, "but not beyond. And you are, I think——"

"Nineteen."

"Quite so. Then in your case I should condemn the muslin. You will permit me to give you a dress, Eleanor, more in accordance with your age and position."

"Thank you very much, grandpapa," says Molly, with a little ominous gleam in her blue eyes. "You are too good. I am deeply sensible of all your kindness, but I really cannot see how my position has altered of late. As you have just discovered, I am now nineteen, and for so many years I have managed to look extremely well in white muslin."

As she finishes her modest speech she feels she has gone too far. She has been almost impertinent, considering his age and relationship to her; nay, more, she has been ungenerous.

Her small taunt has gone home. Mr. Amherst rises from his chair; the dull red of old age comes painfully into his withered cheeks as he stands gazing at her, slight, erect, with her proud little head upheld so haughtily.

For a moment anger masters him; then it fades, and something as near remorse as his heart can hold replaces it.

Molly, returning his glance with interest, knows he is annoyed. But she does not know that, standing as she now does, with uplifted chin and gleaming eyes, and just a slight in-drawing of her lips, she is the very image of the dead-and-gone Eleanor, that, in spite of her Irish father, her Irish name, she is a living, breathing, defiant Amherst.

In silence that troubles her she waits for the next word. It comes slowly, almost entreatingly.

"Molly," says her grandfather, in a tone that trembles ever so little,—it is the first time he has ever called her by her pet name,—"Molly, I shall take it as a great favor if you will accede to my request and accept—this."

As he finishes he holds out to her a check, regarding her earnestly the while.

The "Molly" has done it. Too generous even to hesitate, she takes the paper, and, going closer to him, lays her hand upon his shoulder.

"I have been rude, grandpapa,—I beg your pardon,—and I am very much obliged to you for this money."

So saying, she bends and presses her soft sweet lips to his cheek. He makes no effort to return the caress, but long after she leaves the room sits staring vaguely before him out of the dreary window on to the still more dreary landscape outside, thinking of vanished days and haunting actions that will not be laid, but carry with them their sure and keen revenge, in the knowledge that to the dead no ill can be undone.

Molly, going back to the drawing-room, finds Cecil there, serene as usual.

"Well, and where is my book?" asks that innocent. "I thought you were never coming."

"Cecil, why did you tell grandpapa to offer me a dress?" demands Molly, abruptly.

"My dearest girl!——" exclaims Cecil, and then has the grace to stop and blush, a little.

"You did. There is no use your denying it."

"You didn't refuse it? Oh, Molly, after all my trouble!"

"No,"—laughing, and unfolding her palm, where the paper lies crushed,—"but I was very near it. But that his manner was so kind, so marvelously gentle, for him, I should have done so. Cecil, I couldn't help thinking that perhaps long ago, before the world hardened him, grandpapa was a nice young man."

"Perhaps he was, my dear,—there is no knowing what any of us may come to,—though you must excuse me if I say I rather doubt it. Well, and what did he say?"

"Very little, indeed; and that little a failure. When going about it you might have given him a few lessons in his *rôle*. So bungling a performance as the leading up to it I never witnessed; and when he wound up by handing me a check ready prepared beside him on the desk I very nearly laughed."

"Old goose! Never mind; 'they laugh who win.' I have won."

"So you have."

"Well, but look, Molly, look. I want to see how far his unwonted 'gentleness' has carried him. I am dying of curiosity. I do hope he has not been shabby."

Unfolding the paper, they find the check has been drawn for a hundred pounds.

"Very good," says Cecil, with a relieved sigh. "He is not such a bad old thing, when all is told."

"It is too much," says Molly, aghast. "I can't take it, indeed. I would have thought twenty pounds a great deal, but a *hundred* pounds! I must take it back to him."

"Are you mad," exclaims Cecil, "to insult him? He thinks *nothing* of a hundred pounds. And to give back money,—that scarce commodity,—how could you bring yourself to do it?" In tones of the liveliest reproach. "Be reasonable, dear, and let us see how we can spend it fast enough."

Thus adjured, Molly succumbs, and, sinking into a chair, is soon deep in the unfathomable mysteries of silks and satins, tulle and flowers.

"And, Cecil, I should like to buy Letitia a silk dress like that one of yours up-stairs I admire so much."

"The navy blue?"

"No, the olive-green; it would just suit her. She has a lovely complexion, clear and tinted, like your own."

"Thank you, dear. It is to be regretted you are of the weaker sex. So delicately veiled a compliment would not have disgraced a Chesterfield."

"Was it too glaring? Well, I will do away with it. I was thinking entirely of Letty. I was comparing her skin very favorably with yours. That reminds me I must write home to-day. I hope John won't be offended with me about this money. Though, after all, there can't be much harm in accepting a present from one's grandfather."

"I should think not, indeed. I only wish I had a grandfather, and wouldn't I utilize him! But I am an unfortunate,—alone in the world."

Even as she speaks, the door in the next drawing-room opens, and through the folding-doors, which stand apart, she sees her husband enter, and make his way to a davenport.

"That destroys your argument," says Molly, with a low laugh, as she runs away to her own room to write her letters.

For a few minutes Cecil sits silently enjoying a distant view of her husband's back. But she is far too much of a coquette to let him long remain in ignorance of her near proximity. Going softly up to him, and leaning lightly over his shoulder, she says, in a half-whisper, "What are you doing?"

He starts a little, not having expected to see so fair an apparition, and lays one of his hands over hers as it rests upon his shoulder.

"Is it you?" he says. "I did not hear you coming."

"No? That was because I was farthest from your thoughts. You are writing? To whom?"

"My tailor, for one. It is a sad but certain fact that, sooner or later, one's tailor must be paid."

"So must one's *modiste*." With a sigh. "It is that sort of person who spoils one's life."

"Is your life spoiled?"

"Oh, yes, in many ways."

"Poor little soul!" says he, with a half laugh, tightening his fingers over hers. "Is your dressmaker hardhearted?"

"Don't get me to begin on that subject, or I shall never leave off. The wrongs I have suffered at that woman's hands! But then why talk of what cannot be helped?"

"Perhaps it may. Can I do nothing for you?"

"I am afraid not." Moving a little away from him. "And yet, perhaps, if you choose, you might. You are writing; I wish"—throwing down her eyes, as though confused (which she isn't), and assuming her most guileless air—"you would write something for *me*."

"What a simple request! Of course I will—anything."

"Really? You promise?"

"Faithfully."

"It is not, perhaps, quite so simple a request as it appears. I want you, in fact, to—write me—a check!"

Sir Penthony laughs, and covers the white and heavily-jeweled little hand that glitters before him on the table once more with his own.

"For how much?" he asks.

"Not much,—only fifty pounds. I want to buy something particular for this ball: and"—glancing at him—"being a lone woman, without a protector, I dread going too heavily into debt."

"Good child," says Sir Penthony. "You shall have your check." Drawing the book toward him as it lies before him on the davenport, he fills up a check and hands it to her.

"Now, what will you give me for it?" asks he, holding the edge near him as her fingers close upon the other end.

"What have I to give? Have I not just acknowledged myself insolvent? I am as poor as a church mouse."

"You disparage yourself. I think you as rich as Crœsus. Will you—give me a kiss?" whispers her husband, softly.

There is a decided pause. Dropping the check and coloring deeply, Cecil moves back a step or two. She betrays a little indignation in her glance,—a very little, but quite perceptible. Stafford sees it.

"I beg your pardon," he says, hastily, an expression of mingled pain and shame crossing his face. "I was wrong, of course. I will not buy your kisses. Here, take this bit of paper, and—forgive me."

He closes her somewhat reluctant fingers over the check. She is still blushing, and has her eyes fixed on the ground, but her faint anger has disappeared. Then some thought—evidently a merry one—occurs to her; the corners of her mouth widen, and finally she breaks into a musical laugh.

"Thank you—very much," she says. "You are very good. It is something to have a husband, after all. And—if you would really care for it—I—don't mind letting you have one——Oh! here is somebody coming."

"There always is somebody coming when least wanted," exclaims Sir Penthony, wrathfully, pushing back his chair with much suppressed ire, as the door opens to admit Mr. Potts.

"'I hope I don't intrude,'" says Potts, putting his comfortable face and rosy head round the door; "but I've got an idea, and I must divulge it or burst. You wouldn't like me to burst, would you?" This to Lady Stafford, pathetically.

"I would not,—here," replies she, with decision.

"For fear you might, I shall take my departure," says Sir Penthony, who has not yet quite recovered either his disappointment or his temper, walking through the conservatory into the grounds beyond.

"I really wish, Plantagenet," says Lady Stafford, turning upon the bewildered Potts with most unaccountable severity, "you could manage to employ your time in some useful way. The dreadful manner in which you spend your days, wandering round the house without aim or reason, causes me absolute regret. *Do* give yourself the habit of reading or—or doing something to improve your mind, whenever you have a spare moment."

So saying, she sweeps past him out of the room, without even making an inquiry about that priceless idea, leaving poor Potts rooted to the ground, striving wildly, but vainly, to convict himself of some unpardonable offense.

CHAPTER XXII

"Love, thou art bitter."

—Blaine.

Mr. Amherst, having in a weak moment given his consent to the ball, repays himself by being as unamiable afterward as he can well manage.

"You can have your music and the supper from London, if you wish it," he says to Marcia, one day, when he has inveighed against the whole proceeding in language that borders on the abusive; "but if you think I am going to have an army of decorators down here, turning the house into a fancy bazar, and making one feel a stranger in one's own rooms, you are very much mistaken."

"I think you are right, dear," Marcia answers, with her customary meekness: "people of that kind are always more trouble than anything else. And no doubt we shall be able to do all that is necessary quite as well ourselves."

"As to that you can, of course, please yourself. Though why you cannot dance without filling the rooms with earwigs and dying flowers I can't conceive."

Mr. Amherst's word being like the law of the Medes and Persians, that altereth not, no one disputes it. They couple a few opprobrious epithets with his name just at first, but finally, putting on an air of resolution, declare themselves determined and ready to outdo any decorators in the kingdom.

"We shall wake up in the morning after the ball to find ourselves famous," says Lady Stafford. "The county will ring with our praises. But we must have help: we cannot depend upon broken reeds." With a reproachful glance at Sir Penthony, who is looking the picture of laziness. "Talbot Lowry, of course, will assist us; *he* goes without saying."

"I hope he will come without saying," puts in Sir Penthony; "it would be much more to the purpose. Any smart young tradesmen among your fellows, Mottie?"

"Unless Grainger. You know Grainger, Lady Stafford?"

"Indeed I do. What! is he stationed with you now? He must have re-joined very lately."

"Only the other day. Would he be of any use to you?"

"The very greatest."

"What! Spooney?" says Tedcastle, laughing. "I don't believe he could climb a ladder to save his life. Think of his pretty hands and his sweet little feet."

"And his lisp,—and his new eyeglass," says Stafford.

"Never mind; I *will* have him here," declares Cecil, gayly. "In spite of all you say, I positively adore that Grainger boy."

"You seem to have a passion for fools," says Sir Penthony, a little bitterly, feeling some anger toward her.

"And you seem to have a talent for incivility," retorts she, rather nettled. This ends the conversation.

Nevertheless Mr. Grainger is asked to come and give what assistance he can toward adorning Herst, which, when they take into consideration the ladylike whiteness of his hands and the general imbecility of his countenance, is not set at a very high value.

He is a tall, lanky youth, with more than the usual allowance of bone, but rather less of intellect; he is, however, full of ambition and smiles, and is amiability itself all round. He is also desperately addicted to Lady Stafford. He has a dear little moustache, that undergoes much encouragement from his thumb and first finger, and he has a captivating way of saying "How charming!" or, "Very sweet," to anything that pleases him. And, as most things seem to meet his approbation, he makes these two brilliant remarks with startling frequency.

To Cecil he is a joy. In him she evidently finds a fund of amusement, as, during the three days it takes them to convert the ball-room, tea-room, etc., into perfumed bowers, she devotes herself exclusively to his society.

Perhaps the undisguised chagrin of Sir Penthony and Talbot Lowry as they witness her civility to Grainger goes far to add a zest to her enjoyment of that young man's exceedingly small talk.

After dinner on the third day all is nearly completed. A few more leaves, a few more flowers, a wreath or two to be distributed here and there, is all that remains to be done.

"I hate decorating in October," Cecil says. "There is such a dearth of flowers, and the gardeners get so greedy about the house plants. Every blossom looks as if it had been made the most of."

"Well, I don't know," replies Mr. Grainger, squeezing his glass into his eye with much difficulty, it being a new importation and hard to manage. When he has altered all his face into an appalling grin, and completely blocked the sight of one eye, he goes on affably: "I think all this—er—very charming."

"No? Do you? I'm *so* glad. Do you know I believe you have wonderful taste? The way in which you tied that last bunch of trailing ivy had something about it absolutely artistic."

"If it hadn't fallen to pieces directly afterward, which rather spoiled the effect," says Sir Penthony, with an unkind smile.

"Did it? How sad! But then the idea remains, and that is everything. Now, Mr. Grainger, please stand here—(will you move a little bit, Sir Penthony? Thanks)—just here—while I go up this ladder to satisfy myself about these flowers. By the bye,"—pausing on one of the rungs to look back,—"suppose I were to fall? Do you think you could catch me?"

"I only wish you would give me the opportunity of trying," replies he, weakly.

"Beastly puppy!" mutters Sir Penthony, under his breath.

"Perhaps I shall, if you are good. Now look. Are they straight? Do they look well?" asks Cecil.

"Very sweet," replies Mr. Grainger.

"Potts, hand me up some nails," exclaims Lowry, impatiently, who is on another ladder close by, and has been an attentive and disgusted listener; addressing Potts, who stands lost in contemplation of Grainger. "Look sharp, can't you? And tell me what you think of this." Pointing to his design on the wall. "Is it 'all your fancy painted it?' Is it 'lovely' and 'divine?' Answer."

"Very sour, I think," returns Mr. Potts, hitting off Grainger's voice to a nicety, while maintaining a countenance sufficiently innocent to border on the imbecile.

Both Sir Penthony and Lowry laugh immoderately, while Cecil turns away to hide the smile that may betray her. Grainger himself is the only one wholly unconscious of any joke. He smiles, indeed, genially, because they smile, and happily refrains from inquiry of any sort.

Meantime in the tea-room—that opens off the supper-room, where the others are engaged—Molly and Philip are busy arranging bouquets chosen from among a basketful of flowers that has just been brought in by one of the under-gardeners.

Philip is on his knees,—almost at Molly's feet,—while she bends over him searching for the choicest buds.

"What a lovely ring!" says Philip, presently, staying in his task to take her hand and examine the diamond that glitters on it. "Was it a present?"

"Of course. Where could such a 'beggar-maid' as I am get money enough to buy such a ring?"

"Will you think me rude if I ask you the every-day name of your King Cophetua?"

"I have no King Cophetua."

"Then tell me where you got it?"

"What a question!" Lightly. "Perhaps from my own true love. Perhaps it is the little fetter that seals my engagement to him. Perhaps it isn't."

"Yet you said just now——"

"About that eccentric king? Well, I spoke truly. Royalty has not yet thrown itself at my feet. Still,"—coquettishly,—"that is no reason why I should look coldly upon all commoners."

"Be serious, Molly, for one moment," he entreats, the look of passionate earnestness she so much dislikes coming over his face, darkening instead of brightening it. "Sometimes I am half mad with doubt. Tell me the truth,—now,—here. Are you engaged? Is there anything between you and—Luttrell?"

The spirit of mischief has laid hold of Molly. She cares nothing at all for Shadwell. Of all the men she has met at Herst he attracts her least. She scarcely understands the wild love with which she has inspired him; she cannot sympathize with his emotion.

"Well, if you compel me to confess it," she says, lowering her eyes, 'there is."

"It is true, then!" cries he, rising to his feet and turning deadly pale. "My fears did not deceive me."

"Quite true. There is a whole long room 'between me' and Mr. Luttrell and"—dropping her voice—"you." Here she laughs merrily and with all her heart. To her it is a jest,—no more.

"How a woman—the very best woman—loves to torture!" exclaims he, anger and relief struggling in his tone. "Oh, that I dared believe that latter part of your sentence,—that I could stand between you and all the world!"

"'Fain would I climb, but that I fear to fall,'" quotes Molly, jestingly. "You know the answer? 'If thy heart fail thee, do not climb at all.'"

"Is that a challenge?" demands he, eagerly, going nearer to her.

"I don't know." Waving him back. "Hear the oracle again. I feel strong in appropriate rhyme to-night:

"'He either fears his fate too much,

Or his deserts are small,

Who fears to put it to the touch

To win or lose it all.'"

They are quite alone. Some one has given the door leading to the adjoining apartment a push that has entirely closed it. Molly, in her white evening gown and pale-blue ribbons, with a bunch of her favorite roses at her breast, is looking up at him, a little mocking smile upon her lips. She is cold,—perhaps a shade amused,—without one particle of sentiment.

"I fear nothing," cries Philip, in a low impassioned tone, made unwisely bold by her words, seizing her hands and pressing warm, unwelcome kisses on them; "whether I win or lose, I will speak now. Yet what shall I tell you that you do not already know? I love you,—my idol,—my darling! Oh, Molly! do not look so coldly on me."

"Don't be earnest, Philip," interrupts she, with a frown, and a sudden change of tone, raising her head, and regarding him with distasteful hauteur; "there is nothing I detest so much; and *your* earnestness especially wearies me. When I spoke I was merely jesting, as you must have known. I do not want your love. I have told you so before. Let my hands go, Philip; your touch is *hateful* to me."

He drops her hands as though they burned him; and she, with flushed cheeks and a still frowning brow, turns abruptly away, leaving him alone,— angered, hurt, but still adoring.

Ten minutes later, her heart—a tender one—misgives her. She has been unjust to him,—unkind. She will return and make such reparation as lies in her power.

With a light step she returns to the tea-room, where she left him, and, looking gently in, finds he has neither stirred nor raised his head since her cruel words cut him to the heart. Ten minutes,—a long time,—and all consumed in thoughts of her! Feeling still more contrite, she approaches him.

"Why, Philip," she says, with an attempt at playfulness, "still enduring 'grinding torments?' What have I said to you? You have taken my foolish words too much to heart. That is not wise. Sometimes I hardly know myself what it is I have been saying."

She has come very near to him,—so near that gazing up at him appealingly, she brings her face in dangerously close proximity to his. A mad desire to kiss the lips that sue so sweetly for a pardon fills him, yet he dares not do it. Although a man not given to self-restraint where desire is at elbow urging him on, he now stands subdued, unnerved, in Molly's presence.

"Have I really distressed you?" asks she, softly, his strange silence rendering her still more remorseful. "Come,"—laying her hand upon his arm,—"tell me what I have done."

"'Sweet, you have trod on a heart,'" quotes Philip, in so low a tone as to be almost unheard. He crosses his hand tightly over hers for an instant; a moment later, and it is she who—this time—finds herself alone.

In the next room success is crowning their efforts. When Molly re-enters, she finds the work almost completed. Just a finishing touch here and there, and all is ended.

"I suppose I should consider myself in luck: I have still a little skin left," says Sir Penthony, examining his hand with tender solicitude. "I don't think I fancy decorating: I shan't take to the trade."

"You—should have put on gloves, you know, and that," says Grainger, who is regarding his dainty fingers with undisguised sadness,—something that is *almost* an expression on his face.

"But isn't it awfully pretty?" says Lady Stafford, gazing round her with an air of pride.

"Awfully nice," replies Molly.

"Quite too awfully awful," exclaims Mr. Potts, with exaggerated enthusiasm, and is instantly suppressed.

"If you cannot exhibit greater decorum, Potts, we shall be obliged to put your head in a bag," says Sir Penthony, severely. "I consider 'awfully' quite the correct word. What with the ivy and the gigantic size of those paper roses, the room presents quite a startling appearance."

"Well, I'm sure they are far prettier than Lady Harriet Nitemair's; and she made such a fuss about hers last spring," says Cecil, rather injured.

"Not to be named in the same day," declares Luttrell, who had not been at Lady Harriet Nitemair's.

"Why, Tedcastle, you were not there; you were on your way home from India at that time."

"Was I? By Jove! so I was. Never mind, I take your word for it, and stick to my opinion," replies Luttrell, unabashed.

"I really think we ought to christen our work." Mr. Potts puts in dreamily, being in a thirsty mood; and christened it is in champagne.

Potts himself, having drunk his own and every one else's health many times, grows gradually gayer and gayer. To wind up this momentous evening without making it remarkable in any way strikes him as being a tame proceeding. "To do or die" suddenly occurs to him, and he instantly acts upon it.

Seeing his two former allies standing rather apart from the others, he makes for them and thus addresses them:

"Tell you what," he says, with much geniality, "it feels like Christmas, and crackers, and small games, don't it? I feel up to anything. And I have a capital idea in my head. Wouldn't it be rather a joke to frighten the others?"

"It would," says Cecil, decidedly.

"Would it?" says Molly, diffidently.

"I have a first-rate plan; I can make you both look so like ghosts that you would frighten the unsuspecting into fits."

"First, Plantagenet, before we go any further into your ghostly schemes, answer me this: *is* there any gunpowder about it?"

"None." Laughing. "You just dress yourselves in white sheets, or that, and hold a plate in your hands filled with whiskey and salt, and—there you are. You have no idea of the tremendous effect. You will be more like a corpse than anything you can imagine."

"How cheerful!" murmurs Cecil. "You make me long for the 'sheets and that.'"

"Do the whiskey and the salt ever blow up?" asks Molly, cautiously. "Because if so——"

"No, they don't; of course not. Say nothing about it to the others, and we shall astonish them by and by. It is an awfully becoming thing, too," says Potts, with a view to encouragement; "you will look like marble statues."

"We are trusting you again," says Cecil, regarding him fixedly. "Plantagenet, if you should again be our undoing——"

"Not the slightest fear of a *fiasco* this time," says Potts, comfortably.

CHAPTER XXIII

"Here's such a coil! Come, what says Romeo?"
—Shakespeare.

As eleven o'clock strikes, any one going up the stairs at Herst would have stopped with a mingled feeling of terror and admiration at one particular spot, where, in a niche, upon a pedestal, a very goddess stands.

It is Molly, clad in white, from head to heel, with a lace scarf twisted round her head and shoulders, and with one bare arm uplifted, while with the other she holds an urn-shaped vase beneath her face, from which a pale-blue flame arises.

Her eyes, larger, deeper, bluer than usual, are fixed with sad and solemn meaning upon space. She scarcely seems to breathe; no quiver disturbs her frame, so intensely does she listen for a coming footstep. In her heart she hopes it may be Luttrell's.

The minutes pass. Her arm is growing tired, her eyes begin to blink against her will; she is on the point of throwing up the game, descending from her pedestal, and regaining her own room, when a footfall recalls her to herself and puts her on her mettle.

Nearer it comes,—still nearer, until it stops altogether. Molly does not dare turn to see who it is. A moment later, a wild cry, a smothered groan, falls upon her ear, and, turning her head, terrified, she sees her grandfather rush past her, tottering, trembling, until he reaches his own room, where he disappears.

Almost at the same instant the others who have been in the drawing-room, drawn to the spot by the delicate machinations of Mr. Potts, come on the scene; while Marcia, who has heard that scared cry, emerges quickly from among them and passes up the stairs into her grandfather's room.

There follows an awkward silence. Cecil, who has been adorning a corner farther on, comes creeping toward them, pale and nervous, having also been a witness to Mr. Amherst's hurried flight; and she and Molly, in their masquerading costumes, feel, to say the least of it, rather small.

They cast a withering glance at Potts, who has grown a lively purple; but he only shakes his head, having no explanation to offer, and knowing himself for once in his life to be unequal to the occasion.

Mrs. Darley is the first to break silence.

"What is it? What has happened? Why are you both here in your night-dresses?" she asks, unguardedly, losing her head in the excitement of the moment.

"What do you mean?" says Cecil, angrily. "'Nightdresses'! If you don't know dressing-gowns when you see them, I am sorry for you. Plantagenet, what has happened?"

"It was grandpapa," says Molly, in a frightened tone. "He came by, and I think was upset by my—appearance. Oh, I hope I have not done him any harm! Mr. Potts, *why* did you make me do it?"

"How could I tell?" replies Potts, who is as white as their costumes. "What an awful shriek he gave! I thought such a stern old card as he is would have had more pluck!"

"I was positive he was in bed," says Cecil, "or I should never have ventured."

"He is never where he ought to be," mutters Potts gloomily.

Here conversation fails them. For once they are honestly dismayed, and keep their eyes fixed in anxious expectation on the bedchamber of their host. Will Marcia *never* come?

At length the door opens and she appears, looking pale and *distraite*. Her eyes light angrily as they fall on Molly.

"Grandpapa is very much upset. He is ill. It was heartless, a cruel trick," she says, rather incoherently. "He wishes to see you, Eleanor, instantly. You had better go to him."

"Must I?" asks Molly, who is quite colorless, and much inclined to cry.

"Unless you wish to add disobedience to your other unfeeling conduct," replies Marcia, coldly.

"No, no; of course not. I will go," says Molly, nervously.

With faltering footsteps she approaches the fatal door, whilst the others disperse and return once more to the drawing-room,—all, that is, except Lady Stafford, who seeks her own chamber, and Mr. Potts, who, in an agony of doubt and fear, lingers about the corridor, awaiting Molly's return.

As she enters her grandfather's room she finds him lying on a couch, half upright, an angry, disappointed expression on his face, distrust in his searching eyes.

"Come here," he says, harshly, motioning her with one finger to his side, "and tell me why you, of all others, should have chosen to play this trick upon me. Was it revenge?"

"Upon you, grandpapa! Oh, not upon you," says Molly, shocked. "It was all a mistake,—a mere foolish piece of fun; but I never thought *you* would have been the one to see me."

"Are you lying? Let me look at you. If so, you do it cleverly. Your face is honest. Yet I hear it was for me alone this travesty was enacted."

"Whoever told you so spoke falsely," Molly says, pale but firm, a great indignation toward Marcia rising in her breast. She has her hands on the back of a chair, and is gazing anxiously but openly at the old man. "Why should I seek to offend you, who have been so kind to me,—whose bread I have eaten? You do not understand: you wrong me."

"I thought it was your mother," whispers he, with a quick shiver, "from her grave, returned to reproach me,—to remind me of all the miserable past. It was a senseless thought. But the likeness was awful,—appalling. She was my favorite daughter, yet she of all creatures was the one to thwart me most; and I did not forgive. I left her to pine for the luxuries to which she was accustomed from her birth, and could not then procure. She was delicate. I let her wear her heart out waiting for a worthless pardon. And what a heart it was! *Then* I would not forgive; now—*now* I crave forgiveness. Oh, that the dead could speak!"

He covers his face with his withered hands, that shake and tremble like October leaves, and a troubled sigh escapes him. For the moment the stern old man has disappeared; only the penitent remains.

"Dear grandpapa, be comforted," says Molly, much affected, sinking on her knees beside him. Never before, by either brother or grandfather, has her dead mother been so openly alluded to. "She did forgive. So sweet as she was, how could she retain a bitter feeling? Listen to me. Am I not her only child? Who so meet to offer you her pardon? Let me comfort you."

Mr. Amherst makes no reply, but he gently presses the fingers that have found their way around his neck.

"I, too, would ask pardon," Molly goes on, in her sweet, low, *trainante* voice, that has a sob in it here and there. "How shall I gain it after all that I have done—to distress you so, although unintentionally?—And you think hardly of me, grandpapa? You think I did it to annoy you?"

"No, no; not now."

"I have made you ill," continues Molly, still crying; "I have caused you pain. Oh, grandpapa! do say you are not angry with me."

"I am not. You are a good child, and Marcia wronged you. Go now, and forget all I may have said. I am weak at times, and—and—— Go, child; I am better alone."

In the corridor outside stands Mr. Potts, with pale cheeks and very pale eyes. Even his hair seems to have lost a shade, and looks subdued.

"Well, what did he say to you?" he asks, in what he fondly imagines to be a whisper, but which would be distinctly audible in the hall beneath. "Was he awfully mad? Did he cut up very rough? I wouldn't have been in your shoes for a million. Did he—did he—say anything about—*me*?"

"I don't believe he remembered your existence," says Molly, with a laugh, although her eyelids are still of a shade too decided to be becoming. "He knew nothing of your share in the transaction."

Whereupon Mr. Potts declares himself thankful for so much mercy in a devout manner, and betakes himself to the smoking-room.

Here he is received with much applause and more congratulations.

"Another of Mr. Potts's charming entertainments," says Sir Penthony, with a wave of the hand. "Extraordinary and enthusiastic reception! Such success has seldom before been witnessed! Last time he blew up two young women; to-night he has slain an offensive old gentleman! Really, Potts, you must allow me to shake hands with you."

"Was there ever anything more unfortunate?" says Potts, in a lachrymose tone. He has not been inattentive to the requirements of the inner man since his entrance, and already, slowly but surely, the brandy is doing its work. "It was all so well arranged, and I made sure the old boy was gone to bed."

"He is upset," murmurs Sir Penthony, with touching concern, "and no wonder. Such tremendous exertion requires the aid of stimulants to keep it up. My dear Potts, do have a little more brandy-and-soda. You don't take half care of yourself."

"Not a drop,—not a drop," says Mr. Potts, drawing the decanter toward him. "It don't agree with me. Oh, Stafford! you should have seen Miss Massereene in her Greek costume. I think she is the loveliest creature I ever saw. She *is*," goes on Mr. Potts, with unwise zeal, "by *far* the loveliest, 'and the same I would rise to maintain.'"

"I wouldn't, if I were you," says Philip, who is indignant. "There is no knowing what tricks your legs may play with you."

"She was just like Venus, or—or some of those other goddesses," says Mr. Potts, vaguely.

"I can well believe it," returns Stafford; "but don't let emotion master you. 'There's naught, no doubt, so much the spirit calms as rum and true religion.' Try a little of the former."

"There's nothing in life I wouldn't do for that girl,—nothing, I declare to you, Stafford," goes on Potts, who is quite in tears by this time; "but she wouldn't look at me."

Luttrell and Philip are enraged; Stafford and the others are in roars.

"Wouldn't she, Potts?" says Stafford, with a fine show of sympathy. "Who knows? Cheer up, old boy, and remember women never know their own minds at first. She may yet become alive to your many perfections, and know her heart to be all yours. Think of that. And why should she not?" says Sir Penthony, with free encouragement. "Where could she get a better fellow? 'Faint heart,' you know, Potts. Take my advice and pluck up spirit, and go in for her boldly. Throw yourself at her feet."

"I will," says Mr. Potts, ardently.

"To-morrow," advises Sir Penthony, with growing excitement.

"Now," declares Potts, with wild enthusiasm, making a rush for the door.

"Not to-night; wait until to-morrow," Sir Penthony says, who has not anticipated so ready an acceptance of his advice, getting between him and the door. "In my opinion she has retired to her room by this; and it really would be rather sketchy, you know,—eh?"

"What do you say, Luttrell?" asks Potts, uncertainly. "What would you advise?"

"Bed," returns Luttrell, curtly, turning on his heel.

And finally the gallant Potts is conveyed to his room, without being allowed to lay his hand and fortune at Miss Massereene's feet.

About four o'clock the next day,—being that of the ball,—Sir Penthony, strolling along the west corridor, comes to a standstill before Cecil's door, which happens to lie wide open.

Cecil herself is inside, and is standing so as to be seen, clad in the memorable white dressing-gown of the evening before, making a careful choice between two bracelets she holds in her hands.

"Is that the garment in which you so much distinguished yourself last night?" Sir Penthony cannot help asking; and, with a little start and blush, she raises her eyes.

"Is it you?" she says, smiling. "Yes, this is the identical robe. Won't you come in, Sir Penthony? You are quite welcome. If you have nothing better to do you can stay with and talk to me for a little."

"I have plenty to do," —coming in and closing the door,—"but nothing I would not gladly throw over to accept an invitation from you."

"Dear me! What a charming speech! What a courtier you would have made! Consider yourself doubly welcome. I adore pretty speeches, when addressed to myself. Now, sit there, while I decide on what jewelry I shall wear to-night."

"So this is her sanctum," thinks her husband, glancing around. What a dainty nest it is, with its innumerable feminine fineries, its piano, its easel, its pretty pink-and-blue *crêtonnne,* its wealth of flowers, although the season is of the coldest and bleakest.

A cozy fire burns brightly. In the wall opposite is an open door, through which one catches a glimpse of the bedroom beyond, decked out in all its pink-and-white glory. There is a very sociable little clock, a table strewn with wools and colored silks, and mirrors everywhere.

As for Cecil herself, with honest admiration her husband carefully regards her. What a pretty woman she is! full of all the tender graces, the lovable caprices, that wake the heart to fondness.

How charming a person to come to in grief or trouble, or even in one's gladness! How full of gayety, yet immeasurable tenderness, is her speaking face! Verily, there is a depth of sympathy to be found in a pretty woman that a plain one surely lacks.

Her white gown becomes her *à merveille,* and fits her to perfection. She cannot be called fat, but as certainly she cannot be called thin. When people speak of her with praise, they never fail to mention the "pretty roundness" of her figure.

Her hair has partly come undone, and hangs in a fair, loose coil, rather lower than usual, upon her neck. This suits her, making still softer her soft though *piquante* face.

Her white and jeweled fingers are busy in the case before her as, with puckered brows, she sighs over the difficulty of making a wise and becoming choice in precious stones for the evening's triumphs.

At last—a set of sapphires having gained the day—she lays the casket aside and turns to her husband, while wondering with demure amusement on the subject of his thoughts during these past few minutes.

He has been thinking of her, no doubt. Her snowy wrapper, with all its dainty frills and bows, is eminently becoming. Yes, beyond all question he has been indulging in sentimental regrets.

Sir Penthony's first remark rather dispels the illusion.

"The old boy puts you up very comfortably down here, don't he?" he says, in a terribly prosaic tone.

Is this all? Has he been admiring the furniture during all these eloquent moments of silence, instead of her and her innumerable charms? Insufferable!

"He do," responds she, dryly, with a careful adaptation of his English.

Sir Penthony raises his eyebrows in affected astonishment, and then they both laugh.

"I do hope you are not going to say rude things to me about last night," she says, still smiling.

"No. You may remember once before on a very similar occasion I told you I should never again scold you, for the simple reason that I considered it language thrown away. I was right, as the sequel proved. Besides, the extreme becomingness of your toilet altogether disarmed me. By the bye, when do you return to town?"

"Next week. And you?"

"I shall go—when you go. May I call on you there?"

"Indeed you may. I like you quite well enough," says her ladyship, with unsentimental and therefore most objectionable frankness, "to wish you for my friend."

"Why should we not be more than friends, Cecil?" says Stafford, going up to her and taking both her hands in a warm, affectionate clasp. "Just consider how we two are situated: you are bound to me forever, until death shall kindly step in to relieve you of me, and I am bound to you as closely. Why, then, should we not accept our position, and make our lives one?"

"You should have thought of all this before."

"How could I? Think what a deception you practiced on me when sending that miserable picture. I confess I abhor ugliness. And then, your own conditions,—what could I do but abide by them?"

"There are certain times when a woman does not altogether care about being taken so completely at her word."

"But that was not one of them." Hastily. "I do not believe you would have wished to live with a man you neither knew nor cared for."

"Perhaps not." Laughing. "Sometimes I hardly know myself what it is I do want. But are we not very well as we are? I dare say, had we been living together for the past three years, we should now dislike each other as cordially as—as do Maud Darley and her husband."

"Impossible! Maud Darley is one person, you are quite another; while I—well"—with a smile—"I honestly confess I fancy myself rather more than poor Henry Darley."

"He certainly *is* plain," says Cecil, pensively, "and—he snores,—two great points against him, Yes, on consideration, you are an improvement on Henry Darley." Then, with a sudden change of tone, she says, "Does all this mean that you love me?"

"Yes I confess it, Cecil," answers he, gravely, earnestly. "I love you as I never believed it possible I should love a woman. I am twenty-nine, and—think me cold if you will—but up to this I never yet saw the woman I wanted for my wife except you."

"Then you ought to consider yourself the happiest man alive, because you have the thing you crave. As you reminded me just now, I am yours until death us do part."

"Not all I crave, not the best part of you, your heart," replies he, tenderly. "No man loving as I do, could be contented with a part."

"Oh, it is too absurd," says Cecil, with a little aggravating shake of the head. "In love with your own wife in this prosaic nineteenth century! It savors of the ridiculous. Such mistaken feeling has been tabooed long ago. Conquer it; conquer it."

"Too late. Besides, I have no desire to conquer it. On the contrary, I encourage it, in hope of some return. No, do not dishearten me. I know what you are going to say; but at least you like me, Cecil?"

"Well, yes; but what of that? I like so many people."

"Then go a little further, and say you—love me."

"That would be going a *great* deal further, because I love so few."

"Never mind. Say 'Penthony, I love you.'"

He has placed his hands upon her shoulders, and is regarding her with anxious fondness.

"Would you have me tell you an untruth?"

"I would have you say you love me."

"But supposing I cannot in honesty?"

"Try."

"Of course I can try. Words without meaning are easy things to say. But then—a lie; that is a serious matter.

"It may cease to be a lie, once uttered."

"Well,—just to please you, then, and as an experiment—and—— You are *sure* you will not despise me for saying it?"

"No."

"Nor accuse me afterward of deceit?"

"Of course not."

"Nor think me weak-minded?"

"No, no. How could I?"

"Well, then—Penthony—I—*don't love you the least bit in the world!*" declares Cecil, with a provoking, irresistible laugh, stepping backward out of his reach.

Sir Penthony does not speak for a moment or two; then "'Sweet is revenge, especially to women,'" he says, quietly, although at heart he is bitterly chagrined. To be unloved is one thing—to be laughed at is another. "After all, you are right. There is nothing in this world so rare or so admirable as honesty. I am glad you told me no untruth, even in jest."

Just at this instant the door opens, and Molly enters. She looks surprised at such an unexpected spectacle as Cecil's husband sitting in his wife's boudoir, *tête-à-tête* with her.

"Don't be shy, dear," says Cecil, mischievously, with a little wicked laugh; "you may come in; it is only my husband."

The easy nonchalance of this speech, the only half-suppressed amusement in her tone, angers Sir Penthony more than all that has gone before. With a hasty word or two to Molly, he suddenly remembers a pressing engagement, and, with a slight bow to his wife, takes his departure.

CHAPTER XXIV

"Take, oh! take those lips away,

That so sweetly were foresworn;

And those eyes, the break of day,

Lights that do mislead the morn:

But my kisses bring again,

Seals of love, but seal'd in vain."

—Shakespeare.

The longed-for night has arrived at last; so has Molly's dress, a very marvel of art, fresh and pure as newly-fallen snow. It is white silk with tulle, on which white water-lilies lie here and there, as though carelessly thrown, all their broad and trailing leaves gleaming from among the shining folds.

Miss Massereene is in her own room, dressing, her faithful Sarah on her knees beside her. She has almost finished her toilet, and is looking more than usually lovely in her London ball-dress.

"Our visit is nearly at an end, Sarah; how have you enjoyed it?" she asks, in an interval, during which Sarah is at her feet, sewing on more securely one of her white lilies.

"Very much, indeed, miss. They've all been excessive polite, though they do ask a lot of questions. Only this evening they wanted to know if we was estated, and I said, 'Yes,' Miss Molly, because after all, you know, miss, it *is* a property, however small; and I wasn't going to let myself down. And then that young man of Captain Shadwell's ast me if we was 'county people,' which I thought uncommon imperent. Not but what he's a nice young man, miss, and very affable."

"Still constant, Sarah?" says Molly, who is deep in the waves of doubt, not being able to decide some important final point about her dress.

"Oh, law! yes, miss, he is indeed. It was last night he was saying as my accent was very sweet. Now there isn't one of them country bumpkins, miss, as would know whether you had an accent or not. It's odd how traveling do improve the mind."

"Sarah, you should pay no attention to those London young men,—(pin it more to this side),—because they never mean anything."

"Law, Miss Molly, do you say so?" says her handmaid, suddenly depressed. "Well, of course, miss, you—who are so much with London gentlemen—ought to know. And don't they mean what they say to you, Miss Molly?"

"I, eh?" says Molly, rather taken aback; and then she bursts out laughing. "Sarah, only I know you to be trustworthy, I should certainly think you sarcastic."

"What's that, miss?"

"Never mind,—something thoroughly odious. You abash me, Sarah. By all means believe what each one tells you. It may be as honestly said to you as to me. And now, how do I look, Sarah? Speak," says Molly, sailing away from her up the room like a "white, white swan," and then turning to confront her and give her a fair opportunity of judging of her charms.

"Just lovely," says Sarah, with the most flattering sincerity of tone. "There is no doubt, Miss Molly, but you look quite the lady."

"Do I really? Thank you, Sarah," says Molly, humbly.

"I agree with Sarah," says Cecil, who has entered unnoticed. She affects blue, as a rule, and is now attired in palest azure, with a faint-pink blossom in her hair, and another at her breast. "Sarah is a person of much discrimination; you do look 'quite the lady.' You should be grateful to me, Molly, when you remember I ordered your dress; it is almost the prettiest I have ever seen, and with you in it the effect is maddening."

"Let me get down-stairs, at all events, without having my head turned," says Molly, laughing. "Oh, Cecil, I feel so happy! To have a really irreproachable ball-dress, and to go to a really large ball, has been for years the dream of my life."

"I wonder, when the evening is over, how you will look on your dream?" Cecil cannot help saying. "Come, we are late enough as it is. But first turn round and let me see the train. So; that woman is a perfect artist where dresses are concerned. You look charming."

"And her neck and arms, my lady!" puts in Sarah, who is almost tearful in her admiration. "Surely Miss Massereene's cannot be equaled. They are that white, Miss Molly, that no one could be found fault with for comparing them to the dribbling snow."

"A truly delightful simile," exclaims Molly, merrily, and forthwith follows Cecil to conquest.

They find the drawing-rooms still rather empty. Marcia is before them, and Philip and Mr. Potts; also Sir Penthony. Two or three determined ball-goers have arrived, and are dotted about, looking over albums, asking each other how they do, and thinking how utterly low it is of all the rest of the county to be so late. "Such beastly affectation, you know, and such a putting on of side, and general straining after effect."

"I hope, Miss Amherst, you have asked a lot of pretty girls," says Plantagenet, "and only young ones. Old maids make awful havoc of my temper."

"I don't think there are 'lots' of pretty girls anywhere; but I have asked as many as I know. And there are among them at least two acknowledged belles."

"You don't say so!" exclaims Sir Penthony. "Miss Amherst, if you wish to make me eternally grateful you will point them out to me. There is nothing so distressing as not to know. And once I was introduced to a beauty, and didn't discover my luck until it was too late. I never even asked her to dance! Could you fancy anything more humiliating? Give you my honor I spoke to her for ten minutes and never so much as paid her a compliment. It was too cruel, — and she the queen of the evening, as I was told afterward."

"You didn't admire her?" asks Cecil, interested. "Never saw her beauty?"

"No. She was tall and had arched brows, — two things I detest."

The ball is at its height. Marcia, dressed in pale maize silk, — which suits her dark and glowing beauty, — is still receiving a few late guests in her usual stately but rather impassive manner. Old Mr. Amherst, standing beside her, gives her an air of importance. Beyond all doubt she will be heavily dowered, — a wealthy heiress, if not exactly the heir.

Philip, as the supposed successor to the house and lands of Herst, receives even more attention; while Molly, except for her beauty, which outshines all that the room contains, is in no way noticeable. Though, when one holds the ace of trumps, one feels almost independent of the other honors.

The chief guest—a marquis, with an aristocratic limp and only one eye—has begged of her a square dance. Two lords—one very young, the other distressingly old—have also solicited her hand in the "mazy dance." She is the reigning belle; and she knows it.

Beautiful, sparkling, brilliant, she moves through the rooms. A great delight, a joyous excitement, born of her youth, the music, her own success, fills her. She has a smile, a kindly look, for every one. Even Mr. Buscarlet, in the blackest of black clothes and rather indifferent linen, venturing to address her as she goes by him, receives a gracious answer in return. So does Mrs. Buscarlet, who is radiant in pink satin and a bird-of-paradise as a crown.

"Ain't she beautiful?" says that substantial matron, with a beaming air of approbation, as though Molly was her bosom friend, addressing the partner of her joys. "Such a lovely-turned jaw! She has quite a look of my sister Mary Anne when a girl. I wish, my dear, she was to be heiress of Herst, instead of that stuck-up girl in yellow."

"So do I; so do I," replies Buscarlet, following the movements of Beauty as she glides away, smiling, dimpling on my lord's arm. "And—ahem!"— with a meaning and consequential cough—"perhaps she may. Who knows? There is a certain person who has often a hold of her grandfather's ear! Ahem!"

Meantime the band is playing its newest, sweetest strains; the air is heavy with the scent of flowers. The low ripple of conversation and merry laughter rises above everything. The hours are flying all too swiftly.

"May I have the pleasure of this waltz with you?" Sir Penthony is saying, bending over Lady Stafford, as she sits in one of the numberless small, dimly-lit apartments that branch off the hall.

"Dear Sir Penthony, do you think I will test your good-nature so far? You are kind to a fault, and I will not repay you so poorly as to avail myself of your offer. Fancy condemning you to waste a whole dance on your— wife!"

The first of the small hours has long since sounded, and she is a little piqued that not until now has he asked her to dance. Nevertheless, she addresses him with her most charming smile.

"I, for my part, should not consider it a dance wasted," replies he, stiffly.

"Is he not self-denying?" she says, turning languidly toward Lowry, who, as usual, stands beside her.

"You cannot expect me to see it in that light," replies he, politely.

"May I hope for this waltz?" Sir Penthony asks again, this time very coldly.

"Not this one; perhaps a little later on."

"As you please, of course," returns he, as, with a frown and an inward determination never to ask her again, he walks away.

In the ball-room he meets Luttrell, evidently on the lookout for a missing partner.

"Have you seen Miss Massereene?" he asks instantly. "I am engaged to her, and can see her nowhere."

"Try one of those nests for flirtation," replies Stafford, bitterly, turning abruptly away, and pointing toward the room he has just quitted.

But Luttrell goes in a contrary direction. Through one conservatory after another, through ball-room, supper-room, tea-room, he searches without success. There is no Molly to be seen anywhere.

"She has forgotten our engagement," he thinks, and feels a certain pang of disappointment that it should be so. As he walks, rather dejectedly, into a last conservatory, he is startled to find Marcia there alone, gazing with silent intentness out of the window into the garden beneath.

As he approaches she turns to meet his gaze. She is as pale as death, and her dark eyes are full of fire. The fingers of her hand twitch convulsively.

"You are looking for Eleanor?" she says, intuitively, her voice low, but vibrating with some hidden emotion. "See, you will find her there."

She points down toward the garden through the window where she has been standing, and moves away. Impelled by the strangeness of her manner, Luttrell follows her direction, and, going over to the window, gazes out into the night.

It is a brilliant moonlight night; the very stars shine with redoubled glory; the chaste Diana, riding high in the heavens, casts over "tower and stream" and spreading parks "a flood of silver sheen;" the whole earth seems bright as gaudy day.

Beneath, in the shrubberies, pacing to and fro, are Molly and Philip Shadwell, evidently in earnest conversation. Philip at least seems painfully intent and eager. They have stopped, as if by one impulse, and now he has taken her hand. She hardly rebukes him; her hand lies passive within his; and now,—*now*, with a sudden movement, he has placed his arm around her waist.

"Honor or no honor," says Luttrell, fiercely, "I will see it out with her now."

Drawing a deep breath, he folds his arms and leans against the window, full of an agonized determination to know the worst.

Molly has put up her hand and laid it on Philip's chest, as though expostulating, but makes no vehement effort to escape from his embrace.

Philip, his face lit up with passionate admiration, is gazing down into the lovely one so near him, that scarcely seems to shrink from his open homage. The merciless, cruel moon, betrays them all too surely.

Luttrell's pulses are throbbing wildly, while his heart has almost ceased to beat. Half a minute—that is a long hour—passes thus; a few more words from Philip, an answer from Molly. Oh, that he could hear! And then Shadwell stoops until, from where Luttrell stands, his face seems to grow to hers.

Tedcastle's teeth meet in his lip as he gazes spell-bound. A cold shiver runs through him, as when one learns that all one's dearest, most cherished hopes are trampled in the dust. A faint moisture stands on his brow. It is the bitterness of death!

Presently a drop of blood trickling slowly down—the sickly flavor of it in his mouth—rouses him. Instinctively he closes his eyes, as though too late to strive to shut out the torturing sight, and, with a deep curse, he presses his handkerchief to his lips and moves away as one suddenly awakened from a ghastly dream.

In the doorway he meets Marcia; she, too, has been a witness of the garden scene, and as he passes her she glances up at him with a curious smile.

"If you wish to keep her you should look after her," she whispers, with white lips.

"If she needs looking after, I do *not* wish for her," he answers, bitterly, and the next moment could kill himself, in that he has been so far wanting in loyalty to his most disloyal love.

With his mind quite made up, he waits through two dances silently, almost motionless, with his back against a friendly wall, hardly taking note of anything that is going on around him, until such time as he can claim another dance from Molly.

It comes at last: and, making his way through the throng of dancers, he reaches the spot where, breathless, smiling, she sits fanning herself, an adoring partner dropping little honeyed phrases into her willing ear.

"This is our dance," Luttrell says, in a hard tone, standing before her, with compressed lips and a pale face.

"Is it?" with a glance at her card.

"Never mind your card. I know it is ours," he says, and, offering her his arm, leads her, not to the ball-room, but on to a balcony, from which the garden can be reached by means of steps.

Before descending he says,—always in the same uncompromising tone:

"Are you cold? Shall I fetch you a shawl?"

And she answers:

"No, thank you. I think the night warm," being, for the moment, carried away by the strangeness and determination of his manner.

When they are in the garden, and still he has not spoken, she breaks the silence.

"What is it, Teddy?" she asks, lightly. "I am all curiosity. I never before saw you look so angry."

"'Angry'?—no,—I hardly think there is room for anger. I have brought you here to tell you—I will not keep to my engagement with you—an hour longer."

Silence follows this declaration,—a dead silence, broken only by the voices of the night and the faint, sweet, dreamy sound of one of Gungl's waltzes as it steals through the air to where they stand.

They have ceased to move, and are facing each other in the narrow pathway. A few beams from the illumined house fall across their feet; one, more adventurous than the rest, has lit on Molly's face, and lingers there, regardless of the envious moonbeams.

How changed it is! All the soft sweetness, the gladness of it, that characterized it a moment since, is gone. All the girlish happiness and excitement of a first ball have vanished She is cold, rigid, as one turned to stone. Indignation lies within her lovely eyes.

"I admit you have taken me by surprise," she says, slowly. "It is customary—is it not?—for the one who breaks an engagement to assign some reason for so doing?"

"It is. You shall have my reason. Half an hour ago I stood at that window,"—pointing to it,—"and saw you in the shrubberies—with—Shadwell!"

"Yes? And then?"

"Then—then!" With a movement full of passion he lays his hands upon her shoulders and turns her slightly, so that the ray which has wandered once more rests upon her face. "Let me look at you," he says; "let me see how bravely you can carry out your deception to its end. Its *end*, mark you; for you shall never again deceive me. I have had enough of it. It is over. My love for you has died."

"Beyond all doubt it had an easy death," replies she, calmly. "There could never have been much life in it. But all this is beside the question. I have yet to learn my crime. I have yet to learn what awful iniquity lies in the fact of my being with Philip Shadwell."

"You are wonderfully innocent," with a sneer. "Do you think then that my sight failed me?"

"Still I do not understand," she says, drawing herself up, with a little proud gesture. "What is it to me whether you or all the world saw me with Philip? Explain yourself."

"I will." In a low voice, almost choked with passion and despair. "You will understand when I tell you I saw him with his arms around you—you submitting—you—— And then—I saw him—kiss you. That I should live to say it of you!"

"*Did* you see him kiss me?" still calmly. "Your eyesight is invaluable."

"Ah! you no longer deny it? In your inmost heart no doubt you are laughing at me, poor fool that I have been. How many other times have you kissed him, I wonder, when I was not by to see?"

"Whatever faults you may have had, I acquitted you of brutality," says she, in a low, carefully suppressed tone.

"You never loved me. In that one matter at least you were honest; you never professed affection. And yet I was mad enough to think that after a time I should gain the love of a flirt,—a coquette."

"You were mad to *care* for the love of 'a flirt,—a coquette.'"

"I have been blind all these past weeks," goes on he, unheeding, "determined not to see (what all the rest of the world, no doubt, too plainly saw) what there was between you and Shadwell. But I am blind no longer. I am glad,—yes, thankful," cries the young man, throwing out one hand, as though desirous of proving by action the truth of his sad falsehood,— "thankful I have found you out at last,—before it was too late."

"I am thankful too; but for another reason. I feel grateful that your suspicions have caused you to break off our engagement. And now that it is broken,—irremediably so,—let me tell you that for once your priceless sight has played you false. I admit that Philip placed his arm around me (but not unrebuked, as you would have it); I admit he stooped to kiss me; but," cries Molly, with sudden passion that leaves her pale as an early snow-drop, "I do *not* admit he kissed me. Deceitful, worthless, flirt, coquette, as you think me, I have not yet fallen so low as to let one man kiss me while professing to keep faith with another."

"You say this—after——"

"I do. And who is there shall dare give me the lie? Beware, Tedcastle; you have gone far enough already. Do not go too far. You have chosen to insult me. Be it so. I forgive you. But, for the future, let me see, and hear, and know as little of you as may be possible."

"Molly, if what you now——"

"Stand back, sir," cries she, with an air of majesty and with an imperious gesture, raising one white arm, that gleams like snow in the dark night, to wave him to one side.

"From henceforth remember, I am deaf when you address me!"

She sweeps past him into the house, without further glance or word, leaving him, half mad with doubt and self-reproach, to pace the gardens until far into the morning.

When he does re-enter the ball-room he finds it almost deserted. Nearly all the guests have taken their departure. Dancing is growing half-hearted; conversation is having greater sway with those that still remain.

The first person he sees—with Philip beside her—is Molly, radiant, sparkling, even more than usually gay. Two crimson spots burn upon either cheek, making her large eyes seem larger, and bright as gleaming stars.

Even as Luttrell, with concentrated bitterness, stands transfixed at some little distance from her, realizing how small a thing to her is this rupture between them, that is threatening to break his heart, she, looking up, sees him.

Turning to her companion, she whispers something to him in a low tone, and then she laughs,—a soft, rippling laugh, full of mirth and music.

"There go the chimes again," says Mr. Potts, who has just come up, alluding to Molly's little cruel outburst of merriment. "I never saw Miss Massereene in such good form as she is in to-night. Oh!"—with a suppressed yawn—"'what a day we're 'aving!' I wish it were all to come over again."

"Plantagenet, you grow daily more dissipated," says Cecil Stafford, severely. "A little boy like you should be in your bed hours ago; instead of which you have been allowed to sit up until half-past four, and——"

"And still I am not 'appy?' How could I be when you did me out of that solitary dance you promised me? I really believed, when I asked you with such pathos in the early part of the evening to keep that one green spot in your memory for me, you would have done so."

"Did I forget you?" remorsefully. "Well, don't blame me. Mr. Lowry *would* keep my card for me, and, as a natural consequence, it was lost. After that, how was it possible for me to keep to my engagements?"

"I think it was a delightful ball," Molly says, with perhaps a shade too much *empressement*. "I never in all my life enjoyed myself so well."

"Lucky you," says Cecil. "Had I been allowed I should perhaps have been happy too; but"—with a glance at Stafford, who is looking the very personification of languid indifference—"when people allow their tempers to get the better of them——" Here she pauses with an eloquent sigh.

"I hope you are not alluding to me," says Lowry, who is at her elbow, with a smile that awakes in Stafford a mild longing to strangle him.

"Oh, no!"—sweetly. "How could you think it? I am not ungrateful; and I know how carefully you tried to make my evening a pleasant one."

"If I succeeded it is more than I dare hope for," returns he, in a low tone, intended for her ears alone.

She smiles at him, and holds out her arm, that he may refasten the eighth button of her glove that has mysteriously come undone. He rather lingers over the doing of it. He is, indeed, strangely awkward, and finds an unaccountable difficulty in inducing the refractory button to go into its proper place.

"Shall we bivouac here for the remainder of the night, or seek our beds?" asks Sir Penthony, impatiently. "I honestly confess the charms of that eldest Miss Millbanks have completely used me up. Too much of a good thing is good for nothing; and she *is* tall. Do none of the rest of you feel fatigue? I know women's passion for conquest is not easily satiated,"—with a slight sneer—"but at five o'clock in the morning one might surely call a truce."

They agree with him, and separate, even the tardiest guest having disappeared by this time, with a last assurance of how intensely they have enjoyed their evening; though when they reach their chambers a few of them give way to such despair and disappointment as rather gives the lie to their expressions of pleasure.

Poor Molly, in spite of her false gayety,—put on to mask the wounded pride, the new sensation of blankness that fills her with dismay,—flings herself upon her bed and cries away all the remaining hours that rest between her and her maid's morning visit.

"Alas! how easily things go wrong:
A sigh too much or a kiss too long."

For how much less—for the mere suspicion of a kiss—have things gone wrong with her? How meagre is the harvest she has gathered in from all her anticipated pleasure, how poor a fruition has been hers!

Now that she and her lover are irrevocably separated, she remembers, with many pangs of self-reproach, how tender and true and honest he has proved himself in all his dealings with her; and, though she cannot accuse herself of actual active disloyalty toward him, a hidden voice reminds her how lightly and with what persistent carelessness she accepted all his love, and how indifferently she made return.

With the desire to ease the heartache she is enduring, she tries—in vain—to encourage a wrathful feeling toward him, calling to mind how ready he was to believe her false, how easily he flung her off, for what, after all, was but a fancied offense. But the very agony of his face as he did so disarms her, recollecting as she does every change and all the passionate disappointment of it.

Oh that she had repulsed Philip on the instant when first he took her hand, as it had been in her heart to do!—but for the misery he showed that for the moment softened her. Mercy on such occasions is only cruel kindness, so she now thinks,—and has been her own undoing. And besides, what is his misery to hers?

An intense bitterness, a positive hatred toward Shadwell, who has brought all this discord into her hitherto happy life, grows within her, filling her with a most unjust longing to see him as wretched as he has unwittingly made her; while yet she shrinks with ever-increasing reluctance from the thought that soon she must bring herself to look again upon his dark but handsome face.

Luttrell, too,—she must meet him; and, with such swollen eyes and pallid cheeks, the bare idea brings a little color into her white face.

As eight o'clock strikes, she rises languidly from her bed, dressed as she is, disrobing hurriedly, lest even her woman should guess how wakeful she had been, throws open her window, and lets the pure cold air beat upon her features.

But when Sarah comes she is not deceived. So distressed is she at her young mistress's appearance that she almost weeps aloud, and gives it as her opinion that balls and all such nocturnal entertainments are the invention of the enemy.

CHAPTER XXV

"Ah, starry hope, that didst arise
But to be overcast!"
—Edgar A. Poe.
"The ring asunder broke."
—*German Song.*

At breakfast Molly is very pale, and speaks little. She toys with her toast, but cannot eat. Being questioned, she confesses herself fatigued, not being accustomed to late hours.

She neither looks at Luttrell, nor does he seek to attract her attention in any way.

"A good long walk will refresh you more than anything," says Talbot Lowry, who has been spending the past few days at Herst. He addresses Molly, but his eyes seek Cecil's as he does so, in the fond hope that she will take his hint and come with him for a similar refresher to that he has prescribed for Molly.

Cecil's unfortunate encouragement of the night before—displayed more with a view to chagrining Sir Penthony than from a mere leaning toward coquetry—has fanned his passion to a very dangerous height. He is consumed with a desire to speak, and madly flatters himself that there is undoubted hope for him.

To throw himself at Lady Stafford's feet, declare his love, and ask her to leave, for him, a husband who has never been more to her than an ordinary acquaintance, and to renounce a name that can have no charms for her, being devoid of tender recollections or sacred memories, seems to him, in his present over-strained condition, a very light thing indeed. In return, he argues feverishly, he can give her the entire devotion of a heart, and, what is perhaps a more practical offer, a larger income than she can now command.

Then, in the present day, what so easily, or quietly, or satisfactorily arranged, as a divorce in high life, leaving behind it neither spot nor scar, nor anything unpleasant in the way of social ostracism? And this might— nay, *should*—follow.

Like Molly, he has lain awake since early dawn arranging plans and rehearsing speeches; and now, after breakfast, as he walks beside the object of his adoration through the shrubberies and outer walks into the gardens beyond, carried away by the innate vanity of him, and his foolish self-esteem, and not dreaming of defeat, he decides that the time has come to give voice to his folly.

They are out of view of the windows, when he stops abruptly, and says rashly,—with a pale face, it is true, but a certain amount of composure that bespeaks confidence,—"Cecil, I can keep silence no longer. Let me speak to you, and tell you all that is in my heart."

"He has fallen in love with Molly," thinks Cecil, wondering vaguely at the manner of his address, he having never attempted to call her by her Christian name before.

"You are in love?" she says, kindly, but rather uncertainly, not being able at the moment to call to mind any tender glances of his cast at Molly or any suspicious situations that might confirm her in her fancy.

"Need you ask?" says Lowry, taking her hand, feeling still further emboldened by the gentleness with which she has received his first advance. "Have not all these months—nay, this year past—taught you so much?"

"'This year past?'" Cecil repeats, honestly at sea, and too much surprised by the heat of his manner to grasp at once the real meaning of his words. Though I think a second later a faint inkling of it comes to her, because she releases her hand quickly from his clasp, and her voice takes a sharper tone. "I do not understand you," she says, "Take care you understand—yourself."

But the warning comes too late. Lowry, bent on his own destruction, goes on vehemently:

"I do—too well. Have I not had time to learn it?" he says, passionately. "Have I not spent every day, every hour, in thoughts of you? Have I not lived in anticipation of our meeting? While you, Cecil, surely you, too, were glad when we were together. The best year I have ever known has been this last, in which I have grown to love you."

"Pray cease," says Cecil, hurriedly, stepping back and raising her hand imperiously. "What can you mean? You must be out of your senses to speak to me like this."

Although angry, she is calm, and, indeed, scarcely cares to give way to indignation before Lowry, whom she has always looked upon with great kindness and rather in the light of a boy. She is a little sorry for him, too, that he should have chosen to make a fool of himself with her, who, she cannot help feeling, is his best friend. For to all the moodiness and oddity of his nature she has been singularly lenient, bearing with him when others would have lost all patience. And this is her reward. For a full minute Lowry seems confounded. Then, "I must indeed be bereft of reason," he says, in a low, intense voice, "if I am to believe that you can receive like this the assurance of my love. It cannot be altogether such a matter of wonder—my infatuation for you—as you would have me think, considering how you"—in a rather choked tone—"led me on."

"'Led you on'! My dear Mr. Lowry, how can you talk so foolishly? I certainly thought I knew you very well, and"—docketing off each item on her fingers—"I let you run my messages now and then; and I danced with you; and you sent me the loveliest flowers in London or out of it; and you were extremely kind to me on all occasions; but then so many other men were kind also, that really beyond the flowers,"—going back to her second finger,—"(which were incomparably finer than those I ever received from any one else), I don't see that you were more to me than the others."

"Will you not listen to me? Will you not even let me plead my cause?"

"Certainly not, considering what a cause it is. You must be mad."

"You are cold as ice," says he, losing his head. "No other woman but yourself would consent to live as you do. A wife, and yet no wife!"

"Mr. Lowry," says Lady Stafford, with much dignity but perfect temper, "you forget yourself. I must really beg you not to discuss my private affairs. The life I lead might not suit you or any single one of your acquaintance, but it suits me, and that is everything. You say I am 'cold,' and you are right: I am. I fancied (wrongly) my acknowledged coldness would have prevented such a scene as I have been forced to listen to, by you, to-day. You are the first who has ever dared to insult me. You are, indeed, the first man who has ever been at my feet, metaphorically speaking or otherwise; and I sincerely trust," says Lady Stafford, with profound earnestness, "you may be the last, for anything more unpleasant I never experienced."

"Have you no pity for me?" cries he, passionately. "Why need you scorn my love? Every word you utter tears my heart, and you,—you care no more than if I were a dog! Have you no feeling? Do you never wish to be as other women are, beloved and loving, instead of being as now——"

"Again, sir, I must ask you to allow my private life to *be* private," says Cecil, still with admirable temper, although her color has faded a good deal, and the fingers of one hand have closed convulsively upon a fold of her dress. "I may, perhaps, pity you, but I can feel nothing but contempt for the love you offer, that would lower the thing it loves!"

"Not lower it," says he, quickly, grasping eagerly at what he vainly hopes is a last chance. "Under the circumstances a divorce could be easily obtained. If you would trust yourself to me there should be no delay. You might easily break this marriage-tie that can scarcely be considered binding."

"And supposing—I do not wish to break it? How then? But enough of this. I cannot listen any longer. I have heard too much already. I must really ask you to leave me. Go."

"Is this how your friendships end?" asks he, bitterly. "Will you deny I was even so much to you?"

"Certainly not. Though I must add that had I known my friendship with you would have put me in the way of receiving so much insult as I have received to-day, you should never have been placed upon my list. Let me pray you to go away now, to leave Herst entirely for the present, because it would be out of the question my seeing you again,—at least until time has convinced you of your folly. You are an old friend, Talbot, and I would willingly try and forget all that has happened to-day, or at all events to remember it only as a passing madness."

"Am I a boy, a fool, that you speak to me like this?" cries he, catching her hand to detain her as she moves away. "And why do you talk of 'insult'? I only urge you to exchange indifference for love,—the indifference of a husband who cares no more for you than for the gravel at your feet."

"And pray, sir, by what rule do you measure the amount of my regard for Lady Stafford?" exclaims Sir Penthony, walking through an open space in the privet hedge that skirts this corner of the garden, where he has been spell-bound for the last two minutes. A short time, no doubt, though a great deal can be said in it.

He is positively livid, and has his eyes fixed, not on his enemy, but on his wife.

Lowry changes color, but gives way not an inch; he also tightens his grasp on Cecil's unwilling hand, and throws up his head defiantly.

"Let my wife's hand go directly," says Stafford, in a low but furious tone, advancing.

By a quick movement Cecil wrenches herself free and gets between the two men. She does not fling herself, she simply gets there, almost—as it seems—without moving.

"Not another word, Sir Penthony," she says, quietly. "I forbid it. I will have no scene. Mr. Lowry has behaved foolishly, but I desire that nothing more be said about it. Go," —turning to Lowry, who is frowning ominously, and pointing imperiously to a distant gate,—"and do as I asked you a few moments since,—leave Herst without delay."

So strong is her determination to avoid an *esclandre*, and so masterly is her manner of carrying out her will, that both men instinctively obey her. Sir Penthony lowers his eyes and shifts his aggressive position; Lowry, with bent head, and without another word, walks away from her down the garden-path out of the gate, and disappears—for years.

When he has quite gone, Sir Penthony turns to her.

"Is this the way you amuse yourself?" he asks, in a compressed voice.

"Do not reproach me," murmurs she, hurriedly; "I could not bear it now." She speaks clearly, but her tone has lost its firmness, because of the little tremor that runs through it, while her face is white as one of the pale blossoms she holds within her hand. "Besides, it is not deserved. Were you long here before you spoke?"

"Long enough." With a world of meaning in his tone.

"Then you heard my exculpation. 'Cold as ice,' he called me. And he was right. As I am to you, Sir Penthony, so am I to all men. No one yet has touched my heart."

"For myself I can answer," replies he, bitterly; "but for the others——"

"Not another word," she breaks in, vehemently. "Do not say—do not even hint at—what I might find it impossible to forgive. Not even to you will I seek to justify myself on such a point. And you," she says, tears of agitation arising from all she has undergone, mingled with much pent-up wounded feeling, coming thickly into her eyes, "you should be the last to blame me for what has happened, when you remember who it was placed me in such a false position as makes men think they may say to me what they choose."

"You are unjust," he answers, nearly as white as herself. "I only followed out your wishes. It was your own arrangement; I but acceded to it."

"You should not have done so," cries she, with subdued excitement. "You were a man of the world, capable of judging; I was a foolish girl, ignorant of the consequences that must follow on such an act. Our marriage was a wretched mistake."

"Cecil, you know you can escape from your false position as soon as you choose. No one loves you as I do."

"Impossible." Coldly. "In this world a thing once done can never be undone. Have you lived so long without learning that lesson?"

As she speaks she turns from him, and, walking quickly away, leaves him alone in the garden. Much as he has grown to love her, never until now has the very tenderness of affection touched him,—now, when the laughter-loving Cecil has changed for him into the feeling, accusing woman; although a woman dead to him, with a heart locked carefully, lest he should enter it.

How can he tell, as she goes so proudly along the garden-path, that her bosom is heaving with shame and unconfessed longing, and that down her cheeks—so prone to dimple with joyous laughter—the bitter tears are falling?

Almost as she reaches the house she encounters Tedcastle, and turns hastily aside, lest he should mark the traces of her recent weeping. But so bent is he on his own dismal thoughts that he heeds her not, but follows aimlessly the path before him that leads to the balcony from, which the smaller drawing-room may be reached.

He is depressed and anxious, the night's vigil having induced him to believe himself somewhat hasty in his condemnation of Molly. As he gains the boudoir he starts, for there in the room, with the light flashing warmly upon her, stands Molly Bawn alone.

She is dressed in a long trailing gown of black velveteen,—an inexpensive dress, but one that suits her admirably, with its slight adornment of little soft lace frillings at the throat and wrists. Pausing irresolutely, Luttrell makes as though he would retrace his steps.

"Do not go," says Molly's voice, clear and firm. "As you are here, I wish to speak to you."

She beckons him to come a little nearer to her, and silently he obeys the gesture. There is a small round table between them, upon which Molly is leaning rather heavily. As he approaches, however, and waits, gazing curiously at her for her next word, she straightens herself and compels her eyes to meet his.

"Here is your ring," she says, drawing the glittering treasure from her finger and placing it before him.

There is not the extremest trace of excitement or feeling of any kind in her tone. Luttrell, on the contrary, shrinks as though touched by fire.

"Keep it," he says, involuntarily, coloring darkly.

"No—no."

"Why?" he urges. "It will not hurt you, and"—with a quickly-suppressed sigh—"it may perhaps compel you to think of me now and then."

"I have neither wish nor desire ever to think of you again," returns she, still in the same cold, even tone, pushing the ring still closer to him with her first finger. There is something of contempt in the action. A ray from the dancing sun outside falls through the glass on to the diamonds, making them flash and sparkle in their gold setting.

"That admits of no answer," says Luttrell, with low but passionate bitterness; and, taking up the ring, he flings it lightly into the very heart of the glowing fire.

With a sudden loss of self-restraint Molly makes a movement forward as though to prevent him; but too late,—already the greedy flames have closed upon it.

Not all the agitation, not all his angry words of the night before, have affected her so keenly as this last act. She bursts into a very storm of tears.

"Oh! what have you done?" cries she. "You have destroyed it; you have burned it,—my pretty ring!"

She clasps her hands together, and gazes with straining eyes into the cruel fire. Something within her heart feels broken. Surely some string has snapped. The ring, in spite of all, was a last link between them; and now, too, it has gone.

"Molly!" says he, taking a step toward her, and holding out his hands, softened, vanquished by her tears, ready to throw himself once more an abject slave at her feet.

"Do not speak to me," returns she, still sobbing bitterly. "Have you not done enough? I wish you would leave me to myself. Go away. There is nothing more that you *can* do."

Feeling abashed, he scarcely knows why, he silently quits the room.

Then down upon her knees before the fire falls Molly, and with the poker strives with all her might to discover some traces of her lost treasure. So diligent is her search that after a little while the ring, blackened, disfigured, altered almost beyond recognition, lies within her hand. Still it is her ring, however changed, and some small ray of comfort gladdens her heart.

She is still, however, weeping bitterly, and examining sadly the precious relic she has rescued from utter oblivion, and from which the diamond, soiled, but still brilliant, has fallen into her palm, when Philip enters.

"Molly, what has happened?" he asks, advancing toward her, shocked at her appearance, which evinces all the deepest signs of woe. "What has distressed you?"

"You have," cries she, with sudden vehement passion, all her sorrow and anger growing into quick life as she sees him. "You are the cause of all my misery. Why do you come near me? You might, at least, have grace enough to spare me the pain of seeing you."

"I do not understand," he says, his face very pale. "In how have I offended,—I, who would rather be dead than cause you any unhappiness? Tell me how I have been so unfortunate."

"I hate you," she says, with almost childish cruelty, sobbing afresh. "I wish you had died before I came to this place. You have come between me and the only man I love. Yes,"—smiting her hands together in a very agony of sorrow,—"he may doubt it if he will, but I *do* love him; and now we are separated forever. Even my ring"—with a sad glance at it—"is broken, and so is—my heart."

"You are alluding to—Luttrell?" asks he,—his earliest suspicions at last confirmed,—speaking with difficulty, so dry his lips have grown.

"I am."

"And how have I interfered between you and—him?"

"Why did you speak to me of love again last night," retorts she, "when you must know how detestable a subject it is to me? He saw you put your arm around me; he saw—ah! why did I not tell you then the truth (from which through a mistaken feeling of pity I refrained), that your mere touch *sickened* me? Then you stooped, and he thought—you know what he thought—and yet," cries Molly, with a gesture of aversion, "how could he have thought it possible that I should allow *you* of *all men* to—kiss me?"

"Why speak of what I so well know?" interrupts he hoarsely, with bent head and averted eyes. "You seldom spare me. You are angered, and for what? Because you still hanker after a man who flung you away,—you, for whose slightest wish I would risk my all. For a mere chimera, a fancy, a fear only half developed, he renounced you."

"Say nothing more," says Molly, with pale lips and eyes large and dark through regretful sorrow; "not another word. I think he acted rightly. He thought I was false, and so thinking he was right to renounce. I do not say this in his defense or because—or for any reason only——" She pauses.

"Why not continue? Because you—love him still."

"Well, and why not?" says Molly. "Why should I deny my love for him? Can any shame be connected with it? Yes," murmurs she, her sweet eyes filling with tears, her small clasped hands trembling, "though he and I can never be more to each other than we now are, I tell you I love him as I never have and never shall love again."

"It is a pity that such love as yours should have no better return," says he, with an unlovely laugh. "Luttrell appears to bear his fate with admirable equanimity."

"You are incapable of judging such a nature as his," returns she, disdainfully. "He is all that is gentle, and true, and noble: while you——" She stops abruptly, causing a pause that is more eloquent than words, and, with a distant bow, hurries from the room.

Philip's star to-day is not in the ascendant. Even as he stands crushed by Molly's bitter reproaches, Marcia, with her heart full of a settled revenge toward him, is waiting outside her grandfather's door for permission to enter.

That unlucky shadow of a kiss last night has done as much mischief as half a dozen real kisses. It has convinced Marcia of the truth of that which for weeks she has been vainly struggling to disbelieve, namely, Philip's mad infatuation for Molly.

Now all doubt is at an end, and in its place has fallen a despair more terrible than any uncertainty.

All the anguish of a heart rejected, that is still compelled to live on loving its rejector, has been hers for the past two months, and it has told upon her slowly but surely. She is strangely altered. Dark hollows lay beneath her eyes, that have grown almost unearthly in expression, so large are they, and so sombre is the fire that burns within them. There is a compression about the lips that has grown habitual; small lines mar the whiteness of her forehead, while among her raven tresses, did any one mark them closely enough, fine threads of silver may be traced.

Pacing up and down her room the night before, with widely-opened eyes, gazing upon the solemn blackness that surrounds her, all the wrongs and slights she has endured come to her with startling distinctness. No sense of weariness, no thought of a necessity for sleep, disturbs her reverie or breaks in upon the monotonous misery of her musings. She is past all that. Already her death has come to her,—a death to her hope, and joy, and peace,—even to that poor calm that goes so far to deceive the outer world.

Oh, the cold, quiet night, when speech is not and sleep has forgotten us! when all the doubts and fears and jealousies that in the blessed daylight slumber, rise up to torture us when even the half-suspected sneer, the covert neglect, that some hours ago were but as faintest pin-pricks, now gall and madden as a poisoned thrust!

A wild thirst for revenge grows within her breast as one by one she calls to mind all the many injuries she has received. Strangely enough,—and unlike a woman,—her anger is concentrated on Philip, rather than on the one he loves, instinct telling her he is not beloved in return.

She broods upon her wrongs until, as the first bright streak of yellow day illumes the room, flinging its glories profusely upon the wall and ceiling, pretty knickknacks that return its greeting, and angry, unthankful creature alike, a thought comes to her that promises to amply satisfy her vengeful craving. As she ponders on it a curious light breaks upon her face, a smile half triumph, half despair.

Now, standing before her grandfather's room, with a folded letter crushed within her palm, and a heart that beats almost to suffocation, she hears him bid her enter.

Fatigued by the unusual exertions of a ball, Mr. Amherst is seated at his table in a lounging-chair, clad in his dressing-gown, and looking older, feebler, than is his wont.

He merely glances at his visitor as she approaches, without comment of any description.

"I have had something on my mind for some time, grandpapa," begins Marcia, who is pale and worn, through agitation and the effects of a long and hopeless vigil. "I think it only right to let you know. I have suppressed it all this time, because I feared distressing you; but now—now—will you read this?"

She hands him, as she speaks, the letter received by Philip two months before relative to his unlucky dealings with some London Jews.

In silence Mr. Amherst reads it, in silence re-reads it, and finally, folding it up again, places it within his desk.

"You and Philip have quarreled?" he says, presently, in a quiet tone.

"No, there has been no quarrel."

"Your engagement is at an end?"

"Yes."

"And is this the result of last night's vaunted pleasures?" asks he, keenly. "Have you snatched only pain and a sense of failure from its fleeting hours? And Eleanor, too,—she was pale at luncheon, and for once silent,—has she too found her coveted fruit rotten at its core? It is the universal law," says the old man, grimly, consoling himself with a pinch of snuff, taken with much deliberation from an exquisite Louis Quinze box that rests at his elbow, and leaning back languidly in his chair. "Life is made up of hopes false as the *ignis-fatuus*. When with the greatest sense of security and promise of enjoyment we raise and seek to drain the cup of pleasure, while yet we gaze with longing eyes upon its sparkling bubbles, and, stooping thirstily, suffer our expectant lips at length to touch it, lo! it is then, just as we have attained to the summit of our bliss, we find our sweetest draught has turned to ashes in our mouth."

He stops and drums softly on the table for a moment or two, while Marcia stands before him silently pondering.

"So Philip is already counting on my death," he goes on, meditatively, still softly tapping the table. "How securely he rests in the belief of his succession! His father's son could scarcely fail to be a spendthrift, and I will have—no—prodigal at Herst—to hew—and cut—and scatter. A goodly heritage, truly, as Buscarlet called it. Be satisfied, Marcia: your revenge is complete. Philip shall not inherit Herst."

"I do not seek revenge," says Marcia, unsteadily, now her wish is fulfilled and Philip hopelessly crushed, a cold, troubled faintness creeping round her heart. An awful sense of despair, a fruitless longing to recall her action, makes her tremble. "Only I could not bear to see you longer deceived,—you, after all the care—the trouble—you bestowed upon him. My conscience compelled me to tell you all."

"And you, Marcia,"—with an odd smile she is puzzled to explain,— "*you* have never deceived me, have you? All your pretty speeches and tender cares have been quite sincere?"

"Dear grandpapa, yes."

"You have not wished me dead, or spoken or thought evilly of the old tyrant at Herst, who has so often crossed and thwarted you?"

"Never, dear: how could I—when I remember——"

"Ay, quite so. When one remembers! And gratitude is so common a thing. Will you oblige me by sending a line to Mr. Buscarlet, asking him to come to me without delay?"

"You are going to alter your will?" she asks, faintly, shocked at the speedy success of her scheme.

"Yes," coolly. "I am going to cut Philip out of it."

"Grandpapa, do not be too hard on him," she says, putting her hand across her throat, and almost gasping. "He is young. Young men sometimes——"

"I was once a young man myself, you seem to forget, and I know all about it. Why did you give me that letter?" he asks, grimly. "Are you chicken-hearted, now you have done the deed, like all women? It is too late for remorse to be of use: you *have* done it. Let it be your portion to remember how you have willfully ruined his prospects."

A choking sigh escapes her as she quits the room. Truly she has bought her revenge dearly. Not the poorest trace of sweetness lingers in it.

By this time it will be perceived that the house is in a secret turmoil. Every one is at daggers drawn with every one else. Molly and Lady Stafford have as yet exchanged no confidences, though keenly desirous of doing so, each having noticed with the liveliest surmisings the depression of the other.

Mr. Potts alone, who is above suspicion (being one of those cheerful people who never see anything—no matter how closely under their noses—until it is brought before them in the broadest language), continues blissfully unconscious of the confusion that reigns around, and savors his conversation throughout the evening with as many embarrassing remarks as he can conveniently put in.

"Eaten bread is soon forgotten," says he, sententiously, during a pause. "You all seem strangely oblivious of the fact that last night there was a ball in this house. Why shirk the subject? I like talking," says Mr. Potts, superfluously, "and surely you must all have something to communicate concerning it. Thanks to our own exertions, I think it was as good a one as ever I was at; and the old boy"—(I need scarcely say Mr. Amherst has retired to rest)—was uncommon decent about giving us the best champagne."

"You took very good care to show him how you appreciated his hospitality," says Sir Penthony, mildly.

"Well, why shouldn't I do honor to the occasion? A ball at Herst don't come every day. As a rule, an affair of the kind at a country house is a failure, as the guests quarrel dreadfully among themselves next day; but ours has been a brilliant exception."

"Brilliant indeed," says Lady Stafford, demurely.

"But what became of Lowry?" demands this wretched young man, who has never yet learned that silence is golden. "He told me this morning he intended staying on until the end of the week, and off he goes to London by the midday train without a word of warning. Must have heard some unpleasant news, I shouldn't wonder, he looked so awfully cut up. Did he tell you anything about it?" To Lady Stafford.

"No." In a freezing tone. "I see no reason why I, in particular, should be bored by Mr. Lowry's private woes."

"Well, you were such a friend, you know, for one thing," says Potts, surprised, but obtuse as ever.

"So I am of yours; but I sincerely trust the fact of my being so will not induce you to come weeping to me whenever you chance to lose your heart or place all your money on the wrong horse."

"Did he lose his money, then?"

"Plantagenet, dancing has muddled your brain. How should I know whether he lost his money or not? I am merely supposing. You are dull to-night. Come and play a game at écarté with me, to see if it may rouse you."

They part for the night rather earlier than usual, pleading fatigue,— all except Mr. Potts, who declares himself fresh as a daisy, and proposes an impromptu dance in the ball-room. He is instantly snubbed, and retires gracefully, consoling himself with the reflection that he has evidently more "go" in his little finger than they can boast in their entire bodies.

Sir Penthony having refused to acknowledge his wife's parting salutation,—meant to conciliate,—Cecil retires to her room in a state of indignation and sorrow that reduces her presently to tears.

Her maid, entering just as she has reached the very highest pinnacle of her wrongs, meets with anything but a warm reception.

"How now, Trimmins? Did I ring?" asks she, with unwonted sharpness, being unpleasantly mindful of the redness of her eyes.

"No, my lady; but I thought——"

"Never think," says Cecil, interrupting her with unreasoning irritation.

"No, my lady. I only thought perhaps you would see Miss Massereene," persists Trimmins, meekly. "She wishes to know, with her love, if you can receive her now."

"Miss Massereene? Of course I can. Why did you not say so before?"

"Your ladyship scarcely gave me time," says Trimmins, demurely, taking an exhaustive survey of her cambric apron.

"True; I was hasty," Cecil acknowledges, in her impulsive, honest, haughty way. "Tell Miss Massereene I shall be delighted to see her at once."

Presently Molly enters, her eyelids pink, the corners of her mouth forlornly curved, a general despondency in her whole demeanor.

Cecil, scarcely more composed, advances to meet her.

"Why, Molly!" she says, pathetically.

"You have been crying," says Molly, in the same breath, throwing herself into her arms.

"I have indeed, my dear," confesses Cecil, in a lachrymose tone, and then she begins to cry again, and Molly follows suit, and for the next five minutes they have a very comfortable time of it together.

Then they open their hearts to each other and relate fluently, as only a woman can, all the intolerable wrongs and misjudgment they have undergone at the hands of their lovers.

"To accuse me of anything so horrible!" says Molly, indignantly. "Oh, Cecil! I don't believe he could care for me one bit and suspect me of it."

"'Care for you!' Nonsense, my dear! he adores you. That is precisely why he has made such a fool of himself. You know—

Trifles light as air,

Are to the jealous confirmations strong

As proofs of holy writ.

"I like a man to be jealous,—in reason. Though when Sir Penthony walked out from behind that hedge, looking as if he could, with pleasure, devour me and Talbot at a bite, I confess I could gladly have dispensed with the quality in him. You should have seen his face: for once I was honestly frightened."

"Poor Cecil! it must have been a shock. And all because that tiresome young man wouldn't go away."

"Just so. All might have been well had he only seen things in a reasonable light. Oh, I was so angry! The most charming of your charms, Molly," says Cecil, warmly, "is your ability to sympathize with one. You can feel so thoroughly with and for me; and you never season your remarks with unpalatable truths. You never say, 'I told you so,' or 'I knew how it would be,' or 'didn't I warn you?' or anything else equally objectionable. I really would rather a person boxed my ears outright than give way to such phrases as those, pretending they know all about a catastrophe, after it has happened. And," says her ladyship, with a pensive sigh, "you *might* perhaps (had you so chosen) have accused me of flirting a leetle bit with that stupid Talbot."

"Well, indeed, perhaps I might, dear," says Molly, innocently.

"What, are you going to play the traitor after all that flattery? and if so, what am I to say to you about your disgraceful encouragement of Captain Shadwell?"

"I wonder if I did encourage him?" says Molly, contritely. "At first, perhaps unconsciously, but lately I am sure I didn't. Do you know, Cecil, I positively dislike him? he is so dark and silent, and still persistent. But when a man keeps on saying he is miserable for love of you, and that you are the cause of all his distress, and that he would as soon be dead as alive, because you cannot return his affection, how can one help feeling a little sorry for him?"

"I don't feel in the least sorry for Talbot. I thought him extremely unpleasant and impertinent, and I hope with all my heart he is very unhappy to-night, because it will do him good."

"Cecil, how cruel you are!"

"Well, by what right does he go about making fierce love to married women, compelling them to listen to his nonsense whether they like it or not, and getting them into scrapes? I don't break my heart over Sir Penthony, but I certainly do not wish him to think badly of me."

"At least," says Molly, relapsing again into the blues, "you have this consolation: you cannot lose Sir Penthony."

"That might also be looked on as a disadvantage. Still, I suppose there is some benefit to be gained from my position," says Cecil, meditatively. "*My* lover (if indeed he is my lover) cannot play the false knight with *me*; I defy him to love—and to ride away. There are no breakers ahead for me. He is mine irrevocably, no matter how horribly he may desire to escape. But you need not envy me; it is sweeter to be as you are,—to know him yours without the shadow of a tie. He is not lost to you."

"Effectually. What! do you think I would submit to be again engaged to a man who could fling me off for a chimera, a mere trick of the imagination? If he were to beg my pardon on his knees,—if he were to acknowledge every word he said to me a lie,—I would not look at him again."

"I always said your pride would be your bane," says Cecil, reprovingly. "Now, just think how far happier you would be if you were friends with him again, and think of nothing else. What is pride in comparison with comfort?"

"Have you forgiven Sir Penthony?"

"Freely. But he won't forgive me."

"Have you forgiven him the first great crime of all,—his indifference toward his bride?"

"N—o," confesses her ladyship, smiling; "not yet."

"Ah! then don't blame me. I could have killed myself when I cried," says Molly, referring again to the past, with a little angry shiver; "but I felt so sorry for my poor, pretty, innocent ring. And he looked so handsome, so determined, when he flung it in the fire, with his eyes quite dark and his figure drawn up; and—and—I could not help wondering," says Molly, with a little tremble in her tone, "who next would love him—and who—he—would love."

"I never thought you were so fond of him, dearest," says Cecil, laying her hand softly on her friend's.

"Nor I,—until I lost him," murmurs poor Molly, with a vain attempt at composure. Two tears fall heavily into her lap; a sob escapes her.

"Now you are going to cry again," interposes Cecil, with hasty but kindly warning. "Don't. He is not going to fall in love with any one so long as you are single, take my word for it. Nonsense, my dear! cheer yourself with the certainty that he is at this very moment eating his heart out, because he knows better than I do that, though there may be many women, there is only one Molly Bawn in the world."

This reflection, although consolatory, has not the desired effect. Instead of drying her eyes and declaring herself glad that Luttrell is unhappy, Molly grows more and more afflicted every moment.

"My dear girl," exclaims Lady Stafford, as a last resource, "do pray think of your complexion. I have finished crying; I shall give way to crying no more, because I wish to look my best to-morrow, to let him see what a charming person he has chosen to quarrel with. And my tears are not so destructive as yours, because mine arise from vexation, yours from feeling."

"I hardly know," says Molly, with an attempt at *nonchalance* she is far from feeling, "I really think I cried more for my diamond than for—my lover. However, I shall take your advice; I shall think no more about it. To-morrow"—rising and running to the glass, and pushing back her disordered hair from her face, that is lovely in spite of marring tears—"to-morrow I shall be gayer, brighter than he has ever yet seen me. What! shall I let him think I fret because of him! He saw me once in tears; he shall not see me so again."

"What a pity it is that grief should be so unbecoming!" says Cecil, laughing. "I always think what a guy Niobe must have been if she was indeed all tears."

"The worst thing about crying, I think," says Molly, "is the fatal desire one feels to blow one's nose: that is the horrid part of it. I knew I was looking odious all the time I was weeping over my ring, and that added to my discomfort. By the bye, Cecil, what were you doing at the table with a pencil just before we broke up to-night? Sir Penthony was staring at you fixedly all through,—wondering, I am sure, at your occupation, as, to tell the truth, was I."

"Nothing very remarkable. I was inditing a 'sonnet to your eyebrow,' or rather to your lids, they were so delicately tinted, and so much in unison with the extreme dejection of your entire bearing. I confess, unkind as it may sound, they moved me to laughter. Ah! that reminds me," says Cecil, her expression changing to one of comical terror, as she starts to her feet, "Plantagenet came up at the moment, and lest he should see my composition I hid it within the leaves of the blotting-book. There it is still, no doubt. What shall I do if any one finds it in the morning? I shall be read out of meeting, as I have an indistinct idea that, with a view to making you laugh, I rather caricatured every one in the room, more or less."

"Shall I run down for it?" says Molly. "I won't be a moment, and you are quite undressed. In the blotting-book, you said? I shan't be any time."

"Unless the ghosts detain you."

"Or, what would be much worse, any of our friends."

CHAPTER XXVI

"A single stream of all her soft brown hair
Poured on one side.

Half light, half shade,

She stood, a sight to make an old man young."
    —*Gardener's Daughter.*

Thrusting her little bare feet into her slippers, she takes up a candle and walks softly down the stairs, past the smoking and billiard-rooms, into the drawing-room, where the paper has been left.

All the lamps have been extinguished, leaving the apartment, which is immense, steeped in darkness. Coming into it from the brilliantly-lighted hall outside, with only a candle in her hand, the gloom seems even greater, and overcomes her sight to such a degree that she has traversed at least one-half its length before she discovers she is not its only occupant.

Seated before a writing-table, with his hand, indeed, upon the very blotting-book she seeks, and with only another candle similar to hers to lend him light, sits Luttrell.

As her eyes meet his she starts, colors violently, and is for the moment utterly abashed.

Involuntarily she glances down at the soft blue dressing-gown she wears, over which her hair—brushed and arranged for the night—falls in soft, rippling, gold-brown masses, and from thence to the little naked feet that peep out shamelessly from their blue slippers.

The crimson blood rises to her face. Covered with a painful though pretty confusion, she stands quite still, and lets her tell-tale eyes seek the ground.

Luttrell has risen, and, without any particular design, has advanced toward her. Perhaps the force of habit compels him to do so; perhaps intense and not altogether welcome surprise. For the future to see her is but to add one more pang to his intolerable regret.

"I was writing to you," he says, indicating with a slight movement of the hand the chair on which he has been sitting, and thus breaking the awful silence which threatens to last until next day, so mute has Molly grown. With a delicate sense of chivalry he endeavors to appear oblivious of her rather scanty and disconcerting—however becoming—costume. "But as it is, perhaps I may as well say to you what is on my mind,—if you will permit me."

"I cannot forbid your speech." Coldly.

"I will not keep you long. But"—with a slight, almost imperceptible, glance at her dressing-gown—"perhaps you are in a hurry?"

"I am—rather." At this juncture, had they been friends, Molly would undoubtedly have laughed. As it is, she is profoundly serious. "Still, if it is anything important, I will hear you."

"Can I do anything for you?" asks he, hesitating, evidently fearing to approach the desired subject.

"Nothing, thank you. I came only for a paper,—left in the blotting-book. If you wish to speak, do so quickly, as I must go." Then, as he still hesitates, "Why do you pause?"

"Because I fear incurring your displeasure once again; and surely the passages between us have been bad enough already."

"Do not fear." Coldly. "It is no longer in your power to wound me."

"True. I should not have allowed that fact to escape me. Yet hear me. It is my love urges me on."

"Your—love!" With slow and scornful disbelief.

"Yes,—mine. In spite of all that has come and gone, you know me well enough to understand how dear you still are to me. No, you need not say a word. I can see by your face that you will never pardon. There is no greater curse than to love a woman who gives one but bare tolerance in return."

"Why did you not think of all this while there was yet time?"

"One drifts—until it is too late to seek for remedies. My heaviest misfortune lies in the fact that I cannot root you from my heart."

"A terrible misfortune, no doubt,"—with a little angry flash from her azure eyes,—"but one that time will cure."

"Will it?" Wistfully. "Shall I indeed learn to forget you, Molly,—to look back upon my brief but happy past as an idle dream? I hardly hope so much."

"And would you waste all your best days," asks she, in tones that tremble ever so little, "in thinking of me? Remember all you said,—all you meant,—how 'thankful you were to find me out in time.'"

"And will you condemn forever because of a few words spoken in a moment of despair and terrible disappointment?" pleads he. "I acknowledge my fault. I was wrong; I was too hasty. I behaved like a brute, if you will; but then I believed I had grounds for fear. When once I saw your face, heard your voice, looked into your eyes, I knew how false my accusations were; but it was then too late."

"Too late, indeed."

"How calmly you can say it!" with exquisite reproach. "Have five minutes blotted out five months? Did you know all the anguish I endured on seeing you with—Shadwell—I think you might forgive."

"I might. But I could not forget. Would I again consent to be at the mercy of one who without a question pronounced me guilty? A thousand times no!"

"Say at once you are glad to be rid of me," breaks he in bitterly, stung by her persistent coldness.

"You are forgetting your original purpose," she says, after a slight pause, declining to notice his last remark. "Was there not something you wished to say to me?"

"Yes." Rousing himself with an impatient sigh. "Molly," blanching a little, and trying to read her face, with all his heart in his eyes,—"are you going to marry Shadwell?"

Molly colors richly (a rare thing with her), grows pale again, clasps and unclasps her slender fingers nervously, before she makes reply. A prompting toward mischief grows within her, together with a sense of anger that he should dare put such a question to her under existing circumstances.

"I cannot see by what right you put to me such a question—now," she says, at length, haughtily. "My affairs can no longer concern you." With an offended gleam at him from under her long lashes.

"But they do," cries he, hotly, maddened by her blush, which he has attributed jealously to a wrong cause. "How can I see you throwing yourself away upon a *roué*—a blackleg—without uttering a word of warning?"

"'A *roué*—a blackleg'? Those are strong terms. What has Captain Shadwell done to deserve them? A blackleg! How?"

"Perhaps I go too far when I say that," says Luttrell, wishing with all his heart he knew something vile of Shadwell; "but he has gone as near it as any man well can. You and he cannot have a thought in common. Will you sacrifice your entire life without considering well the consequences?"

"He is a gentleman, at all events," says Miss Massereene, slowly, cuttingly. "He never backbites his friends. He is courteous in his manner; and—he knows how to keep—his temper. I do not believe any of your insinuations."

"You defend him?" cries Luttrell, vehemently. "Does that mean that you already love him? It is impossible! In a few short weeks to forget all the vows we interchanged, all the good days we spent at Brooklyn, before we ever came to this accursed place! There at least you liked me well enough,— you were willing to trust to me your life's happiness; here!—And now you almost tell me you love this man, who is utterly unworthy of you. Speak. Say it is not so."

"I shall tell you nothing. You have no right to ask me. What is there to prevent my marrying whom I choose? Have you so soon forgotten that last night you—*jilted* me?" She speaks bitterly, and turns from him with an unlovely laugh.

"Molly," cries the young man, in low tones, full of passion, catching her hand, all the violent emotion he has been so painfully striving to suppress since her entrance breaking loose now, "listen to me for one moment. Do not kill me. My whole heart is bound up in you. You are too young to be so cruel. Darling, I was mad when I deemed I could live without you. I have been mad ever since that fatal hour last night. Will you forgive me? *Will* you?"

"Let my hand go, Mr. Luttrell," says the girl, with a dry sob. Is it anger, or grief, or pride? "You had me once, and you would not keep me. You shall never again have the chance of throwing me over: be assured of that."

She draws her fingers from his burning clasp, and once more turns away, with her eyes bent carefully upon the carpet, lest he shall notice the tears that threaten to overflow them. She walks resolutely but slowly past where he is standing, with folded arms, leaning against the wall, toward the door.

Just as her fingers close on the handle she becomes aware of footsteps on the outside coming leisurely toward her.

Instinctively she shrinks backward, casts a hasty, horrified glance at her dressing-gown, her bare feet, her loosened hair; then, with a movement full of confidence, mingled with fear, she hastens back to Luttrell (who, too, has heard the disconcerting sound) and glances up at him appealingly.

"There is somebody coming," she breathes, in a terrified whisper.

The footsteps come nearer,—nearer still; they reach the very threshold, and then pause. Will their owner come in?

In the fear and agony and doubt of the moment, Molly lays her two white hands upon her bosom and stands listening intently, with wide-open gleaming eyes, too frightened to move or make any attempt at concealment; while Luttrell, although alarmed for her, cannot withdraw his gaze from her lovely face.

Somebody's hand steals along the door as though searching for the handle. With renewed hope Luttrell instantly blows out both the candles near him, reducing the room to utter darkness, and draws Molly behind the window-curtains.

There is a breathless pause. The door opens slowly,—slowly. With a gasp that can almost be heard, Molly puts out one hand in the darkness and lays it heavily upon Luttrell's arm. His fingers close over it.

"Hush! not a word," whispers he.

"Oh, I am so frightened!" returns she.

His heart has begun to beat madly. To feel her so close to him, although only through unwished-for accident, is dangerously sweet. By a supreme effort he keeps himself from taking her in his arms and giving her one last embrace; but honor, the hour, the situation, all alike forbid. So he only tightens his clasp upon her hand and smothers a sigh between his lips.

Whoever the intruder may be, he, she, or it, is without light; no truth-compelling ray illumines the gloom; and presently, after a slight hesitation, the door is closed again, and the footsteps go lightly, cautiously away through the hall, leaving them once more alone in the long, dark, ghostly drawing-room.

Molly draws her hand hurriedly away, and moving quietly from Luttrell's side, breathes a sigh, half relief, half embarrassment; while he, groping his way to the writing-table, finds a match, and, striking it, throws light upon the scene again.

At the same moment Molly emerges from the curtains, with a heightened color, and eyes, sweet but shamed, that positively refuse to meet his.

"I suppose I can trust you—to—say nothing of all this?" she murmurs, unsteadily.

"I suppose you can." Haughtily.

His heart is still throbbing passionately; almost, he fears, each separate beat can be heard in the oppressive stillness.

"Good-night," says Molly, slowly.

"Good-night."

Shyly, and still without meeting his gaze, she holds out her hand. He takes it softly, reverently, and, emboldened by the gentleness of her expression, says impulsively:

"Answer me a last question, darling,—answer me—*Are* you going to marry Philip?"

And she answers, also impulsively:

"No."

His face changes; hope once more shines within his blue eyes. Involuntarily he draws up his tall, slight figure to its full height, with a glad gesture that bespeaks returning confidence; then he glances longingly first at Molly's downcast face, then at the small hand that lies trembling in his own.

"May I?" he asks, and, receiving no denial, stoops and kisses it warmly once, twice, thrice, with fervent devotion.

"My dear, how long you have been!" says Cecil, when at length Molly returns to her room. "I thought you were never coming. Where have you been?"

"In the drawing-room; and oh, Cecil! *he* was there. And he would keep me, asking me question after question."

"I dare say," says Cecil, looking her over. "That blue *négligée* is tremendously becoming. No doubt he has still a good many more questions he would like to put to you. And you call yourself a nice, decorous, well-behaved— —"

"Don't be silly. You have yet to hear the 'decorous' and thrilling part of my tale. Just as we were in the middle of a most animated discussion, what do you think happened? Somebody actually came to the door and tried to open it. In an instant Tedcastle blew out both our candles and drew me behind the curtain."

"'"Curiouser and curiouser," said Alice.' I begin to think I'm in Wonderland. Go on. The plot thickens; the impropriety deepens. It grows more interesting at every word."

"The 'somebody,' whoever it was, opened the door, looked in,—fortunately without a light, or we might have been discovered,—and——"

"You fainted, of course?" says Cecil, who is consumed with laughter.

"No, indeed," answers Molly; "I neither fainted nor screamed."

"Tut! nonsense. I think nothing of you. Such a golden opportunity thrown away! In your place I should have been senseless in half a minute in Tedcastle's arms."

"Forgive my stupidity. I only turned and caught hold of Teddy's arm, and held him as though I never meant to let him go."

"Perhaps that was your secret wish, were the truth known. Molly, you are wiser than I am. What is a paltry fainting fit to the touch of a soft, warm hand? Go on."

"Well, the invader, when he had gazed into space, withdrew again, leaving us to our own devices. Cecil, if we had been discovered! I in my dressing-gown! Not all the waters of the Atlantic would have saved me from censure. I never was so terrified. Who *could* it have been?"

"'Oh! 'twas I, love;

Wandering by, love,'"

declares Cecil, going off into a perfect peal of laughter. "Never, never have I been so entertained! And so I frightened you? Well, be comforted. I was terrified in my turn by your long absence; so much so that, without a candle, I crept down-stairs, stole along the hall, and looked into the drawing-room. Seeing no one, I retreated, and gained my own room again as fast as I could. Oh, how sorry I am I did not know! Consider your feelings had I stolen quietly toward your hiding-place step by step! A splendid situation absolutely thrown away."

"You and Mr. Potts ought to be brother and sister, you both revel so in the bare idea of mischief," says Molly, laughing too.

And then Cecil, declaring it is all hours, turns her out of her room, and presently sleep falls and settles upon Herst and all its inmates.

CHAPTER XXVII

"Death is here, and death is there;
Death is busy everywhere;
All around, within, beneath,
Above is death,—and we are death.

Fresh spring, and summer, and winter hoar,
Move my faint heart with grief, but with delight
No more, O never more."

                                        —Shelley.

It is just two o'clock, and Sunday. They have all been to church. They have struggled manfully through their prayers. They have chanted a depressing psalm or two to the most tuneless of ancient ditties. They have even sat out an incomprehensible sermon with polite gravity and many a weary yawn.

The day is dull. So is the rector. So is the curate,—unutterably so.

Service over, they file out again into the open air in solemn silence, though at heart glad as children who break school, and wend their way back to Herst through the dismantled wood.

The trees are nearly naked: a short, sad, consumptive wind is soughing through them. The grass—what remains of it—is brown, of an unpleasant hue. No flowers smile up at them as they pass quietly along. The sky is leaden. There is a general air of despondency over everything. It is a day laid aside for dismal reflection; a day on which hateful "might have beens" crop up, for "melancholy has marked it for its own."

Yet just as they come to a turn in the park, two magpies (harbingers of good when coupled; messengers of evil when apart) fly past them directly across their path.

"'Two for joy!'" cries Molly, gayly, glad of any interruption to her depressing thoughts. "I saw them first. The luck is mine."

"I think *I* saw them first," says Sir Penthony, with no object beyond a laudable desire to promote argument.

"Now, how could you?" says Molly. "I am quite twenty yards ahead of you, and must have seen them come round this corner first. Now, what shall I get, I wonder? Something worth getting, I do hope."

"'Blessed are they that expect nothing, for they shall not be disappointed,'" says Mr. Potts, moodily, who is as gloomy as the day. "I expect nothing."

"You are jealous," retorts Molly. "Sour grapes,"—making a small *moue* at him. "But you have no claim upon this luck; it is all my own. Let nobody for a moment look upon it as his or hers."

"You are welcome to it. I don't envy you," says Cecil, little thinking how prophetic are her words.

They continue their walk and their interrupted thoughts,—the latter leading them in all sorts of contrary directions,—some to love, some to hate, some to cold game-pie and dry champagne.

As they enter the hall at Herst, one of the footmen steps forward and hands Molly an ugly yellow envelope.

"Why, here is my luck, perhaps!" cries she, gayly. "How soon it has come! Now, what can be in it? Let us all guess."

She is surprised, and her cheeks have flushed a little. Her face is full of laughter. Her sweet eyes wander from one to another, asking them to join in her amusement No thought, no faintest suspicion of the awful truth occurs to her, although only a thin piece of paper conceals it from her view.

"A large fortune, perhaps," says Sir Penthony; while the others close round her, laughing, too. Only Luttrell stands apart, calmly indifferent.

"Or a proposal. That would just suit the rapid times in which we live."

"I think I would at once accept a man who proposed to me by telegraph," says Molly, with pretty affectation. "It would show such flattering haste,—such a desire for a kind reply. Remember,"—with her finger under the lap of the envelope,—"if the last surmise proves correct I have almost said yes."

She breaks open the paper, and, smiling still, daintily unfolds the enclosure.

What a few words!—two or three strokes of the pen. Yet what a change they make in the beautiful, *debonnaire* countenance! Black as ink they stand out beneath her stricken eyes. Oh, cruel hand that penned them so abruptly!

"Come home at once. Make no delay. Your brother is dead."

Gray as death grows her face; her body turns to stone. So altered is she in this brief space, that when she raises her head some shrink away from her, and some cry out.

"Oh, Molly! what is it?" asks Lady Stafford, panic-stricken, seizing her by the arm; while Luttrell, scarcely less white than the girl herself, comes unconsciously forward.

Molly's arms fall to her sides; the telegram flutters to the floor.

"My brother is dead," she says, in a slow, unmeaning tone.

"He is dead," she says again, in a rather higher, shriller voice, receiving no response from the awed group that surrounds her. Their silence evidently puzzles her. Her large eyes wander helplessly over all their faces, until at length they fall on Luttrell's. Here they rest, knowing she has found one that loves her.

"Teddy—Teddy!" she cries, in an agonized tone of desolation; then, throwing up her arms wildly toward heaven, as though imploring pity, she falls forward senseless into his outstretched arms.

All through the night Cecil Stafford stays with her, soothing and caressing her as best she can. But all her soothing and caressing falls on barren soil.

Up and down the room throughout the weary hours walks Molly, praying, longing for the daylight; asking impatiently every now and then if it "will never come." Surely on earth there is no greater cross to bear than the passive one of waiting when distress and love call loudly for assistance.

Her eyes are dry and tearless; her whole body burns like fire with a dull and throbbing heat. She is composed but restless.

"Will it soon be day?" she asks Cecil, almost every half hour, with a fierce impatience,—her entire being full of but one idea, which is to reach her home as soon as possible.

And again:

"If I had not fainted I might have been there now. Why did I miss that train? Why did you let me faint?"

In vain Cecil strives to comfort; no thought comes to her but a mad craving for the busy day.

At last it comes, slowly, sweetly. The gray dawn deepens into rose, the sun flings abroad its young and chilly beams upon the earth. It is the opening of a glorious morn. How often have we noticed in our hours of direst grief how it is then Nature chooses to deck herself in all her fairest and best, as though to mock us with the very gayety and splendor of her charms!

At half-past seven an early train is starting. Long before that time she is dressed, with her hat and jacket on, fearful lest by any delay she should miss it; and when at length the carriage is brought round to the door she runs swiftly down the stairs to meet it.

In the hall below, awaiting her, stands Luttrell, ready to accompany her.

"Are you going, too?" Cecil asks, in a whisper, only half surprised.

"Yes, of course. I will take her myself to Brooklyn."

"I might have known you would," Cecil says, kindly, and then she kisses Molly, who hardly returns the caress, and puts her into the carriage, and, pressing Luttrell's hand warmly, watches them until they are driven out of her sight.

During all the long drive not one word does Molly utter. Neither does Luttrell, whose heart is bleeding for her. She takes no notice of him, expresses no surprise at his being with her.

At the station he takes her ticket, through bribery obtains an empty carriage, and, placing a rug round her, seats himself at the farthest end of the compartment from her,—so little does he seek to intrude upon her grief. And yet she takes no heed of him. He might, indeed, be absent, or the veriest stranger, so little does his presence seem to affect her. Leaning rather forward, with her hands clasped upon her knees, she scarcely stirs or raises her head throughout the journey, except to go from carriage to train, from train back again to carriage.

Once, during their last short drive from the station to Brooklyn, moved by compassion, he ventures to address her.

"I wish you could cry, my poor darling," he says, tenderly, taking her hand and fondling it between his own.

"Tears could not help me," she answers. And then, as though aroused by his voice, she says, uneasily, "Why are you here?"

"Because I am his friend and—yours," he returns, gently, making allowance for her small show of irritation.

"True," she says, and no more. Five minutes afterward they reach Brooklyn.

The door stands wide open. All the world could have entered unrebuked into that silent hall. What need now for bars and bolts? When the Great

Thief has entered in and stolen from them their best, what heart have they to guard against lesser thefts?

Luttrell follows Molly into the house, his face no whit less white than her own. A great pain is tugging at him, —a pain that is almost an agony. For what greater suffering is there than to watch with unavailing sympathy the anguish of those we love?

He touches her lightly on the arm to rouse her, for she has stood stock-still in the very middle of the hall,—whether through awful fear, or grief, or sudden bitter memory, her heart knoweth.

"Molly," says her lover, "let me go with you."

"You still here?" she says, awaking from her thoughts, with a shiver. "I thought you gone. Why do you stay? I only ask to be alone."

"I shall go in a few minutes," he pleads, "when I have seen you safe with Mrs. Massereene. I am afraid for you. Suppose you should—suppose—you do not even know—*the* room," he winds up, desperately. "Let me guard you against such an awful surprise as that."

"I do," she answers, pointing, with a shudder, to one room farther on that branches off the hall. "It—is there. Leave me; I shall be better by myself."

"I shall see you to-morrow?" he says, diffidently.

"No; I shall see no one to-morrow."

"Nevertheless, I shall call to know how you are," he says, persistently, and kissing one of her limp little hands, departs.

Outside on the gravel he meets the old man who for years has had care of the garden and general out-door work at Brooklyn.

"It is a terrible thing, sir," this ancient individual says, touching his hat to Luttrell, who had been rather a favorite with him during his stay last summer. He speaks without being addressed, feeling as though the sad catastrophe that has occurred has leveled some of the etiquette existing between master and man.

"Terrible indeed." And then, in a low tone, "How did it happen?"

"'Twas just this," says the old man, who is faithful, and has understood for many years most of John Massereene's affairs, having lived with him from boy to man; "'twas money that did it. He had invested all he had, as it might be, and he lost it, and the shock went to his heart and killed him. Poor soul! poor soul!"

"Disease of the heart. Who would have suspected it? And he has lost all. Surely something remains?"

"Only a few hundreds, sir, as I hear,—nothing to signify,—for the poor mistress and the wee bits. It is a fearful thing, sir, and bad to think of. And there's Miss Molly, too. I never could abide them spickilations, as they're called."

"Poor John Massereene!" says Luttrell, taking off his hat. "He meant no harm to any one,—least of all to those who were nearest to his kindly heart."

"Ay, ay, man and boy I knew him. He was always kind and true, was the master,—with no two ways about him. When the letter came as told him all was gone, and that only beggary was before him, he said nothing, only went away to his study dazed like, an' read it, an' read it, and then fell down heart-broken upon the floor. Dead he was—stone dead—afore any of us came to him. The poor missis it was as found him first."

"It is too horrible," says Luttrell, shuddering. He nods his head to the old man and walks away from him down to the village inn, depressed and saddened.

The gardener's news has been worse than even he anticipated. To be bereft of their dearest is bad enough, but to be thrown penniless on the mercies of the cold and cruel—nay, rather thoughtless—world is surely an aggravation of their misery. Death at all times is a calamity; but when it leaves the mourners without actual means of support, how much sadder a thing it is! To know one's comforts shall remain unimpaired after the loss of one's beloved is—in spite of all indignant denial—a solace to the most mournful.

CHAPTER XXVIII

"As the earth when leaves are dead,
As the night when sleep is sped,
As the heart when joy is fled,
I am left lone—alone."
—Shelley.

Meantime, Molly, having listened vaguely and without interest, yet with a curious intentness, to his parting footfalls, as the last one dies away draws herself up and, with a sigh or two, moves instinctively toward the door she had pointed out to Luttrell.

No one has told her, no hint has reached her ears. It is not his usual bedroom, yet she knows that within that door lies all that remains to her of the brother so fondly loved.

With slow and lagging steps, with bent head and averted eyes, she creeps tardily near, resting with her hand upon the lock to summon courage to meet what must be before her. She feels faint,—sick with a bodily sickness,—for never yet has she come face to face with Death.

At last, bringing her teeth firmly together, and closing her eyes, by an immense effort she compels herself to turn the handle of the door, and enters.

Letitia is seated upon the floor beside the bed, her head lowered, her hands folded tightly in her lap. There is no appearance of mourning so far as garments are concerned. Of course, considering the shortness of the time, it would be impossible: yet it seems odd, out of keeping, that she should still be wearing that soft blue serge, which is associated with so many happy hours.

She is not weeping: there are no traces, however faint, of tears. Her cheeks look a little thinner, more haggard, and she has lost the delicate girlish color that was her chief charm; but her eyes, though black circles surround them,—so black as to suggest the appliance of art,—have an unnatural brilliancy that utterly precludes the possibility of crying.

Some one has pulled a piece of the blind to one side, and a fitful gleam of sunlight, that dances in a heartless manner, flickers in and out of the room, nay, even strays in its ghastly mirth across the bed where the poor body lies.

As Molly walks, or rather drags her limbs after her, into the chamber (so deadly is the terror that has seized upon her), Letitia slowly raises her eyes.

She evinces no surprise at her sister's home-coming.

"There is all that is left you," she says, in a hard, slow voice, that makes Molly shiver, turning her head in the direction of the bed, and opening and shutting her hands with a peculiarly expressive, empty gesture. Afterward she goes back to her original position, her face bent downward, her body swaying gently to and fro.

Reluctantly, with trembling steps and hidden eyes, Molly forces herself to approach the dreaded spot. For the first time she is about to look on our undying foe,—to make acquaintance with the last great change of all.

A cold hand has closed upon her heart; she is consumed by an awesome, unconquerable shrinking. She feels a difficulty in breathing; almost she thinks her senses are about to desert her.

As she reaches the side of the bed opposite to where Letitia crouches, she compels herself to look, and for the moment sustains a passionate feeling of relief, as the white sheet that covers all alone meets her gaze.

And yet not all. A second later, and a dread more awful than the first overpowers her, for there, beneath the fair, pure linen shroud, the features are clearly marked, the form can be traced; she can assure herself of the shape of the head,—the nose,—the hands folded so quietly, so obediently, in their last eternal sleep upon the cold breast. But no faintest breathing stirs them. He is dead!

Her eyes grow to this fearful thing. To steady herself she lays her hand upon the back of a chair. Not for all the world contains would she lean upon that bed, lest by any chance she should disturb the quiet sleeper. The other hand she puts out in trembling silence to raise a corner of the sheet.

"I *cannot*," she groans aloud, withdrawing her fingers shudderingly. But no one heeds. Three times she essays to throw back the covering, to gaze upon her dead, and fails; and then at last the deed is accomplished, and Death in all its silent majesty lies smiling before her.

Is it John? Yes, it is, of course. And yet—*is it*? Oh, the changeless sweetness of the smile,—the terrible shading,—the moveless serenity!

Spell-bound, heart-broken, she gazes at him for a minute, and then hastily, though with the tenderest reverence, she hides away his face. A heavy, bursting sigh escapes her; she raises her head, and becomes conscious that Letitia is upon her knees and is staring at her fixedly across the bed.

There is about her an expression that is almost wild in its surprise and horror.

"*You* do not cry either," says she, in a clear, intense whisper. "I thought I was the only thing on earth so unnatural. I have not wept. I have not lost my senses. I can still think. I have lost my all,—my husband,—John!—and yet I have not shed one single tear. And you, Molly,—he loved you so dearly, and I fancied you loved him too,—and still you are as cold, as poor a creature as myself."

There is no reply. Molly is regarding her speechlessly. In truth, she is dumb from sheer misery and the remembrance of what she has just seen. Are Letitia's words true? *Is* she heartless?

There is a long silence,—how long neither of them ever knows,—and then something happens that achieves what all the despair and sorrow have failed in doing. In the house, through it, awakening all the silence, rings a peal of childish laughter. It echoes; it trembles along the corridor outside; it seems to shake the very walls of the death-chamber.

Both the women start violently. Molly, raising her hands to her head, falls back against the wall nearest to her, unutterable horror in her face. Letitia, with a quick, sharp cry, springs to her feet, and then, running to Molly, flings her arms around her.

"Molly, Molly," she exclaims, wildly, "am I going mad? That cannot—it cannot be *his* child."

Then they cling to each other in silent agony, until at length some cruel band around their hearts gives way, and the sorrowful, healing, blessed tears spring forth.

The last sad scene is over; the curtain has fallen. The final separation has taken place. Their dead has been buried out of their sight.

The room in which he lay has been thrown open, the blinds raised, the windows lifted. Through them the sweet, fresh wind comes rushing in. The heartless sun—now grown cold and wintry—has sent some of its rays to peer curiously where so lately the body lay.

The children are growing more demonstrative. More frequently, and with less fear of reproof, the sound of their mirth is heard throughout the silent house. Only this very morning the boy Lovat—the eldest born, his father's idol—went whistling through the hall. No doubt it was in a moment of forgetfulness he did it; no doubt the poor lad checked himself an instant later, with a bitter pang of self-reproach; but his mother heard him, and the sound smote her to the heart.

Mr. Buscarlet (who is a kind little man, in spite of his "ways and his manners" and a few eccentricities of speech), at a word from Molly comes to Brooklyn, and, having carefully examined letters, papers, and affairs generally, turns their fears into unhappy certainty. One thousand pounds is all that remains to them on which to live or starve.

The announcement of their ruin is hardly news to Letitia. She has been prepared for it. The letter found crushed in her dead husband's hand, although suppressing half the truth, did not deceive her. Even at that awful moment she quite realized her position. Not so Molly. With all the unreasoning trust of youth she hoped against hope until it was no longer possible to do so, trying to believe that something forgotten would come to light, some unremembered sum, to relieve them from absolute want. But Mr. Buscarlet's search has proved ineffective.

Now, however, when hope is actually at an end, all her natural self-reliance and bravery return to her; and in the very mouth of despair she makes a way for herself and for those whom she loves to escape.

After two nights' wakeful hesitation, shrinking, doubt, and fear, she forms a resolution, from which she never afterward turns aside until compelled to do so by unrestrainable circumstances.

"It is a very distressing case," says Mr. Buscarlet, blowing his nose oppressively,—the more so that he feels for her very sincerely; "distressing, indeed. I don't know one half so afflicting. I really do—not—see what is to be done."

"Do not think me presumptuous if I say I do," says Molly. "I have a plan already formed, and, if it succeeds, I shall at least be able to earn bread for us all."

"My dear young lady, how? You with—ahem!—you must excuse me if I say—your youth and beauty, how do you propose to earn your bread?"

"It is my secret as yet,"—with a faint wan smile. "Let me keep it a little longer. Not even Mrs. Massereene knows of it. Indeed, it is too soon to proclaim my design. People might scoff it; though for all that I shall work it out. And something tells me I shall succeed."

"Yes, yes, we all think we shall succeed when young," says the old lawyer, sadly, moved to keenest compassion at sight of the beautiful, earnest face before him. "It is later on, when we are faint and weary with the buffetings of fortune, the sad awakening comes."

"I shall not be disheartened by rebuffs; I shall not fail," says Molly, intently. "However cold and ungenerous the world may prove, I shall conquer it at last. Victory shall stay with me."

"Well, well, I would not discourage any one. There are none so worthy of praise as those who seek to work out their own independence, whether they live or die in the struggle. But work—of the sort you mean—is hard for one so young. You have a plan. Well, so have I. But have you never thought of your grandfather? He is very kindly disposed toward you; and if he——"

"I have no time for 'buts' and 'ifs,'" she interrupts him, gently. "My grandfather may be kindly disposed toward *me*, but not toward *mine*,—and that counts for much more. No, I must fall back upon myself alone. I have quite made up my mind," says Molly, throwing up her small proud head, with a brave smile, "and the knowledge makes me more courageous. I feel so strong to do, so determined to vanquish all obstacles, that I know I shall neither break down nor fail."

"I trust not, my dear; I trust not. You have my best wishes, at least."

"Thank you," says Molly, pressing his kind old hand.

CHAPTER XXIX

"I fain would follow love, if that could be."

—Tennyson.

Letitia in her widowed garments looks particularly handsome. All the "trappings and the signs" of woe suit well her tall, full figure, her fair and placid face.

Molly looks taller, slenderer than usual in her mourning robes. She is one of those who grow slight quickly under affliction. Her rounded cheeks have fallen in and show sad hollows; her eyes are larger, darker, and show beneath them great purple lines born of many tears.

She has not seen Luttrell since her return home,—although Letitia has,—and rarely asks for him. Her absorbing grief appears to have swallowed up all other emotions. She has not once left the house. She works little, she does not read at all; she is fast falling into a settled melancholy.

"Molly," says Letitia, "Tedcastle is in the drawing-room. He particularly asks to see you. Do not refuse him again. Even though your engagement, as you say, is at an end, still remember, dearest, how kind, how more than thoughtful, he has been in many ways since—of late——"

Her voice breaks.

"Yes, yes, I will see him," Molly says, wearily, and, rising, wends her way slowly, reluctantly, to the room which contains her lover.

At sight of him some chords that have lain hushed and forgotten in her heart for many days come to life again. Her pulses throb, albeit languidly, her color deepens; a something that is almost gladness awakes within her. Alas! how human are we all, how short-lived our keenest regrets! With the living love so near her she for the first time (though only for a moment) forgets the dead one.

In her trailing, sombre dress, with her sorrowful white cheeks, and quivering lips, she goes up to him and places her hand in his; while he, touched with a mighty compassion, stares at her, marking with a lover's careful eye all the many alterations in her face. So much havoc in so short a time!

"How changed you are! How you must have suffered!" he says, tenderly.

"I have," she answers; and then, grown nervous, because of her trouble and the fluttering of her heart, and that tears of late are so ready to her, she covers her face with her hands, and, with the action of a tired and saddened child, turning, hides it still more effectually upon his breast.

"It is all very miserable," he says, after a pause, occupied in trying to soothe.

"Ah! is it not? What trouble can be compared with it? To find him dead, without a word, a parting sign!" She sighs heavily. "The bitterest sting of all lies in the fact that but for my own selfishness I might have seen him again. Had I returned home as I promised at the end of the month I should have met my brother living; but instead I lingered on, enjoying myself," — with a shudder, — "while he was slowly breaking his heart over his growing difficulties. It must all have happened during this last month. He had no care on his mind when I left him; you know that. You remember how light-hearted he was, how kindly, how good to all."

"He was indeed, poor—poor fellow!"

"And some have dared to blame him," she says, in a pained whisper. "You do not?"

"No—*no*."

"I have been calculating," she goes on, in a distressed tone, "and the very night I was dancing so frivolously at that horrible ball he must have been lying awake here waiting with a sick heart for the news that was to— kill him. I shall never go to a ball again; I shall never dance again," says Molly, with a passionate sob, scorning, as youth will, the power of time to cure.

"Darling, why should you blame yourself? Such thoughts are morbid," says Luttrell, fondly caressing the bright hair that still lies loosely against his arm. "Which of us can see into the future? And, if we could, do you think it would add to our happiness? Shake off such depressing ideas. They will injure not only your mind, but your body."

"I do not think I should feel it all quite so much," says Molly, in a low, miserable, expressionless voice, "if I could only see him now and then. No, not in the flesh—I do not mean that,—but if I could only bring his face before my mind I might be content. For hours together I sit, with my hands clasped before my eyes, trying to conjure him up, and I cannot. Almost every casual acquaintance I possess, all the people whose living or dying matters to me not at all, rise at my command; but he never. Is it not curious?"

"Perhaps it is because your mind dwells too much upon him. But tell me of your affairs," says Luttrell, abruptly but kindly, leading her to a sofa and seating himself beside her, with a view of drawing her from her unhappy thoughts. "Are they as bad as Mrs. Massereene says?"

"Quite as bad."

"Then what do they mean to do?" In a tone of the deepest commiseration.

"'They'? We, you mean. What others, I suppose, have learned to do before us—work for our daily bread."

An incredulous look comes into his eyes, but he wisely subdues it.

"And what do you propose doing?" he asks, calmly, meaning in his own mind to humor her.

"You are like Mr. Buscarlet,—he would know everything," says Molly, with a smile; "but this is a question you must not ask me,—just yet. I have a hope,—perhaps I had better say an idea; and until it is confirmed or rejected I shall tell no one of it. No, not even you."

"Well, never mind. Tell me instead when you intend leaving Brooklyn."

"In a fortnight we must leave it. Is it not a little while?—only two short weeks in which to say good-bye forever to my home,—(how much that word comprises!)—to the place where all my life has been spent,—where every stone, and tree, and path is endeared to me by a thousand memories."

"And after?"

"We go to London. There I hope to work out my idea."

"You have forgotten to tell me," says Luttrell, slowly, "my part in all these arrangements."

"Yours? Ah, Teddy, you put an end to our engagement in good time. Now it must have been broken, whether we liked it or not."

"Meaning that I must not throw in my lot with yours? Do you know what folly you are talking?" says Luttrell, almost roughly. "Ours, I am assured, is an engagement that *cannot* be broken. Not all the cruel words that could be spoken—that have been spoken"—in a low tone of reproach—"have power to separate us. You are mine, Molly, as I am yours, forever. I will never give you up. And now—now—in the hour of your trouble——" Breaking off, he gets up from his seat and commences to pace the room excitedly.

She has risen too, and is standing with her eyes fixed anxiously upon him. At length, "Let us put an end now to all misconceptions and doubts," he says, stopping before her. "Your manner that last evening at Herst, your greeting of to-day, have led me to hope again. I would know without further delay whether I am wrong in thinking you care more for me than for any other man. Am I? Speak, Molly, tell me now—here—if you love me."

"I do—I do!" cries she, bursting into tears again, and flinging herself in an abandonment of grief into his longing arms. "And that is what makes my task so hard. That is why I have not allowed myself to see you all these past days. It was not coldness, Teddy, it was love. I dared not see you, because all must be at an end between us."

"Do you think, with you in my arms like this, with the assurance of your love fresh upon your lips, and now"—stooping—"upon mine, I can do anything but laugh at such treason as that?"

"Nay, but you must listen, Teddy, and believe that I am earnest in all that I say. For the future I shall neither see you nor hear from you: I must even try to forget you, if I would succeed in what lies before me. From henceforth I shall do my best to regard you as a stranger, to keep you at arm's length."

"Never," says Luttrell, emphatically, tightening his arms around her, as though to enforce the meaning of the word and show the absurdity of her last remark. "You talk as though you meant to convince me, but unhappily you don't. The more you say the more determined I am to marry you at once, and put a stop to all such nonsense as your trying to work."

"And are you going to marry Letitia also, and Lovat, and the two little girls, and the baby?" asks she, quietly. "Who is talking nonsense now? You seem to forget that they and I are one."

"Something must be done," says Luttrell, wretchedly.

"I quite agree with you; but who is going to do it?"

"I will"—decidedly; "I shall cut the army. My father has been a member and a staunch Conservative for years, and surely he must have some interest. I have heard of posts under government where one has little or nothing to do, and gets a capital salary for doing it; why should not I drop into one of them? Then we might all live together, and perhaps you might be happy."

"But in the meantime"—sadly—"we poor folks must live."

"That is the worst of it," says Luttrell, with questionable taste, biting his moustache. "Well"—angrily—"I see you are as bent on having your own way as ever. Tell me about this mighty plan of yours."

"I cannot, indeed, and you must not ask me. If I did tell you, probably you would scoff at it, or perhaps be angry, and I will not let myself be discouraged. It is quite useless your pressing me about this matter. I will not tell."

"And do you mean to tell me you purpose going alone into the great London world to seek your fortune, without a protector? You must be mad."

"I have Letitia."

"Letitia"—indignantly—"is a very handsome woman, not more than ten years older than yourself. *She* a protector!"

"I can't help that."

"Yes, you can; but your—obstinacy—won't allow you. Do you, then, intend to let no one know of your affairs?"

"I shall confide in Cecil Stafford, because I can't avoid it. But I know she will keep my secret until I give her leave to speak."

"It comes to this, then, that you consider every one before me. It is nothing to you whether I eat my heart out in ignorance of whether you are alive or dead."

"Cecil"—hastily—"may tell you so much."

"Thank you; this is a wonderful concession."

"Why should I concede at all, when, as I have said, you are no longer bound to me?"

"But I am,—more strongly so than ever; and I insist, I desire you, Molly, to let me know what it is you intend doing."

He looks sterner than one would have conceived possible for him; Miss Massereene evidently thinks him inhumanly so.

"Don't speak to me like that," she says, with quivering lips. "You should not. I have made a vow not to disclose my secret to you of all people, and would you have me break it?"

"But why?" impatiently.

"Because—have I not told you already?—because"—with a little dry sob—"I love you so dearly that to encourage thoughts of you would unfit me for my work. And it is partly for your own sake I do it, for something tells me we shall never marry each other; and why should you spend your life dreaming of a shadow?"

"It is the cruelest resolution a woman ever formed," replies he, ignoring as beneath notice the latter part of her speech, and, putting away her hands, takes once more to his irritable promenade up and down the room.

Molly is crying, silently, exhaustedly. "My burden is too heavy for me," she murmurs, faintly.

"Then why not let me help you to bear it?"

"If it will comfort you, Teddy"—brokenly—"I will give in so far as to promise to write to you in six months. I ask you to wait till then. Is it too long? If so, remember you are free—believe me it will be better so—and I perhaps shall be happier in the thought——" And here incontinently she breaks down.

"Don't," says Luttrell, hurriedly, whose heart grows faint within him at the sight of her distress. "Molly, I give in. I am satisfied with your last promise. I shall wait forever, if that will please you. Who am I, that I should add one tear to the many you have already shed? Forgive me, my own love."

"Yes, but do not say anything more to me to-day; I am tired," says Molly, submitting to his caresses, though still a little sore at heart.

"Only one thing more," says this insatiable young man, who evidently holds in high esteem the maxim to "strike while the iron is hot." "You agree to a renewal of our engagement?"

"I suppose so. Although I know it is an act of selfishness on my part. Nothing can possibly come of it."

"And if it is selfishness in you, what is it in me?" asks he, humbly. "You know as well as I do I am no match for you, who, with your face, your voice" (Molly winces perceptibly), "your manner, might marry whom you choose. Yet I do ask you to wait"—eagerly—"until something comes to our aid, to be true to me, no matter what happens, until I can claim you."

"I will wait; I *will* be true to you," she answers, with dewy eyes uplifted to his, and a serene, earnest face. As she gives her promise a little sigh escapes her, more full of content, I think, than any regret.

After coming to this conclusion they talk more rationally for an hour or so (a lover's hour, dear reader, is not as other hours; it never drags; it is not full of yawns; it does not make us curse the day we were born); and then Luttrell, by some unlucky chance, discovers he must tear himself away.

As Molly rises to bid him good-bye, she catches her breath, and presses her hand to her side.

"I have such a pain here," she says.

"You don't go out," says her lover, severely; "you want air. I shall speak to Letitia if you won't take more care of yourself."

"I have not been out of the house for so long, I quite dread going."

"Then go to-morrow. If you will walk to the wood nearest you,—where you will see no one,—I will meet you there."

"Very well," says Molly, obediently; and when they have said good-bye for the fifth time, he really takes his departure.

How to reveal her weighty secret to Letitia troubles Molly much,—an intimate acquaintance with her sister-in-law's character causing her to know its disclosure will be received not only with discouragement, but with actual disapproval. And yet—disclose it she must.

But how to break it happily. Having thought of many ways and means, and rejected them all, she decides, with a sigh, that plain speaking will be best.

"Letitia," she says, this very evening,—Luttrell having been gone some hours,—"do you know Signor Marigny's address?"

She is leaning her elbows on the writing-table, and has let her rounded chin sink into her palms' embrace; while her eyes fix themselves steadily upon the pen, the paper, anything but Letitia.

"Signor Marigny! Your old singing-master? No. Why do you ask, dear?"

"Because I want to write to him."

"Do you? And what——? No, I have not got his address; I don't believe I ever had it. How shall you manage?"

"I dare say I have it somewhere myself; don't trouble," says Molly, knowing guiltily it lies just beneath her hand within the table-drawer. She is glad of a respite, Letitia having forborne to press the question.

Not for long, however; human nature can stand a good many things, but curiosity conquers most.

"Why are you writing to Signor Marigny?" Letitia asks, in a gentle tone of indifference, after a full five minutes' pause, during which she has been devoured with a desire to know.

"Because I believe he will help me," says Molly, slowly. "I have been thinking, Letty,—thinking very seriously,—and I have decided upon making my fortune—*our* fortune—out of my voice."

"Molly!"

"Well, dear, and why not? Do not dishearten me, Letty; you know we must live, and what other plan can you suggest?"

"In London I thought perhaps we might get something to do,"—mournfully,—"and there no one would hear of us. I have rather a fancy for millinery, and one of those large establishments might take me, while you could go as a daily governess," regarding her sister doubtfully.

"Governess! oh, no! The insipidity, the drudgery of it, would kill me. I should lose sight of the fact that I was my own mistress in such genteel slavery. Besides, as a concert singer (and I *can* sing), I should earn as much in one night, probably, as I should otherwise in a year."

"Oh, Molly!"—clasping her hands—"I cannot bear to think of it. It is horrible; the publicity,—the dreadful ordeal. And you of all others,—my pretty Molly——"

"It is well I am pretty," says Molly, with a supreme effort at calmness; "they say a pretty woman with a voice takes better."

"Every word you say only convinces me more and more how cruel a task it would be. And Molly, darling, I know he would not wish it."

"I think he would wish me to do my duty," says Molly, gazing with great tearless eyes through the window into space, while her slender fingers meet and twine together nervously. "Letitia, why cannot you be thankful, as I am, that I have a voice,—a sure and certain provision?—because I know I can sing as very few can. (I say this gratefully, and without any vanity.) Why, without it we might starve."

"And what will Tedcastle say? For, in spite of all your arguments, Molly, I am sure he is devoted to you still."

"That must not matter. Our engagement, to all intents and purposes, is at an end, because"—sighing—"we shall never marry. He is too poor, and I am too poor, and, besides"—telling her lie bravely,—"I do not wish to marry him."

"I find it hard to believe you," says Letitia, examining the girl's face critically. "Do you mean to tell me you have ceased to care for him?"

"How do I know?"—pettishly, her very restlessness betraying the truth. "At times I am not sure myself. At all events, everything is at an end between us, which is the principal thing, as he cannot now interfere with my decision."

"Do not think you can deceive me," says Letitia, in a trembling tone. "Ah, how cruel it all is! Death when it visits most homes, leaves at least hope behind, but here there is none. Other women lose fortune, or perhaps position, or it may be love; but I have lost all; while you—with all your young life before you—would sacrifice yourself for us. I am not wholly selfish, Molly; I refuse to accept your offer. I refuse to take your happiness at your hands."

"My happiness is yours," returns Molly, tenderly; "refuse to let me help you, and the little shred of comfort that still remains to me vanishes with the rest. Letitia, you are my home now: do not reject me."

Two sad little tears run down her pale cheeks unchecked. Letitia, unable to bear the sight, turns away; and presently two kindred drops steal down her face, and fall with a faint splashing sound upon her heavy crape.

"It would be such a hateful life for you," she says, with a sigh.

"I don't think so. I like singing; and the knowledge that by it I was actually helping you—who all my life have been my true and loving sister— would make my task sweet. What shall I say to Signor Marigny, Letty?" with a sudden air of business. "He has a great deal to do with concerts and that; and I know he will assist me in every way."

"Tell him you are about to sacrifice your love, your happiness, everything that makes life good, for your family," says Letitia, who has begun to cry bitterly, "and ask him what will compensate you for it; ask him if gold, or fame, or praise, will fill the void that already you have begun to feel."

"Nonsense, my dear! he would justly consider me a lunatic, were I to write to him in such a strain. I shall simply tell him that I wish to make use of the talent that has been given me, and ask him for his advice how best to proceed. Don't you think something like that would answer? Come now, Letty," cheerfully and coaxingly, kneeling down before Mrs. Massereene, "say you are pleased with my plan, and all will be well."

"What would become of me without you?" says Letitia, irrelevantly, kissing her; and Molly, taking this for consent, enters into a long and animated discussion of the subject of her intended *début* as a public singer.

CHAPTER XXX

"Who ne'er have loved, and loved in vain,

Can neither feel nor pity pain."

—Byron.

True to her promise, the next day Molly wraps herself up warmly and takes her way toward the wood that adjoins but does not belong to Brooklyn.

At first, from overmuch inactivity and spiritless brooding, a sort of languor—a trembling of the limbs—oppresses her; but presently, as the cold, crisp air creeps into her young blood, she quickens her steps, and is soon walking with a brisk and healthy motion toward the desired spot.

Often her eyes fill with unbidden tears, as many a well-remembered place is passed, and she thinks of a kindly word or a gay jest uttered here by lips now cold and mute.

There is a sadness in the wood itself that harmonizes with her thoughts. The bare trees, the fast-decaying leaves beneath her feet, all speak of death and change. Swinburne's exquisite lines rise involuntarily to her mind:

"Lo, the summer is dead, the sun is faded,

Even like as a leaf the year is withered.

All the fruit of the day from all her branches

Gathered, neither is any left to gather.

All the flowers are dead, the tender blossoms,

All are taken away; the season wasted

Like an ember among the fallen ashes."

Seating herself upon a little grassy mound, with her head thrown back against the trunk of a gnarled but kindly beech, she waits her lover's coming. She is very early, almost by her own calculation half an hour must elapse before he can join her. Satisfied that she cannot see him until then, she is rapidly falling into a gentle doze, when footsteps behind her cause her to start into a sitting posture.

"So soon," she says, and, rising, finds herself face to face with—Philip Shadwell.

"You see, I have followed you," he says, slowly.

He does not offer to shake hands with her; he gives her no greeting; he only stands before her, suffering his eyes to drink in hungrily her saddened but always perfect beauty.

"So I see," she answers, quite slowly.

"You have been in trouble. You have grown thin," he says, presently, in the same tone.

"Yes."

She is puzzled, dismayed, at his presence here, feeling an unaccountable repugnance to his society, and a longing for his departure, as she notes his unwonted agitation,—the unknown but evident purpose in his eyes.

"When last we met," says Philip, with a visible effort at calmness, and with his great dark, moody eyes bent upon the ground, "you told me you— hated me."

"Did I? The last time? How long ago it seems!—years—centuries. Ah!"— clasping her hands in a very ecstasy of regret—"how happy I was then! and yet—I thought myself miserable! That day I spoke to you" (gazing at him as one gazes at something outside and beyond the question altogether), "I absolutely believed I knew what unhappiness meant; and now——"

"Yes. You said you hated me," says the young man, still bent upon his own wrongs to the exclusion of all others. He is sorry for her, very sorry; but what is her honest grief for her beloved dead compared with the desperate craving for the unattainable that is consuming him daily,—hourly?

"I hardly remember," Molly says, running her slender fingers across her brow. "Well,"—with a sigh,—"I have fallen into such low estate since then that I think I have no power within me now to hate any one."

"You did not mean it, perhaps?" still painfully calm, although he knows the moments of grace are slipping surely, swiftly, trying vainly to encourage hope. "You said it, perhaps, in an instant of passion? One often does. One exaggerates a small offense. Is it not so?"

"Yes,"—with her thoughts as far from him as the earth is from the heavens,—"it may be so."

"You think so? You did *not* mean it?" with a sudden gleam of misplaced confidence. "Oh! if you only knew how I have suffered since that fatal word passed your lips!—but you did not mean it. In time—who knows?—you may even bring yourself to care for me a little. Molly,"—seizing her hand,— "speak—speak, and say it will be so."

"No, no," exclaims she, at last, coming back to the present, and understanding him. "Never. Why do you so deceive yourself? Do not think it; do not try to believe it. And"—with a quick shudder—"to speak to me so now,—at this time——"

"Perhaps, had I known you first, you might have loved me," persists he.

"I am sure not," replies she, gently but decidedly. "Your dark looks, your vehemence,—all—frighten me."

"Once assured of your love, I could change all that," he perseveres, unwisely, in a low tone, his passionate, gloomy eyes still fixed upon the ground, his foot uneasily stirring the chilled blades of grass beneath him. "In such a case, what is it I could not do? Molly, will you not take pity on me? Will you not give me a chance?"

"I cannot. Why will you persist? I tell you, if we two were to live forever, you are the very last man I should ever love. It is the kindest thing I can do for you to speak thus plainly."

"Kind!"—bitterly; "*can* you be kind? With your fair, soft face, and your angel eyes, you are the most bitterly cruel woman I ever met in my life. I curse the day I first saw you! You have ruined my happiness."

"Philip, do not speak like that. You cannot mean it. In a few short months you will forget you have ever uttered such words,—or felt them. See, now,"—laying the tips of her fingers kindly upon his arm,—"put away from you this miserable fancy, and I will be your friend—if you will."

"Friend!" retorts he, roughly. "Who that had seen and loved you could coldly look upon you as a friend? Every thought of my heart, every action of my life, has you mixed up in it. Your face is burned into my brain. I live but in recollection of you, and you speak to me of friendship! I tell you," says Philip, almost reducing himself again to calmness through intensity of emotion, "I am fighting for my very existence. I must and will have you."

"Why will you talk so wildly?"—turning a little pale, and retreating a step: "you know what you propose, to be impossible."

"There is nothing impossible, if you will only try to look upon me more kindly."

"Am I to tell you again," she says, still gently, but with some natural indignation, "that if I knew you for ever and ever, I could not feel for you even the faintest spark of affection of the kind you mean! I would not marry you for all the bribes you could offer. It is not your fault that it is so, nor is it mine. You say 'try' to love you. Can love be forced? Did ever any one grow to love another through trying? You know better. The more one would have to try, the less likely would one be to succeed. Love is free, and yet a very tyrant. Oh, Philip, forget such vain thoughts. Do not waste your life hoping for what can never be."

"It shall be," cries he, vehemently, suddenly, with an unexpected movement catching her in his arms. "Molly, if I cannot buy your love, let me at least buy yourself. Remember how you are now situated. You do not yet know the horrors of poverty—real poverty; and I—at least I have prospects. Herst will be mine beyond all doubt (who can be preferred before me?), and that old man cannot live forever. Think of your sister and all her children; I swear I will provide for all; not one but shall be to me as my own, for your sake. You shall do what you like with me. Body and soul I am yours for good or evil. Let it be for good."

"How dare you speak to me like this?" says Molly, who has tried vainly to escape from his detested embrace during the short time it has taken him to pour forth his last words. "Let me go instantly. Do you hear me, Philip?—release me."

Her blue eyes have turned almost black with a little fear and unlimited anger, her lips are white but firm, her very indignation only making her more fair.

"I will, when you have given me some ground for hope. Promise you will consider my words."

"Not for a single instant. When a few moments ago I hinted how abhorrent you are to me, I spoke truly; I only lied when I tried to soften my words. I would rather ten thousand times be *dead* than your wife. Now I hope you understand. Your very touch makes me shudder."

She ceases, more from want of breath than words, and a deep silence falls between them. Even through the bare and melancholy trees the wind has forgotten to shiver. Above, the clouds, rain-filled, scud hurriedly. A storm is in the air. Upon Philip's face a deadlier storm is gathering.

"Have you anything more to say?" he asks, an evil look coming into his eyes. Not for a second has he relaxed his hold.

Molly's heart sinks a little lower. Oh! if Tedcastle would only come! yet with a certain bravery she compels herself to return without flinching the gaze of the dark passionate face bent above hers. She knows every limb in her body is trembling, that a deadly sickness is creeping over her, yet by a supreme effort she maintains her calmness.

"Nothing," she answers, quietly, with just a touch of scorn. "I should have thought I had said enough to convince any *man*. Now will you let me go home? You cannot want to keep me here after what I have said."

"I wonder you are not afraid of me," says Shadwell, who is absolutely beside himself with anger. "Do not put unlimited faith in my forbearance. A worm, you know, will turn. Do you think you can goad a man to desperation and leave him as cool as when you began? I confess I am not made of such stuff. Do you know you are in my power? What is to prevent my killing you here, now, this moment?"

He speaks slowly, as though his breath comes with difficulty, so much has anger overmastered him; yet her eyes have never fallen before his, and he knows, in spite of his words, he has not the smallest mastery over her, he has gained no triumph.

"I wish you were dead," he goes on, in a compressed tone, "and myself too. To be sure, that if you were not mine you would never be another's, has in it a sweetness that tempts me. They say extremes meet. I hardly know, now, where my love for you ends, or where my hatred begins."

His violence terrifies Molly.

"Philip, be generous," she says, laying her hand against his chest with a vain attempt to break from him; "and—and—try to be calm. Your eyes have madness in them. Even if you were to kill me, what good would it do you? And think of the afterward. Oh, what have I ever done to you that you should seek to—to—unnerve me like this?"

"'What have you done?' Shall I tell you? You have murdered me surely as though your knife had entered my heart. You have killed every good thought in me, every desire that might perhaps have had some element of nobleness in it. I was bad enough before I met you, I dare say; but you have made me ten times worse."

"It is all false. I will not listen to you,"—covering her ears with her hands. But he takes them down again, gently but determinedly, and compels her to hear him.

"When you first came to Herst for your own amusement, to pass away the hours that perhaps hung a little heavily upon your hands, or to rouse a feeling of jealousy in the heart of Luttrell, or to prove the power you have over all men by the right of your fatal beauty, you played off upon me all the pretty airs and graces, all the sweet looks and tender words, that come so easy to you, never caring what torment I might have to endure when your dainty pastime had palled upon you. Day by day I was led to believe that I was more to you than those others who also waited on your words."

"That is false,—false. Your own vanity misled you."

"I was the one singled out to escort you here, to bear your messages there. Now and again you threw me flowers, not half so honeyed as your smiles. And when you had rendered me half mad—nay, I think wholly so—for love of you, and I asked you to be my wife, you asked me in return 'what I meant,' pretending an innocent ignorance of having done anything to encourage me."

"I do not think I have done all this," says Molly, with a little gasping sigh; "but if I have I regret it. I repent it. I pray your forgiveness."

"And I will grant it on one condition. Swear you will be my wife."

She does not answer. He is so vehement that she fears to provoke him further; yet nothing but a decided refusal can be given. She raises her head and regards him with a carefully-concealed shudder, and as she does so Luttrell's fair, beautiful face—even more true than beautiful, his eyes so blue and earnest, his firm but tender mouth—rises before her. She thinks of his devotion, his deep, honest love, and without thinking any further she says, "No," with much more decided emphasis than prudence would have permitted.

"'No!'" repeats he, furiously. "Do you still defy me? Are you then so faithful to the memory of the man who cast you off? Have you, perhaps, renewed your engagement with him? If I thought that,—if I was sure of that—— Speak, and say if it be so."

The strain is too great. Molly's brave heart fails her. She gives a little gasping cry, and with it her courage disappears. Raising her face in mute appeal to the bare trees, to the rushing, comfortless wind, to the murky sky, she bursts into a storm of tears.

"Oh, if my brother were but alive," cries she, in passionate protest, "you would not dare treat me like this! Oh, John, John, where are you? It is I, your Molly Bawn. *Why* are you silent?"

Her sobs fall upon the chilly air. Her tears drop through her fingers down upon the brown-tinged grass, upon a foolish frozen daisy that has outlived its fellows,—upon her companion's heart!

With a groan he comes to his senses, releases her, and, moving away, covers his face with his hands.

"Don't do that," he says. "Stop crying. What a brute I am! Molly, Molly, be silent, I desire you. I am punished enough already."

Hardly daring to believe herself free, and dreading a relapse on Philip's part, and being still a good deal over-strung and frightened, Miss Massereene sobs on very successfully, while even at this moment secretly reproaching herself in that she did not pocket her pride half an hour ago, and give way to the tears that have had such a fortunate effect.

Just at this juncture, Luttrell, clearing a stile that separates him from them, appears upon the scene. His dismay on seeing Molly in tears almost obliterates the displeased amazement with which he regards Philip's unexpected appearance.

"Molly," he calls out to her, even from the distance, some undefined instinct telling him she will be glad of his presence. And Molly, hearing him, raises her head, and without a word or cry runs to him, and flings herself into the fond shelter of his arms.

As he holds her closely in his young, strong, ardent embrace, a great peace—a joy that is almost pain—comes to her. Had she still any lingering doubts of her love for him, this moment, in which he stands by her as a guardian, a protector, a true lover, would forever dispel them.

"You here," says Luttrell, addressing Philip with a frown, while his face flames, and then grows white as Shadwell's own, "and Miss Massereene in tears! Explain——"

"Better leave explanation to another time," interrupts Philip, with insolent *hauteur*, his repentant mood having vanished with Luttrell's arrival, "and take Miss Massereene home. She is tired."

So saying, he turns coolly on his heel, and walks away.

Luttrell makes an angry movement as though to follow him; but Molly with her arms restrains him.

"Do not leave me," she says, preparing to cry again directly if he shows any determination to have it out with Shadwell. "Stay with me. I feel so nervous and—and faint."

"Do you, darling?" Regarding her anxiously. "You do look pale. What was Shadwell saying to you? Why were you crying? If I thought he——"

"No, no,"—laying five hasty, convincing little fingers on his arm,—"nothing of the kind. Won't you believe me? He only reminded me of past days, and I was foolish, and—that was all."

"But what brought him at all?"

"To see me," says Molly, longing yet fearing to tell him of Philip's unpardonable behavior. "But do not let us talk of him. I cannot bear him. He makes me positively nervous. He is so dark, so vehement, so—uncanny!"

"The fellow isn't much of a fellow, certainly," says Luttrell, with charming explicitness.

For the mile that lies between them and home, they scarcely speak,—walking together, as children might, hand in hand, but in a silence unknown to our household pests.

"How quiet you are!" Molly says, at length awakening to the fact of her lover's dumbness. "What are you thinking about?"

"You, of course," he answers, with a rather joyless smile. "I have received my marching orders. I must join my regiment in Dublin next Saturday."

"And this is Tuesday!" Aghast at the terrible news. "Oh, Teddy! Could they not have left us together for the few last days that remain to us?"

"It appears they could not," replies he, with a prolonged and audible sigh.

"I always said your colonel was a bear," says Miss Massereene, vindictively.

"Well, but you see, he doesn't know how matters stand; he never heard of *you*," replies Luttrell, apologetically.

"Well, he ought to know; and even if he did, he would do it all the more. Oh, Teddy! dear Teddy!"—with a sudden change of tone, thoroughly appreciated by one individual at least,—"what shall I do without you?"

CHAPTER XXXI

"When we two parted in silence and tears,

Half broken-hearted, to sever for years,

Pale grew thy cheek, and cold, colder thy kiss."

—Byron.

They have wandered down once more by the river-side where first he told her how he loved her. To-night, again the moon is shining brightly, again the stream runs rippling by, but not, as then, with a joyous love-song; now it sounds sad as death, and "wild with all regret," as though mourning for the flowers—the sweet fond forget-me-nots—that used to grace its banks.

Their hands are clasped, his arm is round her; her head drooping, dejected (unlike the gay capricious Molly of a few months back), is leaning on his breast.

Large tears are falling silently, without a sob, down her white cheeks, because to-night they say their last farewell. It is one of those bitter partings, such as "press the life from out young hearts" and makes them doubt the good that this world conceals even in the very core of its disappointments.

"I feel as though I were losing all," says Molly, in a despairing tone. "First John, and now—you. Oh, how difficult a thing is life! how hard, how cruel!" Yet only a month before she was singing its praises with all the self-confidence of foolish ignorant youth.

"While I am alive you do not lose me," he answers, pressing his lips to her soft hair and brow. "But I am unhappy about you, my own: at the risk of letting you think me importunate, I would ask you again to reconsider your decision, and let me know how it is you propose fighting this cold world."

Unable to refuse him audibly, and still determined to adhere to her resolution to let nothing interfere with her self-imposed task, she maintains a painful silence, merely turning her head from side to side upon his chest uneasily.

"You still refuse me? Do you not think, Molly," —reproachfully,—"your conduct toward me is a little cold and unfeeling?"

"No, no. Do not misjudge me: indeed I am acting for the best. See," — placing two bare white arms around his neck, that gleam with snowy softness in the moonlight against the mournful draperies that fall away from them, — "if I were cold and unfeeling would I do this?" pressing her tender lips to his. "Would I? You know I would not. I am a coward too, and fear you would not look upon my plan as favorably as I do. Darling, forgive and trust me."

"Are you going on the stage?" asks he, after a pause, and with evident hesitation.

"Why?" with a forlorn little smile. "If I were, would you renounce me?"

"Need I answer that? But you are so young, so pretty, — I am afraid, my darling, it — it would be unpleasant for you."

"Be satisfied: I am not thinking of the stage. But do not question me, Teddy. I shall write to you, as I have promised, in six months, — if I succeed."

"And if you fail?"

"I suppose then — I shall write to you too," she answers, with a sigh and a faint smile. "But I shall not fail. After all, success will bring me no nearer to you: I shall always have the children to provide for," she says, despondingly.

"We can at least live and hope."

He draws her shawl, which has slipped to the ground, close round her, and mutely, gloomily, they stand listening to the murmuring of the sympathetic stream.

"I always think of this spot as the dearest on earth," he says, after a pause. "Here I picture you to myself with your hands full of forget-me-nots. I have a large bunch of them yet, the same you gathered; faded, it is true, to others, but never so to me. They will always be as fresh in my eyes as on the evening I took them from you. 'My sweet love's flowers.' Darling, darling," pressing her to his heart in a very agony of regret, "when shall we two stand here again together?"

"Never," she whispers back, in a prophetic tone, and with a trembling, sobbing sigh more sad than any tears.

"Give me something to remember you by, — something to remind me of to-night."

"Shall you need it?" asks she, and then raising her hands she loosens all her pretty hair, letting it fall in a bright shower around her. "You shall have one little lock all to yourself," she says. "Choose, and cut it where you will."

Tenderly he selects a shining tress,—a very small one, so loath is he, even for his own benefit, to lessen the glory of her hair,—and, severing it, consigns it to the back case of his watch.

"That is a good place to keep it," she says, with an upward glance that permits him to see the love that lives for him in her dewy eyes. "At least every night when you wind your watch you must think of me."

"I shall think of you morning, noon, and night, for that matter."

"And I,—when shall I think of you? And yet of what avail?" cries she, in despair; "all our thought will be of no use. It will not bring us together. We must be always separate,—always apart. Not all our longing will bring us one day nearer to each other. Our lives are broken asunder."

"Do not let us waste our last moments talking folly," replies he, calmly; "nothing earthly shall separate us."

"Yet time, they say, kills all things. It may perhaps—kill—even your love."

"You wrong me, Molly, in even supposing it. 'They sin, who tell us love can die,'" quotes he, softly, in a tender, solemn tone. "My love for you is deathless. Beloved, be assured of this, were we two to live until old age crept on us, I should still carry to my grave my love for you."

He is so earnest that in spite of herself a little unacknowledged comfort comes into her heart. She feels it is no flimsy passion of an hour he is giving her, but a true affection that will endure forever.

"How changed you are!" he says presently; "you, who used to be so self-reliant, have now lost all your courage. Try to be brave, Molly, for both our sakes. And—as I must soon go—tell me, what is your parting injunction to me?"

"The kindest thing I can say to you is—forget me."

"Then say something unkind. Do you imagine I shall take two such hateful words as a farewell?"

"Then don't forget me; be *sure* you don't," cries she, bursting into tears.

The minutes are flying: surely never have they flown with such cruel haste.

"Come, let us go in-doors," she says, when she has recovered herself. "I suppose it is growing late."

"I shall not go in again; I have said good-bye to Mrs. Massereene. It only remains to part from you."

They kiss each other tenderly.

"I shall walk as far as the gate with you," says Molly; and, with a last lingering glance at their beloved nook, they go silently away.

When they reach the gate they pause and look at each other in speechless sorrow. Like all partings, it seems at the moment final, and plants within their hearts the germs of an unutterable regret.

"Good-bye, my life, my darling," he whispers, brokenly, straining her to him as though he never means again to let her go: then, almost pushing her away, he turns and leaves her.

But she cannot part from him yet. When he has gone a hundred yards or more, she runs after him along the quiet moonlit road and throws herself once more into his arms.

"Teddy, Teddy," she cries, "do not go yet," and falls to weeping as though her heart would break. "It is the bitterness of death," she says, "and it *is* death. I know we shall never meet again."

"Do not speak like that," he entreats, in deep agitation. "I know—I believe—we shall indeed meet again, and under happier circumstances."

"Ah, you can find comfort!" Reproachfully. "You are not half sorry to part from me."

"Oh, Molly, be reasonable."

"If you can find *any* consolation at this moment, you are not. And—if you meet any one—anywhere—and—like her better than me—you will kill me: remember that."

"Now, where," argues he, in perfect sincerity, "could I meet any one to be compared with you?"

"But how shall I know it—not hearing from you for so many months?" She says this as though he, not she, had forbidden the correspondence.

"Then why not take something from those wretched six months?" he says, craftily.

"I don't know. Yes,"—doubtfully,—"it is too long a time. In four months, then, I shall write,—yes, in four months. Now I do not feel quite so bad. Sixteen weeks will not be so long going by."

"One would be shorter still."

"No, no." Smiling. "Would you have me break through all my resolution? Be faithful to me, Teddy, and I will be faithful to you. Here,"—lifting her hands to her neck,—"I am not half satisfied with that stupid lock of hair: it may fall out, or you may lose it some way. Take this little chain"—loosening it from round her throat and giving it to him—"and wear it next your heart until we meet again,—if indeed"—sighing—"we ever do meet again. Does not all this sound like the sentiment of a hundred years ago? But do not laugh at me: I mean it."

"I will do as you bid me," replies he, kissing the slender chain as though it were some sacred relic,—and as such, indeed, he regards it,—while ready tears spring to his eyes. "It and I shall never part."

"Well, good-bye really now," she says, with quivering lips. "I feel more cheerful, more hopeful. I don't feel as if—I were going to cry—another tear." With this she breaks into a perfect storm of tears, and tearing herself from his embrace, runs away from him down the avenue out of sight of his longing eyes.

CHAPTER XXXII

"Why, look you, how you storm!
I would be friends with you, and have your love."
—*Merchant of Venice.*

"She is indeed perfection."
—*Othello.*

The fourth day before that fixed upon for leaving Brooklyn, Molly, coming down to breakfast, finds upon her plate a large envelope directed in her grandfather's own writing,—a rather shaky writing now, it is true, but with all the remains of what must once have been bold and determined calligraphy.

"Who can it be from?" says Molly, regarding the elaborate seal and crest with amazement,—both so scarlet, both so huge.

"Open it, dear, and you will see," replies Letitia, who is merely curious, and would not be accused of triteness for the world.

Breaking the alarming seal, Molly reads in silence; while Letitia, unable to bear suspense, rises and reads it also over her sister's shoulder.

It consists of a very few lines, and merely expresses a desire—that is plainly a command—that Molly will come the following day to Herst, as her grandfather has something of importance to say to her.

"What can it be?" says Molly, glancing over her shoulder at Mrs. Massereene, who has taken the letter to re-read it.

"Something good, perhaps." Wistfully. "There may be some luck in store for you."

"Hardly. I have ceased to believe in my own good luck," says Molly, bitterly. "At all events, I suppose I had better go. Afterward I might reproach myself for having been inattentive to his wishes."

"Go, by all means," says Letitia; and so it is arranged.

Feeling tired and nervous, she arrives the next day at Herst, and is met in the hall by her friend the housekeeper in subdued spirits and the unfailing silk gown, who receives her in a good old motherly fashion and bestows upon her a warm though deferential kiss.

"You have come, my dear, and I am glad of it," she says in a mysterious tone. "He has been asking for you incessant. Miss Amherst, she is away from home." This in a pleased, confidential tone, Miss Amherst being distinctly unpopular among the domestics, small and great. "Mr. Amherst he sent her to the Latouches' for a week,—against her will, I must say. And the captain, he has gone abroad."

"Has he?" Surprised.

"Yes, quite suddent like, and no one the wiser why. When last he come home, after being away a whole day, he seemed to me daft like,—quite," says Mrs. Nesbitt, raising her eyes and hands, whose cozy plumpness almost conceals the well-worn ring that for twenty years of widowhood has rested there alone, "quite as though he had took leave of his senses."

"Yes?" says Molly, in a faltering tone, feeling decidedly guilty.

"Ah, indeed, Miss Massereene, and so 'twas. But you are tired, my dear, no doubt, and a'most faint for a glass of wine. Come and take off your things and rest yourself a bit, while I tell Mr. Amherst of your arrival."

In half an hour, refreshed and feeling somewhat bolder, Molly descends, and, gaining the library door, where her grandfather awaits her, she opens it and enters.

As, pale, slender, black-robed, she advances to his side, Mr. Amherst looks up.

"You have come," he says, holding out his hand to her, but not rising. There is a most unusual nervousness and hesitancy about his manner.

"Yes. You wrote for me, and I came," she answers simply, stooping, as in duty bound, to press her lips to his cheek.

"Are you well?" he asks, scrutinizingly, struck by the difference in her appearance since last he saw her.

"Yes, thank you, quite well."

"I am sorry to see you in such trouble." There is a callousness about the way in which these words are uttered that jars upon Molly. She remembers on the instant all his narrow spleen toward the one now gone.

"I am,—in sore trouble," she answers, coldly.

A pause. Mr. Amherst, although apparently full of purpose, clearly finds some difficulty about proceeding. Molly is waiting in impatient silence.

"You wished to speak to me, grandpapa?" she says, at length.

"Yes,—yes. Only three days ago I heard you had been left—badly provided for. Is this so?"

"It is."

"And that"—speaking slowly—"you had made up your mind to earn your own living. Have I still heard correctly?"

"Quite correctly. Mr. Buscarlet would be sure to give you a true version of the case."

"The news has upset me." For the first time he turns his head and regards her with a steady gaze. "I particularly object to your doing anything of the kind. It would be a disgrace, a blot upon our name forever. None of our family has ever been forced to work for daily bread. And I would have you remember you are an Amherst."

"Pardon me, I am a Massereene."

"You are an Amherst." With some excitement and considerable irritation. "Your mother must count in some way, and you—you bear a strong resemblance to every second portrait of our ancestors in the gallery upstairs. I wrote, therefore, to bring you here that I might personally desire you to give up your scheme of self-support and come to live at Herst as its mistress."

"'Its mistress'!" repeats Molly, in utter amazement. "And how about Marcia?"

"She shall be amply portioned,—if you consent to my proposal."

She is quite silent for a moment or two, pondering slowly; then, in a low, curious tone, she says:

"And what is to become of my sister?"

"Your step-sister-in-law, you mean." Contemptuously. "I dare say she will manage to live without your assistance."

Molly's blue eyes here show signs of coming fight; so do her hands. Although they hang open and motionless at her sides, there is a certain tension about the fingers that in a quick, warm temperament betokens passion.

"And my dead brother's children?"

"They too can live, no doubt. They are no whit worse off than if you had never been among them."

"But I *have* been among them," cries she, with sudden uncontrollable anger that can no longer be suppressed. "For all the years of my life they have been my only friends. When I was thrown upon the world without father or mother, my brother took me and gave me a father's care. I was left to him a baby, and he gave me a mother's love. He fed me, clothed me, guarded me, educated me, did all that man could do for me; and now shall I desert those dear to him? They are his children, therefore mine. As long as I can remember, he was my true and loving friend, while you—you—what are you to me? A stranger—a mere——"

She stops abruptly, fearing to give her passion further scope, and, casting her eyes upon the ground, folds one hand tightly over the other.

"You are talking sentimental folly," replies he, coolly. "Listen. You shall hear the truth. I ill-treated your mother, as you know. I flung her off. I refused her prayer for help, although I knew that for months before your birth she was enduring absolute want. Your father was in embarrassed circumstances at that time. Now I would make reparation to her, through her child. I tell you"—vindictively—"if you will consent to give up the family of the man who stole my Eleanor from me I will make you my heiress. All the property is unentailed. You shall have Herst and twenty thousand pounds a year at my death."

"Oh! hush, hush!"

"Think it over, girl. Give it your fullest consideration. Twenty thousand pounds a year! It will not fall to your lot every day."

"You strangely forget yourself," says Molly, with chilling *hauteur*, drawing herself up to her full height. "Has all your vaunted Amherst blood failed to teach you what honor means? You bribe me with your gold to sell myself, my better feelings, all that is good in me! Oh, shame! Although I am but a Massereene, and poor, I would scorn to offer any one money to forego their principles and betray those who loved and trusted in them!"

"You refuse me?" asks he, in tones that tremble with rage and disappointment.

"I do."

"Then go," cries he, pointing to the door with uplifted fingers that shake perceptibly. "Leave me, and never darken my doors again. Go, earn your bread. Starve for those beggarly brats. Work until your young blood turns to gall and all the youth and freshness of your life has gone from you."

"I hope I shall manage to live without all you predict coming to pass," the girl replies, faintly though bravely, her face as white as death. Is it a curse he is calling down upon her?

"May I ask how you intend doing so?" goes on this terrible old man. "Few honest paths lie open to a woman. You have not yet counted the cost of your refusal. Is the stage to be the scene of your future triumphs?"

She thinks of Luttrell, and of how differently he had put the very same question. Oh, that she had him near her now to comfort and support her! She is cold and trembling.

"You must pardon me," she says, with dignity, "if I refuse to tell you any of my plans."

"You are right in refusing. It is no business of mine. From henceforth I have no interest whatsoever in you or your affairs. Go,—go. Why do you linger, bandying words with me, when I bid you begone?"

In a very frenzy of mortification and anger he turns his back upon her, and sinking down into the chair from which in his rage he has arisen, he lets his head fall forward into his hands.

A great and sudden sadness falls on Molly. She forgets all the cruel words that have been said, while a terrible compassion for the loneliness, the utter barrenness of his drear old age, grows within her.

Crossing the room with light and noiseless footsteps, treading as though in the presence of one sick unto death, she comes up to him, lays her hands upon his shoulders, and stooping, presses her fresh young lips to his worn and wrinkled forehead.

"Good-bye, grandpapa," she says, softly, kindly. Then, silently, and without another farewell, she leaves him—forever.

She hardly remembers how she makes the return journey; how she took her ticket; how cavalierly she received the attentions of the exceedingly nice young man with flaxen hair suggestive of champagne who *would* tuck his railway rug around her, heroically unmindful of the cold that penetrated his own bones. Such trifling details escaped her then and afterward, leaving not so much as the smallest track upon her memory. Yet that yellow-haired young man dreamt of her for a week afterward, and would not be comforted, although all that could be done by a managing mother with two marriageable daughters was done to please him and bring him to see the error of his ways.

All the way home she ponders anxiously as to whether she shall or shall not reveal to Letitia all that has taken place. To tell her will be beyond doubt to grieve her; yet not to tell her,—how impossible that will be! The very intensity of her indignation and scorn creates in her an imperative desire to open her heart to somebody. And who so sympathetic as Letitia? And, after all, even if she hides it now, will not Letitia discover the truth sooner or later? Still——

She has not yet decided on her line of action when Brooklyn is reached. She is still wavering, even when Letitia, drawing, her into the parlor, closes the door, and, having kissed her, very naturally says, "Well?"

And Molly says "Well" also, but in a different tone; and then she turns pale, and then red,—and then she makes up her mind to tell the whole story.

"What did he want with you?" asks Letitia, while she is still wondering how she shall begin.

"Very little." Bitterly. "A mere trifle. He only wanted to buy me. He asked me to sell myself body and soul to him,—putting me at a high valuation, too, for he offered me Herst in exchange if I would renounce you and the children."

"Molly!"

"Yes. Just that. Oh, Letty! only a month ago I thought how sweet and fair and good a thing was life, and now—and now—that old man, tottering into his grave, has taught me the vileness of it."

"He offered you Herst? He offered you twenty thousand pounds a year?"

"He did, indeed. Was it not noble? Does it not show how highly he esteems me? I was to be sole mistress of the place; and Marcia was to be portioned off and—I saw by his eyes—banished."

"And you—*refused*?"

"Letty! How can you ask me such a question? Besides refusing, I had the small satisfaction of telling him exactly what I thought of him and his proposal. I do not think he will make such overtures to me again. Are you disappointed, Letty, that you look so strangely? Did you think, dear, I should bring you home some good news, instead of this disgraceful story?"

"No." In a low tone, and with a gesture of impatience. "I am not thinking of myself. Last week, Molly, you relinquished your love—for us; to-day you have resigned fortune. Will you never repent? In the days to come, how will you forgive us? Before it is too late, think it over and——"

"Letitia," says Molly, laying her hand upon her sister's lips, "if you ever speak to me like that again I shall—*kill you*."

CHAPTER XXXIII

"Mute and amazed was Alden; and listen'd and look'd at Priscilla,

Thinking he never had seen her more fair, more divine in her beauty."

—Longfellow.

It is the 2d of March—four months later (barely four months, for some days must still elapse before that time is fully up)—and a raw evening,—very raw, and cold even for the time of year,—when the train, stopping at the Victoria Station, suffers a young man to alight from it.

He is a tall young man, slight and upright, clad in one of the comfortable long coats of the period, with an aristocratic face and sweet, keen blue eyes. His moustache, fair and lengthy, is drooping sadly through dampness and the general inclemency of the weather.

Pushing his way through the other passengers, with a discontented expression upon his genial face that rather misbecomes it, he emerges into the open air, to find that a smart drizzle, unworthy the name of rain, is falling inhospitably upon him.

There is a fog,—not as thick as it might be, but a decided fog,—and everything is gloomy to the last degree.

Stumbling up against another tall young man, dressed almost to a tie the same as himself, he smothers the uncivil ejaculation that rises so naturally to his lips, and after a second glance changes it to one of greeting.

"Ah, Fenning, is it you?" he says. "This beastly fog prevented my recognizing you at first. How are you? It is ages since last we met."

"Is it indeed you, Luttrell?" says the new-comer, stopping short and altering his sour look to one of pleased astonishment. "You in the flesh? Let us look at you?" Drawing Luttrell into the neighborhood of an unhappy lamp that tries against its conscience to think it is showing light and grows every minute fainter and more depressed in its struggle against truth. "All the way from Paddyland, where he has spent four long months," says Mr. Fenning, "and he is still alive! It is inconceivable. Let me examine you.

Sound, I protest,—sound in wind and limb; not a defacing mark! I wouldn't have believed it if I hadn't seen it. I am awful glad to see you, old boy. What are you going to do with yourself this evening?"

"I wish I knew. I am absolutely thrown upon the world. You will take me somewhere with you, if you have any charity about you."

"I'm engaged for this evening." With a groan. "Ain't I unlucky? Hang it all, something told me to refuse old Wiggins's emblazoned card, but I wouldn't be warned. Now, what can I do for you?"

"You can at least advise me how best to kill time to-night."

"The Alhambra has a good thing on," says young Fenning, brightening; "and the Argyll——"

"I'm used up, morally and physically," interrupts Luttrell, rather impatiently. "Suggest something calmer—musical, or that."

"Oh, musical! That *is* mild. I have been educated in the belief that a sojourn in Ireland renders one savage for the remainder of his days. I blush for my ignorance. If it is first-class music you want, go to hear Wynter sing. She does sing this evening, happily for you, and anything more delicious, both in face and voice, has not aroused London to madness for a considerable time. Go, hear her, but leave your heart at your hotel before going. The Grosvenor, is it, or the Langham? The Langham. Ah, I shall call to-morrow. By-bye, old man. Go and see Wynter, and you will be richly rewarded. She is tremendously lovely."

"I will," says Luttrell; and having dined and dressed himself, he goes and does it.

Feeling listless, and not in the slightest degree interested in the coming performance, he enters the concert room, to find himself decidedly late. Some one has evidently just finished singing, and the applause that followed the effort has not yet quite died away.

With all the air of a man who wonders vaguely within himself what in the world has brought him here, Luttrell makes his way to a vacant chair and seats himself beside an elderly, pleasant-faced man, too darkly-skinned and too bright-eyed to belong to this country.

"You are late,—late," says this stranger, in perfect English, and, with all the geniality of most foreigners, making room for him. "She has just sung."

"Has she?" Faintly amused. "Who?"

"Miss—Wynter. Ah! you have sustained a loss."

"I am unlucky," says Luttrell, feeling some slight disappointment,— very slight. Good singers can be heard again. "I came expressly to hear her. I have been told she sings well."

"Well—*well*!" Disdainfully. "Your informant was careful not to overstep the truth. It is marvelous—exquisite—her voice," says the Italian, with such unrepressed enthusiasm as makes Luttrell smile. "These antediluvian attachments," thinks he, "are always severe."

"You make me more regretful every minute," he says, politely. "I feel as though I had lost something."

"So you have. But be consoled. She will sing again later on."

Leaning back, Luttrell takes a survey of the room. It is crowded to excess, and brilliant as lights and gay apparel can make it. Fans are flashing, so are jewels, so are gems of greater value still,—black eyes, blue and gray. Pretty dresses are melting into other pretty dresses, and there is a great deal of beauty everywhere for those who choose to look for it.

After a while his gaze, slowly traveling, falls on Cecil Stafford. She is showing even more than usually bonny and winsome in some *chef-d'œuvre* of Worth's, and is making herself very agreeable to a tall, lanky, eighteenth century sort of man who sits beside her, and is kindly allowing himself to be amused.

An intense desire to go to her and put the fifty questions that in an instant rise to his lips seizes Luttrell; but she is unhappily so situated that he cannot get at her. Unless he were to summon up fortitude to crush past three grim dowagers, two elaborately-attired girls, and one sour old spinster, it cannot be done; and Tedcastle, at least, has not the sort of pluck necessary to carry him through with it.

Cecil, seeing him, starts and colors, and then nods and smiles gayly at him in pleased surprise. A moment afterward her expression changes, and something so like dismay as to cause Luttrell astonishment covers her face.

Then the business of the evening proceeds, and she turns her attention to the singers, and he has no more time to wonder at her sudden change of countenance.

A very small young lady, hidden away in countless yards of pink silk, delights them with one of the ballads of the day. Her voice is far the biggest part of her, and awakens in one's mind a curious craving to know where it comes from.

Then a wonderfully ugly man, with a delightful face, plays on the violin something that reminds one of all the sweetest birds that sing, and is sufficiently ravishing to call forth at intervals the exclamation, "Good, good!" from Luttrell's neighbor.

Then a very large woman warbles a French *chansonnette* in the tiniest, most flute-like of voices; and then — —

Who is it that comes with such grave and simple dignity across the boards, with her small head proudly but gracefully upheld, her large eyes calm and sweet and steady?

For a moment Luttrell disbelieves his senses. Then a mist rises before him, a choking sensation comes into his throat. Laying his hand upon the back of the chair nearest him, he fortunately manages to retain his composure, while heart, and mind, and eyes, are centred on Molly Bawn.

An instantaneous hush falls upon the assembly; the very fans drop silently into their owners' laps; not a whisper can be heard. The opening chords are played by some one, and then Molly begins to sing.

It is some new, exquisite rendering of Kingsley's exquisite words she has chosen:

"Oh, that we two were maying! — "

and she sings it with all the pathos, the genius, of which she is capable.

She has no thought for all the gay crowd that stays entranced upon her tones. She looks far above them, her serene face — pale, but full of gentle self-possession — more sweet than any poem. She is singing with all her heart for her beloved, — for Letitia, and Lovat, and the children, and John in heaven.

A passionate longing to be near her — to touch her — to speak — to be answered back again — seizes Luttrell. He takes in hungrily all the minutiæ of her clothing, her manner, her expression. He sees the soft, gleaming bunches of snow-drops at her bosom and in her hair. Her hands, lightly crossed before her, are innocent of rings. Her simple black gown of some clinging, transparent material — barely opened at the neck — makes even more fair the milk-white of her throat (that is scarcely less white than the snowy flowers).

Her hair is drawn back into its old loose knot behind, in the simple style that suits her. She has a tiny band of black velvet round her neck. How fair she is, — how sweet, yet full of a tender melancholy! He is glad in his heart for that little pensive shade, and thinks, though more fragile, she never looked so lovely in her life.

She has commenced the last verse:

"Oh, that we two lay sleeping
In our nest in the church-yard sod,
With our limbs at rest

On the quiet earth's breast,

And our souls at home with God!"

She is almost safely through it. There is such a deadly silence as ever presages a storm, when by some luckless chance her eyes, that seldom wander, fall full on Luttrell's upturned, agitated face.

His fascinated, burning gaze compels her to return it. Oh, that he should see her here, singing before all these people! For the first time a terrible sense of shame overpowers her; a longing to escape the eyes that from all parts of the hall appear to stare at her and criticise her voice—herself!

She turns a little faint, wavers slightly, and then breaks down.

Covering her face with her hands, and with a gesture of passion and regret, she falls hurriedly into the background and is gone.

Immediately kindly applause bursts forth. What has happened to the favorite? Is she ill, or faint, or has some lost dead chord of her life suddenly sounded again? Every one is at a loss, and every one is curious. It is interesting,—perhaps the most interesting part of the whole performance,—and to-morrow will tell them all about it.

Tedcastle starts to his feet, half mad with agitation, his face ashen white. There is no knowing what he might not have done in this moment of excitement had not his foreign neighbor, laying hands upon him, gently forced him back again into his seat.

"My friend, consider *her*," he whispers, in a firm but soft voice. Then, after a moment's pause, "Come with me," he says, and, leading the way, beckons to Luttrell, who rises mechanically and follows him.

Into a small private apartment that opens off the hall the Italian takes him, and, pushing toward him a chair, sinks into another himself.

"She is the woman you love?" he asks, presently, in such a kindly tone as carries away all suspicion of impertinence.

"Yes," answers Luttrell, simply.

"Well, and I love her too,—as a pupil,—a beloved pupil," says the elder man, with a smile, removing his spectacles. "My name is Marigny."

Tedcastle bows involuntarily to the great teacher and master of music.

"How often she has spoken of you!" he says warmly, feeling already a friendship for this gentle preceptor.

"Yes, yes; mine was the happiness to give to the world this glorious voice," he says, enthusiastically. "And what a gift it is! Rare,—wonderful. But you, sir,—you are engaged to her?"

"We were—we are engaged," says Luttrell, his eyes dark with emotion. "But it is months since we have met. I came to London to seek her; but did not dream that here—here—— Misfortune has separated us; but if I lived for a hundred years I should never cease—to——"

He stops, and, getting up abruptly, paces the room in silent impatience.

"You have spoiled her song," says the Italian, regretfully. "And she was in such voice to-night! Hark!" Raising his hand as the clapping and applause still reach him through the door. "Hark! how they appreciate even her failures!"

"Can I see her?"

"I doubt it. She is so prudent. She will speak to no one. And then madame her sister is always with her. I trust you, sir,—your face is not to be disbelieved; but I cannot give you her address. I have sworn to her not to reveal it to any one, and I must not release myself from my word without her consent."

"The fates are against me," says Luttrell, drearily.

Then he bids good-night to the Signor, and, going out into the night, paces up and down in a fever of longing and disappointment.

At length the concert is over, and every one is departing. Tedcastle, making his way to the private entrance, watches anxiously, though with little hope for what may come.

But others are watching also to catch a glimpse of the admired singer, and the crowd round the door is immense.

Insensibly, in spite of his efforts, he finds himself less near the entrance than when first he took up his stand there; and just as he is trying, with small regard to courtesy, to retrieve his position, there is a slight murmur among those assembled, and a second later some one, slender, black-robed, emerges, heavily cloaked, and with some light, fleecy thing thrown over her head, so as even to conceal her face, and quickly enters the cab that awaits her.

As she places her foot upon the step of the vehicle a portion of the white woolen shawl that hides her features falls back, and for one instant Luttrell catches sight of the pale, beautiful face that, waking and sleeping, has haunted him all these past months, and will haunt him till he dies.

She is followed by a tall woman, with a full *posée* figure also draped in black, whom even at that distance he recognizes as Mrs. Massereene.

He makes one more vigorous effort to reach them, but too late. Almost as his hand touches the cab the driver receives his orders, whips up his emaciated charger, and disappears down the street.

They are gone. With a muttered exclamation, that savors not of thanksgiving, Luttrell turns aside, and, calling a hansom, drives straight to Cecil Stafford's.

Whether Molly slept or did not sleep that night remains a mystery. The following morning tells no tales. There are fresh, faint roses in her cheeks, a brightness in her eyes that for months has been absent from them. If a little quiet and preoccupied in manner, she is gayer and happier in voice and speech once her attention is gained.

Sitting in her small drawing-room, with her whole being in a very tumult of expectation, she listens feverishly to every knock.

It is not yet quite four months since she and Luttrell parted. The prescribed period has not altogether expired; and during their separation she has indeed verified her own predictions,—she has proved an undeniable success. Under the assumed name of Wynter she has sought and obtained the universal applause of the London world.

She has also kept her word. Not once during all these trying months has she written to her lover; only once has she received a line from him.

Last Valentine's morning Cecil Stafford, dropping in, brought her a small packet closely sealed and directed simply to "Molly Bawn." The mere writing made poor Molly's heart beat and her pulses throb to pain, as in one second it recalled to mind all her past joys, all the good days she had dreamed through, unknowing of the bitter wakening.

Opening the little packet, she found inside it a gold bracelet, embracing a tiny bunch of dead forget-me-nots, with this inscription folded round them:

"There shall not be one minute in an hour

Wherein I will not kiss my sweet love's flower."

Except this one token of remembrance, she has had nothing to make her know whether indeed she still lives in his memory or has been forgotten,— perhaps superseded, until last night. Then, as she met his eyes, that told a story more convincing than any words, and marking the passionate delight and longing on his face, she dared to assure herself of his constancy.

Now, as she sits restlessly awaiting what time may bring her, she thinks, with a smile, that, sad as her life may be and is, she is surely blessed as few are in a possession of which none can rob her, the tender, faithful affection of one heart.

She is still smiling, and breathing a little glad sigh over this thought, when the door opens and Lady Stafford comes in. She is radiant, a very sunbeam, in spite of the fact that Sir Penthony is again an absentee from his native land, having bidden adieu to English shores three months ago in a fit of pique, brought on by Cecil's perversity.

Some small dissension, some trivial disagreement, anger on his part, seeming indifference on hers, and the deed was done. He left her indignant, enraged, but probably more in love with her than ever; while she — — But who shall fathom a woman's heart?

"You saw him last night?" asks Molly, rising, with a brilliant blush, to receive her visitor. "Cecil, did you know he was coming? You might have told me." For her there is but one "he."

"So I should, my dear, directly; but the fact is, I *didn't* know. The stupid boy never wrote me a line on the subject. It appears he got a fortnight's leave, and came posthaste to London to find you. Such a lover as he makes. And where should he go by the merest chance, the very first evening, but into your actual presence? It is a romance," says her ladyship, much delighted; "positively it is a shame to let it sink into oblivion. Some one should recommend it to the Laureate as a theme for his next production."

"Well?" says Molly, who at this moment is guilty of irreverence in her thoughts toward the great poet.

"Well, now, of course he wants to know when he may see you."

"You didn't give him my address?" With an amount of disappointment in her tone impossible to suppress.

"I always notice," says Cecil, in despair, "that whenever (which is seldom) I do the right thing it turns out afterward to be the wrong thing. You swore me in to keep your secret four months ago, and I have done so religiously. To-day, sorely against my will, I honestly confess, I still remained faithful to my promise, and see the result. You could almost beat me, — don't deny it, Molly; I see it in your eyes. If we were both South Sea Islanders I should be black and blue this instant. It is the fear of scandal alone restrains you."

"You were quite right." Warmly. "I admire you for it; only — —"

"Yes, just so. It was all I could do to refuse the poor dear fellow, he pressed me so hard; but for the first (and now I shall make it the last) time in my life, I was firm. I'm sure I wish I hadn't been. I earned both your displeasure and his."

"Not mine, dearest."

"Besides, another motive for my determination was this: both he and I doubted if you would receive him until the four months were verily up, — you are such a Roman matron in the way of sternness."

"My sternness, as you call it, is a thing of the past. Yes, I will see him whenever he may choose to come."

"Which will be in about two hours precisely; that is, the moment he sees me and learns his fate. I told him to call again about one o'clock, when I supposed I should have news for him. It is almost that now." With a hasty glance at her watch. "I must fly. But first, give me a line for him, Molly, to convince him of your fallibility."

"Have you heard anything of Sir Penthony?" asks Molly, when she has scribbled a tiny note and given it to her friend.

"Yes; I hear he either is in London or was yesterday, or will be to-morrow,—I am not clear which." With affected indifference. "I told you he was sure to turn up again all right, like a bad halfpenny; so I was not uneasy about him. I only hope he will reappear in better temper than when he left."

"Now, confess you are delighted at the idea of so soon seeing him again," says Molly, laughing.

"Well, I'm not in such radiant spirits as somebody I could mention." Mischievously. "And as to confessing, I never do that. I should make a bad Catholic. I should be in perpetual hot water with my spiritual adviser. But if he comes back penitent, and shows himself less exigeant, I shan't refuse his overtures of peace. Now, don't make me keep your Teddy waiting any longer. He is shut up in my boudoir enduring grinding torments all this time, and without a companion or the chance of one, as I left word that I should be at home to no one but him this morning. Good-bye, darling. Give my love to Letitia and the wee scraps. And—these bonbons—I had almost forgotten them."

"Oh, by the bye, did you hear what Daisy said the other day *apropos* of your china?"

"No."

"When we had left your house and walked for some time in a silence most unusual where *she* is, she said, in her small, solemn way, 'Molly, why does Lady Stafford have her kitchen in her drawing-room?' Now, was it not a capital bit of china-mania? I thought it very severe on the times."

"It was cruel. I shall instantly send my plates and jugs, and that delicious old Worcester tureen down-stairs to their proper place," says Cecil, laughing. "There is no criticism so cutting as a child's."

CHAPTER XXXIV

"Ask me no more; thy fate and mine are sealed.

I strove against the stream, and all in vain.

Let the great river take me to the main.

No more, dear love, for at a touch I yield;

Ask me no more."

— *The Princess.*

Almost as Cecil steps into her carriage, Sir Penthony Stafford is standing on her steps, holding sweet converse with her footman at her own hall-door.

"Lady Stafford at home?" asks he of the brilliant but supercilious personage who condescends to answer to his knock.

"No, sir." Being a new acquisition of Cecil's, he is blissfully ignorant of Sir Penthony's name and status. "My lady is hout."

"When will she be home?" Feeling a good deal of surprise at her early wanderings, and, in fact, not believing a word of it.

"My lady won't be at home all this morning, sir."

"Then I shall wait till the afternoon," says Sir Penthony, faintly amused, although exasperated at what he has decided is a heinous lie.

"Lady Stafford gave strict horders that no one was to be admitted before two," says flunkey, indignant at the stranger's persistence, who has come into the hall and calmly divested himself of his overcoat.

"She will admit *me*, I don't doubt," says Sir Penthony, calmly. "I am Sir Penthony Stafford."

"Oh, indeed! Sir Penthony, I beg your pardon. Of course, Sir Penthony, if you wish to wait——"

Here Sir Penthony, who has slowly been mounting the stairs all this time, with Chawles, much exercised in his mind, at his heels—(for Cecil's commands are not to be disputed, and the situation is a good one, and she has distinctly declared no one is to be received)—Sir Penthony pauses on the landing and lays his hand on the boudoir door.

"Not there, Sir Penthony," says the man, interposing hurriedly, and throwing open the drawing-room door, which is next to it. "If you will wait here I don't think my lady will be long, as she said she should be 'ome at one to keep an appointment."

"That will do." Sternly. "Go!—I dare say," thinks Stafford, angrily, as the drawing-room door is closed on him, "if I make a point of it, she will dismiss that fellow. Insolent and noisy as a parrot. A well-bred footman never gets beyond 'Yes' or 'No' unless required, and even then only under heavy pressure. But what appointment can she have? And who is secreted in her room? Pshaw! Her dressmaker, no doubt."

But, for all that, he can't quite reconcile himself to the dressmaker theory, and, but that honor forbids, would have marched straight, without any warning, into "my lady's chamber."

Getting inside the heavy hanging curtains, he employs his time watching through the window the people passing to and fro, all intent upon the great business of life,—the making and spending of money.

After a little while a carriage stops beneath him, and he sees Cecil alight from it and go with eager haste up the steps. He hears her enter, run up the stairs, pause upon the landing, and then, going into the boudoir, close the door carefully behind her.

He stifles an angry exclamation, and resolves, with all the airs of a Spartan, to be calm. Nevertheless, he is *not* calm, and quite doubles the amount of minutes that really elapse before the drawing-room door is thrown open and Cecil, followed by Luttrell, comes in.

"Luttrell, of all men!" thinks Sir Penthony, as though he would have said, "Et tu, Brute?" forgetting to come forward,—forgetting everything,— so entirely has a wild, unreasoning jealousy mastered him. The curtains effectually conceal him, so his close proximity remains a secret.

Luttrell is evidently in high spirits. His blue eyes are bright, his whole air triumphant. Altogether, he is as unlike the moony young man who left the Victoria Station last evening as one can well imagine.

"Oh, Cecil! what should I do without you?" he says, in a most heartfelt manner, gazing at her as though (thinks Sir Penthony) he would much like to embrace her there and then. "How happy you have made me! And just as I was on the point of despairing! I owe you all,—everything,—the best of my life."

"I am glad you rate what I have done for you so highly. But you know, Tedcastle, you were always rather a favorite of mine. Have you forgiven me my stony refusal of last night? I would have spoken willingly, but you know I was forbidden."

"What is it I would *not* forgive you?" exclaims Luttrell, gratefully.

("Last night; and again this morning: probably he will dine this evening," thinks Sir Penthony, who by this time is black with rage and cold with an unnamed fear.)

Cecil is evidently as interested in her topic as her companion. Their heads are very near together,—as near as they can well be without kissing. She has placed her hand upon his arm, and is speaking in a low, earnest tone,—so low that Stafford cannot hear distinctly, the room being lengthy and the noise from the street confusing. How handsome Luttrell is looking! With what undisguised eagerness he is drinking in her every word!

Suddenly, with a little movement as though of sudden remembrance, Cecil puts her hand in her pocket and draws from it a tiny note, which she squeezes with much *empressement* into Tedcastle's hand. Then follow a few more words, and then she pushes him gently in the direction of the door.

"Now go," she says, "and remember all I have said to you. Are the conditions so hard?" With her old charming, bewitching smile.

"How shall I thank you?" says the young man, fervently, his whole face transformed. He seizes her hands and presses his lips to them in what seems to the looker-on at the other end of the room an impassioned manner. "You have managed that we shall meet,—and alone?"

"Yes, alone. I have made sure of that. I really think, considering all I have done for you, Tedcastle, you owe me something."

"Name anything," says Luttrell, with considerable fervor. "I owe you, as I have said, everything. You are my good angel!"

"Well, that is as it may be. All women are angels,—at one time or other. But you must not speak to me in that strain, or I shall mention some one who would perhaps be angry." ("That's me, I presume," thinks Sir Penthony, grimly.) "I suppose"—archly—"I need not tell you to be in time? To be late under such circumstances, with *me*, would mean dismissal. Good-bye, dear boy: go, and my good wishes will follow you."

As the door closes upon Luttrell, Sir Penthony, cold, and with an alarming amount of dignity about him, comes slowly forward.

"Sir Penthony! you!" cries Cecil, coloring certainly, but whether from guilt, or pleasure, or surprise, he finds it hard to say. He inclines, however, toward the guilt. "Why, I thought you safe in Algiers." (This is not strictly true.)

"No doubt. I thought *you* safe in London—or anywhere else. I find myself mistaken!"

"I am, dear, perfectly safe." Sweetly. "Don't alarm yourself unnecessarily. But may I ask what all this means, and why you were hiding behind my curtains as though you were a burglar or a Bashi-Bazouk? But that the pantomime season is over, I should say you were practicing for the Harlequin's window trick."

"You can be as frivolous as you please." Sternly. "Frivolity suits you best, no doubt. I came in here a half an hour ago, having first almost come to blows with your servant before being admitted,—showing me plainly the man had received orders to allow no one in but the one expected."

"That is an invaluable man, that Charles," murmurs her ladyship, *sotto voce*. "I shall raise his wages. There is nothing like obedience in a servant."

"I was standing there at that window, awaiting your arrival, when you came, hurried to your boudoir, spent an intolerable time there with Luttrell, and finally wound up your interview here by giving him a billet, and permitting him to kiss your hands until you ought to have been ashamed of yourself and him."

"You ought to be ashamed of yourself, lying *perdu* in the curtains and listening to what wasn't meant for you." Maliciously. "You ought also to have been a detective. You have wasted your talents frightfully. *Did* Teddy kiss my hands?" Examining the little white members with careful admiration. "Poor Ted! he might be tired of doing so by this. Well,—yes; and—you were saying——"

"I insist," says Sir Penthony, wrathfully, "on knowing what Luttrell was saying to you."

"I thought you heard."

"And why he is admitted when others are denied."

"My dear Sir Penthony, he is my cousin. Why should he not visit me if he likes?"

"Cousins be hanged!" says Sir Penthony, with considerable more force than elegance.

"No, no," says Cecil, smoothing a little wrinkle off the front of her gown, "not always; and I'm sure I hope Tedcastle won't be. To my way of thinking, he is quite the nicest young man I know. It would make me positively wretched if I thought Marwood would ever have him in his clutches. You,"—reflectively—"are my cousin too."

"I am,—and something more. You seem to forget that. Do you mean to answer my question?"

"Certainly,—if I can. But do sit down, Sir Penthony. I am sure you must be tired, you are so dreadfully out of breath. Have you come just now, this moment, straight from Algiers? See, that little chair over there is so comfortable. All my gentlemen visitors adore that little chair. No? You won't sit down? Well——"

"Are you in the habit of receiving men so early?"

"I assure you," says Cecil, raising her brows with a gentle air of martyrdom, and making a very melancholy gesture with one hand, "I hardly know the hour I don't receive them. I am absolutely persecuted by my friends. They *will* come. No matter how disagreeable it may be to me, they arrive just at any hour that best suits them. And I am so good-natured I cannot bring myself to say 'Not at home.'"

"You brought yourself to say it this morning."

"Ah, yes. But that was because I was engaged on very particular business."

"What business?"

"I am sorry I cannot tell you."

"You shall, Cecil. I will not leave this house until I get an answer. I am your husband. I have the right to demand it."

"You forget our little arrangement. I acknowledge no husband," says Cecil, with just one flash from her violet eyes.

"Do you refuse to answer me?"

"I do," replies she, emphatically.

"Then I shall stay here until you alter your mind," says Sir Penthony, with an air of determination, settling himself with what in a low class of men would have been a bang, in the largest arm-chair the room contains.

With an unmoved countenance Lady Stafford rises and rings the bell.

Dead silence.

Then the door opens, and a rather elderly servant appears upon the threshold.

"Martin, Sir Penthony will lunch here," says Cecil, calmly. "And—stay, Martin. Do you think it likely you will dine, Sir Penthony?"

"I do think it likely," replies he, with as much grimness as etiquette will permit before the servant.

"Sir Penthony thinks it likely he will dine, Martin. Let cook know. And—can I order you anything you would specially prefer?"

"Thank you, nothing. Pray give yourself no trouble on my account."

"It would be a pleasure,—the more so that it is so rare. Stay yet a moment, Martin. May I order you a bed, Sir Penthony?"

"I am not sure. I will let you know later on," replies Stafford, who, to his rage and disgust, finds himself inwardly convulsed with laughter.

"That will do, Martin," says her ladyship, with the utmost *bonhommie*. And Martin retires.

As the door closes, the combatants regard each other steadily for a full minute, and then they both roar.

"You are the greatest little wretch," says Sir Penthony, going over to her and taking both her hands, "it has ever been my misfortune to meet with. I am laughing now against my will,—remember that. I am in a frantic rage. Will you tell me what all that scene between you and Luttrell was about? If you don't I shall go straight and ask him."

"What! And leave me here to work my wicked will? Reflect—reflect. I thought you were going to mount guard here all day. Think on all the sins I shall be committing in your absence."

She has left her hands in his all this time, and is regarding him with a gay smile, under which she hardly hides a good deal of offended pride.

"Don't be rash, I pray you," she says, with a gleam of malice.

"The man who said pretty women were at heart the kindest lied," says Sir Penthony, standing over her, tall, and young, and very nearly handsome. "You know I am in misery all this time, and that a word from you would relieve me,—yet you will not speak it."

"Would you"—very gravely—"credit the word of such a sinner as you would make me out to be?"

"A sinner! Surely I have never called you that."

"You would call me anything when you get into one of those horrid passions. Come, are you sorry?"

"I am more than sorry. I confess myself a brute if I ever even hinted at such a word,—which I doubt. The most I feared was your imprudence."

"From all I can gather, that means quite the same thing when said of a woman."

"Well, *I* don't mean it as the same. And, to prove my words, if you will only grant me forgiveness, I will not even mention Tedcastle's name again."

"But I insist on telling you every word he said to me, and all about it."

"If you had insisted on that half an hour ago you would have saved thirty minutes," says Stafford, laughing.

"*Then* I would not gratify you; *now*—Tedcastle came here, poor fellow, in a wretched state about Molly Massereene, whose secret he has at length discovered. About eleven o'clock last night he rushed in here almost distracted to get her address; so I went to Molly early this morning, obtained leave to give it,—and a love-letter as well, which you saw me deliver,—and all his raptures and tender epithets were meant for her, and not for me. Is it not a humiliating confession? Even when he kissed my hands it was only in gratitude, and his heart was full of Molly all the time."

"Then it was not you he was to meet alone?"—eagerly.

"What! Still suspicious? No, sir, it was not your wife he was to meet 'alone,' Now, are you properly abashed? Are you satisfied?"

"I am, and deeply contrite. Yet, Cecil, you must know what it is causes me such intolerable jealousy, and, knowing, you should pardon. My love for you only increases day by day. Tell me again I am forgiven."

"Yes, quite forgiven."

"And"—stealing his arm gently round her—"are you in the smallest degree glad to see me again?"

"In a degree,—yes." Raising to his, two eyes, full of something more than common gladness.

"Really?"

"Really."

He looks at her, but she refuses to understand his appealing expression, and regards him calmly in return.

"Cecil, how cold you are!" he says, reproachfully. "Think how long I have been away from you, and what a journey I have come."

"True; you must be hungry." With willful ignorance of his meaning.

"I am not." Indignantly. "But I think you might—after three weary months, that to me, at least, were twelve—you might——"

"You want me to—kiss you?" says Cecil, promptly, but with a rising blush. "Well, I will, then."

Lifting her head, she presses her lips to his with a fervor that takes him utterly by surprise.

"Cecil," whispers he, growing a little pale, "do you mean it?"

"Mean what?" Coloring crimson now, but laughing also. "I mean this: if we don't go down-stairs soon luncheon will be cold. And, remember, I hold you to your engagement. You dine with me to-day. Is not that so?"

"You know how glad I shall be."

"Well, I hope now," says Cecil, "you intend to reform, and give up traveling aimlessly all over the unknown world at stated intervals. I hope for the future you mean staying at home like a respectable Christian."

"If I had a home. You can't call one's club a home, can you? I would stay anywhere,—with you."

"I could not possibly undertake such a responsibility. Still, I should like you to remain in London, where I could look after you a little bit now and then, and keep you in order. I adore keeping people in order. I am thrown away," says Cecil, shaking her flaxen head sadly. "I know I was born to rule."

"You do a great deal of it even in your own limited sphere, don't you?" says her husband, laughing. "I know at least one unfortunate individual who is completely under your control."

"No. I am dreadfully cramped. But come; in spite of all the joy I naturally feel at your safe return, I find my appetite unimpaired. Luncheon is ready. Follow me, my friend. I pine for a cutlet."

They eat their cutlets *tête-à-tête*, and with evident appreciation of their merits; the servants regarding the performance with intense though silent admiration. In their opinion (and who shall dispute the accuracy of a servant's opinion?), this is the beginning of the end.

When luncheon is over, Lady Stafford rises.

"I am going for my drive," she says. "But what is to become of you until dinner-hour?"

"I shall accompany you." Audaciously.

"You! What! To have all London laughing at me?"

"Let them. A laugh will do *them* good, and *you* no harm. How can it matter to you?"

"True. It cannot. And after all to be laughed at one must be talked about. And to be talked about means to create a sensation. And I should like to create a sensation before I die. Yes, Sir Penthony,"—with a determined air,—"you shall have a seat in my carriage to-day."

"And how about to-morrow?"

"To-morrow probably some other fair lady will take pity on you. It would be much too slow,"—mischievously—"to expect you to go driving with your wife every day."

"I don't think I can see it in that light. Cecil,"—coming to her side, and with a sudden though gentle boldness, taking her in his arms,—"when are you going to forgive me and take me to your heart?"

"What is it you want, you tiresome man?" asks Cecil, with a miserable attempt at a frown.

"Your love," replies he, kissing the weak-minded little pucker off her forehead and the pretended pout from her lips, without this time saying, "by your leave," or "with your leave."

"And when you have it, what then?"

"I shall be the happiest man alive."

"Then *be* the happiest man alive," murmurs she, with tears in her eyes, although the smile still lingers round her lips.

It is thus she gives in.

"And when," asks Stafford, half an hour later, all the retrospective confessions and disclosures having taken some time to get through,—"when shall I install a mistress in the capacious but exceedingly gloomy abode my ancestors so unkindly left to me?"

"Do not even think of such a thing for ever so long. Perhaps next summer I may——"

"Oh, nonsense! Why not say this time ten years?"

"But at present my thoughts are full of my dear Molly. Ah! when shall I see her as happy as—as—I am?"

Here Sir Penthony, moved by a sense of duty and a knowledge of the fitness of things, instantly kisses her again.

He has barely performed this necessary act when the redoubtable Charles puts his head in at the door and says:

"The carriage is waiting, my lady."

"Very good," returns Lady Stafford, who, according to Charles's version of the affair, a few hours later, is as "red as a peony." "You will stay here, Penthony,"—murmuring his name with a grace and a sweet hesitation quite irresistible,—"while I go and make ready for our drive."

CHAPTER XXXV

"When I arose and saw the dawn,
I sigh'd for thee;
When light rode high, and the dew was gone,
And noon lay heavy on flower and tree,
And the weary day turn'd to his rest,
Lingering like an unloved guest,
I sighed for thee."
—Shelley.

In her own small chamber, with all her pretty hair falling loosely round her, stands Molly before her glass, a smile upon her lips. For is not her lover to be with her in two short hours? Already, perhaps, he is on his way to her, as anxious, as eager to fold her in his arms as she will be to fly to them.

A sweet agitation possesses her. Her every thought is fraught with joy; and if at times a misgiving, a suspicion of the hopelessness of it all, comes as a shadow between her and the sun of her content (for is not her marriage with Luttrell a thing as remote now as when they parted?), she puts it from her and refuses to acknowledge a single flaw in this one day's happiness.

She brushes out her long hair, rolling it into its usual soft knot behind, and weaves a kiss or two and a few tender words into each rich coil. She dons her prettiest gown, and puts on all the bravery she possesses, to make herself more fair in the eyes of her beloved, lest by any means he should think her less worthy of regard than when last he saw her.

With a final, almost dissatisfied, glance at the mirror she goes downstairs to await his coming, all her heart one glad song.

She tries to work to while away the time, but her usually clever fingers refuse their task, and the canvas falls unheeded to the floor.

She tries to read; but, alas! all the words grow together and form themselves into one short sentence: "He is coming—coming—coming."

Insensibly Tennyson's words come to her, and, closing her eyes, she repeats them softly to herself:

"O days and hours, your work is this,

To hold me from my proper place

A little while from his embrace,

For fuller gain of after-bliss.

"That out of distance might ensue

Desire of nearness doubly sweet,

And unto meeting, when we meet,

Delight a hundredfold accrue!"

At length the well-known step is heard upon the stairs, the well-known voice, that sends a very pang of joy through every pulse in her body, sounds eagerly through the house. His hand is on the door.

With a sudden trembling she says to herself:

"I will be calm. He must not know how dearly he is loved."

And then the door opens. He is before her. A host of recollections, sweet and bitter, rise with his presence; and, forgetful of her determination to be calm and dignified as well for his sake as her own, she lets the woman triumph, and, with a little cry, sad from the longing and despair of it, she runs forward and throws herself, with a sob, into his expectant arms.

At first they do not speak. He does not even kiss her, only holds her closely in his embrace, as one holds some precious thing, some priceless possession that, once lost, has been regained.

Then they do kiss each other, gravely, tenderly, with a gentle lingering.

"It is indeed you," she says, at last, regarding him wistfully with a certain pride of possession, he looks so tall, and strong, and handsome in her eyes. She examines him critically, and yet finds nothing wanting. He is to her perfection, as, indeed (unhappily), a man always is to the woman who loves him. Could she at this moment concentrate her thoughts, I think she would apply to him all the charms contained in the following lines:

"A mouth for mastery and manful work;

A certain brooding sweetness in the eyes;

A brow the harbor of fair thought, and hair

Saxon in hue."

"You are just the same as ever," she says, presently, "only taller, I really think, and broader and bigger altogether." Then, in a little soft whisper, "My dear,—my darling."

"And you," he says, taking the sweet face he has so hungered for between his hands, the better to mark each change time may have wrought, "you have grown thinner. You are paler. Darling,"—a heavy shadow falling across his face,—"you are well,—quite well?"

"Perfectly," she answers, lightly, pleased at his uneasiness. "Town life—the city air—has whitened me; that is all."

"But these hollows?" Touching gently her soft cheeks with a dissatisfied air. They are a little sunk. She is altogether thinner, frailer than of yore. Her very fingers as they lie in his look slenderer, more fragile.

"Perhaps a little fretting has done it," she answers, with a smile and a half-suppressed sigh.

He echoes the sigh; and it may be a few tears for all the long hours spent apart gather in their eyes, "in thinking of the days that are no more."

Presently, when they are calmer, more forgetful of their separation, they seat themselves upon a sofa and fall into a happy silence. His arm is round her; her hand rests in his.

"Of what are you thinking, sweetheart?" he asks, after a while, stooping to meet her gaze.

"A happy thought," she answers. "I am realizing how good a thing it is 'to feel the arms of my true love round me once again.'"

"And yet it was of your own free will they were ever loosened."

"Of my free will?" Reproachfully. "No; no." Then, turning away from him, she says, in a low tone, "What did you think when you saw me singing last night?"

"That I had never seen you look so lovely in my life."

"I don't mean that, Teddy. What did you think when you saw me singing—so?"

"I wished I was a millionaire, that I might on the instant rescue you from such a life," replies he, with much emotion.

"Ah! you felt like that? I, too, was unhappy. For the first time since I began my new life it occurred to me to be ashamed. To know that you saw me reminded me that others saw me too, and the knowledge brought a flush to my cheek. I am singing again on Tuesday; but you must not come to hear me. I could not sing before you again."

"Of course I will not, if it distresses you. May I meet you outside and accompany you home?"

"Better not. People talk so much; and—there is always such a crowd outside that door."

"The nights *you* sing. Have you had any lovers, Molly?" asks he, abruptly, with a visible effort.

"Several,"—smiling at his perturbation,—"and two *bona fide* proposals. I might have been the blushing bride of a baronet now had I so chosen."

"Was he—rich?"

"Fabulously so, I was told. And I am sure he was comfortably provided for, though I never heard the exact amount of his rent-roll."

"Why did you refuse him?" asks Luttrell, moodily, his eyes fixed upon the ground.

"I shall leave you to answer that question," replies she, with all her old archness. "I cannot. Perhaps because I didn't care for him. Not but what he was a nice old gentleman, and wonderfully preserved. I met him at one of Cecil's 'at homes,' and he professed himself deeply enamored of me. I might also have been the wife of a very young gentleman in the Foreign Office, with a most promising moustache; but I thought of you,"—laughing, and giving his hand a little squeeze,—"and I bestowed upon him such an emphatic 'No' as turned his love to loathing."

"To-morrow or next day you may have a marquis at your feet, or some other tremendous swell—and——"

"Or one of our own princes. I see nothing to prevent it," says Molly, still laughing. "Nonsense, Teddy; don't be an old goose. You should know by this time how it is with me."

"I am a selfish fellow, am I not?" says Luttrell, wistfully. "The very thought that any one wants to take you from me renders me perfectly miserable. And yet I know I ought to give you up,—to—to encourage you to accept an offer that would place you in a position I shall never be able to give you. But I cannot. Molly, I have come all this way to ask you again to marry me, and——"

"Hush, Teddy. You know it is impossible."

"Why is it impossible? Other people have lived and been happy on five hundred pounds a year. And after a while something might turn up to enable us to help Letitia and the children."

"You are a little selfish now," she says, with gentle reproach. "I could not let Letitia be without my help for even a short time. And would you like your wife to sing in public, for money? Look at it in that light, and answer me truly."

"No," without hesitation. "Not that your singing in public lowers you in the faintest degree in any one's estimation; but I would not let my wife support herself. I could not endure the thought. But might not I——"

"You might not,"—raising her eyes,—"nor would I let you. I work for those I love, and in that no one can help me."

"Are both our lives, then, to be sacrificed?"

"I will not call it a sacrifice on my part," says the girl, bravely, although tears are heavy in her voice and eyes. "I am only doing some little thing for him who did all for me. There is a joy that is almost sacred in the thought. It has taken from me the terrible sting of his death. To know I can still please him, can work for him, brings him back to me from the other world. At times I lose the sense of farness, and can feel him almost near."

"You are too good for me," says the young man, humbly, taking her hands and kissing them twice.

"I am not. You must not say so," says Molly, hastily, the touch of his lips weakening her.

Two large tears that have been slowly gathering roll down her cheeks.

"Oh, Teddy!" cries she, suddenly, covering her face with her hands, "at times, when I see certain flowers or hear some music connected with the olden days, my heart dies within me,—I lose all hope; and then I miss you sorely,—*sorely*."

Her head is on his breast by this time; his strong young arms are round her, holding her as though they would forever shield her from the pains and griefs of this world.

"I have felt just like you," he says, simply. "But after all, whatever comes, we have each other. There should be comfort in that. Had death robbed us—you of me or me of you—then we might indeed mourn. But as it is there is always hope. Can you not try to find consolation in the thought that, no matter where I may be, however far away, I am your lover forever?"

"I know it," says Molly, inexpressibly comforted.

Their trust is of the sweetest and fullest. No cruel coldness has crept in to defile their perfect love. Living as they are on a mere shadow, a faint streak of hope, that may never break into a fuller gleam, they still are almost happy. He loves her. Her heart is all his own. These are their crumbs of comfort,—sweet fragments that never fail them.

Now he leads her away from the luckless subject of their engagement altogether, and presently she is laughing over some nonsensical tale he is telling her connected with the old life. She is asking him questions, and he is telling her all he knows.

Philip has been abroad—no one knows where—for months; but suddenly, and just as mysteriously as he departed, he turned up a few days ago at Herst, where the old man is slowly fading. The winter has been a severe one, and they think his days are numbered.

The Darleys have at last come to an open rupture, and a friendly separation is being arranged.

"And what of my dear friend, Mr. Potts?" asks Molly.

"Oh, Potts! I left him behind me in Dublin. He is uncommonly well, and has been all the winter pottering—by the bye, that is an appropriate word, isn't it?—reminds one of one of his own jokes—after a girl who rather fancies him, in spite of his crimson locks, or perhaps because of them. That particular shade is, happily, rare. She has a little money, too,—at least enough to make her an heiress in Ireland."

"Poor Ireland!" says Molly. "Some day perhaps I shall go there, and judge of its eccentricities myself."

"By the bye, Molly," says Luttrell, with an impromptu air, "did you ever see the Tower?"

"Never, I am ashamed to say."

"I share your sentiments. Never have I planted my foot upon so much as the lowest step of its interminable stairs. I feel keenly the disgrace of such an acknowledgment. Shall we let another hour pass without retrieving our false position? A thousand times 'no.' Go and put your bonnet on, Molly, and we will make a day of it."

And they do make a day of it, and are as foolishly, thoughtlessly, unutterably happy as youth and love combined can be in the very face of life's disappointments.

The first flush of her joy on meeting Luttrell being over, Molly grows once more depressed and melancholy.

Misfortune has so far subdued her that now she looks upon her future, not with the glad and hopeful eyes of old, but through a tearful mist, while dwelling with a sad uncertainty upon its probable results.

When in the presence of her lover she rises out of herself, and for the time being forgets, or appears to forget, her troubles; but when away from him she grows moody and unhappy.

Could she see but a chance of ever being able to alter her present mode of life—before youth and hope are over—she would perhaps take her courage by both hands and compel it to remain. But no such chance presents itself.

To forsake Letitia is to leave her and the children to starve. For how could Luttrell support them all on a miserable pittance of five hundred pounds a year? The idea is preposterous. It is the same old story over again; the same now as it was four months ago, without alteration or improvement; and, as she tells herself, will be the same four years hence.

Whatever Luttrell himself may think upon the subject he keeps within his breast, and for the first week of his stay is apparently supremely happy.

Occasionally he speaks as though their marriage is a thing that sooner or later must be consummated, and will not see that when he does so Molly maintains either a dead silence or makes some disheartening remark.

At last she can bear it no longer; and one day toward the close of his "leave," when his sentiments appear to be particularly sanguine, she makes up her mind to compel him to accept a release from what must be an interminable waiting.

"How can we go on like this," she says, bursting into tears, "you forever entreating, I forever denying? It breaks my heart, and is unfair to you. Our engagement must end. It is for your sake I speak."

"You are too kind. Will you not let me judge what is best for my own happiness?"

"No; because you are mad on this one matter."

"You wish to release me from my promise?"

"I do. For your own good."

"Then I will not be released. Because freedom would not lead to the desired result."

"It would. It must. It is useless our going on so. I can never marry. You see yourself I cannot. If you were rich, or if I were rich, why, then— —"

"If you were I would not marry you, in all probability."

"And why? Should I not be the same Molly then?" With a wan little smile. "Well, if you were rich I would marry you gladly, because I know your love for me is so great you would not feel my dear ones a burden. But as it is—yes—yes—we must part."

"You can speak of it with admirable coolness," says he, rather savagely. "After all, at the best of times your love for me was lukewarm."

"Was it?" she says, and turns away from him hurt and offended.

"Is my love the thing of an hour," he goes on, angry with her and with himself in that he has displeased her, "that you should talk of the good to be derived from the sundering of our engagement? I wish to know what it is you mean. Do you want to leave yourself free to marry a richer man?"

"How you misjudge me?" she says, shrinking as if from a blow. "I shall never marry. All I want to do is to leave you free to"—with a sob—"to choose whom you may."

"Very good. If it pleases you to think I am free, as you call it, be it so. Our engagement is at an end. I may marry my mother's cook to-morrow morning, if it so pleases me, without a dishonorable feeling. Is that what you want? Are you satisfied now?"

"Yes." But she is crying bitterly as she says it.

"And do you think, my sweet," whispers he, folding her in his arms, "that all this nonsense can take your image from my heart, or blot out the remembrance of all your gentle ways? For my part, I doubt it. Come, why don't you smile? You have everything your own way now; you should, therefore, be in exuberant spirits. You may be on the lookout for an elderly merchant prince; I for the dusky heiress of a Southern planter. But I warn you, Molly, you shan't insist upon my marrying her, unless I like her better than you."

"You accept the words, but not the spirit, of my proposition," she says, sadly.

"Because it is a spiritless proposition altogether, without grace or meaning. Come, now, don't martyr yourself any more. I am free, and you are free, and we can go on loving each other all the same. It isn't half a bad arrangement, and so soothing to the conscience! I always had a remorseful feeling that I was keeping you from wedding with a duke, or a city magnate, or an archbishop. In the meantime I suppose I may be allowed to visit your Highness (in anticipation) daily, as usual?"

"I suppose so." With hesitation.

"I wonder you didn't say no, you hard-hearted child. Not that it would have made the slightest difference, as I should have come whether you liked it or not. And now come out—do; the sun is shining, and will melt away this severe attack of the blues. Let us go into the Park and watch for our future prey,—you for your palsied millionaire, I for my swarthy West Indian."

CHAPTER XXXVI

"Turn, Fortune, turn thy wheel, and lower the proud."
                                    —*Idylls of the King.*

The very next morning brings Molly the news of her grandfather's death. He had died quietly in his chair the day before without a sign, and without one near him. As he had lived, so had he died—alone.

The news conveyed by Mr. Buscarlet shocks Molly greatly, and causes her, if not actual sorrow, at least a keen regret. To have him die thus, without reconciliation or one word of forgiveness,—to have him go from this world to the next, hard of heart and unrelenting, saddens her for his soul's sake.

The funeral is to be on Thursday, and this is Tuesday. So Mr. Buscarlet writes, and adds that, by express desire of Mr. Amherst, the will is to be opened and read immediately after the funeral before all those who spent last autumn in his house. "Your presence," writes the attorney, "is particularly desired."

In the afternoon Lady Stafford drops in, laden, as usual, with golden grain (like the Argosy), in the shape of cakes and sweetmeats for the children, who look upon her with much reverence in the light of a modern and much-improved Santa Claus.

"I see you have heard of your grandfather's death by your face," she says, gravely. "Here, children,"—throwing them their several packages,—"take your property and run away while I have a chat with mamma and Auntie Molly."

"Teddy brought us such nice sugar cigars yesterday," says Renee, who, in her black frock and white pinafore and golden locks, looks perfectly angelic: "only I was sorry they weren't real; the fire at the end didn't burn one bit."

"How do you know?"

"Because"—with an enchanting smile—"I put it on Daisy's hand, to see if it would, and it wouldn't; and wasn't it a pity?"

"It was, indeed. I am sure Daisy sympathizes with your grief. There, go away, you blood-thirsty child; we are very busy."

While the children, in some remote corner of the house, are growing gradually happier and stickier, their elders discuss the last new topic.

"I received a letter this morning," Cecil says, "summoning me to Herst, to hear the will read. You, too, I suppose?"

"Yes; though why I don't know."

"I am sure he has left you something. You are his grandchild. It would be unkind of him and most unjust to leave you out altogether, once having acknowledged you."

"You forget our estrangement."

"Nevertheless, something tells me there is a legacy in store for you. I shall go down to-morrow night, and you had better come with me."

"Very well," says Molly, indifferently.

At Herst, in spite of howling winds and drenching showers, Nature is spreading abroad in haste its countless charms. Earth, struggling disdainfully with its worn-out garb, is striving to change its brown garment for one of dazzling green. Violets, primroses, all the myriad joys of spring, are sweetening the air with a thousand perfumes.

Within the house everything is subdued and hushed, as must be when the master lies low. The servants walk on tiptoe; the common smile is checked; conversation dwindles into compressed whispers, as though they fear by ordinary noise to bring to life again the unloved departed. All is gloom and insincere melancholy.

Cecil and Molly, traveling down together, find Mrs. Darley, minus her husband, has arrived before them. She is as delicately afflicted, as properly distressed, as might be expected; indeed, so faithfully, and with such perfect belief in her own powers, does she perform the pensive *rôle*, that she fails not to create real admiration in the hearts of her beholders. Molly is especially struck, and knows some natural regret that it is beyond *her* either to feel or look the part.

Marcia, thinking it wisdom to keep herself invisible, maintains a strict seclusion. The hour of her triumph approaches; she hardly dares let others see the irrepressible exultation that her own heart knows.

Philip has been absent since the morning; so Molly and Lady Stafford dine in the latter's old sitting-room alone, and, confessing as the hours grow late to an unmistakable dread of the "uncanny," sleep together, with a view to self-support.

About one o'clock next day all is over. Mr. Amherst has been consigned to his last resting-place,—a tomb unstained by any tears. At three the will is to be read.

Coming out of her room in the early part of the afternoon, Cecil meets unexpectedly with Mr. Potts, who is meandering in a depressed and aimless fashion all over the house.

"You here, Plantagenet! Why, I thought you married to some fascinating damsel in the Emerald Isle," she cannot help saying in a low voice, giving him her hand. She is glad to see his ugly, good-humored, comical face in the gloomy house, although it *is* surmounted by his offending hair.

"So I was,—very near it," replies he, modestly, in the same suppressed whisper. "You never knew such a narrow escape as I had: they were determined to marry me——"

"'They'! You terrify me. How many of them? I had no idea they were so bad as that,—even in Ireland."

"Oh, I mean the girl and her father. It was as near a thing as possible; in fact, it took me all I knew to get out of it."

"I'm not surprised at that," says Cecil, with a short but comprehensive glance at her companion's cheerful but rather indistinct features.

"I don't exactly mean it was my personal appearance was the attraction," he returns, feeling a strong inclination to explode with laughter, as is his habit on all occasions, but quickly suppressing the desire, as being wicked under the circumstances. The horror of death has not yet vanished from among them. "It was my family they were after,—birth, you know,—and that. Fact is, she wasn't up to the mark,—wasn't good enough. Not but that she was a nice-looking girl, and had a lovely brogue. She had money too— and she had a—father! Such a father! I think I could have stood the brogue, but I could *not* stand the father."

"But why? Was he a lunatic? Or perhaps a Home-ruler?"

"No,"—simply,—"he was a tailor. When first I met Miss O'Rourke she told me her paternal relative had some appointment in the Castle. So he had. In his youthful days he had been appointed tailor to his Excellency. It wasn't a bad appointment, I dare say; but I confess I didn't see it."

"It was a lucky escape. It would take a good deal of money to make me forget the broadcloth. Are you coming down-stairs now? I dare say we ought to be assembling."

"It is rather too early, I am afraid. I wish it was all done with, and I a hundred miles away from the place. The whole affair has made me downright melancholy. I hate funerals: they don't agree with me."

"Nor yet weddings, as it seems. Well, I shall be as glad as you to quit Herst once we have installed Miss Amherst as its mistress."

"Why not Shadwell as its master?"

"If I were a horrible betting-man," says Cecil, "I should put all my money upon Marcia. I do not think Mr. Amherst cared for Philip. However, we shall see. And"—in a yet lower tone—"I hope he has not altogether forgotten Molly."

"I hope not indeed. But he was a strange old man. To forget Miss Massereene——" Here he breathes a profound sigh.

"Don't sigh, Plantagenet: think of Miss O'Rourke," says Cecil, unkindly, leaving him.

One by one, and without so much as an ordinary "How d'ye do?" they have all slipped into the dining-room. The men have assumed a morose air, which they fondly believe to be indicative of melancholy; the women, being by nature more hypocritical, present a more natural and suitable appearance. All are seated in sombre garments and dead silence.

Marcia, in crape and silk of elaborate design, is looking calm but full of decorous grief. Philip—who has grown almost emaciated during these past months—is the only one who wears successfully an impression of the most stolid indifference. He is leaning against one of the windows, gazing out upon the rich lands and wooded fields which so soon will be either all his or nothing to him. After the first swift glance of recognition he has taken no notice of Molly, nor she of him. A shuddering aversion fills her toward him, a distaste bordering on horror. His very pallor, the ill-disguised misery of his whole appearance,—which he seeks but vainly to conceal under a cold and sneering exterior,—only adds to her dislike.

A sickening remembrance of their last meeting in the wood at Brooklyn makes her turn away from him with palpable meaning on his entrance, adding thereby one pang the more to the bitterness of his regret. The meeting is to her a trial,—to him an agony harder to endure than he had even imagined.

Feeling strangely out of place and nervous, and saddened by memories of happy days spent in this very room so short a time ago, Molly has taken a seat a little apart from the rest, and sits with loosely-folded hands upon her knees, her head bent slightly downward.

Cecil, seeing the dejection of her attitude, leaves her own place, and, drawing a chair close to hers, takes one of her hands softly between her own.

Then the door opens, and Mr. Buscarlet, with a sufficiently subdued though rather triumphant and consequential air, enters.

He bows obsequiously to Marcia, who barely returns the salute. Detestable little man! She finds some consolation in the thought that at all events his time is nearly over; that probably—nay, surely—he is now about to administer law for the last time at Herst.

He bows in silence to the rest of the company,—with marked deference to Miss Massereene,—and then involuntarily each one stirs in his or her seat and settles down to hear the will read.

A will is a mighty thing, and requires nice handling. Would that I were lawyer enough to give you this particular one in full, with all its many bequests and curious directions. But, alas! ignorance forbids. The sense lingers with me, but all the technicalities and running phrases and idiotic repetitions have escaped me.

To most of those present Mr. Amherst has left bequests; to Lady Stafford five thousand pounds; to Plantagenet Potts two thousand pounds; to Mrs. Darley's son the same; to all the servants handsome sums of money, together with a year's wages; to Mrs. Nesbit, the housekeeper, two hundred pounds a year for her life. And then the attorney pauses and assumes an important air, and every one knows the end is nigh.

All the rest of his property of which he died possessed—all the houses, lands, and moneys—all personal effects—"I give and bequeath to——"

Here Mr. Buscarlet, either purposely or otherwise, stops short to cough and blow a sonorous note upon his nose. All eyes are fixed upon him; some, even more curious or eager than the others, are leaning forward in their chairs. Even Philip has turned from the window and is waiting breathlessly.

"To my beloved grandchild, Eleanor Massereene!"

Not a sound follows this announcement, not a movement. Then Marcia half rises from her seat; and Mr. Buscarlet, putting up his hand, says, hurriedly, "There is a codicil," and every one prepares once more to listen.

But the codicil produces small effect. The old man at the last moment evidently relented so far in his matchless severity as to leave Marcia Amherst ten thousand pounds (and a sealed envelope, which Mr. Buscarlet hands her), on the condition that she lives out of England; and to Philip Shadwell ten thousand pounds more,—and another sealed envelope,—which the attorney also delivers on the spot.

As the reading ceases, another silence, even more profound than the first, falls upon the listeners. No one speaks, no one so much as glances at the other.

Marcia, ghastly, rigid, rises from her seat.

"It is false," she says, in a clear, impassioned tone. "It is the will of an imbecile,—a madman. It shall not be." She has lost all self-restraint, and is trembling with fear and rage and a terrible certainty of defeat.

"Pardon me, Miss Amherst," says Mr. Buscarlet, courteously, "but I fear you will find it unwise to lay any stress on such a thought. To dispute this will would be madness indeed: all the world knows my old friend, your grandfather, died in perfect possession of his senses, and this will was signed three months ago."

"You drew up this will, sir?" she asks in a low tone, only intended for him, drawing closer to him.

"Certainly I did, madam."

"And during all these past months understood thoroughly how matters would be?"

"Certainly, madam."

"And knowing, continued still—with a view to deceive me—to treat me as the future mistress of Herst?"

"I trust, madam, I always treated you with proper respect. You would not surely have had me as rude to you as you invariably were to me? I may not be a gentleman, Miss Amherst, in your acceptation of that term, but I make it a rule never to be—offensive."

"It was a low—a mean revenge," says Marcia, through her teeth, her eyes aflame, her lips colorless; "one worthy of you. I understand you, sir; but do not for an instant think you have crushed *me*." Raising her head haughtily, she sweeps past him back to her original seat.

Molly has risen to her feet. She is very pale and faint; her eyes, large and terrified, like a fawn's, are fixed, oddly enough, upon Philip. The news has been too sudden, too unexpected, to cause her even the smallest joy as yet. On the contrary, she knows only pity for him who, but a few minutes before, she was reviling in her thoughts. Perhaps the sweetness of her sympathy is the one thing that could have consoled Philip just then.

"'Farewell, a long farewell to all my greatness,'" he says, with a little sneering laugh, shrugging his shoulders. Then, rousing himself, he draws a long breath, and goes straight up to Molly.

"Permit me to congratulate you," he says, with wonderful grace, considering all things. He is standing before her, with his handsome head well up, a certain pride of birth about him, strong enough to carry him successfully through this great and lasting disaster. "It is, after all, only natural that of the three you should inherit. Surprise should lie in the fact that never did such a possibility occur to us. We might have known that even our grandfather's worn and stony heart could not be proof against such grace and sweetness as yours."

He bows over her hand courteously, and, turning away, walks back again to the window, standing with his face hidden from them all.

Never has he appeared to such advantage. Never has he been so thoroughly liked as at this moment. Molly moves as though she would go to him; but Cecil, laying her hand upon her arm, wisely restrains her. What can be said to comfort him, who has lost home, and love, and all?

"It is all a mistake; it cannot be true," says Molly, piteously. "It is a mistake." She looks appealingly at Cecil, who, wise woman that she is, only presses her arm again meaningly, and keeps a discreet silence. To express her joy at the turn events have taken at this time would be gross; though not to express it goes hard with Cecil. She contents herself with glancing expressively at Sir Penthony every now and then, who is standing at the other end of the room.

"I also congratulate you," says Luttrell, coming forward, and speaking for the first time. He is not nearly so composed as Shadwell, and his voice has a strange and stilted sound. He speaks so that Molly and Cecil alone can hear him, delicacy forbidding any open expression of pleasure. "With all my heart," he adds; but his tone is strange. The whole speech is evidently a lie. His eyes meet hers with an expression in them she has never seen there before, — so carefully cold it is, so studiously unloving.

Molly is too agitated to speak to him, but she lifts her head, and shows him a face full of the keenest reproach. Her pleading look, however, is thrown away, as he refuses resolutely to meet her gaze. With an abrupt movement he turns away and leaves the room, and, as they afterward discover, the house.

Meantime, Marcia has torn open her envelope, and read its enclosure. A blotted sheet half covered with her own writing, — the very letter begun and lost in the library last October; that, being found, has condemned her. With a half-stifled groan she lets it flutter to the ground, where it lies humbled in the dust, an emblem of all her falsely-cherished hopes.

Philip, too, having examined his packet, has brought to light that fatal letter of last summer that has so fully convicted him of unlawful dealings with Jews. Twice he reads it, slowly, thoughtfully, and then, casting one quick, withering glance at Marcia (under which she cowers), he consigns it to his pocket without a word.

The play is played out. The new mistress of Herst has been carried away by Cecil Stafford to her own room; the others have dispersed. Philip and Marcia Amherst are alone.

Marcia, waking from her reverie, makes a movement as though she, too, would quit the apartment, but Shadwell, coming deliberately up to her, bars her exit. Laying his hand gently but firmly on her wrist, he compels her to both hear and remain.

"You betrayed me?" he says, between his teeth. "You gave this letter" — producing it—"to my grandfather? I trusted you, and you betrayed me."

"I did," she answers, with forced calmness.

"Why?"

"Because—I loved you."

"You!" with a harsh grating laugh. It is with difficulty he restrains his passion. "*You* to love! And is it by ruining those upon whom you bestow your priceless affection you show the depth of your devotion? Pah! Tell me the truth. Did you want all, and have you been justly punished?"

"I *have* told you the truth," she answers, vehemently. "I was mad enough to love you even then, when I saw against my will your wild infatuation for that designing— —"

"Hush!" he interrupts her, imperiously, in a low, dangerous tone. "If you are speaking of Miss Massereene, I warn you it is unsafe to proceed. Do not mention her. Do not utter her name. I forbid you."

"So be it! Your punishment has been heavier than any I could inflict.— You want to know why I showed that letter to the old man, and I will tell you. I thought, could I but gain *all* Herst, I might, through it, win you back to my side. I betrayed you for that alone. I debased myself in my own eyes for that sole purpose. I have failed in all things. My humiliation is complete. I do not ask your forgiveness, Philip; I crave only—your forbearance. Grant me that at least, for the old days' sake!"

But he will not. He scarcely heeds her words, so great is the fury that consumes him.

"You would have bought my love!" he says, with a bitter sneer. "Know, then, that with a dozen Hersts at your back, I loathe you too much ever to be more to you than I now am, and that is—nothing."

Quietly but forcibly he puts her from him, and leaves the room. Outside in the hall he encounters Sir Penthony, who has been lingering there with intent to waylay him. However rejoiced Stafford may be at Molly's luck, he is profoundly grieved for Philip.

"I know it is scarcely form to express sympathy on such occasions," he says, with some hesitation, laying his hand on Shadwell's shoulder. "But I must tell you how I regret, for your sake, all that has taken place."

"Thank you, Stafford. You are one of the very few whose sympathy is never oppressive. But do not be uneasy about me," with a short laugh. "I dare say I shall manage to exist. I have five hundred a year of my own, and my grandfather's thoughtfulness has made it a thousand. No doubt I shall keep body and soul together, though there is no disguising the fact that I feel keenly the difference between one thousand and twenty."

"My dear fellow, I am glad to see you take it so well. I don't believe there are a dozen men of my acquaintance who would be capable of showing such pluck as you have done."

"I have always had a fancy for exploring. I shall go abroad and see some life; the sooner the better. I thank you with all my heart, Stafford, for your kindness. I thank you—and"—with a slight break in his voice—"good-bye!"

He presses Stafford's hand warmly, and, before the other can reply, is gone.

Half an hour later, Marcia, sweeping into her room in a torrent of passion impossible to quell, summons her maid by a violent attack on her bell.

"Take off this detested mourning," she says to the astonished girl. "Remove it from my sight. And get me a colored gown and a Bradshaw."

The maid, half frightened, obeys, and that night Marcia Amherst quits her English home forever.

CHAPTER XXXVII

"Fare thee well! and if forever,

Still forever, fare thee well!"

—Byron.

"Oh, Cecil! now I can marry Tedcastle," says Molly, at the end of a long and exhaustive conversation that has taken place in her own room. She blushes a little as she says it; but it is honestly her first thought, and she gives utterance to it. "Letitia, too, and the children,—I can provide for them. I shall buy back dear old Brooklyn, and give it to them, and they shall be happy once more."

"I agree with Lord Byron," says Cecil, laughing. "'Money makes the man; the want of it, his fellow.' You ought to feel like some princess out of the Arabian Nights' Entertainments."

"I feel much more like an intruder. What right have I to Herst? What shall I do with so much money?"

"Spend it. There is nothing simpler. Believe me, no one was ever in reality embarrassed by her riches, notwithstanding all they say. The whole thing is marvelous. Who could have anticipated such an event? I am sorry I ever said anything disparaging of that dear, delightful, genial, kind-hearted, sociable, generous old gentleman, your grandfather."

"Don't jest," says Molly, who is almost hysterical. "I feel more like crying yet. But I am glad at least to know he forgave me before he died. Poor grandpapa! Cecil, I want so much to see Letitia."

"Of course, dear. Well,"—consulting her watch,—"I believe we may as well be getting ready if we mean to catch the next train. Will not it be a charming surprise for Letitia? I quite envy you the telling of it."

"I want you to tell it. I am so nervous I know I shall never get through it without frightening her out of her wits. Do come with me, Cecil, and break the news yourself."

"Nothing I should like better," says Cecil. "Put on your bonnet and let us be off."

Ringing the bell, she orders round the carriage, and presently she and Molly are wending their way down the stairs.

At the very end of the long, beautiful old hall, stands Philip Shadwell, taking, it may be, a last look from the window, of the place so long regarded as his own.

As they see him, both girls pause, and Molly's lips lose something of their fresh, warm color.

"Go and speak to him now," says Cecil, and, considerately remembering a hypothetical handkerchief, retraces her steps to the room she had just quitted.

"Philip!" says Molly, timidly, going up to him.

He turns with a start, and colors a dark red on seeing her, but neither moves nor offers greeting.

"Oh, Philip! let me do something for you," says Molly impulsively, without preparation, and with tears in her eyes. "I have robbed you, though unwittingly. Let me make amends. Out of all I have let me give you— —"

"The only thing I would take from you it is out of your power to give," he interrupts her, gently.

"Do not say so," she pleads, in trembling tones. "I do not want all the money. I cannot spend it. I do not care for it. *Do* take some of it, Philip. Let me share— —"

"Impossible, child!" with a faint smile. "You don't know what you are saying." Then, with an effort, "You are going to marry Luttrell?"

"Yes,"—blushing, until she looks like a pale, sweet rose with a drooping head.

"How rich to overflowing are some, whilst others starve!" he says, bitterly, gazing at her miserably, filling his heart, his senses, for the last time, with a view of her soft and perfect loveliness. Then, in a kinder tone, "I hope you will be happy, and"—slowly—"he too, though that is a foregone conclusion." He pales a little here, and stops as though half choking. "Yes, he has my best wishes,—for your sake," he goes on, unsteadily. "Tell him so from me, though we have not been good friends of late."

"I will surely tell him."

"Good-bye!" he says, taking her hand. Something in his expression makes her exclaim, anxiously:

"For the present?"

"No; forever. Herst and England have grown hateful to me. I leave them as soon as possible. Good-bye, my beloved!" he whispers, in deep agitation. "I only ask you not to quite forget me, though I hope—*I hope*—I shall never look upon your sweet face again."

So he goes, leaving his heart behind him, carrying with him evermore, by land and sea, this only,—the vision of her he loves as last he sees her, weeping sad and bitter tears for him.

A quarter of an hour later, as Molly and Cecil are stepping into the carriage meant to convey them to the station, one of the servants, running up hurriedly, hands Miss Massereene a letter.

"Another?" says Cecil, jestingly, as the carriage starts. "Sealed envelopes, like private bomb-shells, seem to be the order of the day. I do hope this one does not emanate from your grandfather, desiring you to refund everything."

"It is from Tedcastle," says Molly, surprised. Then she opens it, and reads as follows:

"Taking into consideration the enormous change that has occurred in your fortunes since this morning, I feel it only just to you and myself to write and absolve you from all ties by which you may fancy yourself still connected with me. You will remember that in our last conversation together in London you yourself voluntarily decided on severing our engagement. Let your decision now stand. Begin your new life without hampering regrets, without remorseful thoughts of me. To you I hope this money may bring happiness; to me, through you, it has brought lasting pain; and when, a few minutes ago, I said I congratulated you from my heart, I spoke falsely. I say this only to justify my last act in your eyes. I will not tell you what it costs me to write you this; you know me well enough to understand. I shall exchange with a friend of mine, and sail for India in a week or two, or at least as soon as I can; but wherever I am, or whatever further misfortunes may be in store for me, be assured your memory will always be my greatest— possibly my only—treasure."

"What can he mean?" says Molly, looking up. She does not appear grieved; she is simply indignant. An angry crimson flames on her fair cheeks.

"Quixotism!" says Cecil, when she, too, has read the letter. "Was there ever such a silly boy?"

"Oh! it is worse than anything,—so cold, so terse, so stupid. And not an affectionate word all through, or a single regret."

"My dear child, that is its only redeeming point. He is evidently sincere in his desire for martyrdom. Had he gone into heroics I should myself have gone to Ireland (where I suppose he soon must be) to chastise him. But as it is—— Poor Tedcastle! He looks upon it as a point of honor."

"It is unbearable," says Molly, angrily. "Does he think such a paltry thing as money could interfere with my affection for him?"

"Molly, beware! You are bordering on the heroics now. Money is not a paltry thing; it is about the best thing going. _I_ can sympathize with Tedcastle if you cannot. He felt he had no right to claim the promise of such a transcendently beautiful being as you, now you have added to your other charms twenty thousand a year. He thinks of your future; he acknowledges you a bride worthy any duke in the land (men in love"—maliciously—"_will_ dote, you know); he thinks of the world and its opinion, and how fond they are of applying the word 'fortune-hunter' when they get the chance, and it is not a pretty sobriquet."

"He should have thought of nothing but me. Had he come into a fortune," says Molly, severely, "I should have been delighted, and I should have married him instantly."

"Quite so. But who ever heard the opprobrious term 'fortune-hunter' given to a woman? It is the legitimate thing for us to sell ourselves as dearly as we can."

"But, Cecil,"—forlornly,—"what am I to do now?"

"If you will take my advice, nothing,—for two or three weeks. He cannot sail for India before then, and do his best. Preserve an offended silence. Then obtain an interview with him by fair means, or, if not, by foul."

"You unscrupulous creature!" Molly says, smiling; but after a little reflection she determines to abide by her friend's counsel. "Horrible, hateful letter," she says, tearing it up and throwing it out of the window. "I wish I had never read you. I am happier now you are gone."

"So am I. It was villainously worded and very badly written."

"I don't know that," begins Molly, warmly; and then she stops short, and they both laugh. "And you, Cecil—what of you? Am I mistaken in thinking you and Sir Penthony are—are——"

"Yes, we are," says Cecil, smiling and coloring brilliantly. "As you so graphically express it, we actually—*are*. At present, like you, we are formally engaged."

"Really?"—delighted. "I always knew you loved him. And so you have given in at last?"

"Through sheer exhaustion, and merely with a view to stop further persecution. When a man comes to you day after day, asking you whether you love him yet, ten to one you say yes in the end, whether it be the truth or not. We all know what patience and perseverance can do. But I desire you, Molly, never to lose sight of the fact that I am consenting to be his only to escape his importunities."

"I quite understand. But, dear Cecil, I am so rejoiced."

"Are you, dear?"—provokingly. "And why?—I thought to have a second marriage, if only for the appearance of the thing; but it seems I cannot. So we are going to Kamtschatka, or Bath, or Timbuctoo, or Hong-Kong, or Halifax, for our wedding tour, I really don't know which, and I would not presume to dictate. That is, if I do not change my mind between that and this."

"And when is that?"

"The seventeenth of next month. He wanted to make it the first of April; but I said I was committing folly enough without reminding all the world of it. So he succumbed. I wish, Molly, you could be married on the same day."

"What am I to do with a lover who refuses to take me?" says Molly, with a rueful laugh. "I dare say I shall be an old maid after all."

CHAPTER XXXVIII

"Why shouldn't I love my love?
Why shouldn't he love me?
Why shouldn't I love my love,
Since love to all is free?"

Three full weeks that, so far as Molly is concerned, have been terribly, wearisomely long, have dragged to their close. Not that they have been spent in idleness; much business has been transacted, many plans fulfilled; but they have been barren of news of her lover.

"In the spring a young man's fancies lightly turn to thoughts of love;" but his thoughts seem far removed from such tender dalliance.

She knows, through Cecil, of his being in Ireland with his regiment for the first two of those interminable weeks, and of his appearance in London during the third, where he was seeking an exchange into some regiment ordered on foreign service; but whether he has or has not been successful in his search she is supremely ignorant.

Brooklyn, her dear old home, having been discovered on her grandfather's death to be still in the market, has been bought back for her by Mr. Buscarlet, and here Letitia—with her children and Molly—feels happier and more contented than she could ever have believed to be again possible.

Seated at breakfast, watched over by the faithful Sarah, without apparent cause for uneasiness, there is, nevertheless, an air of uncertainty and expectation about Mrs. Massereene and her sister that makes itself known even to their attendant on this particular morning in early April of which I write.

In vain does Sarah, with a suppressed attempt at coaxing, place the various dishes under Miss Massereene's eyes. They are accepted, lingeringly, daintily, but are not eaten. The children, indeed, voracious as their kind, come nobly to the rescue, and by a kindly barter of their plates for Molly's, which leaves them an undivided profit, contrive to clear the table.

Presently, Molly having refused languidly some delicate steaming cakes of Sarah's own making, that damsel leaves the room in high dudgeon, and Molly leans back in her chair.

"Tell me again, Letty, what you wrote to him," she says, letting her eyes wander through the window, all down the avenue, up which the postman must come, "word for word."

"Just exactly what you desired me, dear," replies Letitia, seriously. "I said I should like to see him once again for the old days' sake, before he left England, which I heard he was on the point of doing. And I also told him, to please you,"—smiling,—"what was an undeniable lie,—that, but for the children, I was here alone."

"Quite right," says Miss Massereene, unblushingly. Then, with considerable impatience, "Will that postman *never* come?"

All country posts are irregular, and this one is not a pleasant exception. To-day, to create aggravation, it is at least one good half-hour later than usual. When at length, however, it does come, it brings the expected letter from Luttrell.

"Open it quickly,—quickly, Letty," says her sister, and Letitia hastens and reads it with much solemnity.

It is short and rather reckless in tone. It tells them the writer, having effected the desired exchange, hopes to start for India in two weeks at furthest, and that, as he had never at any time contemplated leaving England without bidding Mrs. Massereene good-bye, he would seize the opportunity—she being *now alone* (heavily dashed)—to run down to Brooklyn to see her this very day.

"Oh, Letty! to-day!" exclaims Molly, paling and flushing, and paling again. "How I wish it was tomorrow!"

"Could there be any one more inconsistent than you, my dear Molly? You have been praying for three whole weeks to see him, and now your prayer is answered you look absolutely miserable."

"It is so sudden," says poor Molly. "And—he never mentioned my name. What if he refuses to have anything to say to me even now? What shall I do then?"

"Nonsense, my dear! When once he sees you, he will forget all his ridiculous pride, and throw himself, like a sensible man, at your feet."

"I wish I could think so. Letty,"—tearfully, and in a distinctly wheedling tone,—"wouldn't *you* speak to him?"

"Indeed I would not," says Letitia, indignantly. "What, after writing that lie! No, you must of course see him yourself. And, indeed, my dear child,"—laughing,—"you have only to meet him, wearing the lugubrious expression you at present exhibit, to melt his heart, were it the stoniest one in Europe. See,"—drawing her to a mirror,—"was there ever such a Dolores?"

Seeing her own forlorn visage, Molly instantly laughs, thereby ruining forever the dismal look of it that might have stood her in such good stead.

"I suppose he will dine," says Letitia, thoughtfully. "I must go speak to cook."

"Perhaps he will take the very first train back to London," says Molly, still gloomy.

"Perhaps so. Still, we must be prepared for the worst," wickedly. "Therefore, cook and I must consult. Molly,"—pausing at the door,—"you have exactly four hours in which to make yourself beautiful, as he cannot possibly be here before two. And if in that time you cannot create a costume calculated to reduce him to slavery, I shall lose my good opinion of you. By the bye, Molly,"—earnestly, and with something akin to anxiety,—"do you think he likes meringues?"

"How can you be so foolish?" says Miss Massereene, reprovingly. "Of course if he dines he will be in the humor to like anything I like, and I *love* meringues. But if not,—if not,"—with a heavy sigh,—"you can eat all the meringues yourself."

"Dear, dear!" says Letitia. "She is really very bad."

Almost as the clock strikes two, Molly enters the orchard, having given strict orders to Sarah to send Mr. Luttrell there when he arrives, in search of Mrs. Massereene.

She has dressed herself with great care, and very becomingly, being one of those people who know instantly, by instinct, the exact shade and style that suits them. Besides which, she has too much good taste and too much good sense to be a slave to that tyrant, Fashion.

Here and there the fruit-trees are throwing out tender buds, that glance half shrinkingly upon the world, and show a desire to nestle again amidst their leaves, full of a regret that they have left so soon their wiser sisters.

There is a wonderful sweetness in the air,—a freshness indescribable,—a rare spring perfume. Myriad violets gleam up at her, white and purple, from the roots of apple-trees, inviting her to gather them. But she heeds them not: they might as well be stinging-nettles, for all the notice she bestows upon them. Or is it that the unutterable hope in her own heart overpowers their sweetness?

All her thoughts are centred on the impending interview. How if she shall fail after all? What then? Her heart sinks within her, her hands grow cold with fear. On the instant the blackness of her life in such a case spreads itself out before her like a map,—the lonely pilgrimage,—the unlovely journey, without companionship, or warmth, or pleasant sunshine.

Then she hears the click of the garden gate, and the firm, quick step of him who comes to her up the hilly path between the strawberry-beds.

Drawing a deep breath, she shrinks within the shelter of a friendly laurel until he is close to her; then, stepping from her hiding-place, she advances toward him.

As she does so, as she meets him face to face, all her nervousness, all her inward trembling, vanishes, and she declares to herself that victory shall lie with her.

He has grown decidedly thinner. Around his beautiful mouth a line of sadness has fallen, not to be concealed even by his drooping moustache. He looks five years older. His blue eyes, too, have lost their laughter, and are full of a settled melancholy. Altogether, he presents such an appearance as should make the woman who loves him rejoice, provided she knows the cause.

When he sees her he stops short and grows extremely pale.

"You here!" he says, in tones of displeased surprise. "I understood from Mrs. Massereene you were at Herst. Had I known the truth, I should not have come."

"I knew that; and the lie was mine,—not Letitia's. I made her write it because I was determined to see you again. How do you do, Teddy?" says Miss Massereene, coming up to him, smiling saucily, although a little tremulously. "Will you not even shake hands with me?"

He takes her hand, presses it coldly, and drops it again almost instantly.

"I am glad to see you looking so well," he says, gravely, perhaps reproachfully.

"I am sorry to see you looking so ill," replies she, softly, and then begins to wonder what on earth she shall say next.

Mr. Luttrell, with his cane, takes the heads off two unoffending crocuses that, most unwisely, have started up within his reach. He is the gentlest-natured fellow alive, but he feels a vicious pleasure in the decapitation of those yellow, harmless flowers. His eyes are on the ground. He is evidently bent on silence. On such occasions what is there that can be matched in stupidity with a man?

"I got your letter," Molly says, awkwardly, when the silence has gone past bearing.

"I know."

"I did not answer it."

"I know that too," with some faint bitterness.

"It was too foolish a letter to answer," returns she, hastily, detecting the drop of acid in his tone. "And, even if I had written then, I should only have said some harsh things that might have hurt you. I think I was wise in keeping silence."

"You were. But I cannot see how you have followed up your wisdom by having me here to-day."

There is a little pause, and, then:

"I wanted so much to see you," murmurs she, in the softest, sweetest of voices.

He winces, and shifts his position uneasily, but steadily refuses to meet her beseeching eyes. He visits two more unhappy crocuses with capital punishment, and something that is almost a sigh escapes him; but he will not look up, and he will not trust himself to answer her.

"Have you grown cruel, Teddy?" goes on Molly, in a carefully modulated tone. "You are killing those poor crocuses that have done you no harm. And you are killing me too, and what harm have I done you? Just as I began to see some chance of happiness before us, you ran away (you a soldier, to show the white feather!), and thereby ruined all the enjoyment I might have known in my good fortune. Was that kind?"

"I meant to be kind, Molly; I am kind," replies he huskily.

"Very cruel kindness, it seems to me."

"Later on you will not think so."

"It strikes me, Teddy," says Miss Massereene, reprovingly, "you are angry because poor grandpapa chose to leave me Herst."

"Angry? Why should I be angry?"

"Well, then, why don't you say you are glad?"

"Because I am not glad."

"And why? For months and months we were almost crying for money, and when, by some most fortunate and unlooked-for chance, it fell to my lot, you behaved as though some overpowering calamity had befallen you. Why should not you be as glad of it as I am?"

"Don't speak like that, Molly," says Luttrell, with a groan. "You know all is over between us. The last time we met in London you yourself broke our engagement, and now do you think I shall suffer you to renew it? I am not so selfish as you imagine. I am no match for you now. You must forget me (it will not be difficult, I dare say), and it would be a downright shame to keep you to—to——"

"Then you condemn me to die an old maid, the one thing I most detest; while you, if you refuse to have me, Teddy, I shall insist on your dying an old bachelor, if only to keep me in countenance."

"Think of what the world would say."

"Who cares what it says? And, besides, it knows we were engaged once."

"And also that we quarreled and parted."

"And that we were once more united in London, where you did not despise the poor concert-singer. Were you not devoted to me then, when I had but few friends? Were you ashamed of me then?"

"Ashamed of you!"

"Once you threw me over," says Molly, with a smile that suits the month, being half tears, half sunshine. "Once I did the same by you. That makes us quits. Now we can begin all over again."

"Think of what all your friends will say," says he, desperately, knowing he is losing ground, but still persisting.

"Indeed I will, because all my friends are yours, and they will think as I do."

Two little tears steal from under her heavily-fringed lids, and run down her cheeks. Going nearer to him, she hesitates, glances at him shyly, hesitates still, and finally lays her head upon his shoulder.

Of course, when the girl you love lays her head upon your shoulder, there is only one thing to be done. Luttrell does that one thing. He instantly encircles her with his arms.

"See, I am asking you to marry me," says Molly, raising dewy eyes to his, and blushing one of her rare, sweet blushes. "I *beg* you to take me. If, after that, you refuse me, I shall die of shame. Why don't you speak, Teddy? Say, 'Molly, I will marry you.'"

"Oh, Molly!" returns the young man, gazing down on her despairingly, while his strong arms hold her fast, "if you were only poor. If this cursed money——"

"Never mind the money. What do I care whether I am rich or poor? I care only for you. If you go away, I shall be the poorest wretch on earth!"

"My angel! My own darling girl!"

"No!" with a little sob. "Say, 'My own darling wife!'"

"My own darling wife!" replies he, conquered.

"Then why don't you kiss me?" says Miss Massereene, softly, her face dangerously close to his; and Tedcastle, stooping, forges the last link that binds him to her forever.

"Ah!" says Molly, presently, laughing gayly, although the tears still lie wet upon her cheeks, "did you imagine for one instant you could escape *me*? At first I was so angry I almost determined to let you go,—as punishment; but afterward"—mischievously—"I began to think how unhappy you would be, and I relented."

"Then I suppose I must now buy you another ring for this dear little finger," says he, smiling, and pressing it to his lips.

"No,"—running her hand into her pocket, "at least, not an engagement ring. You may get me any other kind you like, because I am fond of rings; but I shall have no betrothal ring but the first you gave me. Look,"—drawing out a little case, and opening it until he sees within the original diamonds— his first gift to her—lying gleaming in their rich new setting. "These are yours; I saved them from the fire that day you behaved so rudely to them, and have had them reset."

"You rescued them?" he asks, amazed.

"At the risk of burning my fingers: so you may guess how I valued them. Now they are purified, and you must never get into such a naughty temper again. Promise."

"I promise faithfully."

"Now I shall wear it again," says Molly, regarding her ring lovingly, "under happier—oh, how much happier—circumstances. Put it on, Teddy, and say after me, 'Darling Molly, pardon me for having compelled you to ask my hand in marriage!'"

"I will not,"—laughing.

"You must. You are my property now, and must do as I bid you. So you may as well begin at once. Say it, sir, directly!"

He says it.

"Now you know what a horrible hen-pecking there will be for you in the future. I shall rule you with a rod of iron."

"And I shall hug my chains."

"Think what a life I am condemning you to. Are you not frightened? And all because—I cannot do without you. Oh, Teddy," cries Molly Bawn, suddenly, and without a word of warning, bursting into a passion of tears, and flinging herself into his willing arms, "are you not glad—*glad*—that we belong to each other again?"

"Time will show you how glad," replies he, softly. "I know now I could not have lived without you, my sweet,—my *darling*!"